THE LAST DRAGONHEALER

H S SKINNER

Happy reading!
Heidi

D1713660

I come from the earth.
I come from the sky.
I travel on foot,
I fly.
Hand and claw,
Sword and talon.
Heart-twined,
Soul-bound,
Rider and dragon.
Together we soar.

PROLOGUE

Not much could jolt her out of the cloud of pain and fatigue she existed in, but the exuberant cry of *Dragons!* had her staggering to a halt and trying to look up. Almost overbalancing with the effort, planting one hand firmly against the nearest wall, she stopped and scanned the skies just in time to see dragons swoop low and then disappear behind a line of mudbrick buildings.

At last! Dragons!

She had to get to the dragons. It was imperative! She had to tell them…

Tell them what?

The pain in her head nearly drove her to her knees, but she refused to go down. Utilizing every last smidgen of will she had left, she slid and slithered her way through the crowd, fighting her way to the front.

She could see the dragons now, their multi-hued, iridescent scales gleaming in the sunlight, one emerald and one topaz. Giving a passing glance to the topaz, her eyes locked on the emerald.

Their riders, having already dismounted, were heading away from her.

Were these even the dragons and riders she needed to speak with?

Some soul-deep ingrained element of caution had her holding back.

She had to be certain.

There were so few left…

She couldn't trust the wrong ones, and yet…

The emerald's very presence called to her. Ceaselessly.

Demandingly.

Lives were at stake, but whose? Hers?

She wished she could remember past the screaming pain in her head. Something had to be done—she was running out of time.

That she knew without question.

Unbidden, words came from nowhere as a solemn vow imprinted on her mind.

My bow and my sword I pledge to your service. My life is yours to command.

CHAPTER 1

*S*eventeen winters prior

"DRAGONS? Crying in pain? 'Ow many times I gotta tell ya, there ain't no such thing? Now shut yer yap before I really give you something to cry about!" A sharp backhand emphasized the adult male's fury.

Landing against the stone wall with a distinct thud, sliding bonelessly to the floor, Renny covered her throbbing cheek with one hand and used the other to scooch herself away from the enraged man bearing down on her, murder on his face.

"I tol' you not to wake me again with your stupid nonsense, you sniveling brat."

Hunching into the smallest ball possible as he punctuated his roar with kick after kick, rolling and twisting as much as she could, Renny did her best to minimize the blows.

"You stay away from that door! And shut up so's the rest of us can get some sleep! Do you hear me?"

More punctuation, a veritable flurry of it, sent Renny crawling across the filthy flagstones covered in patches of filthier rushes to her sleeping corner in the farthest reaches of the gloomy hall. Lit only by the feeble embers dying in the fireplace, her corner was the darkest, coldest of all.

Keeping her one still functioning eye on the hulking man stomping and kicking his way back to his own pallet across the crowded and dimly lit room, battening down her sobs, Renny banded her arms around her stomach and rocked herself. Over and above the grumbling and muttered curses and shrieks caused by the man stepping willy-nilly on the prone occupants, she could plainly hear a dragon keening.

She wasn't crazy! Even if she'd never seen one, there *were* dragons, and they *were* crying in pain. Broadcasting their agony so loud Renny could barely hear anything else, awake or asleep. Clapping her hands over her ears, she rocked harder. Not that it did any good.

If only she was big enough to lift the heavy bar on the door! That's what she'd been trying to do when he caught her. Again.

She could ignore the dragons during the long days, filled with chores and surviving. Nighttime… Nights were the worst, when the dragons invaded her dreams and her too-small body responded by trying to go to the dragons and aid them.

Nursing her aches and pains, Renny plotted. First light would see her gone from here. No one paid much attention to her anyway. What was one more starving orphan, displaced by the war? One less was simply one less mouth to feed.

She could scrounge scraps from the morning meal and tuck them in the cleanest corner of her tattered shirt. If she grabbed the slop bucket to feed the mud-grunts, no one would pay her any mind. She could slip out the door, left open during the day. Out the even heavier gate, also left open during the day. Mayhap she could even glean a bit more food from the bucket before she made her escape.

Not like she'd be able to eat on the morrow. Her jaw was already too swollen to chew, and her eye, following suit, had puffed so tight she couldn't open it no matter how hard she tried.

It was going to be another long, miserable night, one of many in the endless series of her short life.

Rocking, drifting in and out with the pain, Renny watched as first light at last crept in the high, narrow openings under the eaves, worked its slow way down to the arrow slits.

Waited and bided her time.

Raking the ashes out of the hearth and kindling the day's fire, gathering the slop jars, attempting to re-scatter and fluff the moldering rushes, Renny carefully kept out of everyone's way. First meal over—for everyone but her, she was still in everyone's bad graces—and reeking bucket in hand, Renny limped out the now open door. Head down, she took careful stock with her limited peripheral vision. The whole right side of her head throbbed in time with her heartbeat and felt like an over-full waterskin.

Dumping bucket and all over the crude log fence—not even her grumbling stomach enough to entice her to share the mud-grunt's slops after watching Big Orst's grinning wife tip the fresh contents of a chamberpot in—she sidled into the shadows along the edge of the stable. Cold stone at her back, she slipped closer to the outer wall and freedom.

Eye on her prize, she never saw the hand that appeared from nowhere and snatched her backwards into the dark recesses of the dank stable.

Poorly maintained like everything else around her, the fracture in the stonework was wide enough for a laxamul—one of the dumber than a stump herd-beasts—to easily escape. Her captor had no problem yanking Renny's thin form through the opening. Making sure she banged her head, knees, and elbows in the process, he threw her farther into the darkness.

Cringing as evil laughter clued her in to exactly who was

tormenting her, Rennie figured the apoma didn't fall far from the tree.

Or in Little Orst's case, rotten fruit hanging from a diseased tree. Just like his father, Big Orst, Little O lived to torment.

Little O, ha! The obnoxious snot was nearly as corpulent as his father.

Their time bullying would have been much better invested repairing and—dragons forbid—cleaning what was left of the keep.

Sucking breath after breath into her straining lungs, Renny scuttled sideways.

Not fast enough.

Little O caught her, pinned her, let fly with fists and feet. Pulling back for a breather, he spat, "That's for last night! Da stepped on me face—thanks to you!—and he had laxamul dung all over his boots."

Blinking blood out of her one good eye enough to see his leering, twisted with hate mug, wondering why Big O slept with his boots on, Renny wheezed, "Definitely an improvement."

Another flurry of fists and feet. Fisting Renny's shirt, dragging her up off the floor and bringing them nose to nose, Little O hissed at her, spittle coating her face as he spewed venom. "You little sneak thief! You're useless! Worthless!"

Having heard that and much worse on a regular basis from not just Big O but most of the other adults in the keep, Renny hung in his grip and didn't bother to answer with words.

The well calculated kick to his balls drove Little O to his knees but failed to loosen his grip. About to really lay into Renny, foreign sounds from the courtyard drifted through the break in the wall and halted his fist far more effectively than Renny's doomed strike.

Cocking his head, Little O dropped Renny in favor of a more interesting event, giving her one last kick for good measure before heading outside.

The rhythmic sound of what had to be ride-beasts, followed by the creaking of a cart, the kind usually pulled by slow, stupid laxamuls. Except in this instance, it sounded like fast moving ride-beasts were pulling the cart. Who would... Only the very wealthiest could afford the nearly unheard of and obscenely expensive okumos.

Wincing, Renny hitched herself closer to a door.

Sneaked a peek around the corner at the well fed animals and the richly dressed riders. Too bad she didn't have access to one of the huge okumos. All she had was her own two feet. They'd have to serve her well.

Taking advantage of the crowd's utter fascination with the newcomers, Renny ghosted past a small contingent of bored looking, gasping for air, too weary to care foot soldiers and out the wide open gate with nary a backward glance. She had dragons to find.

And what was up with that cart? Like nothing she'd ever seen, it bore more resemblance to a cell on wheels. Heavy metal bars all the way around, with a solid metal floor and roof to match.

Same with the paltry contingent of soldiers. Lords that wealthy made it a point to travel with as many guards as they could muster. The long legged okumos with their graceful arched necks were all lathered and blowing hard, even this early in the day. So then... Speed was the issue and not safety.

Cocking her head, spinning in a slow circle, Renny froze like a hunt-beast locking in on a hot trail.

That way.

"The girl! I seek a girl!"

Rolling her shoulders, ignoring the words pouring from inside the gate and the pain flaring from every quarter of her battered body, Renny broke into a ground eating lope.

Skipping right over any pretense at pleasantries, the visiting lord moved straight on to bigger and better tactics when the crowd only stared like stupefied laxamuls.

Holding Big O off the ground by the fist clenched in O's shirtfront, the lord's largest and deadliest soldier shook O like the rat he was while the disgruntled lord hurled questions from the back of his okumo.

"Where is she? 'Tis said you have an urchin who can hear dragons. Where. Is. She."

CHAPTER 2

resent day

Covered in soot and smoke and burning scratches, kicking at the vicious heap of thorns and vines, Allar wielded his pitchfork handily and heaved the last remnant of fire-thorn into the pyre. Despite their best efforts, they couldn't seem to rid the area around Dragon's Haven of the noxious weed. The harder they tried to eradicate it, the more vigorously it rebounded.

Same with all the other dragon keeps.

Hands on his knees, coughing and hacking, he wasted precious breath on inventive curses concerning the parentage of the blight he was attempting to destroy. Wheezed, "We might've won the war against the dragonhaters, but this stuff is gonna be the death of us all!"

Choking, he hocked gob after gob of nasty snot into the blaze.

Thrusting a waterskin into Allar's hand, Voya grinned. "I'd

tell you to wash your face, but you need a river, or at least a giant pond."

Looking at his second like looking into a mirror, Allar and Voya burst into ragged laughter, hoarse and croaky as pond singers. Like a couple four legged night-raiders with their matching masks of soot, nothing showing but the whites of their eyes, Voya was right. They'd need the Great Lake and a boatload of soapweed to get all this grime off.

For certain more than a bathing tub at Dragon's Haven, barely visible in the smoky distance.

Chugging a long drink, Allar swiped the back of his hand over his chapped lips as he surveyed the immense patch of scorched earth they'd just finished grubbing and clearing. Just like with the dragonhaters. Even with all their hard work, unless they stayed right on top of it, it would only take the fire-thorn a short while to regrow and cover this plot like they'd never touched it. One missed dragonhater, one missed root…

An old joke claimed fire-thorn grew so fast it could cover a rider on a dragon if they so much as landed long enough to touch claws to soil. Allar believed it. "Wish I knew what set this off. Fire-thorn has always been a royal pain, but the last few years…"

Voya shrugged. "The war devastated many things, and set others on unnatural courses. All we can do is ride it out."

"Speaking of riding, I'm going to head out so I can get cleaned up."

"With you on that. Just have to…"

Letting Voya's words trail off, Allar sent out a mental call, knowing Voya was doing the same. {{*Zantha, you ready?*}}

A lengthy snicker answered him. {{*Good thing I can smell you. All humans look alike covered in soot. Although, right now you reek of kazas smoke.*}}

{{*Yeah, well, any time you can come up with a better way to dispose of this, I'm all ears. Mayhap if you would help instead of running like a scalded pursim...*}}

Silence from Zantha, as always whenever the subject of fire-thorn—kazas in dragonspeak—came up. Dragons were strange creatures. Fearless in battle, loyal to no end, they had distinct lines. Destroying kazas was one they would not cross, no matter the incentive.

Allar shrugged. No matter. Everyone was entitled to their idiosyncrasies. Checking on his men, making sure their wounds were being treated, he angled toward a large clearing far from the roaring fire, Took stock of his own welts and weals. Left untreated they would fester and spread. Already his were burning, the maddening desire to scratch nearly overwhelming.

Speaking of idiosyncrasies…

Having no desire to stay and be poked and prodded by Seon, much less the assistant healers, Allar headed for a perfect waterfall with an abundant supply of soapweed not too far from here.

COMING UP BLOWING AND SNORTING, Allar shook his head, splattering water and soap bubbles every which way. Basking in a patch of sunlight on a sandy bit of shore, wings outstretched, Zantha rolled a huge eye at his antics.

Splatting some water her way with the flat of his hand, Allar sank back down and let himself drift up. Stretching out on the water like he was home in his bed, Allar relaxed and let the water and sunlight soothe him, the burbling murmur of the waterfall an added bonus.

With the bonus drowning out his over-loud, never ending thoughts, Allar allowed himself a small moment of peace. Demands and responsibilities would claim him soon enough.

Nearly asleep, Allar jolted awake at Zantha's call. Foundered like a ship on a reef, inhaling water as he went down.

{{*Mithar is approaching. Voya needs…*}}

Wiping his face, slicking his long hair back, Allar strode out of the water. Digging a clean shirt out of his saddlebag, using it for his towel, Allar was mostly dressed by the time Mithar landed.

Throwing a leg over, Voya slid off, shaking his head. "You always manage to find the best waterfalls. You took off before Seon could slather you in salve. Did you…"

Cocking his head, Allar finished for Voya. "Yes, *mother*. I put salve on before we got here and renewed it after I washed the grunge off."

Taking the teasing in stride, tossing an oilskin-wrapped parcel Allar's way, Voya plopped on a sun warmed boulder and tipped his head to the sun.

Snagging it out of the air one-handed, Allar took a deep sniff and grinned in satisfaction. Roast laxamul and…bread. It would do until he got back to Dragon's Haven and Cook's fine meals.

With the first bite, flavorful meat juices exploded in Allar's mouth and flooded down his throat, so good he paid little heed to Voya's report.

Something along the lines of men all fine, no losses, no traces of kazas. Same old, same old. Tuning him out unless and until he heard anything to the contrary, Allar munched and enjoyed.

Nearly finished, a wad of meat in his cheek and one halfway down his throat, Allar shook his head as Voya mumbled something Allar couldn't hear over Zantha's pain-filled bellow.

White as a chalk lump, unsteady as a drunk standing on a milking stool, Voya repeated, his lips moving but no sound reaching Allar, "Conthar's missing."

The bite in Allar's mouth, the very last bite, might as well have been kazas pulp spiced with soapweed.

{{*Zantha?!*}}

{{'Tis true. Mithar and Mina just broadcast their distress. They can no longer make contact with him.}}

{{How long since we heard from Conthar?}}

{{Over a fortnight. He often takes off by himself. With no mate he can claim, he has little reason to stay close.}}

{{Call out the troops. Full alert.}}

CHAPTER 3

A fortnight later, innumerable missions flown, half a world mercilessly canvassed to no avail, Allar matched Voya step for exhausted step as they climbed the wide stairs to the spacious veranda encircling and overlooking the hot sand courtyard of Dragon's Haven.

Dog-tired warriors moving ahead of them, behind them, all around them, Allar spoke quietly to Voya. "How are Mithar and Mina…"

Nearly a match in size for Allar, brown haired and hazel eyed, Voya retorted bitterly, "…taking the loss of their only offspring? How do you think they're taking it?"

Understanding Voya's surliness, Allar kept his rebuke on the mild side, far more leeway than he would've afforded any other. "I was going to say, holding up, but evidently you've learned to read my mind as well as Zantha."

Reaching out, Voya caught Allar's sleeve. "Forgive me, Allar. My lord. I'm…"

"Distraught, as you should be. There's nothing to forgive. I can't begin to imagine your pain." And he couldn't.

Continuing his climb, harsh thoughts pummeled him like heavy battle axes, ripping and tearing, opening fatal wounds.

For a dragonrider, losing one's dragon was the worst horror imaginable. Riders often followed their dragons into death and the next world, unable to bear the pain and loss of separation. Then too, besides the bond between human and dragon pairs, the spouses and mates of the human and dragon pairs were also bonded.

Doubly bonded, so instead of losing one, usually they lost four. Two humans, two dragons.

Unconscionable.

The only good side to this whole mess, if there was one—Conthar wasn't mated.

Not that losing one of the few remaining dragons wasn't a tragedy in itself.

The dragonhaters, with their rabid, irrational hatred of all things dragonish, had nearly succeeded in eradicating the entire dragon species with their hate filled vendetta.

The dwindling numbers of dragons, especially viable breeding pairs, would most likely finish off the majestic creatures.

That, and a lack of dragonhealers.

Allar heaved a silent sigh. Even if they managed to kill all the dragonhaters, even if they managed to somehow raise the birthrates to acceptable levels, any young dragonlings that hatched were doomed.

Parasites and diseases that had once been virtually eliminated had made a comeback, stronger than ever. With no known dragonhealers left living to work their magic, the few dragons that hatched…

Conthar was the last known hatchling, the lone survivor of his brood. Not that Allar could have any memory of an event that had happened more than thirty winters ago, five before he'd been born, but he'd heard the tales.

Another sigh, and Allar renewed his vow to himself: He would find a way save the dragons.

Clapping Voya on the back, Allar looked his old friend in the eye. "Go spend some time with your woman and your dragons."

~

A HOT BATH, clean clothes, a filling meal prepared by Cook's expert hands, and Allar was once more beginning to feel somewhat human.

Staring at the detailed floor to ceiling map painted on a long section of wall, pacing the length of it repeatedly, Allar shook his head. Mapped with the aid of countless dragons and cartographers, the Great Lake taking up an overwhelming amount of the center in shades of blue, Allar perused what he knew of his home world, Zola.

The vast, uncharted expanse of sand that encompassed the Great Desert, represented by a wide strip of browns and tans and ochers down the right hand side.

Even with the help of dragons, the extent of it had never been mapped. No dragon had ever flown around it, much less across it, and lived to tell the tale.

The rounded, forest covered mountains, like ranks of ever larger upside down bowls that rimmed this side of the never-ending sand dunes. Those bowl shaped mountains flowed seamlessly into innumerable scattered meadows and ever higher and rockier peaks, the peaks where most of the dragon-keeps were located, because that's where the dragons were happiest. Laxamuls and forage without end, unequaled cliffs for taking off and landing as well as building dragon-keeps suitable to humans and dragons alike. Abundant lakes and waterfalls with plentiful sandy beaches just the right texture to scrub itchy dragon hides to glossy perfection.

Pacing back, passing the Great Lake portion yet again,

grimacing at the terrifying, dragon-sized finned ones depicted as living in its unplumbed depths, Allar stopped in front of the far-side mountains. The heights where humans and dragons were most at home were nothing compared to these. Seeming to touch the sky, they rose and fell in jagged ups and downs like world-sized dragon's teeth. Other than far-flung villages and holdings comprised mostly of outcasts, criminals, and those who'd traded any vestiges of civilization for distance from the war, the far mountains were mostly uninhabited. A few fort type outposts, sparsely manned, comprised mostly of dragonriders who'd survived the loss of their dragons, and soldiers too old or too weary to fight any longer.

The unbonded dragons liked to fly those mountains, testing themselves against the elements and hunting elusive vixamas. Fiercely cunning, experts at camouflage, and one of the few land creatures that rivaled the dragons for size, vixamas were the dragon epitome of fine dining on the fly. Perhaps that's where Conthar had disappeared, but the riders who regularly patrolled the far shores had reported nothing.

Rocking on his heels, Allar pondered ancient tales. Some said the dragons had come from other worlds, drawn perhaps by the Dragonhealers native to this world, but why would there be healers if there were no dragons?

Would all the surviving dragons eventually leave if there were no longer healers? Where would they go? And how? How had the dragons gotten here in the first place?

This world seemed custom made for the dragons. The mountains precluded easy travel, the dragons provided a solution. The laxamuls bred so fast, they'd eat all the vegetation on the planet—save for that thrice damned fire-thorn!—if the dragons didn't keep them in check. The dragons and their riders were the perfect partners to patrol the skies and keep the highwaymen and villains from multiplying like rats so law abiding folks could live in peace.

Not to mention the race of vicious human-like creatures who lived in small gangs and terrorized both shores. Small, vaguely humanoid in appearance, feral, and totally lacking in compassion, the Orimjay would rather help themselves to what others had worked hard for than lift a finger themselves. Thankfully, and thanks to the dragons and dragonriders, their numbers were kept to manageable levels. Or had been.

Leaving off pacing and pondering for sitting at his desk and poring over smaller, scrolled maps until his eyes crossed, not giving up, merely rethinking his strategy, Allar leaned his head back for an instant to recalibrate their strategy. Since what they were doing obviously wasn't working, maybe they needed to expand their search. Usually riders from different keeps parceled out territories closest to their keeps. Maybe they should switch off and...

A booted nudge to his foot and the smell of some of Cook's finest jerked him from dark dreams of a world with no dragons.

Blinking at the familiar trappings of his own officium, Allar shook off the nightmares. Someday dragons might disappear from this world entirely, but it would not be on his watch.

Rising, stretching until his neck and back popped, Allar met Voya at the small table and eagerly attacked the fine repast before them like he hadn't just eaten a short time earlier.

Dropping heavily into a chair, scrubbing his hands over his face, Voya shook his head at Allar's silent question. "Nothing. Absolutely nothing. None of the men have reported so much as a scale. How can a dragon just disappear? Never mind, don't answer that. Too many have gone missing and none of the... results were good."

Clicking through options yet again like flipping the pages of a well known book, Allar had to agree.

Best scenario—Conthar died of natural causes.

Crashed into a mountain. Lost the fight to a vixama.

And yet, knowing Conthar, none of those rang true as a viable reason.

At worst, the remnants of the dragonhaters had sunk their evil claws into him.

No matter how hard he tried, Allar couldn't envision, in any of his mental ramblings, any scenario in which Conthar would have failed to call out to Mithar and Mina on their private link. Or any dragon on the common link. Knowing they'd mobilize every dragon and rider at the first hint of distress, knowing a blank slate from him would have his parents envisioning the worst.

Being unmated, Conthar had flown mission after mission searching far and wide for dragons or those few children who had the potential to be riders, his lonely flights taking him far off the beaten path in hopes of finding one or the other. Or even his mate.

If they knew which direction he'd been flying it would give them a better chance of locating him. No help there, either. He'd kept in contact with his parents but nothing that would give any clues to his whereabouts.

If Conthar hadn't been so stubbornly closemouthed, so adamant about flying solo, hadn't been so uncommunicative about his routes…

Allar and all his men, all the dragonriders from the other remaining keeps, had flown ever-widening circles searching for any hint of Conthar's cobalt hide.

Nothing, nothing, and more nothing.

Like flying across the Great Lake. No land in sight, no fishing boats, nothing but water in every direction as far as the eye could see.

Flying and flying and flying and then…just when you felt like giving up, there it was. A glimpse, a hint of a shadow on the far horizon, like an eyelash on the curve of a cheek.

Drumming his fingers, staring at the piles of scrolled maps

heaped on his desk, Allar slanted a look at Voya. "Think Zantha and Mithar are up for a ride?"

Rising so fast he had to throw out a hand behind himself to catch his chair, gaze intent on Allar's, Voya nodded.

CIRCLING LAZILY, drifting with the air currents, Zantha and Mithar hovered high above Lakeside. A fair distance from Dragon's Haven, nestled along the hilly shoreline in one of the few semi-flatter areas and accessible from land or water, the sizable village was a trading magnet.

From their height, dirt paths along the shoreline and rockier ones leading farther inland stood out plainly, ribs and veins on an immense, rumpled leaf. The huge, half-circle bay provided plenty of good anchorage for larger ships and fishing vessels, while multiple docks serried with ranks of smaller skiffs and dinghies resembled nothing so much as a puddle lined with children's toy boats.

Like most keeps and villages on their mountainous world, having chosen a relatively flat space, they'd gone from there and terraced up, taking advantage of every speck of land.

Banking lower, Voya grinned. Trust Allar, especially now, to think of the annual Trader's Fair. People from everywhere would be gathered to trade and barter goods and services and while they might not know Conthar's exact whereabouts, any dragon sighting would be much talked about, fodder for tavern tales and bragging rights.

Another downward spiral and the buildings came into focus. Nicer, better built houses of stone, high up, belonging to the wealthier merchants in town. Warehouses along the shore, also belonging to the merchants. In between, haphazardly stacked like children's building blocks, everything from wooden houses to mudbrick buildings to shacks cobbled together from a conglomeration of materials.

Landing in the stone-walled meadow long ago set aside for dragons and their riders, Allar and Voya dismounted to an already growing crowd. They wouldn't have to travel far through the town to question people. Could, in fact, stay right here and probably get better results.

While most would keep their distance, curiosity and admiration would draw people faster than Allar and Voya could circulate through the clogged stalls and crooked streets.

Patting Zantha on the shoulder, eyeing the crowd, Allar reminded her, {{*You know the deal. At the first hint of danger, fly. All the dragonhaters haven't been caught. I won't have you endangered needlessly.*}}

Huffing a rude snort, Zantha nudged Allar with her nose, intentionally bumping him hard enough to make him stagger a step sideways. Following up with an affectionate nuzzle, like a parent ruffling a child's hair, she rubbed her muzzle up his arm and blew a warm breath into Allar's hair.

A low murmur of delighted laughter from the crowd let Allar know they'd seen the little byplay.

{{*As if I'd leave you. Dragonhaters hate riders almost as much as they hate dragons.*}}

Flaring her wings dramatically, then drawing them close, shifting all four feet like a feline predator readying itself to pounce, Zantha settled watchfully.

Striding over and through the somewhat weedy patches—a far cry from the once pristine landing area with its inlaid dragon mosaic—to the once skillfully laid stone wall, now in disrepair as well, Allar raised a hand. The crowd stopped jostling for position and hushed. "We seek news of a dragon. A cobalt."

A voice from deep in the crowd jeered, "What'll ya give us for the information? A ride on your precious dragon?"

Allar's reply was cool, his stance as alert as Zantha's. Head up, eyes roving, hand on the hilt of his sword, balanced on the balls of his feet. "If you wish. But only if Zantha concurs."

Scorn obvious in his tone at Allar's deferral to a dragon, the same heckler retorted, "How 'bout…protection? Transport? Isn't that what your stupid flying lizards should be used for?"

Remaining calm, Allar considered. One of the dragonhaters? Or merely a disgruntled whiner, jealous of Allar's ability—thanks to Zantha—for easy travel?

The crowd parted to reveal the aggrieved man, arms crossed and head cocked angrily. Overweight, slovenly dressed, he rocked on his heels and demanded, "Why should we have to hump our butts to get goods from one place to another while the likes of you gets to fly around looking pretty?"

Petty jealousy then. Keeping one eye on him, Allar dismissed the man as a threat, scouring the crowd for anyone else who might come forward and actually have information.

Indicating his grungy state with a sweep of his hand, playing to the crowd, the man continued. "Look at me! I've been traveling for days to get here, along with everyone else, and I look it. Filthy, exhausted, and nearly missed the fair altogether because a bridge was out and I had to backtrack and take another route to get here."

Nods and murmurs from a scant minority encouraged him to keep gesturing and venting. "Look at them! All purty in their fancy clothes. Clean clothes. Because all they have to do is sit still and hang on while their flying lizards do all the work."

Accompanied by hoots and hollers, another voice from the crowd heckled the heckler. "Aw, stuff it, Narton. We all want to see the dragons, even if you don't. They're too busy protecting us to play pack-beast."

Bald pate shining, fringe of greasy hair hanging limply, fat jowls in a sallow face quivering indignantly, he bellowed, "Protecting us? *Protecting us?* Against what? Trail dust and biting flies? I've seen no…"

A woman's amused voice chimed in. "…soapweed in a long time."

Titters rippled out and became guffaws.

Wending her way to stand beside the tall man supporting the riders and dragons, planting her hands on ample hips, the gray haired woman looked Narton up and down.

"What you've *seen* is no bandits and no highwaymen robbing you blind. And no Orimjay. If it weren't for the riders patrolling ceaselessly, you wouldn't be here to complain, so shut your yap. Oh, and the bridge committee meets in two days… Should you be interested in actually doing something."

Still spluttering indignantly, the heckler got swallowed by the crowd as they surged forward and halted politely at the waist-high wall, oohing and ahhing.

Repeating his earlier declaration, questioning further, Allar scanned the myriad faces. "A cobalt. Has anyone seen him? Caught a glimpse? Heard someone say they'd seen him?"

Intent on gaining knowledge, no matter how slim or farfetched, Allar jerked around as Zantha blasted out his name.

{{*Allar!*}}

Allar's eyes locked on a scruffy lad, too old to be a boy and too young to be a man. Far more tattered and travel stained than Narton on his worst day, already inside the wall and alarmingly close to Zantha.

Allar stood too far away to aid his beloved dragon.

Voya, on the far side of Mithar and ceaselessly scanning what he could see of the crowd had yet to spot the lad and—for some reason—neither dragon was alerting to danger.

Warning bells ringing a klaxon cry in his head, Allar drew his sword.

{{*Fly, Zantha! Fly now!*}} His heart nearly stopped when Zantha refused.

{{*Wait.*}}

{{*How can you sound so calm?! Fly! Now!*}} Tearing toward Zantha, Allar froze as…

Dropping to one knee, the lad vowed Zantha an oath. "My bow and my sword I pledge to your service. My life is yours to command."

Not the normal Dragonrider's oath—and why on Zola was the lad pledging to a dragon already claimed by a rider?—but a solemn one just the same.

Fixated on the youth, heading toward the boy once more, Allar stumbled when the lad rose, then jolted alertly as if he too heard Zantha's warning.

{{*Ware!!*}}

Allar and the lad both spun to see an attacker coming at the dragons with one of the lethally sharp fishing spears. Battle trained as he was, before Allar could do more than blink, the lad was in motion.

Throwing himself at the assailant, the lad grabbed the haft of the spear.

Shaking him off, getting in a good blow to the lad's head with the haft, the attacker moved toward the dragons once more. Despite the blow, the lad leaped back into the fray, tackling the assassin. Both of them ended up on the ground. Rolling, punching and gouging and kicking, one on top, then the other.

Allar and Voya circled the roil uselessly, attempting to jump in.

Before they could help subdue the attacker, a knife flashed. Both participants lay unmoving as the dark puddle of blood spread on the dusty ground, tracing macabre patterns on the flagstones, trickles filling the cracks and seeming to reach spidery fingers toward Zantha.

Voya stood guard against further attacks as Allar knelt beside the motionless combatants, his heart in his throat.

An undiscovered dragonrider! Beneath their very noses! They couldn't lose the lad. They'd only just found him! The attacker having ended up on top, Allar cautiously heaved him off the young dragonrider. The assailant flopped like the dead vermin he was.

To Allar's vast relief, the blood streamed from the would be assassin's chest, blade still clutched in the lad's fist. The lad's tunic was soaked in blood, one more stain to add to his impressive collection, but he appeared unharmed.

So why wasn't he moving?

Hefting the slight form, rising with the limp body cradled against his chest, Allar kept a wary eye on the approaching couple.

The same rotund woman and tall, lanky young man from earlier—those who had defended the dragons—stepped up at Allar's nod.

Tugging on his dirty blonde forelock, the blue-eyed farmer shook his head. "Not one of ours, M'Lord. Never seen him a'fore."

Eyeing the body distastefully, the well dressed shopkeeper agreed. "Plenty of strangers in town, but never seen the likes o' this scum."

Giving them a nod of assent, Allar issued the young man a direct order. "A rider will be here shortly to sketch the traitor. See that the carcass is not disturbed till he's finished, then haul it to the wilds for the carrion beasts."

Taking up a wide-legged stance, eyes scanning the crowd as he assumed authority, the farmer nodded. As with any criminal, the sketches would be distributed everywhere to see if anyone could identify the traitor.

"Was the lad harmed?" Reaching out to Allar's charge, the woman fisted her hand, snatched it back when Allar curled his lip and snarled.

Giving them a shrug, backing toward Zantha, Allar didn't know what was wrong with the boy, but if the heat radiating off him was any indication, the boy was burning up with fever. Best thing for that was to get the boy back to Dragon's Haven and Seon's expert care as fast as Zantha could fly.

Knew why he'd snarled, although it seemed an over the top reaction. No matter how much the woman seemed to be on their side, dragonhaters came in all shapes and sizes and Allar wouldn't chance this new rider's life on proffered goodwill from a semi-stranger.

{{*Have the dragons alert Seon, Zantha. We need...*}}

{{*Already done.*}}

Mounting while holding an unconscious body presented more of a challenge than vaulting onto Zantha's back. Zantha hunkered down, bending her foreleg enough for Allar to use it as a step. Making sure Allar and his precious cargo were firmly seated, Zantha took to the sky in a swirl of emerald air.

{{*Fly, Zantha! Faster than you've ever flown before! We can't afford to lose him!*}}

Wings taking huge bites of air and propelling them skyward, Zantha leveled off and arrowed for Dragon's Haven.

{{*She will be a fitting mate for you.*}}

An excellent dragonrider, Allar had *never* lost his seat, but Zantha's innocent comment almost sent him tumbling.

{{*She? She who?*}} The gray-haired woman? Allar remembered her now—sister to the glassblower at Dragon's Haven.

Zantha's smug dragon snicker sounded in Allar's head. {{*The dragonrider you are holding.*}}

Recovering his equilibrium, Allar took a closer at the nearly weightless form cradled in his arms while Zantha's wings beat a rapid tattoo.

A slow, thorough perusal of the gaunt face, the dark circles under the eyes. Numerous wounds and bruises beneath the dirt and blood. Shaggy hair that looked as if it had been hacked off with a dull knife.

Events had happened so fast in the landing arena, much like

a battle, he'd only had time to focus on the most important things. Other, secondary memories insisted on coming back full bore. Overlooked in the heat of the moment, details were coming clear.

The slow, over-careful movements of the newly discovered dragonrider—until the fight with the attacker—that betokened unseen wounds and pain forcibly tamped down. The blurring speed once he...no, *she* had leapt into motion. The expert fighting techniques. The sheer grit and determination.

The dead dragonhater, nowhere near as large as Allar or Voya, had still dwarfed the...young dragonrider. Not once had she backed down.

Her fearlessness when confronted by not one, but two real live dragons. Most non-riders were terrified of getting so close.

Not to mention two dragonriders with swords drawn.

She had saved Zantha's life at the risk of her own.

To top all that off—the spark he'd've sworn he'd seen arc between himself and the young dragonrider.

Add all the above to Zantha's strange comment and no wonder Allar was feeling overly possessive, even moreso as they landed and he slid off Zantha.

Striding rapidly toward the Healing Hall, refusing to relinquish the prize he held to the waiting healers and the stretcher they offered, Allar ground his jaw until it ached.

Covertly trying to ascertain the severity of his new patient's wounds, Seon kept pace with Allar. Older than Allar, wiry ginger hair sproinging in every direction, Seon's spritely steps belied the age difference.

"'Tis true, then? A new rider?"

Allar sighed mentally. "Yes, and female to boot."

Dragons could, would, and did gossip worse than old women.

{{*Zantha!*}}

Not sounding in the least repentant, Zantha practically

purred, {{*You told me to alert Seon. He doesn't speak to dragons. I had to tell a dragon, and they had to tell their rider, and...*}}

{{*Now the whole keep knows.*}}

{{*Is that a bad thing?*}}

{{*You know it's not. But she needs to rest, not have every dragon in creation hounding her to see if she's their rider.*}}

{{*Dragons, unlike humans, have manners and protocols.*}}

{{*What's that supposed to mean?*}}

{{*None of the dragons will bother her. About being hers.*}}

Catching something off in Zantha's smug sounding response, Allar had too much on his plate right now to worry about dragon nonsense and double-speak.

Striding down an antiseptic smelling hall Allar normally tried his best to stay far away from, entering a brightly lit room, Allar gently placed the young dragonrider on a high table used for examinations.

If the healers sent to bring the patient to the Healing Hall thought it strange that Allar wouldn't release his charge to their care, they knew better than to voice their disapproval.

Hovering around her prone form like carnage-birds on a battlefield, picking at her tattered clothes and trying to gauge the extent of her injuries, they definitely considered it peculiar and dared to say so this time when Allar refused to leave the room while Seon washed his hands.

Rinkas, a tall, thin healer with fingers like branches of fire-thorn, objected first. Allar knew the healer, knew his reputation. The man had rough hands when bandaging wounds and worse un-bandaging. Allar avoided the man at all costs. No way would he allow the healer close enough to the wounded dragonrider to cause her any more pain.

"My Lord, 'tis most unseemly." Drawing himself up tall—still coming nowhere near Allar's height—wringing his hands, Rinkas shook his head. "Dragonrider she may be, but she is first and foremost an unattached female in need of healing."

Mankan, shorter and stouter, and one of Rinkas' most avid trainees, voiced his concern in a clipped tone. "You must leave so we can treat her. She won't thank you for staring at her unconscious body."

The third healer stood sentinel at the door, one hand on it, waiting for Allar to leave so he could close the door. "Wait in the hall, M'lord. We'll let you…"

Crossing his arms and staring them down one by one, Allar's gaze found Seon's and locked there, silent messages ringing as loud as a shout.

Snorting back laughter, Seon tipped his head. "Out. All of you. Lord Allar will assist me."

Waiting until their grumbling couldn't be heard—through the door Allar slammed on the last healer's heels—Seon looked Allar in the eye. "Since you've negated all my help, make yourself useful. Use plenty of soapweed to wash your hands and then pour some of that solution in the brown jug over them. If you must pass out, make sure you fall where I won't trip over you."

Eyeing the wounded dragonrider, limp on the table, Allar growled, "Mayhap your healers should be trained differently."

"Mayhap. We've grown so used to tending wounds on the battlefield, we've lost the art of gentler healing." Humming a sound of agreement, without giving Allar a second thought, Seon focused all his considerable talent and energy on the battered body in front of him. Cutting her raggedy clothes off, ignoring Allar's explosive curses as each new wound and bruise was exposed, Seon muttered darkly to himself.

A long, long while later, all wounds cleaned and bandaged, the worst ones stitched up, Seon straightened with a groan, hands in the small of his back. "I've done everything I can. The rest…" Shrugged. "…is up to her."

Covering her with a light blanket, Allar edged Seon out of the way and picked up the slight form, cradling her to his chest.

Looking from his patient to his lord, Seon nodded. "Carry

her next door and put her to bed. Let her sleep as long as she will. I suppose you're staying with her."

Allar's only response was to head out into the corridor and into the smaller, dimmer room. Placing his charge gently on the bed, he hooked the room's only chair with his foot and dragged it closer.

Taking a seat, only half listening to Seon's parting instructions, Allar leaned close and whispered fiercely, "You will not die, do you hear me? I forbid it." Raking her from top to toe once more, Allar shook his head. He'd seen warriors fresh from a battlefield less wounded than the female in front of him. Sporting so many bandages she scarcely needed covers, that she still lived at all was a miracle in itself. That she'd been able to exert so much effort to protect Zantha...

If she hadn't been there...

Unable to bear that line of thought, Allar silently catalogued her wounds.

First, and by far the worst, the lump on the back of her head. Not just a lump—she'd been hit hard enough to split her skull open, leaving her hair matted and bloody.

Numerous cuts, some deep, as if she'd been in a knife fight.

Innumerable bumps, scrapes, bruises, possibly a few fractured bones.

And speaking of bones...the newfound dragonrider's skin draped so tightly over her emaciated frame it made her look like one of the desiccated carcasses of some unfortunate creature found in the desert wastes.

Gingerly picking up one of her scarred and calloused hands —the distinct, long-faded scars from Orimjay claws and teeth standing out on her hands and striping up her forearms—Allar gently stroked the single tiny area not bruised or bloodied. A curiosity in itself—all her nails were broken off to the quick, her knuckles and fingertips raw.

Allar could think of nothing that would cause such wounds.

What could she possibly have been doing to cause that kind of damage?

Her boots, dragonhide boots, had been worn through—*worn through!*—in places.

Dragons shed their skin every so often. The immense cast-off skin, once collected and immersed in a mixture of laxamul brains and certain herbs, then worked to supple softness, remained extremely pliable indefinitely. Unlike the nearly impenetrable hide of live dragons, the sheds were easily cut and molded for a variety of uses. Practically indestructible once it was shaped and then treated with another mixture of herbs, prized for making boots, among other things, it would last virtually forever.

Allar knew of many riders who had only gone through a pair or two…in an entire lifetime.

Nothing was adding up.

Not her sudden appearance, not her manner of dress, not… anything about her.

Hers would be a tale worth telling, and he desperately wanted to hear it.

To top it off, certain sure the female was Allar's mate, Zantha had badgered him relentlessly about her condition. Was badgering still.

CHAPTER 4

"*A*llar, it has been two days. Let someone else keep watch. Go and get some sleep." Seon had looked in countless times, checking the rider's wounds and bandages. Both men knew things couldn't go on like this much longer.

Not stopping in his ceaseless motions, hot cloth to bowl of cool water and back to fevered skin, Allar growled, deep and guttural. Dimly heard the night-quiet sounds of the Healing Hall outside the room's door as Seon departed, shaking his head and muttering about stubborn men. Dismissed anything except the female in front of him and started over with his off/on routine for what seemed the millionth time.

Two days, and no change. She hadn't once moved.

While her fever didn't seem quite as high, it hadn't broken either, despite the cool cloths Allar kept on her, and the water he dribbled between her cracked lips.

Settling back in the chair for a moment, booted feet stretched out in front of him, Allar's eyes drifted shut. Asleep in the time it took him to draw a breath, diving deep into the same dark dream as always, Allar twitched and fought in his sleep to no avail. Until suddenly, like that first glimpse of the far off shore when flying over the Great Lake, he caught a glimmer of hope. Far off and nearly indiscernible, and yet, incredibly close at hand, a glowing light like none he'd ever seen.

Awakening with a start, and for a change not drowning in dark thoughts, Allar stretched his aching muscles, scrubbed a hand over his stubble, rubbed his grainy eyes. Opened them and looked to the bed.

Disbelieving, he rubbed his eyes and looked again.

She was gone!

Even before his chair tipped forward and his feet hit the floor, he was calling for Zantha. {{*Zantha! She's gone. She couldn't have gotten far! Find her!*}}

Flying out the door, drawing breath to rouse the entire keep, Zantha's quiet reply filled his head. {{*She is here, with me. Remain calm.*}}

Tearing down the long corridor, Allar began firing questions. {{*How did she get all the way to the caves? How did she even know where to find you? How long has she been there? How…*}}

Giving the mental equivalent of a dragon shrug, Zantha replied. {{*I know not the answers to all your questions. She just this moment appeared. Take care you do not startle her. She has picked up a sword somewhere along the way.*}}

Pounding the length of halls that had become never-ending, vaulting down flights of stairs that seemed to go on forever, Allar burst out onto the verandah ringing the dragon caves. One leap took him from verandah to landing, the next to sand. Racing to the cave Zantha had claimed for her own, sliding to a halt just before reaching the opening, Allar quieted his breathing and peered cautiously around the corner.

A sword wasn't the only thing she'd scrounged. Somewhere along the way she'd acquired a Dragon's Haven overtunic. Falling past her knees, sleeves rolled up and bunched at her wrists, feet bare, she looked like a child playing dress-up.

Facing Zantha, back to him, Allar tried to edge closer without her noticing.

Sensing him despite his stealth, the Dragonrider whirled to face him, sword at the ready, a fierce snarl on her face. "Do not attempt to harm this dragon or I will separate your head from your body."

{{*Allar, do her no harm. She is tangled in a fever dream.*}}

{{*Dragon! Do not speak with him! 'Tis a trap!*}}

Freezing, hands up in the timeless gesture of surrender, Allar's suspicions stood confirmed. He'd thought the Dragonrider had heard Zantha in Laketown, and he'd been right.

Not only could she hear Zantha, she could speak with his dragon!

Impossible!

Only bonded pairs could do so!

Sometimes mates could hear their spouse's dragon, a kind of mental echo, but he had never known a stranger able to hear, much less speak to an unknown dragon and rider.

Now what? If he tried to mindspeak with Zantha, the Dragonrider would hear him. Be-damned if he'd try to use force to take her down. Not after all the time he'd spent the last few days trying to save her scrawny carcass.

If the bloody patches seeping through the tunic were any indication, she'd already reopened some of her wounds.

As the content of her words surpassed the novelty and sank in, Allar sought Zantha's face.

Trap? What the hell did she mean by that?

{{*Dragon! DO NOT make eye contact with him!*}}

Instantly averting his gaze, Allar hesitated to make a move as the female's warnings became stranger and stranger. Quickly becoming more agitated, swaying on her feet and barely able to hold the too-big sword at the ready, she stiffened her stance and whispered over her shoulder to Zantha, "I must protect you from him. Stay behind me until you get a chance to fly. You must fly!"

Nearly giving Allar a heart attack in the process as Zantha's precious neck came altogether too close to the sword, Zantha bent around the girl, surrounding and protecting.

Zantha whispered back, "Allar is a rider. *My* rider. He would never harm me. A rider would never harm a dragon."

Not once taking her eyes off Allar, the girl leaned in close to Zantha and whispered, "That is what all the other dragons thought as well. I could not save them, but I refuse to watch another dragon die. Not while breath remains in my body."

A meteor burning out of the sky and landing in the Great Lake hard enough to turn it into steam would have caused no bigger ripples than the waves of shock vibrating through man and dragon alike.

Fever dream?! This was more along the lines of the nightmare visions that regularly plagued Allar.

Eyes slitted, claws digging into the solid rock of the floor, Zantha hissed, "Explain yourself!"

Placing her calloused palm on the satiny side of Zantha's head, the girl stared deep into Zantha's eyes, searching for truth. What she saw must have satisfied her.

"I am…" She paused and swallowed, her words slurring. "So confused. Hard to tell…what is real and what is nightmare anymore."

Jaw clenched, breathing deeply through her nose, stroking Zantha's eye-ridge, the girl blinked and fought the lethargy overtaking her.

"He truly is your rider, then."

At Zantha's nod, she simply said, "Forgive me. I was afraid to trust him. The dragonhaters are skilled deceivers. The targets are lured in. Once down, the dragonhaters use mindspeak and conversation to distract them, then they make eye contact. I know not how, but the dragons are unable to fly afterwards, and then…"

She choked on the last, her grief evident. "I could not save them. I tried and tried. All I can hear are dragons screaming in pain." Dropping the sword, she clutched her head.

Creeping carefully closer, Zantha nestled the girl between her front legs and chest, offering comfort in the best way she knew how. Bending her head close, and even with a dragon's remarkable hearing, she barely made out the girl's last words.

"Had to be sure. He sent me to find you. Conthar said…"

Due to some quirk in the cave, Allar had heard each and every whisper. The last one nearly floored him.

If the girl was telling the truth, and he had no doubts about the veracity of her tale, heads were going to roll.

As he watched, she crumpled and he leapt.

Gently scooping her up, Allar settled the both of them in the cradle of Zantha's forelegs. He had much thinking to do, and this was a perfect spot. At least now he knew why the girl'd been so adamant about finding Zantha. But why had Conthar needed to send this ragamuffin to Zantha in the first place?

While his first reaction—to rouse everyone in all the dragon keeps that were still functional and wage all out war satisfied the vengeance-hungry side of him—the canny side of him advised it was better to wait and smoke out the traitors.

It had to be a trusted insider passing along information, but who? A terrible thing, not knowing who could be the traitor.

While there had always been an uneasy truce between riders and non-riders, one faction championing the dragons and the other proclaiming the dragons' uselessness, mostly out of jealousy, the long running conflict had erupted into full out war generations ago.

As soon as the female awoke, they were going to have a serious heart to heart. Meanwhile, mind churning furiously, Allar went back over what little he knew.

She hadn't once called Zantha by name, though if she could mindspeak with Zantha, she had to know it. She had warned Zantha not to mindspeak with Allar, nor to make eye contact.

So what it boiled down to was this: Someone—or someones —was using the very things that made the rider's bond with the dragons so special to ensnare and kill the dragons.

Everyone knew there was power in a name, and if someone could mindspeak with a dragon that only gave them more power. As for looking them in the eye, he wasn't sure where that came in, but it definitely involved power.

Until he'd heard the girl speak to Zantha, he'd've said it was totally impossible for anyone not bonded to a dragon to do so.

But he *had* heard her!

And *she* had heard him!

How?

Allar's confused thoughts chased themselves around and around. Spinning fast but going nowhere, a hunt-beast chasing its own tail.

Conthar! Allar's heart soared. Was he still alive?

Dropped like a rock. Or was he one of the ones she'd said she couldn't save?

She'd also mentioned dragon screams. That smacked of not just death, but torture. Why hadn't any of the dragons called for help? No dragon, or rider, would ever ignore such a cry. If one dragon sent out so much as a whimper, all dragons would hear it.

Who could have enough power to silence dragons, and enough hate to torture and kill them?

Breaking into his whirling thoughts, Allar almost laughed out loud at Zantha's sleepy grumble. "My human. You're giving me a headache and you definitely need your beauty sleep."

Safely snugged between Zantha's legs, back against her chest, arms full of courageous female, Allar gave in but not before Zantha caught his mumbled, "Great! Just what I need—two bossy females telling me what to do!"

37

REGAINING HER SENSES SLOWLY, Renny lay still, savoring the warmth around her. For the first time in forever she felt…safe. Not attempting to analyze it, she just enjoyed. Her wounds felt better, the pain in her head, if not entirely gone, vastly diminished.

At least she could remember her own name now. For the last many days, had anyone asked, she couldn't have said. The fever had hit her hard, as hard as the blow to her head.

She could sense dragons nearby but she couldn't hear any dragons screaming, a blessing in itself. Taking a deep breath she smelled healthy dragon and…warm man.

Slitting her eyes just a little she peered up under her lashes at the man holding her. Who…

Oh! The Dragonrider from the village!

At that realization, a full body spark lit her up everywhere their bodies were touching. Tingling her skin and teasing her senses, making Renny fervently wish for…

Things she'd long ago given up hope of ever having for herself.

A man—a true mate—a home and a family. All the normal things regular people took for granted.

He didn't look like any of the scumbags who liked to torture dragons. Large, very large, where they were of much smaller stature.

Midnight hair fell past his shoulders, some of it pooling on her like the finest silk. Renny clenched her hands lightly at the urge to touch it. Her fingers actually itched to do so, or maybe it was just the healing process.

Taking a breath, she risked another look. Deeply tanned face, square jaw that promised more than a little stubbornness, nose that could've been perfect if it didn't look like it'd been broken a time or two, black wings for eyebrows.

Extremely kissable lips.

Whoa, Renny-girl!

What are you thinking? You never look at a man that way! Men are T-R-O-U-B-L-E! Especially when they look like that!

Wondering where her usual combative/self-protective urges concerning men in close proximity had gone, wondering how she could disentangle herself without waking the sleeping giant holding her, Renny blinked and forgot everything when he opened his eyes.

Blue. The bluest blue, as blue as the magnificent cobalt she'd been unable to save. She didn't even know eyes came in that shade of blue. Feeling like she was falling into their depths, Renny actually put up a hand to stop herself.

He smiled, a flash of white, and she was completely lost. Handsome before, the smile made him devastatingly so. "There you are!"

Having awakened the instant her breathing pattern changed, arms full of warm woman and more at peace than he'd been in a long, long time, Allar had given her a few moments to orient herself before slowly opening his eyes. His gaze met the woman's green ones, as green as Zantha, staring up at him from under shaggy bangs.

A look of utter wonder on her face, she reached up as if to cup his cheek.

Knowing he'd make a complete fool of himself if she did, Allar caught her hand with the utmost care and pressed it gently to his heart.

Like that was any better.

He might've mistaken her for a lad at first, but there was no mistaking what he held now.

She might come in a small package, bruised and battered at that, but what a package!

A mop of sun-gilded light brown hair he suspected she deliberately kept hacked short, tip-tilted eyes like green jewels set in a heart-shaped face, lips that…

Stop right there!

Remember the bruised and battered part!

Grinning rakishly, Allar winged a perfect brow. "So! My sleeping beauty has awakened! Does she have a name?"

She had to try twice before she managed to croak, "Renny."

"Small but mighty. Fits you perfectly!"

Another croak. "What?"

"That's what your name means. Mine's Allar. Lord Allar if you want to be technical."

Renny was having trouble tracking. His voice was sinful, a blend of smoky fires and long nights spent naked on soft furs. Alluring. Sucking her further into his web, she could listen to him forever.

That thought panicked her as few could. She didn't have time to become some lord's plaything. She had to…

"Let me up!"

Instantly sobering, Allar shook his head. "Be still. I didn't mean to alarm you. You must take it slow and easy. I'll help you up but you have to be careful or you'll reopen your wounds, what few you didn't manage to tear open last night. This is the first time you haven't looked like death warmed over."

Bristling, about to lay into him, before Renny could frame a suitable comeback, Zantha broke in.

The dragon's soft reprimand, tinged with humor, reminded Renny that she and the rider weren't alone.

{{*May I speak to my rider now?*}}

Having overlooked the dragon's presence completely in favor of the human—something that had *never* happened to her—using the hand still on the rider's rock-hard chest to push herself off and tipping her head back on his muscular arm, Renny made eye contact with Zantha.

{{*I hate to bother you two, but are you going to finish ogling each other any time soon? I need to feed. 'Tis almost midday.*}}

Jerking away from the rider as if they'd been caught doing far more than staring, Renny tried to scramble out of his hold.

Allar simply flexed his arms and held her immobile. "I said I would help you up! Now be still!"

Stiffening, preparing to fire back a blistering retort, Renny held her tongue when he immediately softened his tone.

"I've spent the last two days patching you up. I've helped our finest Healer clean, stitch, salve, and poultice every inch of your scrawny carcass. Neither of us is willing to go through that again, and unless you enjoy pain, neither are you."

Relaxing a smidge, realizing she wore nothing save a tunic that wasn't hers, Renny panicked. "Where are my clothes?"

Allar snorted, "Those filthy rags we cut off you? In the burn pile, I hope."

"Where did I get this?" Renny indicated the tunic with a twitch of her shoulder. It covered her to mid-calf, but still…

Allar answered wryly, "Probably from the same place you stole the sword you threatened to kill me with last night. Speaking of which, I want to know how you found Zantha. And how you avoided the posted guards."

Renny blinked and her eyes shuttered as she mentally withdrew, obviously getting ready to spout some practiced lie, or more likely, tell him nothing at all.

A loud rumble from the region of Zantha's first stomach propelled Allar to his feet, taking Renny with him as he walked deeper into the cave toward a padded bench in the back. "I've procured some clean clothes for you. Do you need help or…"

The scathing look she shot him should have stabbed hotter and deeper than a fire-thorn to the eye.

Not that Allar paid the slightest attention.

"Well enough. Call if you need me. Otherwise, I'm going to be on the far side of Zantha, waiting. Do not move from this seat."

Hidden behind Zantha's bulk, Renny kept shooting barbed glances over her shoulder. Using the tunic like a tent, she managed to get the clean shirt on without showing any unwarranted skin, wiggled into the leggings and out of the bloodied tunic. He'd said he wouldn't peek, but he was a male. A strange male and…

Turning her head to Renny, Zantha blew a warm breath over her human charge. "Allar is most honorable, Renny. He would never break his word to you."

Patting Zantha and easing the huge emerald muzzle out of the way in the same move, Renny slipped the fleece lined foot warmers on, grumbling under her breath all the while. "Don't know why I have to change. There was barely any blood on that tunic."

Snickering, turning her massive head the other way, Zantha announced, "Your lady is finished, Allar."

Stepping around Zantha, Allar let out a low whistle and sketched a bow. "While Zantha feeds, My Lady, we will go see the healer and feed us."

Sucking in a deep breath as soon as he laid eyes on her, Seon lit into Renny non-stop, gave her a thorough going over. "Well, your midnight jaunt didn't seem to cause too much additional damage and your fever has finally broken, but you still need to take it easy. I'll let the stitches you pulled go for now, but you have to keep the wounds…"

Having been the frequent recipient of more than a few of Seon's long-winded monologues, Allar took pity on Renny. "Healer, would you care to join us in the Great Hall for nooning?"

Winking back saucily at the look Renny shot him—partly grateful, partly exasperated, and promising full retribution at some future date—Allar scooped her up and carried her out the door.

Refusing to give him the satisfaction of re-arguing a battle she'd already lost once and wouldn't win this go-round either, Renny fumed silently.

Carrying her! As if she were a babe! The same way he'd carried her from Zantha's lair to the Healer's Hall.

Barely pausing for breath, Seon continued his tirade all the way to the double doors of the Great Hall. "…plenty of bedrest, lots of fluids, no undue exertion…"

At their entrance, silence swept in front of them like a sudden wind blowing in the door. Renny stiffened, all her alarms screeching. Would've squirmed free and bolted if only Allar hadn't tightened his arms like dragonhide bands around a wooden barrel.

What was she thinking? Following along with everything he dictated like she'd lost her wits? Just because Allar's touch on her skin was like striking two pieces of fire-starter together when she'd never known anything but biting cold… She'd let him lull her, dull her self-preservation instincts… No way she could fight her way out of this. She didn't even have her dagger. What…

{{*Peace, little warrior. None here will harm you.*}}

Zantha's quiet comment calmed Renny, held her more surely in place than Allar.

Taking a deep breath, Renny watched in disbelief. Every Dragonrider, every servant, every person in the place, all staring her way—no, staring at *her*—stopped whatever they were doing. The ones seated rose to their feet, and all stood in perfect silence.

A Dragonrider almost as big as Allar stepped forward and bowed from the waist. "My Lady, we are forever in your debt."

At his words, the entire assemblage erupted into thunderous calls, whistling and clapping.

Allar whispered in her ear, "Meet Voya, my second in command. He was with me in the village when you threw yourself at a madman, not once, but twice, to protect Zantha. He —indeed they—do not give their praise lightly."

Blushing profusely, Renny's face darkened even more as Allar

43

added his thanks. Carrying her toward the head table, he kept speaking low in that dangerously gorgeous voice of his, perfectly discernible to her even over the din of the others.

"My Lady, I fear I have been most remiss. I have yet to thank you for saving my dragon's life. I do so now, from the bottom of my heart. Thank you for Zantha's life, and by default, mine.

The hall and everyone around them disappeared as Renny gazed into Allar's bluer than blue eyes, feeling more off kilter—and yet more balanced—than she'd ever been in her entire life.

"I can tell all this…" Indicating the rest of the huge room with a tilt of his head, never slackening stride, Allar continued. "…makes you vastly uncomfortable, but please let them have their moment. You are the first truly good thing that's happened here in ages. Especially since Conthar vanished. Dragon's Haven, among all the remaining keeps, has never lost a dragon—not in this way—until Conthar. We've been called upon to assist in searches for every other keep. Few of the missing dragons have been found, and those that were… My riders—everyone here—are sick at heart with worry. The thought of losing Zantha too… You've managed to give us back our hope, along with a new Dragonrider. Those are precious things indeed."

Settling Renny into a chair beside his own much larger one, Allar seated himself and raised a hand, the one twined with hers.

Quiet descended like a thunderclap, leaving a void where noise had been.

Right before a ringing cheer shook the dust off the rafters, high overhead.

Torn between wanting to dissolve into her seat then drip down under the table like a melting candle, and wanting to gobble everything in sight—she'd never seen this much food in one place!—Renny sat quietly, observing.

Evidently Seon had given orders—a beaming servant had placed a plate of tasteless wafers and a steaming mug of flavorful broth in front of Renny and moved on. Seated between Allar and

44

Seon, she didn't even have a chance to palm some of the real food for later.

Probably a good thing her stomach was so shrunken. Sorely tempted to gobble everything within reach and then work her way down the table, stuffing her pockets for later, Renny tried not to moan in ecstasy with every sip of the broth.

Reining in her singleminded fascination with the laden tables, she began to listen to the conversations around her.

Seon, talking to someone on the far side of himself, discussing treatments and techniques and herbs.

Renny's interest in that got sidetracked as she focused on Allar's conversation with…Voya.

It sounded as if Allar hadn't left her side for days, as if Voya was catching him up on everyday happenings and decisions.

From Zantha's mind, Renny had gleaned that Allar was a most important man, lord of the keep and a warrior to best all others, with never-ending responsibilities.

Renny was nothing to him, not even one of his people.

So why…

As if discerning her thoughts, Allar brushed his thumb gently across her hand, the hand he'd kept possession of throughout the meal. Smiled warmly at her.

About to say something, Allar changed his mind when one of the riders approached the head table.

One by one, each dropping briefly to one knee, head bowed, they rose to give their reports.

Face becoming grimmer and grimmer with each recounting, a long litany of repetitious bad news, Allar turned to Renny when she nudged his foot under the table.

Leaning his way, Renny murmured in his ear, "Allar, I can ease your pain. I know…"

Brushing his thumb lightly across the back of her hand once more, Allar nodded.

Assured the few remaining riders, "I will hear your tales later.

My Lady is not yet recovered and tires easily." Scooping her up, Allar strode from the hall without a backward glance.

Face flaming—again!—Renny sent strident thoughts his way, casting aspersions on his parentage, his manhood, his fighting abilities.

Smirking as if he could read every one of them, Allar told her, "I must finish with the riders, and I have other business to attend to. If I return you to the Healing Hall, I have no doubt you will escape again."

Cocked his head and regarded Renny thoughtfully. "Were you one of my riders, I would order you to stay there for at least a sennight. I suppose I could have you put in restraints…"

Laughing out loud at the mutinous glare that earned him, Renny's emerald eyes heating and flashing with temper, Allar touched his forehead to hers. "My Lady, you wound me with a look."

Renny snarled, "Try to put me in restraints and I will wound you with more than that! And I am *not* your lady! Stop calling me that!"

Sobering even as Zantha's amused chuckles rang in his head, pondering what to do with Renny while he couldn't be at her side, Zantha provided the perfect solution.

{{*I am finished feeding, if you wish to leave Renny with me while you conduct your business.*}}

{{*Are you reading my mind again, Zantha?*}}

Renny answered Zantha, completely bypassing Allar and once again impressing him to no end. {{Renny *needs no nursemaid, but* I *would enjoy time spent in your company, Zantha.*}}

Shoving against Allar's chest, Renny demanded, "Put me down. I can find my own way to Zantha."

"I'm certain sure you could."

"Put. Me. Down." Looking vastly surprised when Allar set her on her feet, swaying for a moment, Renny caught her balance with a hand against his chest.

"Allar, we need to talk. I know…"

Allar put a finger to Renny's lips to silence her. Her soft, warm, lips. Momentarily distracted, he forgot what he'd been about to say. At Zantha's amused snort, he jerked his hand back, spun on his heel, and resumed walking.

Realizing Renny wasn't beside him, Allar turned just in time to see her stumble. Sweeping her into his arms, he ignored her renewed protests. "Forgive me. I was just scolding you for not staying on the Healing Hall and then I go and forget how very battered you truly are. Hush, and allow me to do you this small service."

Dropping her head on his shoulder, Renny took a breath, and went limp in his arms.

She acted so tough—despite her diminutive size—and radiated so much vitality, it was hard to think of her as anything but a pillar of strength.

That she acquiesced so easily told Allar plainer than words how exhausted Renny still was.

Carrying Renny to Zantha, Allar placed Renny between Zantha's legs, cushioned against Zantha's side. Sunning herself in the large, sandy courtyard, Zantha rested on her belly, legs tucked to one side, wings out-spread.

Giving Zantha a good scratch between the eyes, Allar stepped back and had to grin. Renny was already asleep.

Whispered to Zantha, "Guard her well. She is precious to me already."

Butting him gently with her head, Zantha tucked her head around her legs and wrapped her tail around her nose, cocooning Renny. Folding her wings, draping one over Renny like a momma hen sheltering a chick, Zantha blew out a warm breath and followed Renny.

~

RETURNING at dusk to find Renny still sleeping, surprised she'd remained where he left her, Allar scooped her up.

Startling at his touch, realizing without opening her eyes who held her, Renny snuggled closer and promptly fell back asleep.

Holding her close, rejoicing, Allar made his way to his sleeping quarters in Zantha's cave.

Checking her wounds, Allar was astounded once more by how much they'd healed.

Things would progress faster than he'd thought.

Relaying his plans to Zantha, knowing she'd pass them along to Mithar, he set everything in motion.

They would leave at first light.

CHAPTER 5

*A*wakening to an insistent voice calling her name, Renny opened heavy eyes. Allar's face was the first thing, the only thing in her range of vision. Smiling sleepily, she raised a hand and brushed the back of her fingers across his cheek.

Invisible sparks showered over Renny as her hand made contact.

Murmured, "I was having the nicest dream about you." Snuggled closer, closed her eyes, and was promptly asleep once more.

Reveling in her touch, in her words, if Renny looked at him like that again, Allar would be hard pressed not to take her right here, right now.

Silently chastised himself. It was far too soon—she wasn't ready, physically or mentally—but she *was* well worth waiting for.

Frustration, more with himself than her, made Allar's voice gruff as he gently shook her awake. "Renny, My Lady, you must wake."

Her grumpy *not your lady* sounded almost as much sad as defiant and tore at his heart.

Allar made a rude sound. Renny could deny what was between them all she wanted. Denying something didn't lessen its veracity. "Be that as it may, if you want to ride with me, Zantha and I are leaving. Now."

The last got Renny up and moving before her eyes were fully opened, her quick intelligence snapping to attention. Ride? Few who were not dragonriders were accorded the privilege. Renny wasn't about to turn down the offer, and Allar had deliberately put her off about telling him her information. He must be trying to get them out of the keep. Once in the sky, none could overhear and Zantha would never betray a confidence.

Renny knew Zantha was privy to Allar's every thought, but the dragon was as closemouthed as her rider, and Renny would never ask Zantha to betray Allar.

By the time she performed her morning ablutions, which consisted of splashing water on her face from the basin in the corner and cursorily finger combing her short hair, she was feeling marginally more human.

Shaking his head, Allar watched her closely. He'd never seen anyone heal as quickly. Although moving somewhat slowly, Renny didn't seem to be in too much pain. Seon had done a fine job, and Renny's proximity to Zantha seemed to have helped tremendously. Maybe it was just the amount of sleep she'd gotten.

Dragons were good for riders, and riders were good for dragons. That was a known fact.

Time would take care of the rest.

That and Allar.

Renny wasn't getting out of his sight, and he was going to do everything in his power to see that she was well taken care of from here on out.

In that vein…

"I procured shirts that will fit you better, and a warm cloak. You'll need them when we fly. Get dressed and let's be on our way. Seon's cleared you to eat more than broth, and we can do that while Zantha flies."

Rubbing the material between her fingers, Renny shivered in delight. More finely woven than the tunic she'd swiped or the shirt he'd scrounged for her, these were also much softer.

Two shirts! A lighter one to wear underneath, and a heavier overshirt. Definitely more her size and nicer than anything she'd ever worn.

Stroking the fabric, rubbing the downy softness against her cheek, Renny looked up in time to catch a strange look on Allar's face. Making a shooing motion with one hand, Renny waited until he disappeared.

Tugging yesterday's too-big shirt off, slipping the under shirt on, Renny delighted as its softness slithered against her skin. Overshirt next, and she belted them both with a belt Allar had also provided.

The voice in her head, the one that'd kept her alive for so many years, bleated long and loud.

Renny-girl, you're getting entirely too dependent on him. You learned the hard way to depend on none save yourself. You…

Ignoring the clamoring of her inner voice, leaning into Zantha's side, Renny patted the warm hide repeatedly.

Swinging her massive head around close to Renny, Zantha chuffed her approval.

Renny shrugged and patted some more. "I just wanted to thank you. For guarding me while I slept, and for… Well, everything."

Regarding the small human female intently, Zantha replied, "'Tis I who should be thanking you, for far more than you know. Not only did you fight a dragonhater for me, you make Allar laugh. That is a boon without measure. There has been little enough to inspire mirth lately, and his cares are wearing on him."

Renny sagged. "My tale will only add to his burden."

Zantha countered, "Not knowing is far worse."

Straightened like a soldier going into battle. "If he hates me after, I will not blame him."

Zantha's eyes whirled and the sounds she made sounded suspiciously like laughter. "Hate…you? Allar could never hate you."

~

HIGH ABOVE DRAGON'S HAVEN, Allar felt his heart swell to bursting.

He'd known Renny wouldn't be afraid of flying, and she hadn't let him down. Seated in front of him so he could keep a good grip on her in case she lost her balance, Allar kept a tight hold on her hips, mindful of her cracked and wrapped ribs.

Taking to riding like she'd been born on a dragon, Renny's joy was contagious. Eyes wide open, head thrown back, she flung her arms to the side and laughed with sheer delight.

"This is so…perfect! Absolutely perfect!"

Tucking the warm cloak around Renny, Allar secured it between them. "I don't want you to get chilled."

Nodding her understanding, Renny continued to gawk unashamedly—up, down, and all around. Snickered to herself. With the cloak covering the front of her, Allar's heat behind her and Zantha beneath her, she didn't think getting chilled was going to be a problem.

Reaching into the pouch at his hip, having deliberately trapped Renny's arms under the cloak, Allar held something to her lips. Practically daring her to refuse, he fed her bits of soft cheeses, small bites of tender laxamul, berries and fruits, and in between bites, he held a flask of sweet bizzle-berry juice to her lips, urging her to take sip after sip.

Flying steadily higher and higher into the mountains—nowhere near anything like the heights and valleys Renny was used to on the

other side of the Great Lake, and yet still nearly impassable on foot
—Zantha took a winding, circuitous route, as if they were merely
exploring. The terrain becoming ever wilder and more remote,
Zantha at last began circling over a deep, hidden valley. Beautiful,
but they'd flown over a hundred just as breathtaking.

Renny had all ideas she didn't want to know the *why* of this
particular one. She really didn't.

Looking around as Zantha nailed a perfect landing, nary a
jolt, Renny could see nothing remarkable about this place. Cliffs,
trees, rocks, grass, a creek.

Sliding off with Renny in his arms, Allar offered, "Your tale
can be told here with no fear of being overheard by man or
dragon."

All her senses flaring, tamping down even the residual tingles
from being so close to Allar after being held by him and buoyed
by Zantha for the entire flight, Renny shivered.

"What happened here?"

Allar's lungs froze at Renny's astuteness. *Not why, but what, she
asks.* Hoping to avoid an explanation, or at least give her nothing
more than the sanitized version, he should've known better. Not
only was his Renny tough and brave, she was too smart for her
own good.

Sidestepping a direct answer, Allar merely told her, "This
valley prevents dragons from speaking mind to mind if they are
below the surrounding heights."

Knowing he was withholding information to protect her, not
willing to let him shoulder the burden by himself, Renny eyed
him steadily. "And you know this because..."

Turning and walking away, Allar stood wide legged, back
rigid, head thrown back, arms stiff and hands fisted at his sides,
the epitome of rage and guilt.

Released from the need to refrain from mindspeak, Zantha
answered for him. {{*A first time rider and his dragon became lost in a*

terrible storm and crash landed here. They weren't found for...several days.}}

No need to ask who had found the lost pair. Renny swallowed back bile threatening to choke her as she picked the horrible images loud and clear from Zantha's mind.

A young boy, bones shattered, unable to move.

A dragon, wing broken, calling and calling for help.

Neither understanding why no one answered.

Both in unbearable pain, neither able to help the other.

Their newly formed and untried bond echoing and refracting their pain, multiplying it until both were very nearly driven insane.

Feeling his pain to the depths of her soul, Renny wrapped her arms around Allar and pressed her cheek to the middle of his back. Didn't try to soothe him with words. There weren't any.

She simply held him, and waited.

His outburst, when it finally came, frightened the birds from their nesting places in the cliffs.

Renny and Zantha watched in silence as Allar paced and seethed.

"Do you know why Dragon's Haven has never lost dragons when all other keeps have? We don't send out inexperienced riders alone. No rider is trusted by himself until he has proven he can stay seated on his dragon, that he and his dragons know where the danger zones are."

Rolling his shoulders, moving his head side to side and cracking his neck, clenching and unclenching his fists until the muscles in his arms bulged and the veins stood out, Allar lanced more venom from his self-inflicted wounds.

"Leadership of Dragon's Haven isn't passed on because someone's father or grandfather was lord. Dragon's Haven alone has always chosen its lords based on their ability to protect our dragons. No dragons go very far for very long by themselves without keeping in constant contact."

Standing still, breathing hard, Allar looked inward and scowled at whatever he saw.

"We lost Conthar only because he informed me, through Zantha, he was close to finding out why the other dragons were disappearing and I let him search, too far and too long by his lonesome. Nay, in my eagerness to end this madness, I sent him out, most likely to his death. The weight of that decision rests solely on my shoulders."

Renny knew all about that crushing weight. The pain in Allar's voice threatening to break Renny's heart, she also knew better than to show him any pity.

While she wanted to run to him and coddle him, soothe him like a mother with a hurt child, instead, she merely remarked in a very dry tone, "Perhaps you should have restrained him in the Healer's Hall."

It took a moment for Renny's comment to sink in, but it had Zantha chortling and Allar staring, slack jawed.

Saying nothing, Allar strode to Renny, and cupping her face, gently kissed her until they were both breathless, the sparks surrounding them nearly lighting the air on fire.

Wrapping his arms around Renny, Allar drew her against his heart and dropped his head over hers.

"Thank you." A soft, intimate murmur that ruffled Renny's hair and sank into her skin like a soothing balm.

Wanting to savor the closeness just a moment longer, dreading what she had to tell him, Renny pushed away. Knowing after Allar found out the truth about her, he'd never want to touch her again, already missing his touch like she'd miss a severed limb.

Stiffening, Renny looked Allar in the eye. "I, too, share your burden. I have seen more mortally wounded dragons than I can count." Swallowed and blurted, "I hear dragons. Wounded dragons. Dragons in pain. I have always heard dragons. I cannot shut out their cries. And I can not save them. Ever."

Exchanging stupefied glances, Allar and Zantha eased closer.

A Dragonhealer? Their Renny was not merely a dragon*rider*, she was a Dragon*healer*!

Above even the dragons, the Dragonhealers had been targeted by the dragonhaters. Many of the ones not killed outright had been driven insane during the wars from hearing the dragons' cries.

Renny had voiced the same confession in Zantha's cave and neither Allar nor Zantha had picked up on it, too immersed in Renny's deteriorating condition. Or if they'd paid her statement any mind, they'd figured it was the effects of the fever dream tangled around her.

That a healer lived was news indeed! So much so it rendered Allar and Zantha speechless.

Taking their silence for condemnation, gathering her courage around herself like a tattered cloak, Renny confessed, "The last one I heard was Conthar. I could not save any of the others, neither could I save him."

Sounding bitter and defeated, she continued. "He was trapped in a valley like this one so his cries to you went unheard, but even wounded and dying he managed to tell me about Dragon's Haven. Made me promise to find you." As if the staggering pain had become unbearable, Renny spat, "Made me leave him to those butchers so I could carry his warning to you."

Allar stared, stunned, knowing it was just like Conthar, even close to death, to make every effort to relay his knowledge. Eyes riveted to Renny's white face, he commanded, "Take me to him!"

He and Zantha, along with the rest of Dragon's Haven, would deal with the pain of losing Conthar later.

Threading her fingers through the hair at her temples, grabbing a double handful, Renny yanked. Yanked harder and replied miserably, "I...cannot. I have no idea where he is."

Looming over Renny, Allar demanded, "How can you not know?"

Not in the least intimidated, Renny flung back, "Because he knew as long as there was breath in my body, I would never willingly leave him. Conthar lay wounded unto death, trapped, and those butchers were going to finish the job. I couldn't free him and I refused to leave, so Conthar caused a landslide. It buried him in rocks and rubble."

Swallowing as if the very words were choking her, Renny tipped her head back. Took a deep breath and met Allar's gaze. "I tried to dig him out, but I merely succeeded in bringing down more rocks. One hit me on the head, and after that, I remember nothing but coming to with a burning desire, nay, a compulsion, to find you and Zantha and Dragon's Haven as fast as I possibly could."

Shoulders slumping in defeat, Renny shrugged. "I have no idea how long I traveled, and as for the direction, only that I headed east, so Conthar lies somewhere to the west."

Nuzzling Renny, Zantha spoke, her tone reverent. "Dragonhealer..."

Stepping away from Zantha's comfort, her tone filled with self-loathing, Renny charged, "Don't you mean dragonkiller? I told you I could save none of the dragons I heard. Conthar was merely the last in a long line of failures."

"Dragonhealer," Zantha affirmed. "We will discuss what you term failures later. Finding Conthar is of utmost import right now. Perhaps Allar and I can help you remember if you are willing to try."

Staring into Zantha's eyes, her own lighting with a spark of eagerness, Renny declared, "Anything! Anything I can do to help find Conthar. I cannot bear the thought of those butchers being the only ones to know the burial place of one such as he."

Tipping her head deferentially to Renny, Zantha informed her, "If you will permit me to look into your memories, perhaps between us we can figure out where he is. Normally, since we're not bonded, I wouldn't even attempt something like this but you can hear me so well, and you and Allar can hear each other through me. Allar will have to act as anchor. If dragon and healer don't have an anchor, they can both become trapped in the memories. I am full willing to try if you and Allar are agreeable."

"When can we start?" Drawing herself up like she was going into battle, Renny looked ready to walk through fire.

{{*First, we all need to feed.*}} Zantha's verbal reply, if she made one, was lost in the rush of her wings as she took flight. {{*We will all need every iota of strength we can muster to do this.*}}

Renny and Allar watched in silence as Zantha zeroed in on a couple four legged cliff climbers clambering up a sheer rock wall.

Scrubbing her hands over her face, Renny turned away from Allar. He still hadn't spoken, and Renny wasn't picking up on anything through Zantha's link.

How he must hate her!

She'd left Conthar to die, and she had an abysmal track record with precious dragon lives.

Renny'd only know Allar for a couple of days. It shouldn't hurt this much to think he loathed her.

Staring at the slight woman in front of him, awed by her courage and tenacity, Allar's throat had closed at her admissions, and he couldn't begin to find words to express his gratitude and respect.

He'd only rescued one wounded dragon, and the excruciating pain had very nearly destroyed him. He simply couldn't imagine doing it countless times.

{{*Our female—our Dragonhealer—thinks you hate her.*}}

Zantha's comment shocked him into speech.

"Renny. Look at me."

Renny's reply was wooden, devoid of emotion. "You need to eat. Zantha said so."

"As do you, and we will. Look at me."

Giving Renny a moment to comply, Allar tipped her chin up

and kept a firm grip on her soft skin. "You think I blame you for Conthar's death?"

Refusing to look at him, Renny jerked her head and tried to worm out of his hold. Her question came out in a pain-filled whisper. "How could you not? I just stood here and told you I left a wounded, trapped, and defenseless dragon in the hands of dragonhaters. I. Left. Him."

Not slackening his grip, Allar snarked, "You're absolutely right. You should have stayed there and died with Conthar, so that not only would we have lost a dragon, but a Dragonhealer as well."

Renny's head whipped up, eyes finally meeting his.

Softening his tone, rubbing his thumb across her lower lip, Allar shook his head. "Don't you realize the only thing rarer than dragons and dragonriders is dragonhealers? So rare, that in all my years, you are the first I have ever seen or even heard of in anything but tales of the old days? It has long been thought that all perished in the Battle of Pyrajeem whilst I was still in leading strings. The dragonhaters had perfected some new weapon capable of piercing dragon hide like a knife through warm butter, causing a slaughter without parallel."

Mesmerized by the rhythmic stroking on her lip, Renny blurted, "The butchers use such weapons."

Allar nodded, eyes on Renny's lips. Cupping her cheek, he shifted his caresses to her cheekbone. "Conthar recognized what you were, how valuable you are. He knew he had to save you at all costs."

Renny stared at Allar, speechless. Valuable, her? Was it possible? When all her life, she'd been told ceaselessly just exactly how worthless she was?

Turning his back to Renny and leaving her to her own thoughts, Allar dug in his pack and pulled out the provisions he'd brought for their nooning.

Spreading Renny's cloak on the grass, Allar divided the food.

"If you wish to do this thing, you must eat, My..." Changing his mind, Allar finished,"...Renny."

Saying nothing more, he watched Zantha at the far end of the valley as she devoured the cliff climbers.

Watched Renny out of the corner of his eye as she reluctantly joined him, sitting on the barest edge of her cloak and taking miniscule bites. Where, and how, had she been raised that she didn't know dragonhealers were valued above jewels and gold? Renny didn't even think of herself as a Healer. Perhaps that explained why Zantha hadn't picked that vital bit of information out of Renny's head.

Allar silently berated his own thick-headedness. He should've deduced Renny's status from all the clues she'd let slip from the first time he'd laid eyes on her.

Renny could hear and speak to Zantha without being bonded to Zantha. That was a major red flag if ever there was one. Speaking to all dragons was a vitally necessary skill for dragonhealers.

They couldn't very well help dragons if they didn't know what was wrong, and how were they supposed to know what was wrong if they couldn't communicate with more than their own dragon?

Renny had pledged a dragon oath without being bonded, and other than dragonriders, none save Healers pledged to dragons that weren't their own.

Renny had selflessly come between Zantha and danger twice. Once from the dragonhater, and again when she thought Allar was trying to harm Zantha.

Renny hadn't known Zantha, Zantha hadn't been in pain, and yet Renny had arrowed straight to Zantha's lair as if she had a map, to check on Zantha.

A dragonhealer's highest purpose in life was to save dragons, even at the cost of their own lives.

Allar couldn't believe he hadn't put the pieces together.

Zantha intruded on his musings. {{*Mayhap you were too busy ogling her? If you two are finished, we need to get started.*}}

Rising as Zantha landed nearby, pretending not to hear Zantha's mental exchange with Allar, the rosy tint of Renny's cheeks gave her away. "I'm ready when you are. Tell me what to do."

Checking to make sure Renny'd eaten everything he'd put in front of her, Allar grinned. Nothing left, not even stray crumbs.

Zantha eyed her newest human with compassion. Obviously anticipating the worst, standing stiffly, spine rigid, shoulders back, Renny stared off into nothing. Zantha and Allar shared a look.

There was no doubt in either of their minds that if throwing herself off a cliff was what was required to make this work, Renny would already be halfway to the top of the highest one.

Zantha soothed, "Little Warrior, all you have to do is make yourself comfortable. Allar and I will do the rest."

Leaning his back against a large boulder, Allar stretched his long legs out in front of himself and patted the cloak turned blanket beside him. At Renny's skeptical look, he waggled his eyebrows suggestively.

Grinning at the flash of fire in her eyes, he patted the same spot once more.

"Come, sit beside me and relax. I never let a girl kiss me on the first date." Smothering a laugh at her astonished look, Allar tried for prim and proper, failing miserably.

Choking back her own snort of laughter, Renny sat on a corner of the blanket. *Not* beside Allar.

Reaching over, carefully tugging Renny down so her head was in his lap, Allar said, "Relax. Just relax." Running his fingers through her hair, front to back, slowly, over and over, nails barely scraping her scalp and being careful to avoid the sore spots, Allar practiced some soothing of his own.

Zantha's dulcet tones joined Allar's. "Relax, Renny. Think

about the spot where you found Conthar. Tell us how you got there."

Renny's eyes drifted closed, the sun warm on her face. The nearby stream chuckled softly to itself, the wind whispered in the trees, birds called to one another. Allar's unique scent surrounded her—warm man, wind and sunshine, a little leather and dragon thrown in for good measure.

Renny stifled a yawn. She shouldn't be tired. All she'd done the last few days was sleep. How much did she have to relax for this—whatever this was—to work?

Even as she chided herself for being so lazy, Renny was falling asleep, falling…

CHAPTER 6

*L*anding against the wall with a distinct thud, Renny slid
bonelessly to the floor, face already pounding from the
blow that'd launched her.

One hand over her throbbing cheek, Renny used the other to
slide herself away from the enraged man stalking her way.

Counted herself lucky she was still breathing by the time he
finished.

Stifled her sobs, held herself and for the rest of the
interminable night, planned her getaway.

Getting out of the rundown keep had been the easiest part.

Slipping out the gates, past the unknown soldiers and their
weird looking cart and an obviously furious lord, Renny loped
across a field and disappeared into the thick woods on the other
side.

Running became Renny's life. She ran away from the only
home she'd ever known, ran to the dragons.

Quickly finding out an orphan with no skills was unwanted
anywhere, Renny taught herself the necessary skills to survive,
starting with thieving without getting caught.

By the time she became proficient in hunting and fishing and foraging, Renny was wraith thin, making her former half-starved slenderness look well fed.

And always, always, she was drawn to dragons in pain.

Always became her mantra.

Always too late.

Always too young.

Always too unskilled.

Always powerless to combat the horrors that awaited her.

The dragons she found were always too far gone.

By the time she found the third dragon, two summers had passed.

By the time she found the fifth, she had grown more than a foot taller and was unrecognizable as the child who had run away to search for dragons.

Her own two feet her sole means of transport, working her way deeper and deeper into the mountains, Renny wended her way through the tortuous maze of ridges and valleys and passes, her lack of knowledge of the geography of the area hindering her immensely.

Places she could plainly see across a mountain valley took days, sometimes weeks to reach. Renny pushed herself to run faster, run faster, run faster.

Dying dragons her only contact with other species, Renny turned inward, her thoughts her only company.

Realized early on someone was deliberately harming the dragons. Tortured and in some cases poisoned—anything to insure a long, painful death.

Renny couldn't save them, but neither would she abandon them to die alone. Comforting the dragons as much as she was able, she sang to them and stroked them, drawing some small comfort from their presence as well.

Each dragon death broke her heart a little more.

She *would* find the ones responsible.

They *would* pay.

Try as she might to get the dragons to tell her who had committed these atrocities, she always—that word again—fell short, the dragon's memories either destroyed or blurred beyond recalling.

Drifting, avoiding contact with people, attending the dragons whenever and wherever she found them, Renny's mind slipped its mooring a little in those first terrible years.

Emerging from the blessed numbness one day to find herself in the dooryard of a small farm holding, a child's shrill voice had Renny instantly backing up, hands in the air in a gesture of peace.

"Maman, come quick!"

Attention focused on the plump woman in front of her brandishing a twig broom, a gruff voice from behind Renny had her whirling around.

Trapped between the farmwife and the farmer, the pitchfork in his hands pointed at Renny, she froze.

Jabbing the wicked looking implement at her, the farmer bellowed, "Git, boy! Or I'll spit ye like a mud-grunt!"

Shifting her weight, preparing to bolt, another voice stopped Renny in her tracks.

"Leave him be!" Thin and scratchy, but still full of authority, the order had the man returning to the barn and sent the woman scurrying back into the one room house, dragging the child with her and slamming the heavy wooden door.

Unsure whether she was actually seeing these people or if her hallucinations had caught up with her and utterly taken over her mind, Renny stared.

Seated under the canopy of a huge tree was an old woman.

Impossibly old.

Ancient.

Tiny and wizened, looking more like an animated apple doll

than a real person, the old woman beckoned Renny closer with an arthritic claw.

Ordered, and squinted knowingly as Renny moved nearer. "Come here—not a boy, then, are ye—girlie, and make it quick! I don't have all day! Come, come. I won't bite—I don't have any teeth." Wheezing with laughter at her own joke, she patted the bench beside herself.

Edging a few steps closer, Renny cocked her head to one side, staring into the woman's dark button eyes. Mesmerized, Renny did as she was told, the woman with the broom and the man with the pitchfork completely forgotten.

"Rider or healer?" The old woman cackled at Renny's baffled look. "Dragons. Are you a dragonrider or a dragonhealer? I can smell dragon all over you. Faint, but there."

Renny stared in shock. In all her short years, no one had spoken to her about dragons, except to abuse or deride her.

She hadn't spoken in so long—not since the last dragon had died and she'd screamed out her grief and rage until her throat became so raw she remained hoarse for days and days—Renny wasn't sure if she could speak anymore.

Opening her mouth to try, the old woman guessed shrewdly, "You really don't know, do you, child? Orphaned by the wars, I suppose, set adrift with no instruction or guidance."

Looking Renny up and down, the old woman shook her head. "No telling who you are or where you came from, but you're without a doubt from dragon stock."

Sighing as Renny continued to stare with wide eyes, the woman continued, "My mother and her mother before her and hers before that, beyond memory, were Dragonhealers."

Lamented, "Alas, their talent was not passed to me, but I do know the healing plants and words. If you are Dragonhealer and willing to work hard, I can teach you. If you are dragonrider, I know nothing of riding or fighting. You'll have to learn those skills from someone else."

Finding the voice she'd thought forever lost, Renny's words came out a rusty squawk. "You can…teach me to heal dragons?"

Hope returning in a rush—any price would be worth paying —if she could learn how to alleviate the dragons' suffering, or not have to watch another dragon die while she stood by helplessly.

"I can't teach you how to be anything you aren't—I can only teach you how to use what you are."

Throwing herself whole-heartedly into the old woman's lessons, together they studied plant lore and identification, which to use for what and how much.

Days passed, then weeks, then months.

As Renny learned, something blossomed within her. Some deeply buried part of her soul she'd thought withered and dead came flickering back to life, making her more determined than ever that the next dragon she heard would not die.

Sitting under the huge tree in the yard, their usual spot, watching leaves drift down, the old woman patted Renny's knee. "You're a quick learner, Renny-child. Don't know as I've ever taught a youngun with your capabilities. I used to ask my mother why I was so useless. Why the talent skipped me. Why, after generations beyond count, I was the only worthless offspring. My mother always gave me the same response."

Looking Renny up and down as she had the first day, the old woman nodded to herself, lost in memories, seeing people Renny would never see, hearing voices Renny would never hear. "She'd always tell me, 'You are not useless. There is a reason for everything. If you are very lucky, you will live long enough to find the answer to your question. Nothing, no matter how strange it seems, is without purpose.'"

"I've watched you for months now, Renny-child. You've absorbed everything I've taught you like dry sand soaks up water. In my lifetime, I've seen Dragonhealers go from being some of the most revered persons in the land to being hunted down and exterminated like vermin. I haven't heard of a single living healer in more years than I can count. I've outlived three husbands, raised ten children, helped raise three times that many grandchildren and great-grandchildren, and now I'm spending my remaining days with one of my great-great-grandchildren, watching her raise her children."

Listening intently as she usually did when the old woman was imparting knowledge, Renny waited patiently for the woman to make her point.

Taking a deep breath, the old woman focused on Renny. "I switched long ago from thinking my lack of skill was a curse to knowing it was a blessing. This was my reason, to live long enough to teach you, the last Dragonhealer. You are the answer, and my purpose. I've taught you everything I know. I dread it, but any day now, you will hear a dragon and be gone like the wind. As you should."

Gently touching the frail shoulder, Renny sought words to adequately express her thanks. "Old Mother, I am more grateful than you will ever know for your longevity and your teaching prowess. I...hear one now. It is time."

Reaching out a wrinkled hand to softly caress Renny's cheek, the old woman smiled. "Blessings upon you. Be careful, remember what I taught you, and most important, believe in yourself."

Gone like a wisp of smoke, Renny didn't see the oldest child come to check on Gran-gran and go tearing back into the humble home.

Didn't see the family gather around the bench beneath the huge old tree. Didn't see the farmer's wife throw her apron over her face, her husband's arm around her, the children huddled around their parents. Didn't see the tears, or hear the weeping as they bid goodbye to a beloved family member.

Didn't see the beatific smile on the Old Mother's care-worn face.

RENNY COULDN'T SAVE that one either, despite her best efforts, but she came closer than ever before. With the lore imparted by the Old Mother, Renny eased the dragon's suffering, and passing, far more than she had hitherto been able.

Between the other dragons, she'd just drifted and survived, waiting for another summons.

If she was going to stop the ones responsible for these horrible deaths, she'd have to learn to fight with something more than sticks and stones.

THE SOLDIER'S guffaws rang loud in Renny's ears.

"Want to train to be a soldier, do you? A puny little mite like you? Get you gone, boy."

At that, more loud laughter followed as the other soldiers joined in.

Renny ignored their laughter that day, as she did for many days thereafter. She kept her head down, left her face and clothes grimy, made sure her hair stayed unevenly chopped short.

If they made fun of what they thought was a scrawny lad, how much worse would it be if they found out Renny was really a girl?

Making herself useful around the garrison, doing any small chore—no matter how odious—carrying wood and water, running errands, cleaning in general, one of the older soldiers finally took pity on her.

He began to teach her the rudiments of fighting. "You are small, and somehow I don't think you're ever going to get very big. That can be a disadvantage, or you can turn it to your benefit. Because you are small, no one will expect you to be a warrior. You must use other tactics—instead of strength, you must use cunning, in place of brawn, you must use your brain. Instead of brute force, speed is your ally."

To that end, the old soldier helped her fashion a bow to fit her small stature.

Taking careful heed of his words, Renny practiced until long after the others had given up and gone to seek food and rest. If they practiced with their bows until they could sink half their arrows into the target, Renny nocked arrow to bow until she could sink all of hers into the bulls-eye, so close she stripped the fletching off and split the shafts.

Practiced with the small sword—more a long dagger—her mentor forged for her, slashing and stabbing the sacks filled with straw until her arms ached and her body shook with fatigue. Until her feet danced and twitched in her dreams to some unseen opponent's advances and retreats.

Her mentor's advice rang in her head with every stroke, every thrust, every parry.

"Wait until you are close to strike. Dart in, stab and slash, and begone ere your opponent knows you have done damage."

The day came, as Renny knew it would.

Too soon, it seemed.

She wanted to protest, *I don't know enough.*

Answered herself, *I know far more than I did.*

Preparing to leave yet another place, Renny wondered: Was this to be her life? To always hear dragons she couldn't save? To always find friends and teachers, only to have to leave?

She refused to let that be all.

She would find the ones responsible for these atrocities, and they would be held accountable.

CHAPTER 7

*L*ungs heaving like a bellows, heart threatening to explode out of her chest, Renny pushed herself to run harder. It seemed as if she had been running forever. She had to get there in time.

Had to, had to.

The words chanted in time with her labored breaths.

The dragon's cries, so strong at first, were weakening rapidly now, drawing her ever closer like the beacon they were. Stopping at a cold, clear stream to gulp a drink of water and refill her waterskin, taking a moment to catch her breath, Renny paused in her headlong flight long enough to swallow a mouthful of dried fruit.

Crouched over the stream, well hidden amidst the overhanging fronds of a willow tree, she caught a reflection. A dragon carrying his dragonrider.

Heading *away* from the wounded dragon's cries.

Something was very, very wrong.

Resuming her trek far more cautiously, Renny broke over the top of the ridge just in time to see another dragon flying off in the opposite direction. Staying low, concealed in the brush at the edge of the tree line, Renny made her way closer to the wounded dragon she could now see.

Unmoving... *Dead?*

No!

The dragon's cries were faint, barely audible, but still there. So, too, were the torturers. Still there, continuing to poke and prod already horrific injuries, laughing and taunting. Her first instinct was to rush at them, sword singing a sharp song of death and retribution. The faintest of warnings from the dragon held her immobile.

{{*Hold.*}} And then, {{*I will distract them. Use your bow. Stay as far away as you can.*}}

{{*Dragon! Do not waste your strength!*}}

{{*You cannot save me. I am...spent. Do this for me—take out as many of them as you can but do not let them capture you. The others will return soon. You must be far from here ere they do. You* must *live!*}}

Before Renny had time to protest, the dragon semi-reared and swung his bloody head into the crowd of tormentors, scattering them willy-nilly. They attacked mercilessly, a horde of stinging ants going after still-living prey.

Shaking her head to dislodge the tears blurring her vision, streaming down her face, Renny took aim and let silent death take wing. In the midst of their noise and frenetically agitated movements, she took several of the tormentors out before they noticed.

When they did, they turned their attention to Renny, intending to make her their newest target.

Renny's long sessions of bow practice paid off. Finishing them off quickly, one by one, descending toward the dragon with every step and arrow she let fly.

Realizing she could no longer hear him, fairly leaping down the remaining hillside, Renny stumbled to a halt and dropped to her knees, head bowed.

Too late. I am always too late, she thought bitterly, even as she reached a hand out to touch the dragon.

A faint spark tingled her fingertips and hope flared for an instant, then flickered out, a spent candle.

Barely there, as if from a tremendous distance, Renny heard the dragon's pain-wracked praise. {{*Well done, little sister. Ere the others return… Grant…me…mercy.*}}

Shock—followed by rage, the roil coalescing into a hard dark knot in her soul—had Renny protesting even as she drew her sword and plunged it deep into the vulnerable spot just below the dragon's wing, straight into its heart.

The dragon's final, grateful *Ahhhh* rippled in Renny's mind as her sword found its mark.

Withdrawing her sword slowly, her hatred for the butchers who did this knew no bounds. Wiping her blade clean on one of the carcasses, she surveyed the carnage.

None of the dead cowards bore identifying colors or insignia, their dress all motley mismatched common leggings and tunics, nothing any farmer or traveler wouldn't wear.

Her soul in tattered shreds, Renny retrieved her arrows. Leaving the carcasses for the butcher's friend and the carrion beasts—weren't they the same thing?—she made her way back into the forest, leaving a clear trail.

The butchers would come after her.

Let them.

Smiling wolfishly to herself, Renny vowed—hers would be a dangerous and bloody trail to follow.

Let the hunt begin.

"WHAT DO YOU MEAN, *the warrior has struck, and escaped, again?*" The enraged voice came hissing out of the dark, furious and seeking a target.

The only other person there, Din bowed his head as he listened to the rant. Din made no excuses—indeed the owner of the voice would not hear any.

This warrior, this…nithling, plaguing their mission had attained legendary status. None had ever seen him and lived to tell about it. Some said he was a nightmare, a figment, bearing death in his wake like a plague.

He appeared out of nowhere to mete out death and destruction, and returned to the same.

Before this defender of dragons had shown up, Din and his cronies had long wreaked havoc with total impunity. Luring dragons in, torturing them for as long as Din and company could keep them alive, with no fear of being caught.

The warrior had changed all that.

Simply put, their unknown foe was ruining everything.

"He must be stopped! I will not tolerate this hindrance to my plans. We have duped all the other dragonriders into thinking we are as serious as they about finding the guilty parties. They don't even suspect us. If we can fool dragonriders and we can lure dragons to their deaths, surely we can manage to kill a single man, warrior or not. Double the number of men on the next mission."

Listening until he heard the royal *we-are-so-powerful* speech change over to the *this-is-all-your-fault-peasant* spiel before tuning the owner of the voice out, Din mentally listed the names of those to be sacrificed next, making sure his would not be one of them.

AND SO RENNY began a deadly game of cat-and-mouse, never quite sure who was cat and who was mouse. Following the dragon cries, waiting until the perfect moment to strike, killing the traitors.

Making certain sure she killed them all so there would be no tales told, no description given. Careful to retrieve all her arrows, she left little sign of her passing save for the bodies.

Each time doing what little she could for the downed dragons, which meant, more often than not, simply putting them out of their misery, adding to hers.

She remembered each and every one of the dragons she was forced to kill or was simply too late to save.

Either way, their deaths were her fault. Each death engraved another gaping wound on her soul, and most frustrating, each dragon death brought her little closer to finding the identities of those responsible.

The torturers bore no identifying marks on their clothing or weapons. The single thing she had noticed, the one time she'd seen dragonriders leaving the scene, was that those dragons' colors had seemed dull, not jewel bright like the few other dragons she'd seen high above in flight, and the ones she'd tended.

Even wounded unto death, the dragons retained their individual colors, none the same as any other. Although Renny'd been unable to discern their names—all of them too far gone—she knew each color, knew the location of each of the bodies.

Having followed the latest dragon's cries to this remote spot, Renny concealed herself and watched. There was only one way she was going to find out who was responsible. She would have to kill all but one of the butchers and extract information from the survivor.

Watching them, trying to decide who looked the most in charge so she could let him live, trying to ignore what they were doing to the dragon—already far past her meager skills to aid— Renny quickly made up her mind.

There! The traitor standing off to one side, busily giving orders.

Renny's first arrow pierced his thigh. He might yet run but he wouldn't get far, and even if he did, he'd leave a bloody trail an infant could follow.

Shooting slowly and methodically, Renny took the others out save for several hiding behind the bulk of the dragon. Before Renny could shift position and dispatch them as well, the dragon heaved over on her side and crushed the remaining offenders.

Rage at another senseless dragon death shook Renny to her core as she felt the dragon die, having used the last bit of her strength to move.

Stalking down the hill towards the remaining—blubbering like a babe—coward, Renny wondered for the thousandth time: Why were the dragons always in a valley ringed by high cliffs? Concealment? Every dragon she'd found had been in such remote areas it hardly seemed worth the time to hide what they were doing.

Spotting Renny's approach and pegging her identity, accurately gauging the rage on her face, the sniveling coward drew his dagger and slit his own throat.

Leaping to his side, knowing it was too late to question him, Renny screamed anyway. "Who sent you?"

Answered by his death rattle, Renny knew she'd have to be quicker next time.

THIS DRAGON WAS SO FAR GONE Renny couldn't reach it mind to mind. Far beyond help or even pain, its life-spark the faintest glimmer.

Instead of killing all the butchers as she ached to do, though the thought of it left her jaw clenched tight and a bitter taste in her mouth, this time she would let them live.

For awhile.

Allowing them to live and following them when they left was a better choice.

For now.

Waiting till they gave up their gruesome sport on the unresponsive dragon and headed out, Renny efficiently dispatched the dragon with a heartfelt blessing and a well placed thrust. Trotted after the slayers.

Slogging through the mud that had plagued this journey since she left the last dragon's side, Renny dreamt of warm, dry clothes and hot food for the millionth time. Wished it would stop raining.

Chided herself silently and sourly: Wish in one hand and spit in the other. See which one fills up faster.

She'd dutifully followed the murderers for a long while, finally lost most of them in a torrential downpour just outside a large village where they split and went their separate ways.

Still trailing the only one who'd seemed to have a specific destination in mind, Renny decided she'd follow him a bit longer and if he didn't lead her to anything soon, she'd kill him and be done with it.

Go find another.

There were plenty of the scum around.

CHAPTER 8

*D*in slipped into the tavern, careful to keep his face hidden. Easy enough, the pouring rain had everyone ducking their heads and huddling into their cloaks.

A quick glance showed him a shapeless form in the darkest corner of the crowded tavern, seated by himself with a great swath of empty tables surrounding him. Din made his way over and sat.

Not that Din could identify the man.

As usual, *He* was hidden almost completely by the darkness, a flash of hand or sleeve all that was visible.

Staring hungrily at the rapidly disappearing food on *his* plate, Din raised a hand to catch the attention of the serving wench. Pointing at the plate, he held up two fingers to indicate he wanted the same.

She nodded and Din turned back to listen.

"You are certain you were not followed?" Waiting for Din's nod of assent, He continued, "What have you to report? We are becoming impatient. How much longer before you resolve this matter?"

The meaty thump of his fist striking the table, rattling the utensils and making the heavy pewter mug dance, emphasized his barely audible words.

Keeping his face blank and his tone subservient, Din fought down thoughts of the warrior stalking him. The man in front of him couldn't want the warrior's head on a pike any worse than Din himself. Tired of constantly looking over his shoulder, jumping at the slightest noise, flinching at every shadow, Din wanted the warrior dead, pike or no.

"Good news. No sign of him this time. We lost no men at the last site, and our mission was accomplished." Giving more details, stopping for breath only when He asked a question, Din finished his report and heaved a silent sigh of relief when He threw some coin on the table and left.

Pocketing the coin, when the server finally brought his food, Din looked up, disappointed. Where had the curvy wench gotten off to? Nothing special, she'd had a ripe figure, one he'd counted on seeing more of later, willing or not.

Figures they'd send his food out with some raggedy chore boy instead, one who looked as if he'd been out slopping mud-grunts in the rain and not merely fallen down, but been trampled. Beyond that, the boy smelled like he bedded down with the grunts on a regular basis.

Carrying the platter and mug to her mark's table, keeping her head down, Renny remained on full alert. She'd stood outside the inn door for scant heartbeats debating with herself. *Stay out here in the rain and wait, or go in and hope he doesn't realize I've been following him?*

Warm and dry had won, hands down. Walking inside, giving her eyes a moment to adjust, she'd spotted her quarry and moved further into the shadows.

Watching intently without seeming to, Renny observed her quarry looking up and then away when she came in, watched him go right back to listening to the other man at the table.

Catching the leering exchange between her quarry and the serving girl, correctly interpreting the girl's fearful distaste, Renny'd moved swiftly.

Intercepting the girl just before she entered the kitchen, Renny bargained even as she handed over her sopping cloak.

Now, pretending to stumble just as she slid her mark's food onto the table, spilling a good portion of it and receiving a sharp cuff for her clumsiness, Renny proceeded to bobble his ale. Managing to right it before it all spilled out, trying to help clean up won her another blow amid a spate of curses.

She left him, still cursing, what little food left on his platter soggy with ale, his mug practically empty.

Almost as empty as his pockets.

Hiding her grin, Renny wended her way back to the kitchen, knowing she'd found another piece of the puzzle.

Sidling through the kitchen door, Renny was met by the grateful eyes of the serving girl, a burly man who looked to be her father, and an older version of the girl, surely her mother.

Crossing his arms over his barrel chest, the father cocked his head and stared at Renny. "I suppose you had good reason for that oafish display, and my little girl here says you kept her from being mauled by the likes of him, so I'm not going to argue. Best you leave quickly." Jerking his head toward the door behind them, he nodded. "I'll take care of him. Go."

"My thanks." Inclining her head, Renny skirted her way around the room, barely pausing when she passed in front of the man. Grinning cheekily, she tossed him a fat purse. "Take this. It will more than pay for the meal and any inconvenience. Were I you, I'd hide it."

An impudent grin plastered on her face, Renny slipped out the back just as an enraged bellow came from the front room of the tavern.

Still grinning, she strode quickly into the darkness, whirling with dagger drawn when she heard running footsteps behind her. Relaxing as she realized it was only the girl, Renny waited.

Gasping for breath, the girl stammered, "I… Thank you. Here, you forgot your cloak." Thrusting the sodden fabric at Renny, stammering her thanks again, the girl fled.

Amused by her deception, and well pleased with the results, Renny *had* forgotten her cloak. Not that it would do her much good this night, not as wet as it was…

Wait. There was something bundled in it.

Opening the cloak enough to feel an oilskin wrapped package —warm!—Renny started to unwrap it. Scented pastry and meat, and sighed blissfully.

Looking up, she spotted stars twinkling through ragged remnants of clouds.

Still grinning as she retrieved her bow and sword from their hiding place, she couldn't help but think, *sometimes wishes did come true.*

Savoring the food slowly, bite by wonderful bite and saving some for the morrow, Renny refused to gulp it down in its entirety as her stomach loudly demanded.

Wondered, and knew she'd have to wait for daylight to examine her other prize.

Curling into a damp ball, weapons close at hand, Renny slept.

Awakening well after daylight, stretching, Renny couldn't remember the last time she'd slept so long. For that matter, the last time she'd had warm food. Real food.

Unwrapping the last of her bounty—a tart—apoma by the smell, she began munching as she examined her treasure.

Apomas, butter, spices—all wrapped in a flaky crust—melted together on her tongue, drizzled down her throat and appeased her belly.

As fine as the tart tasted, it paled in comparison to what lay spread in front of her.

A map! The fool had carried a map—rare and cherished.

Good for her, bad for him.

Renny couldn't make sense of it, yet.

She'd figure it out.

Places marked with x's. Important places, obviously.

Sucking the last sweet crumbs off her fingers, wiping her hands on her shirt, she turned the supple parchment this way and that, trying to make sense of it.

She'd seen—and studied—an ancient map like this at the soldiers' garrison. Prized beyond belief, it had given Renny a better sense of the scope of the peaks and valleys she'd been scrambling up and down for as long as she could remember.

All she had to do was…

The key hit her like a bolt of lightning.

The x marked spots all seemed to be valleys, spread out over a huge area.

Renny had been in many of these same valleys. Valleys where dragons had been tortured and died.

Many were empty, too.

Why just certain valleys, though?

The mountainous terrain sported as many valleys as peaks.

She was missing something here, something vital.

Renny could feel it.

She just couldn't grasp quite what.

If she could only figure out their pattern, perhaps she could get ahead of the butchers and finally, finally save a dragon.

Renny decided to try the x'd valley closest to the tavern. Since the man she'd been trailing had met an associate, she suspected he was either giving a report or getting one. From his posture and bearing, most likely giving one, as he also seemed to be taking orders.

She probably should've changed targets, but, hey. Why press her luck?

The worst thing that could happen? It would become one more bad decision to add to her long list.

DIN CURSED THE THIEVING PICKPOCKET, his ruined meal, the tavern owner, and the weather, along with all the other patrons who were laughing heartily at his discomfort.

The loss of his coin rankled badly, even though the tavern owner, after much hemming and hawing and blustering, let Din have what was left of his meal free of charge.

Consoling himself with the thought that even if the dim-witted fool of a pickpocket could read, the lad would probably never be able to figure out what the map was for.

Hell's bells. The moron would probably use it to wipe his arse.

No way would Din tell *Him* he'd lost the map, not when he wasn't even supposed to have a map.

Besides marking all the special valleys, it was Din's personal way of keeping track of how many dragons they'd killed—and how many more they were going to.

LOOKING at the widely scattered skeletal remains of the dragon with grim distaste, losing another piece of her heart, Renny bowed her head.

So much for her theory.

This dragon had been dead for a long, long while.

So where next?

Pulling out the map, unrolling it, Renny examined it again. There had to be some clue she was overlooking, some way to figure out where the dragonhaters would strike next.

All those x's couldn't be dead dragons.

The more she stared at the map, the more right that idea felt.

So, then, not only macabre grave markers, but future grave sites.

Reaching the next valley after a grueling five day run, only to find the same thing, there was no way she'd ever be able to keep up this pace and check all these valleys. Not on foot, anyway.

If she was a dragonrider... Renny snorted to herself at that absurd thought.

Speaking of which, Renny wondered why the dragonriders hadn't found these dragons. All these valleys were remote, but not that out of the way, especially from a dragon's perspective.

Something else was going on here.

Something that smacked of conspiracy, treachery, and deceit.

How else could the murderers separate and know where to meet up again in time for the next slaughter? How could they know where to meet in the first place?

Renny was going to have to go back into one of the villages and see if she could find one of the men she hadn't killed and follow him.

Better yet...

CHAPTER 9

"Sir, please. I am looking for work. I'll do anything. I'm stronger than I look." Tugging ingratiatingly on the man's sleeve, Renny earned a kick for her trouble.

"Begone, brat. I've no need of a beggar like you." Barely sparing her a glance, the man turned back to his companion.

Running in front of him, Renny tried again. "Please, sir. I will work very hard for you. I can…"

Bellowing this time, the man reiterated, "Get you gone!"

Renny tried his friend. "Please, kind sir. I…"

Garnering the same negative response, Renny slumped in defeat and began muttering under her breath. "Stupid dragonriders. Stupid dragons. I hate them both. Devil take 'em all. If it wasn't for them, I wouldn't be in this position."

Head down, kicking a rock viciously with each statement, Renny peeled away from the two men.

The first man grabbed her by the arm and shook her. "What say you?"

"Nuthin'! I didn't say nuthin'." Eyes wide, trying to squirm out of his grip, Renny denied, denied, denied.

Shaking Renny harder, gripping hard enough to leave bruises, he repeated his question and then asked another. "Why did you say you hated dragonriders and dragons?"

Renny blurted, "I asked one of the riders for work. He told me I should ask you, that you needed help. He was just playing a cruel joke on me, getting rid of me. I hate him! I hate them all! They pretend to care about the plain folk but they really don't. All they care about is their stupid dragons! Let me go!" Renny tried to twist away again.

The man's head came up and his grip tightened even more as he looked around frantically. "What rider? Where?"

Renny whimpered, "Not here. A few villages back. I've been trailing you 'cause I was afraid to ask you if you needed help. I thought maybe I could find some'at on my own, but nobody needs…"

Dismissing her rambling, the man got a crafty gleam in his eye. "So you hate them, eh? I just might have something for you. Come with me. I know someone who'd like to speak with you."

Renny trotted along, pretending to have to try to keep up with the swift pace the longer legged men set as they headed out of town. Somehow, without arousing suspicion, she had to get back to the spot where she'd hidden her weapons.

And then—talk about off the dragon and into the clouds!

Renny recognized him before he even turned around.

She ought to—she'd spent enough time looking at the back of his balding head as she trailed him.

All she could do was hope the tavern had been too dark for him to recognize her!

Grabbing Renny's arm again and thrusting her forward, the first man she'd approached announced, "Boy here says he needs work and…he has good reason to hate dragons and dragonriders."

Spinning on his heel, Din looked the thin, raggedy boy up

and down and sneered, "What kind of dragon dung is this? What could he possibly do? He looks as if a slight breeze would tumble him head over heels. He can't possibly have any useful skills."

Staring him in the eye—if he showed any sign of recognition! —Renny would need every moment to make good her escape. What a time to have stashed her weapons!

In the enemy's camp, surrounded and unarmed, this had to be at the top of her Stupidest Things I've Ever Done list.

Keeping her face carefully blank while her heart ricocheted around inside her ribs searching for the slightest opening, Renny decided to go for the bold approach and pray it worked.

Puffing up, Renny stared him the eye and stated boldly, "I'm stronger than I look and I'm a quick learner."

Din stared right back. "So, you hate dragons? How much? Enough to watch one die? Enough to *help* it die?"

"I've done both, more times than I can count." Truth, just not his truth.

"Interesting. And exactly where have you committed all this mayhem?"

Renny shrugged. "I've lived in these mountains all my life. I've come across many dragons that were dead or had been left for dead. The ones that were dead…" She shrugged again. "The ones that weren't…some I watched die, and some I finished off."

Truth again. Renny had long ago realized she was no good at lying. Best either to keep her mouth shut or tell a partial truth that could be interpreted as the listener wished.

Din perused the gangly lad again, head to toe, more slowly this time. They were always looking for recruits, especially since the Warrior was constantly thinning their ranks. This scrawny no-account might just prove to be a good one.

"You have no weapons, I assume you *can* fight?"

The chance she'd been waiting for, handed to her on a platter!

"I have weapons, I stashed them before I entered the village. I just have to retrieve them."

"I see." Another sneering glance. "A stick? Or a rock? Or perhaps both?"

The boy made a noncommittal twitch that could've meant anything. Din knew he was taking a chance, letting this boy join them without first clearing it with *Him*.

However, they *were* shorthanded, and they already had the newest ambush set up and ready to go.

Din would just have to take a chance and tell *Him* after the ambush. In fact, they needed to leave now if they wanted to arrive on time.

"What's your name, boy?"

"Ren."

"Wren? Well, you aren't much bigger than a bird. Get a move on, Birdie. We're running out of time."

Retrieving her cached weapons, Renny returned to find the men on the march not too far from where she'd left them. Slipping into their line, ignoring the speculative glances cast her way, Renny knew she'd probably have to fight every last one of them before they'd leave her alone.

Like an extremely rabid colony of Orimjays she'd run afoul of once. Most of the ones she'd run across had left her alone once they figured out she possessed far less than they did. She'd had to kill every single one of that particular nest before they'd leave her to her lonely travails. Not that she had anything worth stealing. She lived, and she wasn't one of them…that was enough to inspire their hatred.

The best she could hope for now? That the challenges would come one at a time. Especially since she'd deliberately have to lose, at least some. Wouldn't do to show them all her skills at once, but darned if she was going to sit back and take getting beaten to a pulp without doing a little damage in return.

The first attack came earlier than she wanted, but no sooner than she expected. They'd covered much distance before dark, keeping to a steady, ground eating trot.

Near the back of the line, eating a lot of dust but having no trouble keeping up the pace, Renny wondered where all the mud from a little over a fortnight ago had disappeared to.

Not trusting her yet, they kept several men in front of her and a few behind. The leader, the one they called Din, raised a hand to halt the column.

Slowing to a walk, Renny was shoved hard from behind into the man in front of her, nearly bringing them both to their knees.

Set-up!

The man she'd caromed into came up swinging and cursing.

The man behind Renny caught her in a bear hug and pinned her arms to her sides. Too savvy to waste time trying to squirm free, Renny dropped her bow and sword and shifted her weight so the man behind her was supporting her.

Picking up both booted feet, throwing her head back, Renny slammed her head into the nose of the man behind her and her feet into the stomach of the man attacking from the front. The frontal attacker went down gasping, breath knocked out of him.

When the man who held her from behind released her to clutch at his nose, Renny landed on her feet, crouched, and rolled sideways just in time to see a knife flash past her face.

She came up with her own dagger in hand, circling warily.

If the others stayed out of this, she might have a chance.

She should've known better. Did know better.

Din stood to one side, watching critically. If the boy made it through their little game alive, he might be worth feeding. So far, their little Birdie was doing an outstanding job against overwhelming odds.

Expecting to see the slight boy end up on the bottom of a

very large pile, Din was pleasantly surprised when Birdie ended up, not on the bottom, but on one knee, the other pressed into the middle of his largest soldier's back.

The soldier, belly to the ground, lay frozen, still as a corpse.

Birdie had him by the hair, head back and neck stretched taut, knife at his throat.

Looking at Din, Renny said, "Choose."

"For being stupid and slow enough for you to best him, I *should* let you kill him. Let him live. This time." Waving the others off, Din slowly, repeatedly clapped. "Congratulations, recruit. You have first watch." Without a second glance at either his men or the new boy, he walked away.

Removing her knife from the soldier's throat, Renny rose and moved away in one swift movement, keeping her eye on the men as she bent to pick up her bow and sword.

There would be other tests, but she'd survived this one.

Not unscathed, she noted ruefully. Tender spots, bruises already forming, and numerous nasty cuts from someone's knife.

Cuts she'd have to doctor lest they become infected. That should prove interesting—she wasn't about to take her shirt off in a camp full of men.

She could feel blood trickling from more than one cut, fairly gushing from a couple of the worst ones. At least none of them were stab wounds. She shuddered to think where those knives had been.

Finding a high spot in a nest of boulders, Renny settled in for what promised to be a long watch. Grinning to herself, she watched as Din's men moved about slowly, nursing their own wounds, setting up a cold camp.

She'd given as good as she'd gotten, and made more than one enemy in the process.

As she knew he would, Renny's replacement took his own sweet time. Finally relieved from guard duty, Renny took her miserable self a good way from the camp. Managed to find, with the help of the nearly full moon, a sheltered and easily defendable nook where she made herself as comfortable as possible and curled up to sleep.

Awakening well before daylight, Renny munched on some dried fruit and jerky she took from one of the hidden pockets inside her cloak. Sipping a little water from her waterskin, she tried to stretch the stiffness out of her body.

The cuts were burning, itching. Not good, but at least they'd stopped bleeding. She'd put a little smarzo she'd scrounged—chewed into a pulp—on the ones she could reach, but she'd used all of the tiny patch she'd found growing close to her night's vantage point.

The blood had dried, and in the process stuck her shirt to the bloody places. Moving was only going to start them bleeding again. Oh, well. Better than not bleeding because she was dead.

Watching the sun rise, Renny tried to get her bearings in relation to the map. She couldn't very well pull it out and check, but she was positive there was an x'd valley nearby.

Up and moving well before anyone else in the camp stirred, Renny dared not let them see just how badly they'd hurt her. She couldn't do anything about the bloodstains, but if she moved confidently enough, perhaps they'd assume the blood was someone else's.

Their blood, she thought with a grin. A worthwhile grin, even if it started her split lip bleeding again.

The motley group continued climbing higher into the mountains, Renny holding her own. Some of the others weren't doing as well. Certain she'd done some serious damage to a couple of them, Renny had no doubt they would repay her in full as soon as possible.

After traveling all day at a hard pace—for them, not for Renny— they set up another cold camp. Tired as they were, Renny could sense their growing excitement.

She drew first watch again, lucky her. Good thing she had

some dried food in her pockets, as this was obviously Bring Your Own.

None of the men showed any inclination to hunt, fish, or set snares, acting as if they had stores cached somewhere close. In fact, they traveled light, almost as light as she did, carrying little but their weapons and rations enough for a few days.

If they had a sure expectation of food ahead, they had no need of packs to weigh them down, slow them down. One more clue in the conspiracy.

Renny was getting close to having some of her questions answered, she could feel it. She wasn't going to like the answers any more than the questions.

The next morning, they broke camp but stayed where they were. Not that there was much to set up or take down, as Din was the only one with a shelter of any kind. He hadn't spoken a word to her since the fight.

Renny wasn't so sure that was a good thing.

Watching him covertly, Renny leapt to her feet as a dragon flew overhead. Something was wrong!

The dragon was flying erratically, as if ill or injured.

About to take off running, Renny remembered where she was and who she was with.

She froze, eyes tracking the dragon until it went out of sight over the next ridge. Looked at the men lounging around what was left of their camp, none of them moving. Some of them staring after the dragon, some eyeing her.

Waiting for a signal.

Din chose that moment to speak to her. "Eager, are you?"

Renny stared at him, not answering.

"We won't have to wait much longer." He scanned the sky and ordered, "Positions, now! Move!"

Din seemed to be expecting another dragon momentarily. Renny watched the men fall to the ground, striking poses as if they'd fallen in battle.

Their diabolical plan became instantly clear.

No dragon would give more than a cursory glance at what looked to be human bodies, not when a live dragon seemed to be in dire trouble.

Hiding would've aroused the dragon's curiosity and invited closer scrutiny, while this…

Sprawled on her back, eyes wide open, Renny watched in awe as a huge cobalt dragon circled them, then flew out of sight over the same ridge the other dragon had gone over.

As soon as he was out of sight, the men sprang to their feet and took off running in the same direction.

Renny followed, careful not to outpace them when she could easily have done so, not sure what to expect but knowing it was going to be bad. Topping the ridge just in time to see the cobalt land beside the pretender, Renny felt like applauding at the performance.

The pretender fluttered one wing, dragged the other, flopped its head and thrashed as if it were truly in distress.

'Twould have been a fine performance, save for one thing.

Renny heard no dragon cries.

Not a single one rang in her head.

Easing down into the valley, wanting so badly to scream out a warning to the cobalt, Renny bit her tongue in order to keep her mouth shut. If she gave herself away now, she'd be of no use to the blue.

Looking closer at the flailing dragon, Renny realized it was one of the curious no-colors she'd seen flying away from one of the other valleys.

Watching in slow motion horror as the cobalt, now on the ground, moved closer and closer, Renny could hear the pretender pleading with the cobalt.

{{*Help me, please.*}}

Wait—how could she hear him? She'd never before been able

to hear a dragon that wasn't in utter distress, as this one so obviously wasn't.

Shaking her head over that anomaly, Rennie continued watching.

Distracted by the antics of the no-color, the cobalt had yet to see the approaching man.

Something alerted the cobalt to the man's presence. Turning his attention from the no-color to the man, Renny watched in dismay as the man hailed the cobalt.

Motioning the cobalt to come nearer, the man pretended to stumble.

The cobalt leaned his great head closer.

Renny couldn't make out what happened next, but when the cobalt was almost nose to nose with the man, Renny saw the man's lips move.

The magnificent cobalt stiffened, collapsed, and went completely still.

Her concentration broken by the whoops and yells of the men she'd forgotten she was with, Renny had no choice but to join them as they picked up their pace and ran down the slope of the high ridge towards the dragon.

Reaching the bottom, they danced a mad jig around the downed cobalt, the no-color miraculously recovered. In a pure frenzy, the men stabbed at the cobalt with their swords and daggers and spears. Poking and prodding until blood ran in rivers down the cobalt's beautiful hide, the bright red a stark contrast to the deep cobalt.

The cobalt didn't so much as twitch.

Why were their weapons effective against the dragon? Normally nothing could pierce dragon hide.

Maybe they'd been treated with something, the same something that'd made Renny's cuts burn and itch.

Renny hung back, trying not to be sick, shaking with the need to go after the men with her own weapons.

Ironically, Din was the one who saved her from certain self-destruction.

"Thought you said you had killed lots of dragons," he said smugly.

Renny glared at him through a bloody haze of anger. "Killed, yes. I said nothing about torturing them first."

"But that's the very best part!" Whistling, Din strolled away to talk to the man beside the no-color.

In shock, helpless to aid the cobalt, Renny had known she wasn't going to like the answers, and she was right.

The dragonhaters were luring dragons in using the no-color, and then doing something to immobilize the dragons before they realized it was a trap.

Was the no-color in on it or a pawn in a deadly game? No way would any self-respecting dragon co-operate in such a manner. Most of them would die before betraying their kind.

Busily talking to the rider of the no-color, Din pointed at Renny and waved her over.

Reluctantly joining them, Renny kept her distance, making sure she didn't come close to touching either one of them.

Din grinned evilly and ambled off, leaving Renny alone with the rider.

No, betrayer. Renny refused to accord him the coveted title.

"Din's newest recruit doesn't care to join in the fun? Afraid it will spoil your appetite? When Renny didn't answer, the betrayer demanded, "What's your name?"

Renny's very soul recoiled from him in horror.

He looked normal—two arms, two legs, two eyes, only one head—but Renny could feel the evil radiating off him in waves. Monstrous evil.

Renny had to force herself to stand still when everything in her was screaming at her to flee.

Looking him in the eye, Renny got another shock as he stared into her eyes, unblinking. She could *feel* him prying around the edges of her mind! Immediately blanking her thoughts, Renny broke eye contact before answering him.

Don't give him your name! That's how he caught the cobalt!

Somehow, before the cobalt crumpled, the man must have discerned the dragon's name.

Dropping her gaze as if his strength was too much for her, Rennie whispered, "Birdie."

"Birdie?"

At his use of Din's nickname, Renny shuddered as she felt his evilness pulling at her soul. How much worse would it've been if she'd given him her real name?

"Well, *Birdie*, we'll teach you to fly later, or maybe we'll clip your wings so you can never fly again."

Renny didn't have a clue what he was talking about and figured she probably didn't want to know.

RENNY STILL DIDN'T KNOW why the cobalt hadn't called for help, but she'd bet her life the betrayer had something to do with it.

The cobalt had lain immobile till long past nooning, more than long enough for them to throw chains over him and anchor him in place.

Heart breaking, Renny had forced herself to help, creating a stain on her soul that would never be erased. She'd tried to speak to him repeatedly using mindspeak, but whatever the betrayer had done seemed to have paralyzed the dragon's mind as well as his beautiful body.

Renny could feel him but she couldn't reach him, couldn't get any response.

Maybe that's why he hadn't called for help. Why none of the others had either.

The more Renny thought about it, the more sense it made.

She didn't know how, but she *was* going to save this dragon or die trying.

She was also going to take the betrayer out, make sure this was the last dragon he hurt.

The evil one finally left, to the vast relief of everyone.

Renny'd overheard the betrayer tell Din he would return around midday tomorrow.

Din had thrown out orders and trotted off shortly after.

Running out of time, even if by some miracle she killed all the butchers here, there was no way Renny could move the cobalt before Din and the betrayer returned.

She could kill them too.

None of which would help the cobalt.

The best thing Renny could do was lay low, play it by ear and keep herself alive.

The comatose dragon seemed to be slowly regaining his senses, if the occasional twitches meant anything.

The torturers, under strict orders to wait until the dragon awoke to inflict any more damage, seemed in no hurry to disobey.

No sense wasting perfectly good torture if the subject couldn't appreciate it.

Heartsick, Renny worked hard to remain calm. Nearly impossible, knowing what they were getting ready to do to this dragon.

The men were all at ease, joking and eating, as relaxed as if they were waiting for a play to begin. They hadn't even posted any guards, despite their fear of the Warrior, because the no-color and the betrayer were flying tight circles around the outer perimeter, just out of sight of this valley.

She'd been right about the food. The betrayer had brought supplies in with him on the no-color.

Why didn't his dragon have any color?

Thoughts chasing themselves in circles until she was dizzy, sunk deep in misery, at first Renny thought the mental words were just one of her stray thoughts, answering itself.

{{*He has no color because his heart is dead.*}}

CHAPTER 10

*C*onthar awoke, to the sound of a bell.

One gloriously pure note, resonating to the depths of his soul.

Strange, he didn't remember any villages nearby, much less any with a bell-tower.

Where was he, anyway?

And why couldn't he move?

Cautiously sending out a thought, seeking to find out what was going on before opening his eyes, he encountered...

Her!

His heart leapt and his body wanted to follow.

Joy, pure joy!

He had found his rider!

That was the source of the bell tone, and not some village bell-tower.

He could feel her sorrow, weighting her down.

Why so sad?

Conthar struggled to remember what'd happened.

Bits and pieces came back to him in a flash—a wounded dragon, and a strange man…

What had they done to him?

Conthar sent up a mighty cry on his private link.

{{*Zantha, I am down! Warn Allar and send aid, now!*}}

That done, confident help was on the way—even though he'd heard no answer from his…from Zantha—Conthar turned his thoughts back to his rider. Tried to read her mind.

Her thoughts were jumbled like a river in flood.

Catching hold of one, like snatching a whirling leaf out of a whirlpool, Conthar held fast.

Why didn't his dragon have any color?

He answered, careful not to startle her. {{*He has no color because his heart is dead.*}}

At first she didn't seem to hear him, and when she did, he felt her get up and move farther away.

What was going on here?

She spoke mind to mind to him, and Conthar heard her words, but he was also getting the backspill from her thoughts. Very confusing, especially when he was muzzy-headed to begin with.

Conthar could sense others around them, feel their evil intent. These must be some of the dragonhaters he'd been trying to find.

He'd found them, alright.

But what was his rider doing here with them?

She wasn't a prisoner, he could feel that.

Why would she be here—with them—voluntarily?

The answer hit him like a boulder falling out of the sky—unexpected and terrifying and utterly devastating.

She was here to help him!

Amazing!

Horrible!

She had to get out of here!

Conthar brushed her mind again, and got sucked deep into the whirlpool of guilt, regret, pain, horror, sorrow, fury, all roiling and tumbling in her head and heart.

What he saw at the very core of her shocked Conthar to his. She wasn't just his rider, didn't even realize she was his rider. She was a...*Dragonhealer!*

REALIZING the answer came from the cobalt, Renny stood slowly and perched on a boulder, facing away from the others, away from the dragon as well lest she alert the others. {{*Do not move! You must be still! They're only waiting for you to wake before they start torturing you again!*}}

The cobalt answered, sounding like his words were coming from the bottom of a deep lake, welling up gradually and breaking the surface in little pops and bubbles. {{*Why are you... with them?*}}

A pause, as if he took a breath.

{{*You are no traitor to dragonkind. You are...*}}

Another pause.

{{*You cannot...think...to save me.*}}

Sounding utterly panicked, he threw out, {{*No! Leave!*}}

Gasped, {{*Before they find out...what you are...*}}

Renny's mind, almost as paralyzed as the dragon's had been, snapped back to awareness. {{*I will not leave you to these butchers!*}}

{{*Riders will be here soon. I have already called them. Until they arrive, you must get yourself out of harm's way!*}}

{{*Riders? What riders? Yours?*}} Renny's heart lifted a bit. A dragon who had a rider would be missed that much more quickly.

An endless pause before the dragon replied. {{*At this time, I have no rider I care to call, nor recognize.*}}

Renny had told enough truthful lies to recognize one when

she heard it, didn't have time to puzzle out the hidden meaning in the dragon's words.

Her tone harshly sympathetic, she told the cobalt, {{*There won't be any riders coming to your rescue. I'm it. If I can't get you out of here, we're both doomed.*}}

{{*What do you mean, no riders will come?*}}

{{*Whatever they did to you blocks your cries.*}} Renny let that sink in. {{*I'm the only one who can hear you.*}}

Not doubting her in the least, the cobalt sounded frantic. {{*Then it is even more imperative that you leave. You cannot help me by staying here. You must leave—find dragons and dragonriders and guide them back here.*}}

Renny huffed a rude noise, amplified through their mental connection. {{*There would be nothing but a bloody, mangled carcass to bring them back to, even if I knew where to find riders or dragons, and I don't. Besides that, I have no idea which ones can be trusted. A dragon as well as a dragonrider helped lure you in, then they did something to you so you couldn't fly or speak.*}}

{{*A rider…helped? I cannot remember. The last thing I remember is seeing a dragon flying erratically, following it and landing here. I remember trying to talk to the downed dragon, and seeing a man, then…nothing till I awoke. Allar. You must find Lord Allar of Dragon's Haven. Or Zantha, she can be trusted.*}}

{{*How do I know I can trust them, supposing I could even find either one?*}}

{{*Where one is, the other will be. I trust Allar with my life. He is the best, the bravest, champion the dragons have ever known—Dragonkind's staunchest ally. Look for a black dragon crossed by a silver sword. Zantha is my… She will help. Now, go!*}}

Yeah, well, this *Allar* might be the greatest thing since dragonhide boots, but Renny didn't think he was going to pop out of the woodwork anytime soon. A man who championed dragons? Renny had never heard of such.

{{*There isn't time, dragon. I have to get you out of here. You don't understand what these dragonhaters are capable of. I've seen what they do to the dragons they capture. I won't let them torture you! I won't have another dragon death on my conscience!*}}

The dragon's voice rang somber, threatening as a huge thunderhead. {{*What do you mean, another death?*}}

Renny's reply chilled him to his core, her sorrow and horror made his heart ache. {{*This is the first time I've actually been in time to help. All the other dragons—I was too late. I pretended to hate dragons so the dragonhaters would let me join with them. It was the only way I could think of to get here in time to save you.*}}

Sounding coldly enraged, the cobalt snarled, {{*How did you know they had targeted me?*}}

Renny answered, sounding defeated and heartsick. {{*I didn't know they had picked you, especially. Just another dragon. I… I helped them put chains on you. I didn't want them to get more suspicious of me than they already are.*}}

The cobalt's continued silence after her admission assured Renny that he now hated her as much as he hated the rest of the butchers. Heart squeezing in her chest, tone devoid of emotion, Renny gave the most beautiful dragon she'd ever seen her solemn vow. {{*Give me a bit of time. Gather your strength while I take out the butchers. I will free you and then you must fly, back to your Allar and your Zantha and freedom and safety. I swear I will never bother you again.*}}

Gathering herself, subtly shifting her weapons while confirming each and every position of the men surrounding her, Renny prepared to unleash death. She could take them all. Maybe.

No maybe about it.

She had to, if this dragon was to live.

She would take out the scum here today, and she would live to take out Din and the betrayer. After that…

The cobalt's distress nearly knocked Renny off her perch, blasting at her like he'd body slammed her. {{*You think to take on all these men? By yourself? I forbid it! I will not lose you when I've only just found you.*}}

{{*What? What are you talking about? Killing these butchers is what I do. My life doesn't matter—only yours.*}}

Abruptly switching gears at this further admission, the dragon demanded, {{*How badly are you hurt?*}}

{{*'Tis nothing. It's you I'm worried about. I have to get you out of here. How soon do you think you can fly once I release the chains?*}}

The pain radiating from her struck Conthar like a flaming arrow. Added to the pain from his wounds and hers, the level was becoming intolerable, unacceptable for both of them.

Conthar would have to keep her from bonding with him. If he opened his mind completely to her, the bond would lock in and the shared pain would destroy them both.

Making sure his barriers were firmly in place so he wouldn't accidentally bond with his rider, he tried to ease her pain a tad.

{{*My name is Conthar.*}}

That teeny bit of information—a powerful bit—widened the crack, opened the door a bit more.

Enough for him to feel each of her injuries, enough that his fury knew no bounds, so that he demanded again, {{*How badly are you hurt? Who did this to you?*}}

{{*It doesn't matter. I've had worse. It's you we've got to worry about.*}}

{{*Open your mind to me!*}} Conthar might have to keep a tight rein on his mind, but that didn't mean his rider couldn't let him in. He needed to know exactly who had done this to her. He would exact retribution to the fullest extent of his not inconsiderable power.

Sensing her reluctance, Conthar wondered what she could possible have to hide from him that was so terrible.

Determined to know, Conthar pressured her until she gave.

No wonder she was so reluctant—she thought he hated her.

Somehow he had to comfort her. Conthar had the distinct feeling there hadn't been much comfort in her life.

Trying to soothe his rider, Conthar cajoled, {{*If you won't open to me, at least tell me your name.*}}

{{*Renny.*}}

With that, all the floodgates in Renny's mind blew wide open.

Her name the last coherent word he heard as he was sucked into her memories, Conthar was whirled into a maelstrom, sucked under, held under, battered beyond belief. He was getting these things secondhand. How much worse had they been to live through?

He felt her determination, her boundless love for dragons, her despair at not being able to help them.

Her loneliness, her need to love and be loved, hidden even from herself. Renny considered herself unloveable.

Fought his way back to the here and now, knowing whatever the cost, he had to force her to leave or what they were going to do to him would destroy her utterly.

If she'd felt the loss of those other dragons so keenly, the loss of her own dragon would shatter Renny irreparably, especially if she was forced to participate, or even watch.

Conthar had to make her leave, give her no choice.

Surreptitiously testing the chains holding him down, Conthar realized the dragonhaters had done an excellent job, due no doubt to their vast experience in such matters.

That would be remedied as well.

Casting his senses further, to his surroundings, Conthar discovered they had chained him close to a cliff.

He remembered it now.

The no-color had been huddled against a pile of talus at the base of the escarpment when Conthar landed. Trying to get close enough to see how badly the no-color had been wounded, Conthar had been right next to the pile when he'd fallen.

If he could find the right pitch, a few good dragon roars would bring an avalanche of loose shale down on top of him.

With any luck at all, he'd manage to crush some, if not all of the torturers at the same time.

Now, how to keep Renny—his rider's name was Renny!—far enough away she wouldn't get hurt.

Knees drawn up to her chest, Renny sat statue still on her boulder. Probing gently, Conthar felt Renny stiffen. She'd mistaken his silence for disgust at what he'd read in her memories. What he felt was anything but.

Admiration, adulation, fear for her safety, all these combined in a heady brew, like the finest nectar.

Because of their situation, Conthar couldn't ease her pain as he longed to do. Couldn't open his mind fully and let her see his admiration, his awe at what she'd accomplished. Couldn't tell her —she wouldn't believe—that what she'd done bordered on miraculous. That even though she felt like she'd failed abysmally, she'd done more for the dragons than anyone else in the history of their world.

Hunching into herself at Conthar's touch, Renny asked, {{*So, are you going to kill me or should I just throw myself on their tender mercies?*}}

Conthar snorted. {{*Why would you think I'd want to harm you, Little Warrior? Because of what I saw in your memories? I think, even though we looked at the same thing, we see different sides of the same world. You see a desert, barren and lifeless. I see a harsh environment where only the strong survive and what seems to be ugly only needs a little encouragement to bloom.*}}

Not giving Renny time to ponder his words, fearing she'd look past his comforting words and see the real truth of the matter, Conthar deliberately stretched and rattled his chains.

He had to get Renny away from here as soon as possible, before the dragonhaters weakened him so much he could do nothing, and before Renny was damaged beyond repair or killed outright.

{{*What are you doing? Be still! Do not move!*}}

Renny's frantic warning hiss seared Conthar's heart and firmed his resolve. He moved again.

As he knew they would, the dragonhaters swarmed, poison coated weapons poised to do the most harm without causing death. Circling Conthar as he opened his eyes and tried again to move, they stabbed and poked and prodded, their shouts of glee filling the air.

Renny sat unnoticed, staring in horror, frozen in place.

Conthar had to act fast, before she ruined his plans.

Straining against his bonds and loosening the one over his muzzle just enough, thrashing his great head as much as his chains would allow, Conthar roared again and again.

The talus slope, unstable at best, began to vibrate.

The torturers paid no attention, overly pleased to have drawn such a response from their prey. Engrossed in their bloody work, they had eyes for nothing but the dragon.

Roaring once more, pulling at his chains, Conthar felt more than heard the low rumble begin. He had just enough time to place the strongest compulsion he could devise in Renny's head, to hope that the men surrounding him would have no time to get away, and then the world disappeared in thundering darkness.

FROZEN in horror as the cobalt dragon—Conthar! His name is Conthar!—deliberately attracted the attention of the butchers, that paralyzing fear was nothing to what swamped Renny as she watched what looked to be half the mountain collapse on top of Conthar with a thunderous roar.

What was he doing? Had he lost his mind?

With the roar still booming, the dust still pluming, Renny was on her feet and running.

Toward the avalanche.

Fighting the overwhelming urge to run in the opposite direction with every leap and bound.

Screaming out his name, over and over.

Choking on the thick cloud, unable to see, Renny stopped and called Conthar mind to mind.

Nothing.

Frantic, she reached the edge of the pile and began clawing at the rocks with her bare hands. It seemed as if the torturers had all been buried along with the dragon. She couldn't hear any of them calling for help, and she still couldn't see anything.

Renny dug, and threw rocks aside as she cried out his name over and over, not believing he was dead.

This dragon death hurt more than all the others combined.

Why? Because she'd seen this one go down?

Because she'd been able to speak with this one before he was so out of his mind with pain he became incoherent?

Because she'd come closer to saving Conthar than any of the others?

Or was it because Conthar had seen inside her soul and hadn't condemned her outright? She'd felt a momentary flash of hope at his words.

Whatever the reason, Renny felt the blackness taking over her soul, blotting out the light, creeping into every crack and crevice, urging her to run and keep running. To anywhere but here.

She had failed again.

Clawing and digging and tossing until her hands were raw and bloody, nails broken off to the quick, Renny was still heaving rocks when the moon came up.

A full moon this night, and Renny gladly used its light to continue.

She hadn't even found a human yet, let alone any sign of Conthar. Her head kept telling her it was hopeless, her heart... Her heart was broken.

This defeat would finish her.

Changing position on the pile—maybe this was closer to where Conthar was buried—Renny left bloody handprints everywhere as she tried to singlehandedly move the mound.

Hard to tell anything with the amount of rock that'd fallen, was still falling in trickles and fits. Grateful for the light of the moon, it distorted things even more.

Concentrating on digging, hearing nothing but her own harsh breathing, Renny didn't hear the ominous rumble until it was too late. Still digging frantically, the secondary avalanche caught Renny unaware.

Rocks landing all around her, some striking her, Renny hunkered down, trying to make herself small.

She never saw the one that knocked her cold.

RENNY CAME to to find the moon—both of them—almost set.

Why were there two moons?

Far too groggy to puzzle it out, Renny tried to move. An explosion of pain—in her head, her ribs, her entire body—rewarded her attempt.

The urge to run hit her harder than ever. She had to leave this place, had to go… Where?

Couldn't leave the dragon.

Had to.

The argument in her head setting off war drums, fighting her way out of the pile of rubble she lay half buried in, Renny managed to stumble-slide her way to solid ground. Tripped and fell to her knees, the pain almost making her pass out again.

Looking over her shoulder, surveying the monstrous heap of rock that had buried the dragon, she wished emphatically it had buried her too.

Starting back to the pile, determined to keep digging, Renny couldn't make herself touch it.

What? So now, in addition to everything else wrong with her, all her other failings, she was going to add cowardice to the list?

Pain had never made her afraid before.

Why now?

Turning away, head ringing and body protesting, she shambled to what had been the campsite, such as it was.

East. She had to go east.

Why east? She'd never gone very far in that direction, preferring to stay in the mountains, close to the dragons calling for help.

Long journey. Days and days.

Not for a dragon, but Renny didn't have a dragon, only her feet.

Befuzzled, Renny shook her pounding head slightly. It seemed as if there were two conversations going on in her head at the same time.

Of course, she *was* seeing double, so maybe that was par for the course.

Food. She would need food.

Rooting through what little remained of the stores the no-color had left, Renny found a few odds and ends. They wouldn't be needing any of the supplies, for sure and for certain.

Good thing. There wasn't much left.

Putting what she scrounged in an abandoned rucksack—a little jerky, some dried fruit, some small rinds of cheese—Renny looked around one last time, her eyes skittering past the heap of stone.

She would be back. With help.

Help? Where was she supposed to find help?

Allar.

Conthar had told Renny Allar would help. Or Zantha. She'd have to trust Conthar knew what he was talking about.

How was she supposed to find them?

Head due east.

Renny took a step. Why would Allar believe her outlandish tale if she did find him?

He'll believe you.

Taking another step, Renny stumbled like a drunk and snorted to herself. Conthar had said *Lord Allar*. One look at her and any self-respecting lord would run the other way as fast as his feet would carry him.

Locating her small pile of belongings, Renny picked up her sword, slung her bow and quiver over her shoulder along with her waterskin, and staggered to the top of the ridge on the opposite side from where she'd come into the valley.

The sun—both of them—just breaking the edge of the world, the sight revealed by the ever increasing light didn't give Renny much encouragement. Even when she squinted enough so she only saw one great glowing orb, it didn't help. Didn't change the reality of the view.

Mountain after mountain, ridge after ridge, as far as she could see, and for every ridge there would be a valley.

Settling her meager supplies, breaking into a shambling trot, Renny headed into the rising sun.

CHAPTER 11

*D*in had slipped away from camp to meet with *Him*, the one who couldn't afford for his face to be seen by the rest of the men. The same *Him* Din had met a short time ago in the dark tavern where that wretch had lifted his purse and ruined his meal.

The same *Him* who'd been giving orders while taking no risks for as long as Din had been playing this game. Din figured He was one of the lords of a great keep, or at least someone very important. Always cloaked and hooded, tending to lurk in heavily shadowed places, Din had never been able to get a good look at the Other—what Din always called Him in his mind.

Reporting in on his latest success, upon revealing the color of the last dragon captured, the Other's unholy glee was startling, even to Din.

Rubbing his hands together, He chortled, "Make this dragon's death even slower and more painful than any who have gone before and you will be rewarded handsomely. Most handsomely. Fail me and you will find out firsthand just how painful a dragon death can be."

Already counting his reward, discounting any thoughts of failure, Din headed back to camp. What could go wrong? The dragon was already captured and chained down.

Arriving the next morning—and just where were the dragon and rider supposed to be keeping watch against the predations of the Warrior?—Din found disaster. Not the kind he'd become so adept at concocting, but a natural disaster of epic proportions.

All that remained of his men and the dragon they'd been set to torture was a mountain sized heap of fallen stone. Assuming all his men had been trapped in the fall, kicking around the scattered packs and the remnants of food brought by the rider, Din found evidence to the contrary.

Someone had survived, but who? And where were they?

Had the rock fall been contrived, then?

Noticing small, bloody handprints, Din cursed. That brat! The new kid! How had he managed to survive when everyone else had perished? Berated himself and avoided thinking about what He'd have to say about this.

Din had known better than to take on a new recruit on such short notice, but he'd also been desperately shorthanded. It took a lot of men to properly torment a dragon.

Birdie would pay. All Din had to do was find the lad and…

Too late, Din heard the approaching rider. Wishing he could hide under the rock pile, Din turned to meet his fate.

Not the rider from yesterday, but the second, more evil than the first.

Landing in a swoosh of wings, not bothering to dismount, Second stared around in disgust. Indicating the heap of stone with a thrust of his chin, he curled his lip in a sneer. "I suppose all your men are there."

Attempting to bluff and mitigate his part in this, Din demanded, "Where's the other rider? Why wasn't he keeping watch like we agreed?"

Second sneered. "Our business is none of yours."

Cocking his head, Second listened for a moment while looking around anxiously. "My dragon says there's been another rider here. He can sense the rider, faintly. Too much mayhem in the air to get a good reading. No other dragon, though. We'll have to report this."

Giving Din a mock salute, Second said, "Nothing left for us here. Better figure out a way to rectify this or you'll be the next sacrifice."

Watching bitterly as dragon and rider took to the sky, Din sincerely wished he had a dragon to torture. Attacking the empty rucksacks with blind fury he cursed and flailed like a madman.

Not only had he taken on a new recruit without permission, one who'd turned out to be a rider in disguise, Din had lost yet another crew *and* the dragon they were supposed to be torturing.

The Other would...

Din had a pretty good idea what the Other would do.

Thoughts circling like carrion birds, there was a slim chance Din could redeem himself yet.

All he needed to do was...

If he followed the lad, sooner or later the boy would lead Din to another dragon. Not only would Din have a chance to torture and kill the boy, maybe he could find another dragon as well.

The Other would be well pleased.

Perhaps enough that He would forget how badly Din had botched this mission.

INTENTLY FOCUSED on putting one foot in front of the other as fast as possible, the water was halfway up Renny's boots before she looked up and realized this was no stream, nor even a river.

Renny gazed at the vast expanse, despair filling her heart.

She'd heard of the Great Lake—who on Zola hadn't.

Hearing about it and seeing it were wildly different.

She couldn't see the other side.

Couldn't even see a haze on the far horizon.

For someone used to mountainous terrain, the flat expanse seemed more a heat-shimmer dream than anything real.

After all the days and days of running, the mountains she'd scaled and the valleys she'd plumbed only to start another climb, Renny refused to be defeated by water.

Looking left, then right, as if a boat or a bridge might magically appear, too tired to care anymore, Renny backed out of the water and plopped down on the sandy shore.

Her meager supplies had run out days ago. At least she had plenty to drink.

Quashing the hysterical laughter bubbling up and threatening to consume her, too exhausted to think, Renny leaned back on her elbows, then stretched out on the sun-warmed sand…and passed out.

AWAKENING SLOWLY, like pushing out from under heavy hides, Renny pried open her gritty eyes and blearily peered in the direction of the lake, an intense sense of urgency gripping her.

Yep, still there.

She wanted to just lie right here for awhile longer, like maybe till the lake dried up. Although she was only seeing one lake. That was an improvement.

One was bad enough.

Sighing, Renny heaved herself to her feet in slow stages.

First rolling to her side, the side with the least hurt ribs, then to all fours, Renny managed to get one knee up and under her. Using it for a prop, she struggled the rest of the way upright.

Looked left, then right. Shoreline and woods receded in both directions forever, no sign of smoke or other indications of human habitation breaking the monotony.

Renny was just going to have to do it.

Surveying her few remaining belongings, this was light, even for her. She hated to leave her sword and bow, but no way could she swim and carry them.

Unwilling to leave them out in the open, Renny looked around for somewhere to stash them.

Spying an odd shaped formation of boulders, feeling like she was abandoning old friends, Renny carefully concealed her weapons in a deep crevice.

Stripping out of her clothes—when had she lost her cloak?—Renny wrapped the map—good thing it was oiled—and her dagger tightly into her shirt.

Rolling her supple boots into a tight ball, she wound her pants around shirt and boots.

The last thing she needed was for her boots to fill with water and add another challenge.

Stuffing the roll into the rucksack she'd liberated and making sure the top was tied securely, sincerely thankful it wasn't the dead of cold season, Renny waded into the water.

TRAILING what he now knew to be a dragonrider—and how come the brat was on foot if he was a rider?—Din couldn't catch up no matter how hard he tried. How was it possible the boy could travel like the wind?

Din knew his men had wounded the lad.

Under strict orders not to kill, Din had watched as they ganged up on the boy, each landing numerous blows. Seen the bloody places left by their knives.

There had been blood, and lots of it, on the pile of rocks covering the cobalt and around what was left of the campsite.

Birdie couldn't have much food, had to be starving. The men, knowing more supplies would be flown in, had devoured nearly every scrap, and the boy hadn't eaten anything at all, preferring to sit off to himself and sulk.

From the tracks and dried blood, Din guessed he was at least three days behind Birdie and falling further behind with every step. Obviously still bleeding, not stopping to hunt or fish, the boy had to be on his last leg.

Losing confidence he would catch up to Birdie shortly, Din couldn't understand how the boy could be outdistancing him.

No matter. Making no effort to hide his tracks, the wounded Birdie would be an easy target once Din finally found him.

Crossing a large clearing in the bottom of a valley, Din saw a dragon shadow racing across the waving grasses ahead of him.

Flinching from the swoosh of wings and First calling his name, tempted to run, there was nowhere for Din to hide.

"Ho, you there! You haven't caught that raggedy boy yet?"

About to spin a lie, Din realized he could turn this encounter to his advantage. "I'm close and getting closer, no thanks to you. Why haven't you flown ahead and located the brat?"

"Ha! I don't answer to the likes of you, and I didn't lose an unapproved recruit."

"Be that as it may, I am in dire need of rations, and you can give me a ride on your beast there."

Holding his breath, surprised when the rider agreed—while the mercenaries Din usually commanded never questioned his orders—the riders barely acknowledged Din's existence. The Other must be throwing a fit indeed for the rider to give in this easily.

Clambering clumsily aboard to curses from the rider and grunts and bellows from the dragon, Din clamped his arms around First in a stranglehold.

What seemed forever later, before they even landed properly, First fairly shoved Din from his precarious perch on the dragon. "You sorry ass son of a dragonrider! Worthless spawn of a dragonhealer! I ain't carrying your pain in the arse self anywhere ever again, no matter what He says."

Having flown due east, the direction Birdie had run steady and true as a compass, First had balked at flying Din across the Great Lake, arguing there was no way the boy could've crossed it without a boat or a dragon.

Din had insisted, invoking His wrath if the boy got away when they were this close. Knew in his black heart the boy had indeed crossed—perhaps he'd grown wings and flown, but Birdie was on the other shore.

Ill-matched and worse-tempered, Din's trio had journeyed across the endless water, culminating in Din being shoved off while the dragon was still a man's height off the ground.

Splashing down into the edge of the lake, shaking his fist, Din threw rocks and hurled epithets as rider and dragon flew away. Why anyone would want to ride a dragon was beyond him.

First had no cause to get upset. Din had only gotten sick four or five times, and as for almost tumbling them both off more than once, well, the stupid rider shouldn't have flown so fast or banked so steeply.

CRAWLING from the shallows onto dry land, Renny lay gasping for breath. Ribs screaming in protest with every bellows-like heave, arms and legs wooden, Renny dragged herself under the shelter of some bushes along the shore and collapsed, face down.

When she could finally breathe again without feeling like she was going to pass out, Renny flopped over onto her back with all the grace and speed of an over-turned hard-shell.

Lying there, staring through the canopy of leaves, she thought she saw a dragon high overhead, a dragon with two riders. Maybe she was seeing double again—but shouldn't there have been two dragons as well?

The deep laceration on the back of Renny's head once more trickling warm and wet down her scalp, and since thinking only made her head hurt worse, Renny stopped thinking

Dragging her wet clothes out of her pack, Renny wrung them out as best she could. Eyeing the branches speculatively, she would've loved to hang her clothes and let them dry, but her sense of urgency, growing stronger with each passing moment, precluded that luxury. They'd dry just as well on her.

Folding the map into a small square and stuffing it into the toe of one of her boots, she abandoned the empty rucksack.

Struggling into her wet clothes, shivering hard enough to make her bones rattle, Renny tucked her dagger into its sheath inside her boot and turned inland, still heading due east.

Forcing her way through the heavy brush along the shore, Renny found an animal trail, which became a path, which led to an actual well-travelled dirt road, rife with human, animal, and cart tracks.

Hoping for a good-sized village, Renny tried to increase her pace, managed to go from a shamble to a stumble. So hot now, burning up, Renny wished her clothes were still wet.

Barely noticing the increasing crowds on the road, Renny did notice when she came to the village proper.

If she looked as bad as she felt…and judging by the looks and the wide berth all the people she encountered were giving Renny, she must look pretty bad.

Now what? The strange compulsion which had pushed Renny beyond the limits of even her endurance seemed to have vanished like a puff of smoke.

Standing still, letting the crowd flow around her, the roaring in her head and the darkness hovering on the edges of her vision threatened to finish what Din and company had started.

Staring mutely at an empty space in a shady alley, contemplating curling up right there, Renny heard the cry chorusing from a multitude of voices, felt it reverberate through her.

Dragons!

Fully engaged again, Renny spotted two dragons and two riders, high above. She didn't think she was seeing double, this time, but she wasn't sure.

The dragons had color, an emerald and a topaz.

She hadn't seen double in different colors before so she was going to assume there were two separate dragons.

But were they the right dragons?

At least the dragons had color.

Wending her way through the crowd, Renny tried to keep one eye on the direction the dragons had headed. Figured out quick it was easier just to go with the flow. Everyone seemed headed one way, the way Renny needed to go.

Cold again, shivering, Renny wondered where all the heat of the day had gone. Breaking out of the narrow, twisty streets, she could see a large meadow, and the dragons, just landing.

A quick glimpse, and then the crowd ringed the riders and she could see nothing.

Being small had its advantages—Renny wormed her way through the crowd until she stood in the front row, the gawking crowd keeping a respectful distance.

Somewhere there must be a very large, very loud drum. Renny's head thumped in time with it, each beat driving spikes into her until her whole body throbbed with pain.

No one else seemed to hear it.

Renny wanted to clap her hands over her ears and curl into a ball.

Shaking it off, it was now or never.

Trying to go to the dragons, Renny received an elbow to her ribs for her trouble. The additional agony almost did her in, and she still wasn't sure these dragons could be trusted.

How could she tell?

The dragonriders were walking toward the crowd, away from Renny and their dragons. One of the riders turned back to his dragon.

The symbols on his tunic—a black dragon crossed by a silver sword—almost made Renny faint with relief.

These riders could be trusted.

She'd bet her life on it. Was betting her life on it. Feeling curiously light, Renny floated toward the emerald.

Approaching the dragons, the emerald turned her head to Renny. The emerald's eyes lit, glowing from within, and heat radiated from the dragon to Renny.

An answering glow emanated from within Renny and a melting sensation enveloped her entire body.

Inclining her head to the dragons, Renny spotted one of the riders pounding back to the dragons. Paid him no mind as she dropped to one knee and spoke words that poured from her heart.

"My sword and my bow I pledge to your service. My life is yours to command."

Regaining her feet, Renny locked eyes with the rider, felt her heart do that curious melting thing again, and all hell broke loose.

The green dragon's warning rang so loud in Renny's skull it was a pure wonder her head didn't explode.

{{*WARE!*}}

Renny spun just in time to see Din coming at the emerald with one of the lethally sharp fishing spears. Throwing herself at him, Renny grabbed the haft.

Shaking her off, Din went after the green again, unable to pass up such an opportunity to kill a dragon, and besides, Birdie wasn't going anywhere fast. He was in too bad a shape. The green—about to be dead—dragon made a perfect precursor to spitted Wren, and Din wasn't getting out of this alive anyway.

Even if he did, The Other would never let him live, so Din would kill the dragon first and then the dratted Birdie.

Redeem himself a little, even if only in his own eyes.

Drawing from some reservoir of strength Renny didn't know she had, she launched herself at Din's back and tumbled them both to the ground.

Din went after the lad that had been such a plague to him, such a detriment to his grandiose plans. Striking all the places he knew his men had hurt the worst, his need to kill the dragon pushed aside in his need to punish the lad.

Fending off Din's blows as best she could, trying to draw her dagger at the same time, rolling and twisting and writhing, Renny ended up on the bottom, being pummeled.

Just as Din rose up to deliver the finishing blow, Renny got her dagger free and plunged it up under his ribs and straight into his black heart. Din collapsed on top of Renny as her world disappeared in a massive explosion of pain.

CHAPTER 12

*A*llar woke with Renny spooned against him, wrapped tight in his arms, Zantha curled protectively around both of them with Renny sandwiched between them.

Thinking back over the memories they'd just shared, no wonder Renny had the look of a hunted she-wolf. A she-wolf fighting for those she loved, battling against incredible odds.

Renny and Zantha were sleeping soundly, and would for awhile yet. They had borne the brunt of the emotional storm, Allar merely acting as anchor.

Tugging Renny closer, still unable to believe what she'd been through, Allar wanted to wrap her up and put her somewhere safe. Somewhere she'd never be hurt again.

Zantha had only meant for them to find Conthar's location but their connection was so strong, their bond so intense, they'd gotten every sordid detail of Renny's life. Her whole journey to this place and time.

Renny wouldn't be pleased about that, no matter how unintentional.

Allar couldn't fathom the sheer courage Renny possessed,

not to mention heart and endurance. A warrior himself, Allar had fought in more than his share of bloody battles and been through some extremely harrowing experiences, but the things he'd seen in Renny's memories had nearly stopped his heart with fear.

Renny had no idea just how special she truly was.

Allar intended to spend the rest of their lives convincing her of that.

DREAMING ABOUT FOOD—DIDN'T she always?—this time Renny could even smell it.

Fish, cooking over an open fire.

Half asleep, Renny remembered one of the best ones she'd dreamed lately in vivid detail.

A great hall. Food of every description covered all the tables and she had eaten to her heart's content. No matter how much she ate, there was more, and more, and more.

She'd been able to stuff enough in her pockets to last her for days.

That must be what the Great Dragon Hall in the sky was like —warm, dry, safe, a full belly and a never-ending supply of food.

Renny fought to stay asleep, not wanting the dream to end.

Not wanting to wake up, cold and starving and alone.

Opening her eyes reluctantly, Renny closed them and reopened them.

A fish—a large fish—cooked to perfection, on a flat rock right in front of her nose.

Renny blinked, certain the fish would disappear.

She'd had realistic dreams before but never quite this real.

Maybe she hadn't made it across the lake after all. Maybe she'd just quit swimming and sunk to the bottom of the lake and simply didn't realize she was dead yet.

Maybe the fish wasn't dead and cooked and was getting ready to eat her instead.

Renny inhaled deeply but didn't move. Sure smelled real enough. Afraid to reach out and touch it, fearing it was a figment of her over-stressed mind and underfed stomach, she kept staring, eyes and mouth watering.

Allar had to look away as Renny stared longingly at the fish. No wonder she'd gazed so blissfully at the laden tables in his great hall.

Like she wanted to eat her way from one end to the other and back again and then wallow amid the leftovers.

Vowing he would see to it she never missed another meal as long as she lived, knowing Renny would reject any signs of pity, Allar coughed lightly.

"Are you going to eat that fish, or just stare at it?"

Shifting her gaze to Allar's face, Renny blinked back tears. "That's…for me?"

At his nod, Renny struggled to sit up.

Allar was at her side instantly, slipping an arm beneath her and helping Renny to a sitting position. She still made no move toward his offering. Puzzled, Allar nudged her.

Meeting his gaze, all sign of tears banished, studiously ignoring the steaming, succulent piscine, Renny swallowed. "I've already eaten today—twice. You eat it."

Making it sound as if eating twice in the same day was an unheard of miracle, and for her, it probably was.

As if she had no right to want nor expect more.

Renny's generosity almost did Allar in. He could hear her stomach growling, but she thought he needed the meal more than she.

There obviously hadn't been much teasing in her life, either. Allar would remedy that lack as well.

Leaning over Renny to break the fish into small pieces, Allar felt more than heard her indrawn breath as he picked up the first morsel. Thinking he was going to eat it, Renny averted her gaze as Allar moved the tasty bite toward his face.

Blowing on it, Allar held the bite to Renny's lips.

Startled emerald eyes met cobalt and they froze, far more sizzling between them than shared food.

"I've already eaten, love. Open your mouth. There's plenty more where this came from." Allar cradled Renny at an angle so he could continue to feed her.

Exhausted, she let him.

Eyes closed, head snugged against his chest, Renny opened her mouth for each bite like a fledgeling bird.

Struggling to remain awake, Renny'd eaten all but the last few bites when Allar felt her drop back into sleep like a rock into a pond. Easing her into a more comfortable position, Allar held Renny to his heart and rocked her gently.

Sharing memories was tiring at any time, but as wounded and wrung out as Renny had been to start with…

Allar honestly didn't know how she'd managed to keep going.

No wonder the dragonhater in the village had died with such an astonished look on his face. The man had been trailing Renny since Conthar and had had help from a rider, barely catching up even then.

Moving his hands ceaselessly over Renny's slight form, Allar watched the gathering dusk and began making plans.

BUGLING from the top of the cliffs, the sky just beginning to shift from black to a lighter shade of midnight, Zantha woke them before first light.

Pillowed against something that felt soft and hard at the same time, Renny savored.

Warm—it felt like a sun warmed boulder covered in soft fabric. Nuzzling her face into whatever it was felt…exquisite.

Sighing, opening her eyes, Renny's warm pillow turned out to be Allar. Trying to push off and away, Renny froze when Allar tightened his arms.

"We already had this discussion and you lost last time, remember? Allar's rumbling chuckle vibrated in Renny's ear, settled deep in her heart.

Allar didn't think now was the time to inform Renny this was the way she was going to wake up every morning for the rest of her life.

Warm and safe and well fed, wrapped in his arms, as close to his heart as Allar could get her.

Indulging in his own bit of nuzzling, Allar rubbed his chin back and forth across the top of Renny's head, amused when strands of her sun-gilded mop caught in his beard stubble.

Engrossed in each other, the couple broke apart when Zantha landed and demanded, "Are you going to stop…"

Allar began warningly, "Do not say…"

"ogling…"

"…that word."

"…her?"

Laughing as he replied, "Renny's mine! I can ogle her all I want!" Allar's and Zantha's combined laughter drowned out Renny's protests.

Taking one last look around the shadowed valley where they'd spent the night, Renny hoped in some small way what had happened here yesterday and last night would help negate the horrible tragedy associated with this place.

All silent, the threesome remained lost in their own thoughts as they hurriedly flew back to Dragon's Haven, no sightseeing this time but a direct flight.

The enormity of the deception, involving not just humans but dragons as well, was hard to take.

The number of people involved, the sheer hatred, boggled the mind.

127

Especially to Allar and Zantha.

Having never known anything else, Renny took it in stride.

Zantha had already taken great care to shield her mind from the other dragons. Not only because they didn't want to alert the traitors, but because the other dragons would seize this information and seek revenge.

Allar wanted the trap well laid before it was sprung. Wanted all those responsible brought to justice, wanted this ended once and for all.

There would be no prisoners taken, no quarter given, no survivors left to perpetuate the hatred.

Flying so rapidly, the wind rushing noisily past them ruined any chance of conversation. Knowing Allar would hear her through his link with Zantha, Renny directed her thoughts to Zantha.

{{*I've never known anything else, never knew any other than myself cared for the dragons—I mean, I'd heard of dragonriders but until Allar, I'd never actually met a real one—but why do the dragonhaters hate dragons so much?*}}

Stiffening beneath her riders, Zantha bellowed her rage.

Allar answered through his link with the dragon. {{*Nothing more than the age old story of greed and jealousy. One faction covets what another has, and not being able to obtain the coveted item, seeks to destroy it instead.*}}

Renny shivered, and Allar tucked the warm cloak tighter around her.

{{*Dragons are not pack animals, to be owned by the highest bidder or the most skillful breeder. Dragons are free spirits. Thinking beings, and they choose their riders. Not the other way around. Dragons cherish their riders but barely pay other humans any mind. The oldest stories say the dragons came to this planet in search of their human counterparts. None of the stories say how the dragons got here, and if the dragons know, they're not telling.*}}

Nestling deeper into Allar's hold, Renny pondered the new

information. While she knew much about healing dragons, she knew little about history.

{{*Tell me more about the wars.*}}

Allar shrugged. Old news to him, he wasn't sure what Renny wanted to hear.

{{*There have always been dissenting factions, those who have dragons and those who crave to have. While laxamuls are thick as fleas, okumos are so rare as to be practically non-existent. On our mountainous world, any means of transportation other than by foot is a blessing. Around a hundred years ago, tensions exploded. The dragons have always been willing couriers, but some of the riders began refusing to use their dragons to help. The dissent which had been brewing reached a boiling point and it became a bitter stew of who was at fault. Relationships disintegrated even more until the riders stayed in their keeps and haters stayed in their towns. Trade between the two ceased. The riders were starving, needing more foodstuffs than the laxamuls the townsfolk were so adept at breeding and tending. Rustling and outright thievery became common, angering the haters even more. The townsfolk had no way to get their goods from place to place as bandits and thieves flourished in the absence of dragon patrols. The Orimjays were breeding like rats and thieving whatever the brigands didn't.*}}

Allar shifted, reached around Renny to pat Zantha's gleaming neck. {{*Some riders and some townspeople continued to honor the ancient treaties, and those keeps and towns prospered while the ones who didn't sunk further and further into poverty and hate.*}}

Renny hunched into herself. {{*Aye, I was raised in one such.*}}

Furious at her admission, even though he'd seen it in her memories, Allar hugged Renny tight enough to make her squeak. {{*At some point, the hatred escalated and the haters targeted Healers as well as dragons. Without Healers, nothing riders do matters. In the last generation, the guerrilla attacks have increased, contributing to the decline of dragons. And not merely attacks to kill, attacks designed to torture and maim, with the aim of causing the most pain they can.*}}

{{*Which is where I come in.*}} Sliding her hand under Allar's and stroking Zantha's neck, reiterating what they'd already seen via her memories, Renny told them, {{*Conthar said the dragons that were helping had no color because their hearts were dead. Seems like someone would've noticed a number of dragons that've lost their color. I know there are at least two, because once I saw two at the same time. There could be more. I couldn't reach them mind to mind. I tried, but there was…nothing. At least two riders are involved, possibly more. The man I saw at the tavern with Din didn't seem to be a rider, but I saw him giving orders to Din. I couldn't get close enough to overhear them, though I tried. While I was with the traitors, I heard Din call the man the Other. He is so evil, bursting with malevolence. He radiates the same feeling I got when the rider in the valley questioned me. Something is drastically wrong with both of them.*}}

Shutting his mind firmly to Zantha lest Renny pick his plans out of the air and take off on her own, her confessions were stated so matter of factly she might've been talking about ways to keep your sword sharp and shiny.

Spying, infiltrating the enemy's camp, going toe to toe with evil with no thought of self-preservation, Renny didn't see anything unusual in what she'd accomplished.

Allar knew there weren't any no-color dragons at Dragon's Haven or anywhere close, but what about human traitors?

Too bad they weren't as easy to spot.

All Renny's memories seemed to center around the far side of the Great Lake, and deep into the wilderness, so there weren't any easy answers there.

Allar couldn't be too careful, all their lives depended on the decisions he was making. Still ruminating, Allar came out of his dark musings when they landed on the cliffs at Dragon's Haven, the guards on the towers, human and dragon calling out a warm welcome.

Voya met them on the ramparts, grinning ear to ear. His second had obviously been informed of certain events by Mithar, who'd been clued in by Zantha. Probably as soon as they'd cleared the rocky cliffs of the valley.

Shaking his head in amusement, Allar gave in to the inevitable dragon gossip.

Trying to rein in his glee at the possessive way Allar kept touching Renny, at the way Allar kept her tucked close to his side, Voya turned his attention to Renny.

Slight to the point of looking frail, Renny seemed as if the merest breeze would blow her right off the ramparts, but she had a core of steel.

Had to have, to even be walking after the horrendous wounds she'd suffered.

Grinning wider, Voya hurried to meet the returning couple.

Renny would need every bit of that steel spine to deal with Allar.

Clasping forearms and falling into a bear hug, pounding each other on the back, Allar and Voya acted as if they'd been apart years instead of only a day.

Renny had the uncomfortable feeling they were celebrating far more than Allar's return. Feeling awkward and in the way, Renny tried to hang back.

Having none of it, gently clasping her small, calloused hand in his much larger one, Allar drew Renny forward.

Much to her consternation, Voya hugged her too.

Thankfully, with much less enthusiasm than he'd shown Allar.

Stepping back, hands on Renny's shoulders, Voya looked deep into her eyes. "Welcome, Little Sister. We have waited long for you."

Thoroughly confused now, Renny looked to Allar for an explanation. Exchanging amused glances with Voya, Allar slung his arm around Renny's shoulder and tucked her close.

Walking toward the keep, Renny sandwiched between the two very large, very protective men, Allar informed Voya, "Renny has told me much, good and bad. There is little time and we must act quickly if we are to make it across the lake this day."

~

ZANTHA SPOKE to the dragons of the riders Allar needed in Council. Voya went to fetch the few who weren't riders while Allar waylaid one of the servants. "Tell Cook I need food sent to the council room with as much haste as she possibly can. Lady Renny needs sustenance."

The food arrived in a blink, well before the members. Seating Renny, Allar made sure her plate stayed full. Renny still looked half afraid the food would disappear out from under her nose.

Plain food, simple food, but Renny gazed upon it as if it were nectar from the gods.

Allar watched in awe as Renny ate slowly, savoring every bite, rarely taking her eyes off what was before her.

Had he been the one to miss so many meals, he had the feeling he'd be gobbling every mouthful, growling like a starving watch beast with each bite.

"The men I have called here are warriors, every one. It will be hard to convince them that riders, much less dragons, are in on this plot to maim, torture, and kill dragons. Most of us cannot conceive of anyone being so twisted, so evil. Perhaps that is why they succeeded so well for so long. We were looking in the wrong places for the responsible parties."

At the heavy guilt in Allar's words, Renny finally looked up from her plate. Told him thoughtfully, "You are not to blame for their atrocities, any more than I am. Each person, each dragon, is accountable for their own actions. Most live good lives. If they do no great deeds, at least they do no harm. Something has happened to these dragons and riders to warp them, like wet boards left too long in the sun. Still wood, but useless for their intended purpose. The only thing you can do is destroy the boards and start over with new wood."

Leaning close, cupping Renny's face in his hands, Allar

brushed a sweet kiss across her lips. Drawing back just a smidge, he rested his forehead against hers.

That same molten buzz she was coming to associate with Allar's touch zapped Renny once more, held her still where normally she'd have jerked away.

Bemused by the kiss, Renny's momentary peace was jarred by the sound of Voya clearing his throat. Looking up to see the same wide grin as before directed at herself and Allar, Renny squirmed out of Allar's hold.

Sobering as he gave his report, Voya said, "All are headed this way. Guards are posted at the ends of the hall and I gave orders for us not to be disturbed."

Straightening with a lingering glance at Renny, Allar nodded. "Well done, Voya. I fear they will not be very happy with the news I have to give them."

Turning back to Renny, pressing his lips to her forehead, Allar breathed in her scent. "Trust me."

Looking deep into Allar's eyes, decision made, Renny nodded slowly, just as the first of the men entered.

Renny came to her feet, too wary to remain seated in a room with this many strange men, even with the massively heavy table between them and her.

Sensing her unease, and wanting—needing—to stay in contact with her person, Allar moved to Renny's side, took her hand in his and greeted the men now pouring into the room.

"All of you know each other, and those of you who weren't flying missions met my Lady Renny two days past at nooning. However, she doesn't know all of you. I ask that each man introduce yourself."

Grumbling and jostling, throwing Renny surreptitious looks the men complied.

Renny's eyes followed the men as one by one they spoke.

"Reeve, rider of Tant."

"Vin, rider of Lees."

"Tarso, rider of Sann."

"Meer, rider of Ashel."

"Awalt, rider of Kell, and Master of Weapons for Dragon's Haven."

"Blan, Master of Supplies."

The last man, one Renny hoped to avoid more contact with, bowed in Renny's direction and grinned wryly. "Seon, Master Healer of Dragon's Haven."

"Be seated, quickly." Allar looked around the room at the select group of men he'd chosen to include in his plans. All of them seemed more than willing to accept Renny.

Except Meer, glaring at Renny suspiciously, but then, he regarded everything that way.

Was it possible one of his most trusted friends was in truth a traitor? Hoping with all his heart it wasn't so, Allar paced away from Renny.

"What is revealed in this room stays in this room. Since the ones gathered here are the only ones who will hear this tale, if word leaks out, until the guilty party is identified, you will all be considered as traitors and treated as such."

Ignoring the outraged gasps and mutters, Allar continued. "The tale Renny has imparted to me, and Zantha, sounds farfetched. Renny didn't actually tell it, Zantha shared Renny's memories. Acting as anchor, I am witness to their truth. I must ask you to shield from your dragons for the time being."

Waiting a beat, getting a nod from each man, Allar clenched a fist, released it. "Renny brings news of terrifying joy, and heartbreak. News of Conthar.

Pausing as the room broke into a loud babble of voices, Allar raised a hand.

"The good news is, Renny found him. The not so good news…" Taking a deep breath and blowing it out, Allar finished. "…he was captured by dragonhaters."

The room went totally silent for the space of several

heartbeats before erupting once more, some of the men jumping to their feet.

"Where is he?"

"Is he still alive?"

And finally, one comment directed accusingly at Renny hushed the others. "You left him?" Meer glared at her, hands fisted on the table and leaning menacingly in her direction.

One look at Renny's white face had Allar moving behind her and placing his hands on her shoulders.

He could feel the fine tremors wracking Renny's body, but she gave no other indication of the pain their questions were inflicting. Drawing Renny back against his chest, Allar wound an arm around her front.

"Renny has come a far distance, on foot, at great peril to herself to find us. Knowing Renny wouldn't leave as long as he drew breath, Conthar buried himself in a landslide of his own making."

Meeting each man's eyes, Allar continued. "Conthar couldn't aid himself, nor help Renny. She can mindspeak with dragons, and Conthar told her how to get here. More than that, he placed a compulsion in Renny's mind to find Dragon's Haven. There was nothing she could do except leave him."

Allar glared at the worst accuser.

Meer. A remarkable soldier but bitter and distrustful to the core. Could he possibly be…

Keeping eye contact with Meer, Allar informed them all as if they hadn't already heard, "Renny protected Zantha using nothing more than her own body and a dagger against a crazed dragonhater who was attacking Zantha with one of Lakeside's fishing spears."

All knew the reputation of those spears. Made by the local blacksmith of some prized metal, honed to razor sharpness, they were nothing to be trifled with.

"Do any of you truly think my Lady Renny would willingly

leave a wounded dragon?" Surveying the grim faces, stopping on each face and making eye contact, at the unanimous head shakes of denial—Meer's slower and more reluctant than the rest—Allar relaxed somewhat.

Voya looked at Renny thoughtfully. "You can hear dragons as well as speak to them?"

Allar grinned to himself, grateful Voya saw straight to the heart of the matter.

At Renny's curt nod, Voya finished his thought, not taking his eyes off Renny. "Only those dragonbonded can do so, and then usually only with their own dragons."

Renny's quiet reply confused the rest of the men even more. "I do not have the honor of being bonded with any dragon."

Voya's slow smile creased his weather face. "Only one other has the privilege of understanding dragons." He bowed from the waist, a deep bow this time, as the room's occupants looked on in befuddled amazement, a glimmer of understanding crossing some of the older rider's features.

Straightening and giving the room at large a wave of his arm, Voya pronounced, "It is with the utmost pleasure that I present to you—Lady Renny. Our very own…Dragonhealer."

The uproar caused by Allar's announcement dimmed in comparison to Voya's.

Peace finally restored, the men began to talk in earnest.

Renny stood to one side, wall at her back, wishing she was anywhere else.

On her way back to Conthar's burial place would be a good start.

Renny twitched with the need to doing something, used to action, used to taking charge and getting the job done, unused to waiting for someone else to discuss and debate every angle of a problem.

Sounding like they wanted proof, Renny's only proof lay buried under a mountain of rubble, far away.

Warily watching one of the older riders approach, Renny stood her ground as he reintroduced himself.

"I am Reeve, Lady. My dragon is the ruby, Tant. Are you truly a dragonhealer?"

Renny shrugged. "So I have been told, once by an old woman and again by Zantha."

"Well, then, it must be so. Dragons are seldom wrong. Welcome to Dragon's Haven. How did you find Conthar?"

"I pretended alliance with the dragonhaters, trying to head off another killing. A no-color dragon lured Conthar in and they captured him. When he came to, we started mindspeaking. I... Excuse me."

Trailing off as she remembered something very important, making her way to Allar, Renny stopped in front of him, intensity pouring from her. "You said you burned my old clothes. What did you do with my boots?"

Allar looked puzzled. "Your boots? Your clothes were beyond rags, but your boots are dragonhide—with holes worn in them. I gave orders for them to be taken to my private chambers so I could..." Glancing down at Renny's shod feet, he raised his eyes back to hers. "Why do you need your boots?"

"Take me to your chambers! Now!"

Winging a brow at her unintentional demand, feeling the heat and ignoring the snickers, a tip of Allar's head dispatched Voya. All of them waiting impatiently for his return, Voya seemed to take forever, but in reality he was back in no time, boots in hand.

Trembling, Renny, reached out and took them. Sliding her hand deep inside one of the boots, Renny sighed with relief when her questing fingers located the object she was seeking.

Tugging it out, she unfolded it and smoothed it out on the table.

"What are we looking at, besides a bunch of x's?" This from

Meer, the same rider who'd practically accused Renny of outright desertion.

Renny swallowed. "All these x's mark valleys where dragons were tortured and killed, or future sites."

"How do you know?" Vin, this time. Not accusing, merely curious.

Straightening a little, not attempting to sugarcoat the truth, Renny told them flat out, "Many of these valleys I have been in, only to find dead dragons. Some held nothing." Locking eyes with Allar, Renny said, "All resembled the valley where we went yesterday." Some wispy connection niggling at her, Renny lost the thought as the next question hammered her.

Frowning, Vin remarked, "Anyone can draw x's on a map. How do we know this map is real, or that the x's are what you say?"

Renny fisted her hands at her side to keep from going off on the lot of them. They had as little reason to trust her as she had to put up with their bullshit. "I stole the map from a dragonhater, but even before, I'd been in many of these valleys. Would you like me to draw you a picture of what I found?"

Meer snarled, "So you're a thief as well? You appear here from out of nowhere and we're supposed to blindly believe everything you say? Just how did you find these valleys before you stole the map?"

Watching as Renny distanced herself from her painful memories, Allar was about to step in when her imperiously raised hand stopped him in his tracks.

"I hear dragons. I have for as long as I can remember. I found the valleys because I was drawn to dragons screaming in pain."

Meer sneered, "You heard dragons screaming in pain and yet you did nothing? Why didn't you contact riders? I'm sure they could've done more than you. And you call yourself a Dragonhealer? Pah!"

Taking a deep breath, Renny reined in her *let's quit the crap and get moving* thoughts. Told him cooly, "I never said I was a Dragonhealer. I didn't know where to find riders, wouldn't have known which ones to trust even if I had. I did what I had to do."

"And just what, pray tell, does that mean?" Meer might as well have slapped Renny, so obvious was his disdain.

Getting right in the larger man's face, so ferocious Meer backed up, Renny cut loose on him. "It means...I have found tortured dragons, dragons in unimaginable pain. Stayed with them as they breathed their last. A few begged me to end their torment and I...obliged."

The only sound was a concerted indrawn breath.

Tarso's tone was horrified, his face equally so. "You...you *murdered* dragons? The penalty for killing a dragon is...death."

Allar stepped forward and the world erupted into sound at the same time. Before he had a chance to defend Renny, the dragons did so in no uncertain terms.

Drowning out the riders' protests, the dragons roared out their displeasure until the walls shook.

All the riders clutched their heads as the dragons' protests rang in the rider's heads and ears, loud and clear.

Thoroughly chastened, the riders sat quietly and regarded Renny with newfound respect.

All the dragons were on Renny's side, agreeing with her even over their own riders.

Allar grimaced. He'd remembered to tell the other riders to shield from their dragons but he hadn't shielded from Zantha completely. Wasn't sure it was possible any more. Not after their little adventure with Renny. That had strengthened an already tight bond into an unbreakable weave.

Zantha had used Allar's little slip to keep the other dragons in the loop about Renny. Ecstatically thrilled to find a dragonhealer, they would brook no criticism, nor would they allow any condemnation of her actions.

Especially when it could've easily happened to any one of

them, and given the choice of being slowly tortured to death or dispatched with their dignity intact, all would've chosen a quick, merciful death.

Renny was humbled by the dragons' faith in her.

Quieting by slow increments as each dragon vied to mindspeak to Renny, they turned out to be much less suspicious and much, much friendlier, much faster than their riders.

Watching as everyone settled back down and he had their full attention, Allar said, "Renny can hear dragons, thankfully. If she couldn't, we might never have known what happened to Conthar, or to the other missing dragons. Armed with what we now know, we're in a position to stop any more dragon deaths. Renny won't be alone the next time she hears a dragon. We're that much closer to finding out who our enemies are, but first, before we do anything else, we are going to retrieve Conthar."

Cheering and whistling and foot stomping drowned Allar out for a long moment. Raising a hand, he waited.

"Conthar lies many days journey to the west. We must leave now if we're going to make it across the lake this day. Make haste!"

Dismissing his men to prepare for the journey, catching Renny's hand in his, Allar headed for the ramparts. Grinning, he stole a kiss.

"Before we leave, we have several things to do as well. First, I have been commanded to take you to the dragons so they can see you for themselves. They are waiting impatiently." Guessing shrewdly, Allar snorted. "But you already know that, don't you?

Renny's delightful blush confirmed his guess.

"More importantly, Seon has to give his stamp of approval before you even think about stepping foot on such a strenuous journey. If he says nay, you will remain here if I have to have you sedated and restrained."

Bracing himself for wrath and reasons, Allar slanted a look at

Renny, knowing that despite his heavy-handed proclamation, if she turned those big green eyes on him, he was a goner.

Renny's laughter had Allar jerking toward her in amazement. The first time he'd heard her laugh, the sound zinged straight to his heart, blazing a path like a beam of sunshine in the darkest valley.

"We already had this conversation and you lost, remember?" Renny teased, throwing Allar's words back at him. If he thought one overly protective cave man was going to keep her from going... "Your worry is for naught, but I thank you for your concern, however misplaced."

Softening her tone, Renny placed one of her scarred hands on Allar's arm. "I do thank you, but if I made it here on foot, badly wounded, I hardly think riding on a dragon's back will do me in. Besides, knowing you, you will carry enough supplies to ensure the entire keep could be fed, so you won't have to worry about me going hungry. None of my wounds are infected and my head doesn't hurt anymore."

Much, Renny amended silently.

Scrutinizing Renny closely—altogether too good at hiding pain what with her lifetime of practice—Allar couldn't tell whether she was in pain or not.

Still, Allar wasn't budging without Seon's approval and Zantha's opinion, which carried far more weight in Allar's eyes.

The only thing Allar knew for sure right now, other than the fact he wanted to kiss Renny senseless, was that he'd never get enough of her laughter.

Standing back, Allar reveled at Renny basking in the admiration of healthy dragons. 'Twould do her self esteem a world of good. While she'd dealt with plenty of wounded and dying dragons, had her soul ripped to shreds with all she'd been through, Renny'd never had the chance to be in the company of any that weren't in pain.

Their approval the best sort of healing balm, Allar

thoroughly enjoyed watching Renny's pleasure at mingling with the dragons.

Totally fearless, Renny had planted herself in the middle of a large circle of very large dragons, scratching and stroking and petting as if they were no more than oversize, friendly hunt-beasts, the whole crowd of them besotted.

Renny's laughter rang out again and again as the dragons made some comment or shared some thought that tickled her.

Zantha stood by, practically beaming, looking for all the world like a proud parent.

Gaze never wavering from the small woman surrounded by dragons as Voya stepped up beside him, Allar asked, "All set?"

"Aye. We await your command." Nodding to himself, Voya remarked happily, "'Tis a wondrous sight, is it not? I never in my lifetime thought to see a Dragonhealer, let alone be able to claim one for our very own. The entire keep will be talking about this for generations to come."

"The entire world." Considering for a moment, Allar rolled his shoulders. "I had thought to keep this secret for awhile, but perhaps news of a Dragonhealer will draw the traitors out quicker than anything. My Lady must be well guarded at all times. If I can't be at her side, you will be."

Voya's inelegant snort mirrored Allar's thoughts exactly. Used to taking care of herself, Renny was not going to like that one bit.

Too bad.

Voya mused, "Other than the two of us, we'll have to trust the dragons to discern friend from foe."

Nodding his agreement, hating to spoil Renny's fun, Allar moved across the courtyard towards her. Alerted by Zantha, Renny said her goodbyes amid heavy protests and headed Allar's way, her wide, delighted smile fading with each step, to be replaced with a look of grim fierceness.

"Time to go?"

Wrapping his arms around Renny, pulling her up and close to

his heart, Allar curled himself over her slight form and nodded against her head.

Renny was beautiful to him, battered and bloody.

Rested, fed, cleaned up and glowing with happiness, she was exquisite.

And he was asking her to give up safety and head back into the wilderness, straight to danger.

CHAPTER 13

hey mounted up, all the dragons carrying heavy-duty panniers slung securely across their withers. Camping gear, foodstuffs, extra weapons, shovels and picks, heavy tarps.

Looking at the baskets and bundles of foodstuffs Cook insisted be taken along, Allar could do nothing but shake his head. Renny already had everyone in the keep—except Meer—wrapped around her finger as tightly as he was.

She had no clue, wouldn't believe him if he told her.

Seon, having given his reluctant approval on the condition that not one, but two, Healers be included in the group of travelers—with specific, detailed instructions for taking care of Lady Renny—the Healers carried pack after pack, stuffed to the brim. Enough to treat at least one army, maybe two.

Amused at the length and depth of Seon's instructions, Allar wondered fleetingly if the Healers would even notice should one of the riders need tending. A lift of Allar's hand sent them winging skyward, a wave sent them heading westward, the dragons flying at top speed.

Renny rode with him, of course.

The Healers rode double with two of the other riders.

Grinning as he thought of the green cast of Seon's skin as they'd lifted off, Allar replayed Voya's joke in his head, sent the thought winging in Zantha's direction with a request to pass it along to Renny.

Straight faced, Voya had informed Seon that Allar expected him, as Head Healer, to join this trip. Sick at the mere thought of riding a dragon, Seon had none the less started listing things he would need, turning greener and greener with every breath until Voya finally relented and took pity on the Healer.

The only thing Seon hated worse than sickness was riding dragon-back.

Renny immediately threw back her head and laughed long and loud. Allar's gut twisted at the sound, storing it up, knowing they all needed all the laughter they could get.

The greens and browns of the hills and vales a blur beneath them, the convoy passed over Lakeside in a blink.

Examining the curve of the shoreline, Renny could almost pick out where she'd come ashore.

They flew and flew and flew, and flew some more, still over water with no shore in sight.

Allar's stomach stayed tangled in knots at the vision of Renny swimming this distance, alone and wounded. Bleeding. At the thought of the dragon sized finned-ones who inhabited this lake. He'd've thought long and hard before crossing it in one of the fishing boats. Unconsciously tightening his grip, Allar grunted when Renny elbowed him.

Finally glimpsing a glimmer of the far shore, the setting sun glinting off it, Zantha eventually zeroed in on a large, clear beach and began a slow, gliding descent.

Looking at the site with barely concealed excitement, as soon as Zantha's feet touched and Renny could wiggle out of Allar's hold, she scrambled off. Throwing her arms around Zantha's neck in a quick hug, Renny took off running down the beach.

Skidding to a halt in front of a pile of boulders, Renny began flinging rocks in every direction.

Dismounting in a more leisurely fashion, stretching and bending to work the riding kinks out, Allar grinned as the other riders watched Renny with unconcealed amusement and not a little worry for her sanity.

Finding what she so desperately sought, Renny shimmied a quick dance of joy and turned to the waiting crowd.

Running back toward them, Renny placed a smacking kiss on Zantha's nose and skidded to a halt in front of Allar clutching a sword, a bow, and a quiver to her heart.

Caressing the weapons the way Allar wished she'd touch him, grinning, Renny told him breathlessly, "I despaired of ever seeing these again. It fair broke my heart to leave them behind."

Spinning to Zantha to thank the dragon once more, Renny missed the look on Allar's face.

Allar remembered wondering where her weapons were when Renny pledged to Zantha. No wonder she hadn't had any weapons! No way could Renny have swum the lake carrying them. 'Twas nothing short of a miracle she'd made it across at all.

No wonder either she was so glad to be reunited with her sword and bow.

Superbly crafted, obviously custom made, definitely well used and well taken care of.

As good a place as any, they made camp for the night. Lighting a fire wouldn't draw any more attention to themselves than a large group of riders heading anywhere would anyway.

Fire lit and food passed around—and thanks in great part to Renny, Cook had supplied them well—they relaxed. The dragons settled comfortably in the sun-warmed sand, the riders and healers content to nestle against them.

During the usual settling down chatter, and amidst the food,

Awalt, Master of Weapons, asked Renny what they'd all been dying to. "Fine weapons, there. How'd you come by them?"

Eyeing him thoughtfully, taking her time swallowing a mouthful of something delicious, Renny glanced around. All eyes were on her, all conversations halted as the others eagerly awaited Renny's answer.

Fighting men all, they knew quality when they saw it.

"I didn't steal them, if that's what you're implying."

Awalt chuffed, roll in one hand, hunk of herdbeast in the other. "Never crossed my mind. 'Tis obvious to a blind man they were made for you. I'm not prying, just curious."

"They were crafted for me by an old soldier. All the normal swords and bows are way too big for me to handle." Renny went silent for a moment, lost in memories.

"He took pity on me when no one else would teach me. Made these for me and taught me how to use them, as well as my size to my advantage. I owe him a debt I can never repay."

"Lady, what was the soldier's name?"

Renny peered in the direction of the voice. Sann's mental nudge supplied {{*Tarso.*}} She was getting better at matching the names to the riders. With lots of help from their dragons.

"Rand, from the garrison at Fort Helve."

Silence, followed by startled exclamations and a babble of voices vying to be heard as the men gathered close to examine Renny's treasures.

"Rand?" An awe filled voice Renny easily identified as the rider of the ruby, Galajk. Another mental nudge, accompanied by a dragon snicker. {{*Reeve.*}} Reeve had spoken to her several times. "I know of him! A warrior of great renown, you were fortunate indeed to have him as mentor."

Renny gave Reeve a sharp nod. "He is an excellent teacher and a true friend."

Practically drooling on himself, Awalt stared with renewed vigor at Renny's weapons, glittering in the firelight.

The men were warming to Renny bit by bit, positively entranced by her gear, if not her story, so she offered up her sword and bow to be passed around.

Watching all the men—except Meer—cluster around Renny, oohing and ahhing over her weapons like women over new babies, Allar decided he'd give Meer one more chance.

Could Meer be the traitor? Or was he just so set in his curmudgeonly ways he didn't know any other way to act?

Either way, Meer's days were numbered. No matter how good a rider or fighter.

Up and gone before first light, eating a cold on-the-fly breakfast of squares of cornmeal mush wrapped around slices of herdbeast, they stopped at nooning to give the dragons a breather and let the dragons hunt.

In pairs only.

They flew all day again, and the next day was a carbon copy.

On the eve of the third day, landed and settling in for the night, Renny noticed Meer heading her way.

Sighed to herself.

Men like him only ever wanted the same thing—to bully and belittle anyone not strong enough to stand up to them.

Tall as Allar, lacking Allar's muscled bulk, whatever Meer had in mind, it wasn't good.

Renny stood her ground, gaze never wavering, hands loose and ready at her sides.

Having chosen to wait until Allar sought a bit of privacy to relieve himself, coming to a stop in front of Renny, Meer looked her up and down, trying to intimidate her much smaller form.

Renny almost wished him luck. She'd stood her ground, and won, against men far tougher than Meer had ever thought about being.

Intent on each other, neither noticed Allar—per Zantha's informing words—returning from the woods on the far side of the camp.

Voice dripping with suspicion and accusation, Meer curled his lip. "You say your wounds are fresh, that you got them trying to protect Conthar."

Renny nodded, not taking her eyes off him, saying nothing, waiting him out.

"We've flown for days, and according to the dragons' calculations we should reach our destination on the morrow."

Renny nodded again, fairly certain where he was headed with his line of questions.

Looking around at the gathering riders, sure of his audience and their compliance without the utterly besotted Allar to steer them wrong, Meer tucked his thumbs in his belt and rocked on his heels. "Yet…Allar told us at Dragon's Haven you tried to dig Conthar out by the light of the full moon."

Renny nodded again, sure now.

Puffing his chest out with self importance, Meer delivered his final argument. "How is that possible? If Conthar was trapped on the full moon, then your wounds can't be as recent as you say. That would've been over a month and a half ago."

Voice rising to a thundering crescendo, Meer hounded Renny. "Your story is just that, a story. Perhaps a trap, hoping to lure us in as you lured Conthar. Perhaps the blow to your head did more damage than Seon thought."

His voice turned sly, implying nasty things. "Perhaps…you are one of those women who will do anything, go to any lengths to bed a rider."

Ignoring the outraged gasps and the shocked glances of the other men, Renny's reply was glacial. She didn't care what they thought of her, or what this sorry excuse for a human called her, but to accuse her of deliberately luring in a dragon and dragonriders…

"Not *that* full moon. The full moon around eighteen days past."

Sure of his audience, sure of himself, Meer accused,

"Preposterous! You've been at Dragon's Haven five, six days. You think you can con us into believing you covered all this distance wounded and on foot, not to mention the fact you claim to have swum across the Great Lake—all that in somewhere around eleven, twelve days at the most? A distance it has taken dragons nearly four days to fly? Bah! I call dragonshit!"

The look on Renny's face would've silenced a saner man. She'd held her temper till now, but it no longer mattered if he was one of Allar's trusted advisors. Meer had crossed the line.

Balling her fists to keep from drawing her blades and using Meer for a straw-target, Renny stalked toward the much larger man, making him stumble backwards.

{{*Renny, Allar is coming up behind you. Take care not to eviscerate him.*}}

Ignoring Zantha's dragon snicker ringing in her head, Renny prepared to launch. Teeth bared like a she-wolf, wound up like a slither-worm getting ready to strike, Renny snarled, "Think you I care whether you believe me or not? The only reason you still breathe is because I would not have your dragon suffer the pain caused by your death. Not killing you leaves me a lot of leeway."

Backing up and backing down at the venom in Renny's tone and her aggressive advance, Meer stared, speechless for once.

Hooking Renny's waist from behind just as her toes left the ground, as much to keep her from launching herself at Meer as to just touch her, Allar snatched Renny out of the air and back against his hard frame. Ignored her furious hiss at her thwarted attempt to neutralize Meer.

Holding Renny against his hip, Allar admitted, "If Zantha and I hadn't shared Renny's memories, I too would find her story hard to believe."

Renny stiffened and Allar tightened his hold, a quick squeeze loaded with *Trust me.*

Reprimanded Meer sternly, and somehow Allar's sword appeared in his right hand, pointed right at Meer. "However, we do believe Renny. If you continue to refute her, I will consider it an act of treason, equal to harming a dragon and punishable by death."

Meer's face, already white at whatever death he'd seen in Renny's eyes, whitened even more.

Allar's tone dropped, lower and deadlier. "Besides which, Renny is my love, my mate, and will soon be Lady over Dragon's Haven. You have two choices: Apologize or leave. Choose. Either way, if my Lady so desires, I will loose her on you in reparation."

Meer backed off, spluttering now in lieu of blustering. Holding his hands out placatingly, shaking his head, eyes wild. "I meant no harm. I only thought to protect you from a charlatan. She herself has confessed to being a thief."

Allar's hand squeezing Renny's hip was gentle, tender even. His voice was harsh, as grim and cold as Renny's a moment ago.

"And so you name My Lady Renny a liar and worse as well?"

Meer backtracked frantically. "I meant no harm, My Lord."

"Then I suggest you apologize right quickly, and mean it. Otherwise, I will see you escorted back to Dragon's Haven…to pack."

The audible, concerted indrawn breath seemed to echo off every rock and tree. Banishment meant a certain death sentence. No other keep would take in an exiled rider and dragon, and an unaffiliated dragon was like tossing a wounded dragon to the dragonhaters.

Throwing a desperate, hate-filled look at Renny, Meer bowed stiffly and grudgingly gritted out, "My apologies."

Without waiting for Allar's permission, Meer spun on his heel and came to a halt. In a half circle facing him were all the dragons, his own included, and all the riders.

Disbelieving, he glared at them. "You side with her?"

Not waiting for an answer, Meer stormed off into the night.

Signaling Voya to follow Meer, Allar turned Renny so they were face to face. "My apologies, My Lady, for Meer's boorish behavior. He is an excellent warrior, even if his attitude has always left much to be desired, but that was too much, even for him."

Allar smiled proudly. "Voya stood right behind you, and I would have stepped in sooner, but you obviously had things under control and I would not undermine your victory. Thank you for not destroying Meer, but you have my full backing if he tries such again. Even were you not mine, not a Dragonhealer, he has no right to belittle you so."

Allar was stunned when Renny merely shrugged off both Meer's behavior and Allar's apology. "He's an ass, but he's just trying to protect you from me. He's right, you know. I admit to being a thief. And worse."

Heart scraped raw, knowing his pity was unacceptable and would drive Renny farther away, Allar answered matter of factly, "Meer's right about one thing—you've already stolen something most precious to me."

Renny's face flashed hurt disbelief just before closing like a slamming door.

Head high, holding his gaze, Renny's throat was tight with the pain his words caused. Why had Allar said he loved her, called her his mate only to turn on her like this? "I have stolen many things, but not a single thing from you."

Allar asserted, "You stole from me."

Jerking as if he'd slapped her, Renny averted her eyes and stiffened in his hold, both his hands wrapped around her upper arms in a gentle but unbreakable grip. She should've known better. All Allar's pretty words, the gentle touches, the way he made sure she had soft clothes and plenty of food—all were just bait he dangled in front of her for information. She'd swallowed every bit of it, hook, line, and sinker.

Was she truly so starved for food and attention she'd fall for the oldest ploys in the book?

Now that Allar had what he wanted—information about

Conthar—she'd served her purpose. But then, why had he defended Renny against Meer's accusations? He'd caught her around the waist, held her, and not once had her abused ribs twinged.

Renny couldn't remember a time when being accused of thievery hurt so much.

Why? Why would Allar…

Wait. Allar hadn't sounded angry. Renny knew all about enraged men. Allar had sounded…like he was teasing.

Her mind still in a whirl at Allar's conflicting words and gestures, she started when he cupped her cheek. Still wouldn't look him in the eye. Her heart hurt. Everything hurt.

Allar's soft words had her astonished gaze meeting his and locking there.

"You stole my heart. My love, my Renny." Allar nodded slowly and then leaned close and kissed her breathless. Melting against Allar, they came up for air only to hear a happy cacophony of whistles, clapping, and bugling dragons.

Renny hid her flaming face against Allar's hard chest while he laughed and laughed.

CHAPTER 14

*A*irborne for some time, with every stroke of dragon wings, Renny felt worse. Her headache, which had been mostly gone, returned with a vengeance. Her wounds throbbed in time with the beat of Zantha's wings, her ribs so tender every shallow breath flamed in agony.

Noticing Renny getting stiffer and stiffer in his arms, Allar thought it merely because she was dreading their arrival at the valley where Conthar lay.

Zantha finally clued him in. {{*Renny is in increasing pain. I have been shouldering much of it for her, but even with my help, she is miserable.*}}

Immediately ordering Zantha to slow enough he could speak to Renny, Allar demanded, "Why did you not tell me you were hurting? I knew this trip would be too much for you." On the verge of ordering a halt so the healers could tend Renny, the scouts returned, dropping over the ridge in front of them, swooping to meet the stragglers. Using real speech instead of letting the dragons communicate took longer but was far safer.

"My Lord! We've found the valley we're seeking—just over the next couple of ridges!"

Muttering an oath, Allar growled in Renny's ear, "You will let the healers attend you as soon as we land."

In too much pain to argue, Renny merely nodded.

If Zantha hadn't picked this place out of Renny's head, they'd never have suspected what'd happened here. Most of the riders didn't fly this far west unless they had to, and to a cursory fly-over, it merely seemed as if part of the mountain had fallen.

There was no sign of the tragedy that had occurred.

No need to summon the healers—the dragons had alerted to Renny's distress and almost before they landed the healers were on their way.

Dismounting as gently as he could, Allar cradled Renny and looked for a soft grassy spot to lay her down. One of the riders supplied a cloak and ere it finished settling to the ground, Allar had Renny on it. Refusing to relinquish his grip on her hand, Allar knelt beside her.

Voice far from his usual authoritative growl, Allar sounded… distraught. "You will take the medicine the healers give you without protest.

Renny nodded slightly, even that small effort costing her. She hurt worse than when her wounds were fresh, and now she could barely breathe, as if a great weight had taken up residence on her chest.

Whatever the healers gave her, foul though it was, eased her pain somewhat.

What really helped the most were the dragons. Zantha gathered them in a huge circle encompassing Renny and Allar. A low, melodious humming filled the air.

No matter how they did what they did, Renny was grateful and Allar moreso as they helped Renny breathe easier.

Zantha's whispered, "We must hurry, Dragonhealer," had Renny struggling to sit up over Allar's vociferous protests.

Gasping through gritted teeth and clenched jaw, Renny managed to get out, "Allar, the only way you will keep me down is to knock me out. Now either help me or get out of my way. We're wasting daylight."

"Tell me what's going on and mayhap I'll think about letting you up." The Great Lake, frozen over, had more give to it than Allar at this moment.

Renny and Zantha shared a long, intense look. Zantha nodded and Renny answered, "I…we…think… No, I *know* Conthar is still alive! The pain I'm feeling is his, and time is running out swiftly. Hurry! We must hurry!"

Allar lifted Renny to a sitting position but absolutely forbade her to set foot near the pile of rocks.

Not as if she could anyway.

Silently cursing herself for her inability to go near Conthar's burial place, Renny had been many things in her lifetime, but never had a pile of rock defeated her so handily, turned her into such a sniveling coward.

Running out of derogatory swear words to direct at herself— and her collection of them was impressive—Zantha connected with Renny.

{{*Help us, Dragonhealer! You are the only one who can get through to Conthar! Find a place of peace deep within yourself and shelter him there. Make him understand we're close. You will have to block the pain. What you are feeling, on top of his own pain will push him over the edge and we'll lose him. Cease berating yourself! You are the bravest human I know. Conthar put a warding compulsion on this place, as well as the compulsion for you to find Allar—'twas the only way he could be sure you'd leave. Trust us and yourself. Believe in yourself!*}}

Renny heard the last like an echo from a far distance.

Others had told her the very same, over and over.

Thinking of all the dragons she'd failed, all the dragons who died because she couldn't save them, Renny renewed the vow she'd vowed to herself: She would not, could not, fail this one.

This dragon she would save.

The first time she'd ever had help, Renny banished all inklings of failures and focused, drawing strength from the living dragons around her and the memories of the ones past helping.

Closing her eyes, Renny thought of Conthar, as he'd been the first time she saw him. Larger than life, so beautiful he took her breath away and brought tears to her eyes.

Cobalt scales shimmering in the early morning light, powerful wings spread wide, heroically coming to the rescue of a wounded dragon.

The way Conthar showed only compassion instead of hate when Renny opened her mind and shared her memories with him.

Conthar, as he looked just before he collapsed the mountain on himself, making sure she was out of harm's way.

The love and respect in Allar and Zantha's voices and memories when they spoke or thought of Conthar.

There! A flicker of life!

Renny latched onto the flicker of Conthar's life flame like a trapped soul in a cave grasps at the faintest glimmer of daylight.

Word that Conthar still lived spread through the riders like wildfire. Beginning in the spot Zantha indicated was closest to Conthar, the men and dragons quickly formed teams.

Unfolding the tarps brought for that purpose, the men hastily filled the tarps with rocks and pulled the corners to meet in the middle. The dragons picked up the tarps and carried them some distance away before dumping them and returning for another load.

All worked steadily, not even stopping to eat. No matter how hard they worked, how many rocks they moved, the pile didn't seem to diminish any in size.

Sitting up as long as she could, Renny gave up and curled on her side, holding onto the glimmer that embodied Conthar so tightly her entire body was rigid with effort.

Aware the dragons were aiding her, sharing their strength, and grateful for it, Renny wrapped her essence around Conthar's, concentrating on weaving a protective cocoon and blocking out everything else.

Allar worked furiously along side the rest. The news that Conthar lived struck him like a huge fist squeezing his heart.

Zantha had known! And kept it from him!

Allar had thought them close, closer even than most dragons and riders. No time to worry about her betrayal now, he would take that hurt out later and examine it.

Pausing, casting a worried glance in Renny's direction—she was so pale and unmoving…{{*Zantha…*}}

Halfway across the clearing with another load to dump, Zantha's assurance came back loud and clear. {{*Renny is fine, as well as she can be right now. Believe in her, and yourself. I will explain everything to you later. Know this—I did not willingly keep this from you.*}}

Contenting himself with Zantha's answers for now, Allar renewed his attack on the unforgiving rocks. No wonder Renny's hands had been raw. She'd been one person attacking this heap.

Throwing a glance at the sky, Allar wished for a full moon. It would be dark soon in this steep valley, even though the sky directly above was still bright. Dusk was rapidly creeping in around the edges, unwilling sleep stealing up on an exhausted soldier standing watch.

Straightening his aching back, Allar looked around at his men and their dragons. Knowing they couldn't continue like this, Allar curled his tongue and let loose a loud whistle.

All eyes turned his way, the whites glaring in the dust covered faces like fire-rock miners coming out of a mine, none willing to let up in their efforts.

"I am as unwilling to stop as the rest of you but we'll break for now—eat something and figure out how we can light enough torches to continue."

Informing their riders not to worry about torches, the

dragons rose as one and disappeared over the ridge. Sparing enough time to hunt a few morsels for each, the dragons returned carrying enough logs and brush to light a fire that would illuminate the entire valley.

While they were gone, the riders dropped in a circle close to Renny. The healers moved among the riders, tending the worst cuts, making the men drink a foul concoction—to stave off infection and to counteract the dragonhater's poison, should they come into contact with any residuals—or so they said.

Having long held the suspicion the healers made the stuff taste as nasty as possible on purpose, Allar choked down his portion without complaint.

The healers passed out food and drink, refilling as fast as the men cleaned their plates and emptied their mugs.

Sitting hip to hip with Renny, Allar panicked when he couldn't rouse her enough to eat.

Only Zantha's timely reassurance kept Allar from losing it completely.

How had this little slip of a female gotten so deep into his heart so quickly? Needing comfort, if just the weight of her body, Allar scooped Renny into his lap, arms a tight circle of love and protection around her, as the dragons had done earlier.

Letting his mind go blank, Allar relaxed a bit and savored the feel of her. This felt right, so right.

{{*Allar. Do not worry so. We will not fail.*}}

Allar twitched and convulsively clasped Renny closer to him as her voice rasped softly in his head, sounding as if she were far, far away instead of in his arms.

How was it possible for him to be hearing her? Deciding Renny must be channeling through Zantha, Allar paid the strange quirk no more mind.

Renny's voice came to him again, fainter and farther away.

{{*Believe.*}}

That was all—just that one word—and then she was gone,

back to wherever she was in her mind, holding onto Conthar with an unbreakable grip.

By firelight, the roaring fire the dragons kept stoked, the riders kept working.

Repeating the same moves over and over until they hardly remembered why they were bending over, picking up the rocks, placing the rocks on tarps.

Their world narrowed to bend, lift, toss, repeat.

Over and over, endlessly, they worked like human ants, destroying a mound instead of building one.

Still working when the sky lightened, unnoticed by the riders at first, the sun finally broke over the top of the ridge and illuminated the infinitesimally diminishing heap of rock.

Had they been able to merely unearth Conthar, they'd've been finished by now. Because the men feared the rest of the scree would collapse on top of them, they'd been forced to start high up and work their way down.

At last beginning to see results, the pile of rock they'd moved was approaching the pile they were removing from in stature.

Desperate to find Conthar, the teams were loath to halt.

Allar insisted.

They all, men and dragons, had to take a break, needed sustenance if they were to continue.

Allar used every moment of the break to cradle Renny.

She was totally unresponsive to touch or voice, and icy cold even though the healers had kept blankets piled on top of her and a fire going as close as they could without cooking Renny.

As Allar's agitation increased heartbeat by heartbeat, Zantha reassured him.

{{*Our Renny is fine, just focused on holding Conthar.*}}

Holding Renny in his lap, rocking her gently, Allar called her name repeatedly. Renny had touched his mind—perhaps with Zantha's help Allar could do the same.

Deep—so deep she doubted she'd ever find her way back—
Renny heard Allar calling her name.

How had he become her world in just a few short days? She
who'd never had anyone, never needed anyone, and now she
couldn't breathe right unless he was close, touching her. She had
to find her way back, if only for long enough to tell Allar she
loved him.

Concentrating on his voice and his arms around her, Renny
opened her mind.

Mustered enough strength to answer.

{{*Allar.*}}

That one word was all she could manage, but Renny poured
a wealth of feeling, every bit of love she felt for him into that one
word.

So faint he thought he imagined it, Allar heard Renny
breathe his name. A mere wisp, Allar latched onto it and followed
it to the source.

{{*Renny, my love, hold on just a little longer. We're almost there.*}}

Allar could see his words reaching Renny, one at a time, rocks
sinking slowly into the depths of a clear, bottomless pool.

Peace filled Allar's soul, so close to touching the very heart of
Renny, as if their souls knew each other intimately, had always
known each other and were just now being fully rejoined after an
interminable absence.

A brilliant light surrounded the two of them, joining them
further, encapsulating them in warmth.

Bright bubbles floated around them, sparkling in the light,
each bearing the essence of a dragon. The dragons offered their
comfort and Allar could feel their strength pouring into Renny…

And Conthar!

The bubble holding Conthar's essence was dim, but there, the
light faint, Zantha's right beside it.

Cradling Renny closer, focused on her and Conthar, Allar
was aware of nothing else.

Not the healers hovering near.

Not the men finishing their break, nor the sounds of them attacking the pile with renewed vigor.

They'd only been at it for a short while when Voya let out a joyful whoop. The last rock he'd moved revealed a tiny patch of dusty cobalt.

At the sight, a reverent hush fell over the entire crowd of men and dragons. The silence lasted only an instant before the air filled with hoots and hollers and the renewed sound of rocks being heaved onto tarps.

Furiously, frantically, the men and dragons moved rocks, exhaustion forgotten. As more and more of Conthar was exposed, so too were the chains holding him down.

Heavy chains snaked over his back, trailed over his neck and tail, trapped his wings close to his body.

The rescue team had come prepared.

Working pieces of dragonhide under the chains—possible only because of the tremendous amount of weight Conthar had dropped since he'd been trapped—acid distilled from those damnable fire-thorn brambles was poured carefully, one drip at a time onto the chains until a link gave way.

Hovering anxiously between Conthar and her humans, when the others had Conthar mostly uncovered, Zantha called urgently to Allar. {{*Listen to me! You must rouse Renny. She has to come back to us without letting go of Conthar, without letting her pain come to the surface. Do you understand?*}}

Blinking groggily, Allar shook his head, as if waking from a deep sleep. {{*Renny is exhausted. She can do no more.*}}

{{*She has no choice. Conthar's life hangs by a thread, and Renny holds that thread.*}}

Renny broke in, almost beyond hearing. {{*Allar, do not fight me on this. If I cannot save Conthar, then I will die trying. I cannot bear to lose another dragon, especially not this one.*}}

{{*I cannot bear to lose you.*}}

Allar's heartfelt declaration warmed Renny as nothing else could've, gave her strength to carry on. She made no movement, but Allar sensed her come back to him like an arrow striking the bullseye.

{{*Allar, I…*}}

Knowing what she wanted, Allar rose with Renny in his arms and strode closer to Conthar. Renny struggled to get out of his arms, wanting to stand.

Using his greater muscle mass, keeping his arms tight around her, Allar insisted Renny kneel beside Conthar. Kneeling behind Renny and holding her in front of him, supporting her physically as well as mentally, Allar brushed a soft kiss across the top of her head.

Reaching out trembling hands, Renny planted both palms on blue silk and stroked Conthar, feeling the same spark that'd zapped her the first time she laid eyes on Allar.

Zantha butted her head in so Renny had one hand on Conthar and one on Zantha. Allar felt the jolt as the four of them connected, melding together.

The air crackled the way it does when a lightning strike is imminent—a hair standing on end, skin prickling, spine tingling quiver.

He/she/they shared pain/joy/despair/hope, unable to tell where one ended and the others began, couldn't tell who felt what.

Slowly, slowly, the emotions swirled and coalesced into a living flame, shared among the foursome.

With the settling came a blinding flash of knowledge, a direct lightning strike melding the four of them together like sand grains fused into fulgurite, sending Conthar's life flame shooting up, burning bright and true. No longer in such dire panic of being snuffed out.

Allar had teased Zantha and Conthar about finding their mates when the answer was right in front of him all the while.

Zantha and Conthar hadn't been looking because they *were* mates, and they both knew it.

So if they were mates, why hadn't they bonded?

That answer came flying in on the heels of the first, another direct strike.

Conthar hadn't been out looking for his own mate—he'd been searching for Allar's!

Had Conthar claimed Zantha while Allar was still unmated...

{{*'Twould have been most difficult for you.*}} Zantha nudged Allar, blew a warm breath across him.

Humbled at the sacrifice the two dragons had made for him, Allar now understood why Conthar hadn't come home much, why he'd insisted on searching farther and farther away from Dragon's Haven, putting himself more and more at risk.

It must've been sheer torture to be so close to his mate and be unable, nay, unwilling, to claim her.

No wonder Zantha hadn't told Allar Conthar still lived. Allar would've questioned how she knew, and rather than lie to her human, Zantha had held her peace.

Sneaky dragon! Allar had always assumed Zantha got her news of Conthar from Mithar and Mina and Zantha had never corrected that assumption.

Leaning into Zantha, Allar rubbed his cheek against her silky scales. {{*Thank you both. I...*}}

Allar swallowed but the words in his head, in his heart, couldn't get past the lump in his throat.

Small wonder Zantha had seemed to be more full of teasing laughter and innuendo than ever since they'd found Renny. Or rather, Renny had found them.

Now that Allar had a mate to bond with, Zantha and Conthar could bond as well. Providing Conthar lived, Allar thought grimly.

Heavy protests hit him from the other three almost before the thought was completed.

Grinning, Allar surrendered to their wisdom. They would allow no other outcome.

Scooping Renny into his arms, Allar eased down what was left of the pile so the rest of the men could finish uncovering Conthar.

Glancing back, Allar frowned.

He knew from Renny's memories the torturers had been close to Conthar when the mountain came crashing down. Even though it might be possible to identify some of the bodies, get them a little closer to tracking down the dragonhaters, he wasn't looking forward to uncovering any of them.

Renny didn't move in his hold, but Allar could feel her mirth and her thoughts came to him clearly.

{{*Conthar says you are a worrywart, that you worry worse than an old woman. He also said to stop obsessing about the traitors. As soon as they heard the rumble of the avalanche, they tried to run. All of them are farther out in the pile, and unless you particularly want to see squashed bugs, they'll be of no use to you. Conthar and I can show you memories of exactly what they looked like whenever you're ready.*}}

Carrying Renny back to the nest of blankets the healers had made for her, Allar could feel Renny's discomfort at being carried around like a child.

"I really, really like the feel of you in my arms, Renny my love. You fit there perfectly."

The healers brought food, a thick broth, along with a mug of something that smelled awful but was no doubt good for Renny.

Chuckling at the expression on Renny's face when she got a whiff of the concoction, leaning close and whispering conspiratorially, Allar murmured, "Anything. I will give you anything if you can make medicine taste better than this swill."

With a furtive glance at the healers, Allar indicated the mug with a knowing, sympathetic thrust of his chin.

Renny almost choked on her laughter. "Ah, but if it tasted good, would it work half as well?"

Grimacing, she drained the cup and started on the broth, savoring the meager meal as she did any food that came her way.

Watching as Renny cleaned out her cup to the last drop, Allar signaled the healers to refill it, knowing Renny would never ask for more. Wouldn't even think to.

Renny would need every sip and then some.

Conthar might be able to see light, but he wasn't out of the deep dark forest yet.

While he might be mostly out from under the pile of rocks, he had grievous injuries Renny would have to tend. Not just the poisoned wounds the torturers had inflicted, probably horribly infected by now, but also wounds gotten from being buried under tons of rocks for weeks.

Good thing dragons had tough hide.

SITTING QUIETLY WHILE SHE ATE, keeping an eye on Conthar— unmoving—and Allar—moving about ceaselessly—Renny gathered both her thoughts and her strength.

She would need medicines, special herbs and salves if she was to save Conthar. The torturers used unusual weapons for their dirty deeds. Incredibly sharp, designed to cut through dragonhide with ease, and treated with poison.

Conthar had been stewing in those poisons for... Far too long.

Renny silently berated herself for taking so long to get back here. For not thinking to bring medicines—and why would she have?—she was expecting to unbury a corpse. For...

Immediate dissent, mental and vocal, came from the other three members of her foursome as well as all the other dragons.

Making an internal note to keep to keep a tighter rein on her mental meanderings, Renny finished her broth and medicine. *What* was in that stuff? Dried Orimjay dung?

Waiting until one of the healers looked her way, Renny motioned him closer. "Healer, I thank you for taking care of me. I need to know what medicinals you carry." Making a come on, hurry up gesture, ignoring the poor man blushing to the roots of his hair, Renny drew the words from him in fits and starts.

Throwing frequent beseeching glances at Allar, like a little boy seeking his father's approval and expecting a beating, the healer stuttered and stammered through the extensive list of supplies Seon had insisted they bring.

Blushing even redder, the tips of his ears going brilliant scarlet, he stammered with a boyish grin, "For you, My Lady Renny."

"Well and good. I will need all those and more if I'm to save Conthar." Using mindspeak to call Zantha—they needed to find those missing herbs and ingredients quickly—Renny stood.

Returning swiftly to Renny's side, stopping her before she could take one step, Allar demanded, "What do you think you're doing?"

Sighing, looking at Allar like he'd lost his mind, Renny shrugged. "If I am to save Conthar, there are things I must do. I need herbs and salves, some of which the healers do not carry. I also need meat, large herdbeasts, cut into chunks small enough for me to pick up easily."

She tried to explain patiently, though her heart was screaming, hurry, hurry! Time's a'wastin'!

Crossing his arms over his—very nice!—chest, Allar spoke to Renny like he would a wayward recruit. All authority and no back down. "Tell us what you need and we will get it for you. You are going nowhere. While you are waiting, you can use what the healers have to get started."

Adamant she obey, Allar would brook no refusal. At Renny's stony stare, he threw out more orders. "Show Zantha exactly what you need and we will search for it. You will remain here, where I know you are well protected." {{*Where I know you have no chance of being abducted or attacked by the dragonhaters.*}}

About to do some attacking of her own, Renny bit back her instant rage, even as she flashed mental pictures to Zantha. Perfectly capable of taking care of herself, Renny tamped down her anger and tried to give in graciously to Allar's concern, something she'd never had before.

Someone who cared if she lived or died. Had food. Was cold. Huh. A warm sensation enveloped Renny and she smiled tentatively.

"This...is difficult...harder than I thought. I do not mean to seem ungrateful. 'Tis only that...I am unused to anyone restricting my movements or giving me orders."

Barking out a laugh, Allar drew Renny into a swift, gentle hug. "We both have much to learn, I think. Being mates means you watch out for each other. You will have to get used to being taken care of, and I... I will try to remember you are stronger than you look."

Scooping up an empty pack, Allar took a step, turned back and kissed Renny. Hard.

"We will work this out. I promise. Stay right here and I'll be back before you miss me." Pressing his forehead against hers for an instant, Allar spun and took a few running steps. Leaping onto Zantha's back, they were airborne in a heartbeat.

Watching until they were out of sight, Renny took a deep breath, as deep as she could with her ribs still sore. Allar and Zantha would be fine. Besides, they had two other dragons and riders as escort.

Switching her gaze from the sky to the ground, Renny knew she would have to hurry. Conthar's body almost completely uncovered, the few rocks remaining around him were dwindling fast and the rest of the men were working diligently.

The healers brought the items she requested of them, some

they had and some growing close by. Renny set to work, mixing, grinding, adding, considering. The healers watched earnestly, quizzing her, why this and not that, seeking to add to their knowledge.

Renny explained as best she could, not fully understanding all the whys herself. The old mother had taught Renny well but some things Renny just knew.

Knew it was right, knew it would work.

Starting to add a particular herb to one of the salves she was mixing, one of the healers questioned her. "My Lady," he began.

"Renny," she corrected absently, focused on her medicines.

"My Lady Renny," he began again.

"Just Renny," she countered without looking up.

"But…" spluttering, at a loss for words, he finally voiced his concern, addressing her without a title. "That plant is a weed. It has no purpose, save to aggravate a farmer. Once it gets in a field, it takes over."

That got Renny's attention. Finally taking her eyes off her work, Renny grinned at the young healer. "All plants are weeds somewhere. You are…Bena?"

At his nod, Renny expounded. "What works on one dragon may not work on another. Sometimes the poisons are different, sometimes 'tis the dragons who are different. Each one is unique."

Without missing a beat, Renny continued, "Before I forget again, I would thank you for the medicines you gave me." Recalling her earlier conversation with Allar and the foul taste of the healer's brew, Renny searched through the herbs scattered on the cloak in front of her.

Picking a pleasant smelling one with a star shaped leaf, giving the goggle-eyed healer a conspiratorial wink, Renny told him, " I know you think this one a weed as well, but next time mix in a pinch or two of this and some sweet-tree, if you have it. 'Twill make the medicine more palatable and the men will not grumble and whine like children in need of a nap."

Suppressing a snicker, the other healer, Sher, moved closer.

"'Tis the truth, some of Seon's concoctions…" Broke off and shuddered. "They work, if the taste doesn't kill you. Everyone will be most grateful to you."

The three healers shared a knowing grin.

Renny's disappeared with Bena's innocent question.

"So, how many dragons have you saved?"

Renny's painful, "None so far," had both healers gaping at her, slack jawed.

Intent on her preparations, Renny'd noticed Zantha's and Allar's return, several feral herd-beasts clutched in Zantha's front claws. Forced herself to stay with her herbs instead of getting up and running to Allar, throwing herself into his arms as her heart demanded.

They'd barely been gone, and she had missed him. Missed both of them like they'd been gone years.

Dismounting, hoping Renny would do more than glance his way, Allar started toward Renny and the healers. Clutching the bag of weeds Renny had requested and he and Zantha had collected, Allar stopped to watch Renny work her magic, fingers flying and nose twitching.

Heads close together, the Dragonhealer and the human healers were grinning, sharing secrets, he supposed.

Too far away to hear more than the murmur of voices, Allar watched as one of the healers asked Renny a question. Her smile vanished to be replaced by a look so grim Allar reacted before he thought.

Fisting Bena's shirtfront, Allar jerked the healer to his feet and shook him. In a voice as grim as Renny's face, Allar snarled, "You will apologize to My Lady Renny."

Leaping to her feet, eyes flashing, Renny faced down Allar. "Release him this instant! Bena merely asked me a question. My reaction is my fault. Bena wanted to know how many dragons I had saved and I told him—none." Repeated bitterly, "None."

Glaring until Allar released Bena to land in a ruffled heap, Renny turned her back to all of them to stand stiffly, hands fisted at her sides, head thrown back.

Struck by the similarities, Allar realized he'd stood in just the same way in the valley when he'd been in agony.

Taking a chance he could soothe Renny in the same manner she'd soothed him, Allar wrapped his arms around Renny from behind. Dropping his head over hers, he held her, not saying anything until he felt some of her tension drain away.

Turning Renny gently, he drew her close.

Renny leaned into him, face pressed into his hard chest, hands bunching his shirt at his waist.

"I've done it again, haven't I? Acted like a lovesick fool and embarrassed you." Allar sighed. "I am a lovesick fool. I've never had a mate to protect before. This will definitely take some getting used to, on both our parts."

Renny made no answer, but Allar could feel how tense she was, walls up and in place. She did not need him beating on his chest, proclaiming his territory before all the world. Renny had enough on her plate trying to hold Conthar.

Allar could feel the tension, taut as a bowstring, humming through Renny's slender body. He could also feel the tremendous drain on her strength.

Healing was hard enough, in and of itself, but Renny had been holding Conthar for a long span, all the while managing to keep the pain level tolerable for both woman and dragon.

Allar shook his head in wonder.

Pulling back as much as Allar would allow, enough to tilt her head back and look him in the face, Renny's voice rang with frustration. "You keep saying we are mates, that we belong together. I've never been close to anyone. Don't even know how to be. Choose someone else, someone who can be whatever it is that you want. I don't know how to be anything but me, just plain Renny."

Swallowing, avoiding rolling her eyes by a bare minimum, Renny worked her shoulders. "You think I'm some weak damsel in distress in need of rescuing—I'm not. Since we've met I haven't exactly been myself, but normally I am a strong person. I don't want or need you hovering over me like a momma cluckit. I won't have it. Now let go of me. I have work to do."

Wanting to draw Renny closer, shelter her with everything he was, Allar recognized her frustration, along with something else.

Fear! Renny kept trying to push him away because she feared for him. The closer they were, the more damage would be done to all of them if she failed.

Fear for herself, also. Renny still couldn't believe Allar actually wanted her.

Not daring to loosen his hold, Allar demanded, "Renny. Look at me."

Voice devoid of emotion, Renny refused. "Let me go."

Smoothing his hands up and down Renny's back Allar told her, "Renny, we're in this together. Crash or fly, whatever happens to you happens to me."

Renny looked at him then, eyes as cold as her tone. "I won't be responsible for your life also. I have enough deaths on my hands already without dragging you down, too."

"Renny, Renny. What am I going to do with you? Haven't you realized yet that you are exactly what I want? Mates aren't chosen—they just are. We have yet to complete the bonding ritual, but we are so entwined, all of us—you, me, Zantha, Conthar—there's no separating us now. What happens to one happens to all."

Panicking, Renny shoved frantically, trying to put some modicum of distance between them. "No! I won't allow my failures to affect the rest of you!"

"Renny. You won't fail. We have complete faith in you."

Changing his grip to just above Renny's elbows, Allar dipped his head and held eye contact, letting everything he felt for her show in his eyes.

Calmer now, shaking her head, Renny replied tremulously, "Don't do this to me. Don't ask me to put any more lives on the line. I have never feared for myself, but the thought of causing harm to any of you... I can't bear it." Doubt creeping in, Renny shuddered. "I've never been able to save a dragon. What makes you think I can save Conthar?"

Time she knew, Allar couldn't believe Renny hadn't seen it for herself. There'd been a lot going on, Renny was stressed and exhausted, and Allar hated to be the one telling her this.

Renny could mindspeak with all dragons and Conthar had shielded from her—why would Renny have realized or even suspected?

With her background, or lack of, Allar doubted if Renny even knew dragons and their riders came in matched pairs.

Human to human, dragon to dragon, both couples being mates.

That same blinding flash of knowledge that'd informed Allar of Zantha's and Conthar's mate status had shown him Conthar's and Renny's at the same time. Allar'd known the truth as soon as they melded, that shining moment while Renny was touching them all.

Couldn't believe Renny hadn't picked it out of one of their minds.

Conthar must've still been shielding Renny.

Assent from Zantha and Conthar on both counts. Yes, Renny needed to know, and yes, Conthar had been shielding Renny.

Walls still firmly in place, isolating herself, Renny didn't pick up on their conversation.

Allar began, paused. There wasn't any easy way to break this to her. "Renny, Conthar isn't just any dragon—he's your dragon."

Dead silence greeted Allar's announcement. Renny's face drained of all color, her eyes wide and shocked. Staring at Allar as if he were insane, the only thing that kept Renny on her feet was Allar's grip on her upper arms.

Dropping her shields, Renny sought truth from the dragons as well as Allar.

Her heart stopped, she couldn't breathe, and there was an entire swarm of angry ground-stingers buzzing in each ear. Looking past Allar to see Conthar's bulk—her dragon!— Renny's elation was matched by her rage, equalled by her despair.

Renny'd asked Conthar if he had a rider and puzzled over his answer. Conthar's words came back to Renny, their true meaning blaring loud and clear.

{{*At this time, I have no rider I care to call, or recognize.*}}

Dragon truth, always with a sub-layer of meaning,

He'd known then and hadn't told her. Had he lied about what he thought of her? Did he find her lacking? Didn't want to claim a defective rider?

Anger filled Renny, from the tips of her dragonhide shod toes to the crown of her about to explode head. Jerking back, radiating pain and fury and intending to pull away from Allar, he wouldn't let go.

Gripping her tighter, he spoke urgently. "Renny. Listen to me. To Conthar. If you'd known Conthar was your dragon, could you have left him? Even to fetch help? Or would you have stayed here and died with him, dooming us all? Not telling you was the only chance for all of us."

What was it with these males protecting her? Did they think her so incompetent…

Conthar chimed in, breaking the vicious circle of Renny's frayed thoughts. {{*Renny, I had only just found you. I couldn't risk losing you, not when you mean so much to me—to all of us! You are so brave, so fiercely loyal—I knew you would die rather than leave me. Finding Zantha*}} *and Allar was the only hope for any of us. I did what I had to do. Heal me and then you can berate me all you want.}}*

Renny's fury cooled as fast as it'd flared, knowing they were right. Still not liking it.

Shaken to the core by their confidence in her, by hearing the echo of her own words in Conthar's *I did what I had to do.* How many times had she said the exact same thing?

Hated what she had to do with all her heart but done it anyway?

Despised herself for committing an act but willingly shouldered the responsibility that went with it?

Thoroughly annoyed, Renny struck out at the most available target. *{{Shut up, Conthar! Just shut up. Why are you wasting your strength by using mindspeak anyway? Never mind, don't you dare answer that! Not a word in his defense, Zantha! I'll deal with you later.}}*

The next closest target being Allar, Renny turned her displeasure on him, all but hissing and spitting. "How long have you known?"

Allar briefly considered lying. "Since you knelt beside Conthar, when you touched all of us at the same time and we melded."

Eyes slitted, Renny ground out, "And you didn't think that little detail was important enough to tell me?"

Hands up, shaking his head, Allar laid the blame squarely where it belonged. "Conthar's decision, not mine."

Before Renny could round on Conthar again, Zantha broke in. *{{Renny, you have let our hardheaded males distract you. Whatever you did earlier helped Conthar tremendously but it is wearing off. He grows weaker as we speak. Gather your medicines and work your magic. He is fading fast.}}*

Tamping down her anger to a simmer, Renny brushed past Allar, snagged her medicines on the fly and ran toward Conthar.

Voya stepped in front of her, arms out to the sides, before she reached her dragon—*her dragon!* "My Lady, 'tis not yet safe."

Sidestepping without slowing, and when Voya matched her move, fluid as mercury, Renny feinted, dodged and slipped around his imposing bulk.

Ignoring Voya's protests, Renny had almost reached Conthar when Allar snagged her low around the waist from behind.

Allar expected Renny to fight, but she froze and hissed, "I don't have time for this! You said you believed in me."

"Renny. I have the utmost faith in you and your abilities. We all do. I merely wanted to remind you to be careful. The rest of the mountain looks as if it will come tumbling down any moment. Can Conthar be moved farther away from the cliff?"

Renny took a deep breath and tamped down a little harder. It seemed…bizarre, having all these people vested in her welfare.

"I have to see his wounds first. How can you move a dragon?"

Heaving a sigh, Allar took a moment to nuzzle her hair. "If it's at all possible to move him, we'll try to roll him over onto the tarps we brought, a sling of sorts. Then the other dragons can lift him out of harm's way. It depends on your recommendation. If he wasn't ringed by rock still, we could just roll him onto the tarps and drag him carefully, but we don't have time"—Allar froze at an ominous grumble from the mountain—"to move the rest of the slide."

Carefully walking around Conthar, trailing hands and eyes all over him, Renny checked out the most obvious rents and gashes in his beautiful skin. Using more than sight and touch, Renny probed with her mind, much the same way she spoke with the dragons.

What she saw sickened her.

Hastily locking those negative thoughts in a deep compartment in her mind, Renny continued her assessment.

Having circled Conthar not once, but twice, Renny returned to Allar. One hand on Conthar, holding the other out to Allar, Renny said, "You must be as gentle as possible. Conthar's wounds are grievous. I'm just glad those butchers didn't have more time to work him over. That, at least, is in our favor. Ready the tarps and I will give Conthar some medicine to dull the pain."

Stroking the deep blue of her dragon, the once beautiful cobalt much dulled by dust and pain, Renny added, "All of you must be extremely careful—Conthar may lash out without meaning to. He is confused, much like I was when the fever was on me. The poisons in his system are wreaking havoc and he is very weak from lack of food, not to mention being under that pile of rocks for so long."

The men and dragons resumed working frantically, scrambling with the tarps and Renny's plan of action.

Renny perched close beside Conthar's great head, crooning to him, stroking him and enticing him to open his mouth, tipping a waterskin so the pain-killer laced liquid dribbled into his mouth. Painstakingly wetting his tongue and throat, Renny began slipping chunks of meat impregnated with more painkillers and medicines between Conthar's massive jaws, putting them as far down his throat as she could reach.

"Open for me just a little more, that's it. Now swallow. Do it for me, big fella. Come on, that's my boy."

Unashamedly eavesdropping, standing watch in case he needed to haul Renny out of there, Allar nearly cheered the first time he saw Conthar's throat convulse.

Conthar managed to down several more servings. Using the waterskin again, Renny switched to a broth she'd concocted, poured small amounts into his maw over and over.

Allar had no doubt Renny'd made it taste better than some of the vile things he'd choked down. Shook his head in consternation. Healers! It didn't matter whether they healed humans, animals, or dragons, they all warned you to be careful and then proceeded to completely ignore their own advice and put themselves at risk.

Wounded, anything could turn on you in a flash, yet there went Renny, sticking practically her whole arm into a wounded dragon's mouth, a dragon who hadn't eaten in quite a while.

A dragon with very large, very sharp teeth. Lots of them.

Nervously eyeing those same teeth, Allar kept his eyes locked on Renny.

"She is something, is she not?" Coming to stand beside Allar, Voya sounded both pleased and proud. "Renny will be an excellent lady, for you and for Dragon's Haven. I have no doubt, if you ever so much as say a harsh word to her, everyone at Dragon's Haven, human and dragon alike will take you to task for it. Not that Lady Renny can't defend herself, you understand, it's just the principle of the thing. She's fearless for herself and brave beyond belief, but there's just something about Lady Renny that makes you want to protect her."

Allar nodded in total agreement. "Renny gives and gives and gives, and never thinks of herself at all." Tipped his head in Renny's direction. "Watching her put food in Conthar's mouth— he could swallow her in one bite, yet she has complete confidence that he won't harm her. That confidence makes you want to live up to her faith in you, makes you more determined not to let her down, because even if you did, she'd never say a word against you. Her very silence would make you feel lower than a slither-worm's belly. When I think of her being alone all her life till now, and risking it over and over for dragons…"

Close to having enough space to lay out the tarps and try to roll Conthar, Allar glanced at the sun. It seemed this day had dragged on for weeks, months, forever, yet the sun had scarce moved since Allar'd roused Renny and gone to fetch the herbs and meats she needed.

The last few rocks were heaved out of the way and everything was in place.

Now…how to get Renny far enough from Conthar's side to be out of harm's way.

Zantha spared Allar the trouble. {{*Renny, you must come over here with me, out of the way, or Conthar will refuse to co-operate, and he is far too weak to waste time and energy arguing. Let the men and dragons do the heavy work and then you can resume treating Conthar. Besides, you must take a moment to rest and eat something for yourself.*}}

Reluctant to leave Conthar's side, however briefly, Renny acquiesced to Zantha's plea.

Heaving a sigh of relief, Allar winged a silent *thank you* Zantha's way.

Sending a mental smirk Allar's way, Zantha made sure Renny moved far enough to keep from being hurt yet still close enough to see.

Bena and Sher talked Renny into sitting, pressed more food on her. For a change, Renny ate absently, paying no attention to what she was eating, all her concentration focused on Conthar.

The healers urged her to drink more laced broth.

Taking a sip, Renny sniffed and took another. Lifted her mug in silent tribute toward the healers. They had listened well, and this batch was definitely more palatable.

Renny watched intently as the men laid out tarps. She'd paid little attention while the men were piling rocks on them, but now she looked closer. Made of dragonhide, they were tough.

Tough enough to lift a dragon? They had to be.

Sensing Renny's worries, Zantha broke into Renny's thoughts. {{*The tarps will hold. The men have carried dragons this way before.*}}

Zantha crouched close to Renny. {{*When they shift him, you must be prepared for his backwash of pain. If you let it, it will swamp you both. You must shut it out, shut it down, for both your sakes and all ours.*}}

Renny nodded grimly, eyes locked on Conthar, lying as he'd fallen. Belly down, wings folded close.

The men were preparing to tie soft ropes to his off side legs in order to roll him when his massive tail twitched, thrashed, lashed out once.

A single man went flying to land heavily in a tangled heap.

On her feet in an instant, restrained by Bena and Sher, Renny could only watch. All work halted as the rest of the men rushed to help the downed man.

Catching the echo of Zantha's snicker, Renny looked closer. Realizing the downed man was Meer, Renny choked back a snicker of her own even as she chided Conthar for wasting strength.

Message delivered, loud and clear. No one, human or dragon, didn't get it.

Resuming what they'd been doing, the men finished tying the ropes. On Allar's count, they pulled while the dragons used their great heads to push.

Too busy blocking pain to watch all of it, when Renny could see again Conthar was on his side, on the tarps. All they had to do now was lift him. The men moved back and the dragons took over.

With two tarps under him—one just behind his front legs, the other just front of his rear legs, the two largest dragons gathered the ends of the tarps in their talons.

Rising slowly, in perfect unison, they took flight, hovering off the ground enough so Conthar's head and legs wouldn't drag, Allar busily calling out commands and keeping watch.

Renny thought she was prepared for the explosion of pain, but even with the painkillers she'd gotten Conthar to swallow, she almost lost it. Hanging by a thread, Zantha and the rest of the dragons shielded Renny as best they could, but it came down to Renny and Conthar.

Renny held until they had Conthar a safe distance away and settled him gently to the ground.

Bena caught Renny as Zantha bellowed for Allar.

~

COMING TO IN HORRIBLE PAIN, striking out at anything within range, Allar caught Renny's flailing fists and locked her in his arms.

"Shh. You're safe. Easy, Renny. I've got you. Fight the pain, Renny. What you're feeling is the backspill from Conthar. Get a grip and tamp it down. Everything either of you feels is magnified by the other. Feel me, I'm right here."

Zantha crowded close, torn between Allar and Renny and her own mate. Zantha's torment finally got through to Renny.

Going limp in Allar's arms, Renny sought Conthar.

He lived, barely.

"Let me up. I have to go to him." Struggling to get free, Renny opened her eyes to stare directly into Allar's. Sinking, drowning in twin blue pools, for that moment, Renny forgot everything except Allar.

"Here, drink this." Offering her a mug, Allar nearly laughed when Renny sniffed it before she'd take so much as a single swallow. "Bena and Sher have taken your lessons to heart, My Renny. I think they're afraid Conthar will flip them with his tail."

A faint smile flickered over Renny's lips and she drained the mug, knowing she'd need every advantage she could glean.

"How long was I out?"

A quick shake of Allar's head reassured her. "No time at all."

The last she spoke to them for a long, tiring while, the rest of the men and dragons could do nothing but stand by and watch helplessly.

Renny was The Dragonhealer, and this battle was hers alone.

She forgot them all, forgot anything existed beyond the wounded dragon in front of her.

Renny's world, her vision, narrowed until she could see nothing but Conthar. Holding him with her will, consoling him with her mind, Renny used the salves she'd mixed earlier on his wounds.

Some to draw out the poisons and some to fight the

infections. Packing the worst wounds with salt and herb poultices, changing them frequently, all the while crooning to Conthar almost inaudibly.

Zantha stayed a ready presence in Renny's mind, relaying to Allar, both of them ready in case Conthar lashed out in pain, or worse.

If Conthar didn't survive...

Renny kept up a running patter with Conthar, uncaring whether he understood or not, knowing the sound of her voice was one more thread binding him to her.

Comforting, cajoling, bullying Conthar into holding on.

"Come on, Beautiful. Live for me. For us. Your wounds aren't that bad. I've seen far worse. They didn't have time for any of the really fun stuff like cutting off your wings or gouging out your eyes. You'll just have some manly scars to brag about every time you and your male friends get together and swap war stories. That's my baby—I didn't run all that way and swim till I almost grew gills just so you can die on me. Besides, it broke my heart the first time I thought you'd died—you're not allowed to break it again. Once per lifetime is my absolute limit."

And so it went, on and on till Renny talked herself hoarse, and still she kept it up.

Round and round, Renny circled Conthar tirelessly, changing poultices over and over, packing more salt and herbs in each time.

Catching her rhythm, Bena and Sher helped as much as they could, though Renny refused to let them actually touch Conthar's wounds or the used poultices.

Renny scarcely acknowledged them, directing with a flick of her hand or a jerk of her head. Everyone else sat back and suffered, unable to do anything else.

Zantha relayed steadily to Allar, and the other dragons, who passed it on to their riders.

If they hadn't loved Renny before this for what she'd

endured, was enduring again for Conthar, this cemented their feelings.

Even Meer grudgingly admitted he *might* have misjudged Renny.

Gray with exhaustion, swaying, nearly asleep on her feet, Renny finally gave in. She'd done all she could. The rest was up to Conthar.

Allar pushed a mug into her hands and urged her to drink. Renny would've been more than surprised had anyone told her he'd been doing the same thing all night.

Allar knew Renny hadn't noticed him pressing drinks on her because she hadn't sniffed them, just drained them and kept going, as if trapped in some never-ending nightmare. For her, he supposed this was.

Renny started to speak and the men gathered close so they could hear.

Without taking her eyes off Conthar's still form, Renny rasped hoarsely, "I've done what I can. Conthar must sleep for awhile. If—*when*—he awakes, he will be starving. Bena and Sher, you must wash, over and over, and rub some of the blue salve on your hands. All these used poultices and herbs must be burned, as well as the tarp they're on. They are full of poisons. You must all wear your gloves and when you're finished, burn the gloves as well. Take care not to get any of the poisons on yourselves or your clothes. Do not let the dragons help, or even get in the smoke from the fires. You must bathe and wash your clothes after. Have the healers make some more of the broth they made the first day we were here, only stronger."

Wrapping a blanket around Renny, Allar caught her as she collapsed, still mumbling orders.

Turning to address the crowd with Renny in his arms, Allar wondered if he looked as bad as they did. The men's faces were gray and grim, the dragons looked off color. The most of a day and then all night long fight for Conthar's life had taken its toll on them, Renny most of all. "I promise you, whatever the outcome of this, whether Conthar lives or dies, we will be avenged for these atrocities. You all heard your Lady's orders. Let's not disappoint her."

The men scattered to do Renny's bidding. Wrapping the tarp tight, they dragged it to the far end of the valley, making sure they were upwind of the dragons before lighting it, going so far as to send the dragons out of the valley to hunt as an added precaution.

The pile smoked and sputtered before catching alight, burning in luminous, putrid shades of greens and nasty shades of yellows, the very flames evil incarnate.

Carrying Renny to the bank of the wide, slow moving creek that wound through the valley, Allar stepped into the icy water. Stripping Renny, leaving her clothes in the water, Allar immersed Renny as much as possible without drowning her. She didn't even flinch at the frigid water enveloping her.

Her hands—all purpley-red—looked as if they'd been scalded. The cold water seemed to help, the horrible tinge slowly fading to a more normal color.

Pushing Renny's clothes away, Allar held her in the water as long as he dared. Stepping up on the bank and placing Renny on the clean blanket Voya'd brought, Allar dried Renny briskly with another until her color was somewhat better. He slathered the the blue ointment all over her hands.

Wrapping Renny in the driest blanket, leaving her clothes in the stream, Allar carried Renny back to Conthar and settled her on a nest of blankets.

Zantha hadn't gone far and had returned quickly, making sure to stay out of the smoke. {{*Allar, I can reach neither of them. They are both worn out and will have to sleep it off. The smoke is mostly gone and the other dragons will return soon. Those were potent poisons indeed. The dragons said to tell you...*}}

Zantha choked. {{*...they said to tell you, if Conthar doesn't make it,* *they place no blame on Renny. No one, human or dragon could have tried harder or done more.*}}

Acknowledging Zantha's comfort, Allar'd never thought any would blame Renny. On the other hand, he had no doubt Renny would attempt to shoulder all the blame if anything went wrong.

The men trickled back, still gray but soaking wet and now tinged blue as well. They'd heeded Renny's words well after seeing what the poisons had done to her and Conthar.

Of all the men, only Vin had gotten a face full of smoke. Green as the nasty smoke, coughing, the healers plied him with all sorts of potions.

BENA AND SHER made everyone a strong mug of medicines, not nearly so vile this time, thanks to Renny. Making sure Bena and Sher had plenty of the same drink and lots of blue salve on their hands, Allar applied more to Renny's hands.

Not returning until the last wisp of the smoke had vanished, the dragons came over the crest of the mountain and landed in the meadow. One at a time, they eased closer for a look at Renny and Conthar.

Satisfied they both lived, the dragons backed off and began settling, tamping down the lush meadow grasses until they were content to bed down in a huge circle around Renny and Conthar.

Allar took first watch, knowing he would find sleep impossible. The rest of the men and dragons, exhausted, had no such problem.

Allar moved between Renny and Conthar, back and forth, checking first one and then the other. The healers had told him what to watch for with instructions to wake them if he had need.

Eyeing Renny's slight form, Allar marveled at the upheaval

such a small woman had brought to all their lives. In little over a sennight, she'd forever changed their world.

It'd taken much less than that for Renny to rock his world to its very foundations. Sitting beside Renny's battered form, Allar did as he'd done in the Healing Hall. Taking one of her hands in his, he stroked it.

So much power in such a small hand!

Allar could still feel a burning tingle from the residual poison. Renny'd been immersed in this same poison a great part of yesterday and all night with nary a word of complaint.

Conthar had been stewing in a mix of this for a long while.

Feeling utterly helpless, Allar could only repeat the words he'd spoken to Renny in the Healing Hall.

"You will not die. I forbid it."

Bedded down beside Conthar, careful not to jar him and disturb his wounds, Zantha sighed in agreement and repeated them to Conthar. Nuzzled her mate and slept.

Trading off with Voya around midday, Allar curled himself around Renny and dropped into sleep.

Woke at dusk to the smell of roasting meat.

The men and dragons had been busy.

Several carcasses of what looked to be mud-grunts were roasting on a spit.

Leaning up on an elbow, Allar looked at Renny. Not even the delicious odors wafting their way could rouse her.

Before Allar could panic, Zantha calmly assured him, {{ *They are healing—at an unbelievable rate. Each feeding off the other and... They will wake when it is time.* }}

Easy for Zantha to say. She lay as close to Conthar as Allar was to Renny, Zantha's head draped protectively over Conthar's shoulder. Opening one great eye, Zantha slowly blinked at Allar. {{ *It is important that they feel us close by.* }}

Allar agreed wholeheartedly.

Closing her eyes, Zantha murmured, {{*Right now, that is all we can do for them.*}}

Untangling himself from Renny, Allar helped himself to a large chunk of steaming meat. Positioning himself so he could see her, Allar sat beside the fire. Looking around at his men, their faces reflected the same grimness and determination he felt.

Awalt was the first to speak, pounding a fist on his knee and giving voice to what they were all thinking. "If not for Lady Renny, those responsible may very well have gotten away with this torture and deception forever. This is wanton destruction, a sadistic attack for no other reason than because they can. Whoever is doing this does so because they enjoy torturing dragons. This scourge must be wiped off the face of our world."

Reese snorted. "Their first mistake was attacking Conthar. Their second, and our great blessing, was Lady Renny surviving and finding us. Otherwise, we might never have figured out what was happening. There has to be some pattern, some rhyme as to what they're doing. Some way we can draw them out or second guess them, maybe beat them to their next planned attack so we can set up an ambush."

Meer asked, "What happened to the map she…" With a nervous glance at Conthar, he hastily corrected himself. "I mean, Lady Renny, showed us? Didn't Lady Renny say that's what she was trying to do?"

Cursing himself for being seven kinds of a fool, Allar jumped to his feet. Grabbing a burning stick, he sprinted to the creek bank. Holding the improvised torch aloft, Allar scanned the water.

Letting out a whoop, he jumped into the water and retrieved Renny's clothes with a long stick. Good thing the current was sluggish, almost completely still here. Throwing the sopping mess on the bank, Allar dropped to his knees and began poking with the stick.

Someone took the torch and handed Allar another branch.

187

Searching frantically, finally sitting back on his heels, ready to conceded defeat, Allar startled his men.

"Her boots! Does anyone see Renny's boots?"

Chuckles broke out all round as the men searched. Retrieving the items in question, they headed back to the fire so they could better see the map.

Digging the map out of the toe of Renny's boot, Allar spread it wide. Heads bumped as they all tried to look at once.

Backing up a tad, they studied the map from every angle, finally conceding defeat.

Rolling the map, Allar stated, "Renny knows these valleys. She said the x's were grave markers—past, present, and future. When she wakes, we'll get more information from her and devise a plan to find out which ones are which and go from there."

CHAPTER 15

*R*egaining consciousness slowly, Renny awoke to the sounds of an armored camp. Disoriented, at first she thought she must be at the garrison at Fort Helve.

No, that had been…forever ago.

The only other such camp she'd known had been with the dragon torturers.

She could smell dragon and feel a dragon in pain.

Freezing in fear and loathing, heart pounding in alarm, Renny was working up enough courage to open her eyes when she realized there was a warm body wrapped around her. A heavy arm draped around her waist.

Allar!

Relief surged through her body, and memory through her bruised brain. Her eyes flew open and she struggled to get up. Conthar! She had to get to Conthar!

"Good morn to you, too. Any other woman would enjoy waking up in my arms, but not you. I always have to fight to keep you here." Nuzzling his face into the crook of Renny's neck, Allar blew a warm breath, making her shiver. "Never have I had a woman try so hard to get away from me. I'm starting to think I have dragon mites or…"

That startled a tiny laugh out of Renny even as she attempted to disentangle herself from his arms. "Your ego can stand a set down. I already told you, I'm not like most women."

Allar nuzzled again and loosened his hold. His turn to laugh when Renny rolled over, and getting to her feet, threw back over her shoulder, "If you value your manhood, I better be the only woman waking up in your arms. Some of the *weeds* I've come across have nasty, *permanent* side effects."

She flounced off in Conthar's direction without a backward glance.

Renny's first sign of possessiveness tickled Allar to no end. Stacking his hands behind his head, grinning hugely, he watched her hurry to Conthar.

Voya's laughter had Allar swiveling his head. "You are well and truly caught, my friend. When a woman threatens your manhood and all you can do is grin…" Shaking his head, Voya offered Allar a loaded plate.

Allar raised his brows in surprise.

Voya grinned. "A tiny village several valleys over. The dragons spotted it on one of their hunting forays. The locals were having a bit of trouble rounding up some escaped livestock. We helped and they shared. A couple small mud-grunts, some eggs, a little fresh bread and cheese. We saved Lady Renny a goodly portion. It's your job to get her to eat it."

Taking the offered plates, Allar headed in Renny's direction.

Circling Conthar's still form, methodically checking each wound, Renny turned to Allar, face glowing. "He is much better this morn. I still can't reach him but he is sleeping, truly sleeping, not merely drugged."

Zantha hovered close beside Conthar, staying just out of Renny's way.

Allar cut his eyes in Zantha's direction. Renny immediately got the message. "Zantha, go find food. You watched over Conthar, over all of us. For that, we thank you. Allow us to take a turn and we will inform you if he so much as stirs. You have my word."

Eyeing her humans solemnly, Zantha spoke aloud. "Renny, again I owe you my thanks. Conthar will live. None other could have accomplished the miracle you wrought here."

Taking a large step backwards, Zantha extended a foreleg and bowed her great head to Renny. In a rush of wings she was gone, Ashel joining Zantha before she got too far.

Watching until the dragons were out of sight, Renny turned to Allar, eyes shining. "Zantha confirmed what I thought— hoped... We did it! Conthar will live!"

Allar's joyous expression mirroring Renny's, he held out a plate. "I heard! Congratulations, and you have my utmost admiration and gratitude. Conthar will wake soon and... You must eat before he wakes. Everyone will be mad at me, human and dragon, if you don't."

As Renny took the plate, grasping her other hand, Allar shook his head. "Your hands..."

Renny tried to snatch her hand out of his grip but Allar held on stubbornly. "'Tis nothing. It will fade in time."

Frowning, Allar raised his eyes to hers. "Still, it looks painful and I do not like it. Why do you not wear gloves?"

Once again trying to curb her impulse to lash out at Allar, trying to swallow her anger at his high-handed tone and instead appreciate his caring, Renny shrugged. "In order to tell what kind of poison was used, I must be able to touch the dragon so I can tell how much and what kind of medicine I need to use to counteract the poison. Gloves interfere."

"Are you still in pain?"

"A little." At Allar's skeptical look, Renny added, "Some. I told you it will ease. 'Tis no worse now than if I'd brushed a single fire-thorn branch."

"Oh, now that's reassuring."

Stung by his sarcasm when she'd been trying so hard, Renny snarked, "Not my fault you're a wuss."

Allar's face clouded, cleared, and he burst into laughter. "A bunch of us boys were skinny dipping…"

Renny smirked, already knowing where this story was headed.

"We'd stolen some mellikins from Old Man Call's garden. He tracked us to the river. Having already eaten all the evidence and thrown the rinds in the river to get rid of the remainder, we thought we were safe. After all, he had no proof it was us. Old Man Call, well, he was screaming and his eyes were bugging out of his head and…"

Renny sniggered.

"Turns out, those weren't just any mellikins—they were his grown-for-the-summer-festival, prize winning, about to beat his neighbor's ten year winning streak for the first time mellikins. We swam the river, crawled out on the other bank, and ran for our lives, minus our clothes. In the dusky dark."

Snorting and choking, Renny was holding back her laughter. Barely.

Shooting Renny a stern look, Allar shook his head woefully. "In our headlong flight from the madman, we ran through a patch of fire-thorn. Needless to say, we were all extremely sorry and more than adequately punished for our transgressions."

Allar shuddered and grimaced. "To this day I associate mellikins with acute pain. The smell alone breaks me out in a cold sweat. And don't even get me started on fire-thorn."

Laughing so hard she had to sit before she dropped her plate, Renny snorted, "I bet you were an incorrigible brat."

Allar tried to look innocent and only succeeded in making

Renny laugh harder. Dropping beside Renny, Allar grinned. "Pretty much so."

Actually looking at what her plate held for the first time, Renny's slight frown informed Allar the wheels were turning in her mind. "Where did you get this?"

Teasing just a bit, Allar answered with a straight face. "Voya handed it to me."

Corners of her lips twitching up, Renny rolled her eyes. "Incorrigible. Seriously, where? The traitors carried no supplies. Didn't even carry any snares or fishing lines. The no-color and his dragon brought foodstuffs when they came. If the supplies were garnered locally... Never mind. They could've been flown in from anywhere."

Chewing thoughtfully on a bite of his sausage before answering, Allar nodded. "No, you're right. If any of the local villages bartered for food with dragonriders, this place is so isolated 'twould be a seven days' wonder. Eat, before your food gets any colder."

Catching Voya's attention, Allar waved him over.

Crouching down in front of Renny and Allar, Voya grinned. "The food pleases you, My Lady Renny?"

Renny halted with a bite almost to her lips. "Just Renny, and food always pleases me. My thanks."

Smirking at Renny, Allar informed Voya, "My Lady says the traitors carried no supplies. The no-color delivered food to them."

Interest piqued, Voya glanced at their plates. "You think the food came from nearby?"

Allar sobered at the thought they might be eating the same food the torturers had enjoyed while they committed their crimes. "Possibly. Take riders and scout out any villages within a couple days' flight."

Directing his question to Renny, Voya asked, "Anything special we're supposed to be looking for?"

Swallowing the mouthful she was chewing, Renny shook her head. "No... Wait! There was this one cheese..." Sounding wistful with the memory, practically drooling, Renny told them, "I've never had anything like it and I only got a small taste, but I would recognize it if I tasted it again."

"So, I'm on a cheese collecting mission." Smiling wryly, Voya stood. Glancing at Conthar's motionless form, his expression turned grim.

Following his gaze, Renny said softly, "Conthar will live."

Voya swung back to Renny, incredulous. "You know this for certain?"

Fidgeting uncomfortably, Renny met Allar's eyes, praise and love shining out of their blue depths, and settled. "As certain as I can be of anything."

Letting out a whoop of delight, Voya spun away and then back and dropped to one knee. Bowed his head. "My Lady, my gratitude knows no bounds. With your permission, I would tell the others."

At Renny's nod, Voya leapt to his feet and dashed off.

Judging from the way the rest of the dragons let loose and filled the air with their mighty trumpeting, as soon as Renny'd given Voya the go ahead, he'd told Mithar, who'd passed the word to the other dragons.

Renny's head abuzz with all the dragons trying to talk to her at once, the men gathered round, wide grins splitting their faces.

Letting the ecstatic men congratulate Renny for a few moments, Allar shooed them off so she could eat in peace. Little did he know the cacophony the dragons were creating in her head.

Renny ate steadily while answering the dragons as best she could.

No, she had no idea when Conthar would wake, but he'd be starving when he did.

No, she didn't know how long it would take him to recover.

She didn't really know anything. Conthar was the first dragon who'd lived so she had no timeline for any of this.

She was going to have to wing it on this one. They all were.

Noticing Renny eating slowly, seeming lost in thought, about the time Allar realized she was conversing with the dragons, Conthar made the slightest of movements.

Renny leapt to her feet, food forgotten.

Calling for Zantha, Allar felt the silent blankness where his dragon should've been.

{{*Zantha?*}}

{{*ZANTHA?*}}

{{*ZANTHA?!*}}

Nothing!

He couldn't reach Zantha!

Freezing mid-step, Renny locked eyes with Allar. Sent out her own puzzled call. {{*Zantha?*}}

Allar covered his ears—like that would help—as Renny bellowed a mental command for the other dragons to {{*GO FIND ZANTHA! SOMETHING IS WRONG!*}}

Taking flight as one, the dragons barely cleared the top of the ridge when they began circling agitatedly.

Dropping back down below the rim, Tant called to Renny.

Her head snapped up as she conferred with him.

Grabbing Allar's wrist, head cocked to one side, Renny squeezed. "Zantha is fine. Tant says… They can hear Zantha as soon as they leave the valley. She's on her way, almost here."

Renny paused, gazing around thoughtfully as vague hunches backed by survival-honed instincts solidified. "I know why the dragonhaters chose this valley, as well as the other ones." Pointed with her chin. "The rocks here—those sparkly ones—are the same as in the valley where you took me so we couldn't be overheard. The rocks…block the dragons' mindspeak."

Warming to her theory, Renny continued, "I never paid any mind before, but I bet you'll find the same type of rock in all those x'd valleys. It wasn't the men the dragons were speaking to that silenced them and kept them from calling for help, it was the valleys themselves and that damnable rock. The men lured the dragons in and immobilized them, but these valleys aid their evil purpose like the valleys were custom made."

Done with talking, and concentrating on Conthar, placing her hands on his noble head, Renny closed her eyes and focused, calling him softly.

"Conthar, wake for me, sweeting." Speaking aloud, strengthening their ties.

Nothing for long, heart stopping moments and then, faintly, {{*Weak. So weak.*}}

"I know, baby. I know." Renny soothed with hands and voice. "You have to wake for just a little while, long enough to eat and swallow some medicine and then you can go back to sleep. Zantha's on her way with fresh meat for you. You wouldn't want to disappoint her, would you?"

{{*Gotta love a female who hunts while her mate just lazes around.*}}

Smiling at Conthar's cocky comment, Renny felt Conthar's raw pain as soon as he tried to touch Zantha's mind and found only blankness.

Conthar's mental bellow—similar to Renny's but with a skilled dragon's force behind it—put Renny on her knees, hands still on his head.

"Conthar! Listen to me! She's fine—I swear it on my life. This valley prevents dragons from speaking mind to mind. That's why no one heard you when you called for help. That's why the dragonhaters only use certain valleys."

Zantha dropped over the edge of the valley with a multiple still-warm carcasses clutched in each of her front claws. Seeking Conthar as soon as she did, Zantha couldn't help but feel the emotional disturbance he was creating.

{{*Conthar, be still. I am here and I am fine.*}}

His relief immediately evident, Conthar relaxed against Renny's hands. Touching her forehead to his head, Renny whispered, "We will get through this, I promise you. Right now, you have to eat and regain your strength, then we'll worry about punishing those responsible."

Zantha dropped all the carcasses save one right in front of Conthar's nose and settled as close as she could get, nuzzling and blowing heated breaths everywhere she could reach.

Pushing away from Conthar the instant Zantha crowded close, Renny went to mix some more medicines.

Eating and additional medicines would go a long way towards speeding the healing process.

Allar watched as Renny skillfully mixed herbs, pinching and sniffing, adding and pondering each addition carefully, using dragon-sized quantities. Satisfied with her concoction, making a long slit in the carcass Zantha had laid aside, Renny packed the cavity with her mixture.

Zantha delicately picked up the herd-beast and placed it in front of Conthar.

In the bare spot where only a few moments ago a heap of steaming herd-beasts had rested.

Conthar must've inhaled them while Allar was engrossed in watching Renny.

Handily disappearing that one too, letting out a contented belch, Conthar promptly fell back asleep.

Rising, careful not to touch anything with her bloody hands, Renny started in the direction of the creek.

Allar paced beside her, thoughts whirling in his head, not saying anything.

"I laced that carcass with as much of a sleeping herb as I dared. Making Conthar stay still for as long as possible will benefit him greatly but I don't have very high hopes on that score. Zantha might be able to bully him a little, but he's extremely hardheaded." Stepping out onto a flat rock, Renny crouched and leaned over the water to wash her hands.

She looked up as Allar snorted in amusement. "Pot, meet kettle."

When Renny stared, open-mouthed, Allar smirked. "I seem to recall someone else hardheaded who won't take proper care of herself and refuses to stay under a healer's care. Sound familiar?"

Renny answered Allar with a soaking spray of cold water delivered via the flat of her hand.

At her response, Allar heard chortles from the dragons and outright guffaws from his men.

Jumping back onto the bank and walking along the creek, Renny halted when she came to a dead, brown area of vegetation. The leaves of the bushes were frizzled higher than her head, the taller trees were shriveled and shrunken and obviously not going to make it. The grass looked like it had been through a devastating wildfire, and the moss… Instead of being verdantly emerald, it poofed at each step like ashes from a fire. Coming up behind her, Allar explained grimly, "This is where I washed you after you tended Conthar. I stripped you, let you soak till you were blue, then dried you off and rubbed on that blue ointment of yours."

Looking down at the clothes she was currently wearing, slowly lifting her gaze to Allar's face, Renny said nothing, merely arched a brow.

Allar began defensively and ended defiantly. "You ordered the men to burn anything touched by the poison. That definitely included your clothes. I had extra packed for you and will order more made for you as soon as we return to Dragon's Haven. Do you think I would let you run around naked in a camp full of men?"

Renny drilled her finger into his chest. "I think…you have an absolute fetish with taking my clothes off every chance you get."

Scooping Renny up, one arm behind her back and one beneath her knees, Allar held her tight against his chest and spun in dizzying circles.

Looping both arms around his neck, Renny laughed, high pitched and carefree.

Pretending to growl, Allar nuzzled his face into her neck. "You're absolutely right, and not just that, I'd love to see you run around naked." Leaning back so he could see Renny's face, Allar waggled his brows lecherously.

Bursting into laughter once more, Renny muttered, "Don't hold your breath on either count."

Allar didn't tell Renny, but he had definite plans for both in the not too distant future.

RENNY AND ZANTHA used every trick in the book, short of actually sitting on Conthar—and Zantha threatened that—to keep him still.

Three days was two more than Renny thought she'd get.

Conthar's wounds were healing as rapidly as Renny's had, but Renny had no idea how long before he'd be fully healed.

Right now, Conthar was sulking, not speaking to Renny or Zantha.

Renny hadn't been out of the valley since they landed, had barely left Conthar's side, but Voya and the others had made continuous forays. Ostensibly for supplies, covertly seeking information.

So far, none of the cheeses they'd returned with were the one Renny remembered, but they'd found some really delicious samples—taste testing being one camp job Renny was more than glad to volunteer for.

Staying close, Allar enjoyed watching Renny. Watching her

move about, totally comfortable being the only female in an armed camp. His men had accepted Renny completely, treating her like their Lady and a revered Healer half the time, the other half like somebody's little sister who happened to tag along.

Meer had even begun singing Renny's praises.

In his watching, Allar noticed with no little satisfaction Renny putting on weight. Abundant, regular meals and staying in one spot for a few days had done wonders, even with all the worrying about Conthar and tending to him.

Losing the gaunt look, her face filling out, Renny no longer resembled a starved wolf. Her visible bruises had healed to the point of being invisible unless you looked closely.

Over Renny's heavy protests, Allar had insisted on checking her ribs and hidden wounds, grinned to himself at her remembered response:

Bena and Sher had already checked her. Several times.

She was fine, Allar didn't need to.

And her final, disgruntled hiss, "You just want to get me naked again."

Allar snickered at the last. He hadn't argued, merely given Renny a heated look and informed her in no uncertain terms, the next time he took her clothes off, Renny would not be unconscious.

Opening and closing her mouth like a landed fish gasping for air, struggling for a suitable answer, Renny glared.

Allar managed to sound stern as he gave Renny a choice.

Himself, here and now, or Seon. Allar would personally escort her back to Dragon's Haven. Either way, her wounds would be rechecked.

No way was Allar going back and facing Seon if Renny came down with the slightest hint of infection.

And that didn't even take into consideration what the dragons would do. The whole lot of them watched Renny's every move like starving hunt beasts eyeing prey.

Today being prime time for Renny's stitches to come out, she'd stonily shut Allar out while he tended her, muttered an ungrateful thanks when he finished, and stomped off to sit sulkily beside Conthar.

The two of them made a good pair, acting like a couple two year olds on a festival night who'd just been told it was time for bed.

Waiting until she was sure Renny wasn't paying them any attention, Zantha informed Allar, {{*You yourself told Renny there had been other women in your life. Now that she's had time to heal a bit and catch her breath, Renny is starting to worry.*}}

Scratching Zantha's eye ridges and drawing a churring sound from his dragon, Allar snorted again. {{*Worry? About what? Those other women are long gone and none of them stayed long anyway. I tried to tell Renny mates just are—there's no rhyme or reason. Renny thinks I want her solely because of that, but I have seen no other woman since I laid eyes on her.*}}

Zantha chuffed and tilted her head under Allar's hand so he could reach an especially itchy spot. {{*Allar, you're thinking as a man. Try to see things from Renny's point of view. A male such as you attracts and chooses beautiful, talented, experienced women. In Renny's mind, she is none of those things. Her body reflects her harsh life. Scars on a male are, well, manly. Scars on a woman are seen as less than a badge of honor. Renny didn't care so much about you seeing her without clothes, what bothered her was you saw her blemishes.*}}

Leaning into Allar's ministrations, Zantha churred louder. {{*Blemishes she regards as faults. Fearing you will compare her to your other women and find her lacking, Renny knows nothing of being Lady of a keep, only of fighting and surviving. If you are not careful, Renny will talk herself into believing she's not good enough for you, that you and Dragon's Haven deserve a more ladylike Lady. She's well on her way down that path or I wouldn't betray her thoughts by discussing this with you. Besides, anger is akin to jealousy. If Renny is jealous, then she cares a great deal more for you than she's willing to let on. Use it to your advantage.*}}

Enlightenment held Allar speechless for a moment. {{*Zantha, you're right, and your advice is sound. To me, Renny is beautiful. As for her scars, I hate them for her sake because of what she's endured but they in no way detract from her appeal. As for the other, there are more than enough useless ladies at every keep. Dragon's Haven needs a strong Lady and Renny is nothing if not strong. That she is inexperienced, well, that I intend to remedy as soon as possible.*}}

Zantha let out a soft hmmph. {{*You better get started quick. You're running out of time.*}}

Still sitting beside Conthar, seething, Renny hadn't moved. Allar had no doubt part of her anger was a direct reflection of Conthar's—no more used to enforced confinement than Renny —disgruntlement. Smiling, Allar snagged food as he walked in their direction.

Dropping down beside Renny, Allar leaned carefully back against Conthar and draped an arm over Renny's shoulders. Taking a bite, offering Renny one—mouth a thin line, head turned away—which she refused, Allar swallowed before speaking.

Flicking bizzle-berries in the air one at a time, Allar tipped his head back and caught them in his mouth, let their sweet essence drizzle down his throat. "So, you want to sneak off somewhere? You can take my clothes off this time."

Renny's sharp elbow dug into Allar's ribs. His startled yelp and the airborne bizzle-berry smacking him between the eyes brought a slight twitch to her lips.

"Take your feast day tricks elsewhere and leave me alone."

Expertly catching another bizzle-berry, Allar offered to throw one at Renny.

Staring straight ahead, Renny kept her mouth clamped shut and crossed her arms.

Letting his head thump back softly against Conthar's hide— no longer dusty but polished and gleaming, thanks to Renny and Zantha—Allar sighed. "Conthar, is Zantha this intractable?"

Swinging his massive head around to his humans, Conthar regarded them solemnly. "Only when she is angry with me, like now. Just because she thinks I am too weak to get up and I happen to disagree…"

"You are" hit Conthar in tandem as Renny and Zantha both objected.

"See what I mean?" Conthar continued to mutter under his breath as both females berated him for being hardheaded.

Allar kept on as if he and Conthar were alone, having a heart to heart about the stubborn females of either species. "But you still love Zantha, right?"

"There is no other for me." Conthar's blunt statement left no room for argument.

Allar slanted a glance at Renny. "So, if Zantha had been the one captured and tortured and had the scars to show for it, would you still want her as your mate?"

Conthar's livid bellow caught them by surprise and had everyone else in camp looking their way. "I would not allow such a thing to happen, but had Zantha been the one caught, there is nothing they could have done to her to make me stop loving her. She is my mate, the other half of my heart and soul. Zantha is the most beautiful dragon I have ever seen, but what the outside looks like is not nearly as important as what's inside. Should Zantha dare to think I don't love her, I would do everything in my power to show her otherwise and I would never stop until she believed me."

Allar persisted. "But what if Zantha, despite what you said and did, felt she was no longer suitable for you?"

Gazing steadily at Zantha, Conthar replied, "Then I would spend the rest of our days convincing her she is perfect for me."

Without taking her eyes off her mate, Zantha bellied closer and touched heads with Conthar.

Throwing a bizzle-berry in the air, watching it rise and fall,

Allar snapped it out of the air like a pond-croaker with a fly. "What about the ones who hurt her?"

Conthar vowed, "There is nowhere they could hide that my wrath would not find them."

Twining their necks and churring in delight, engrossed in each other, the dragons forgot their humans.

Renny slumped. "Point taken."

Allar pulled her closer. Sinking one hand in Renny's short mop, palming her head, Allar turned her face up for his kiss. Brushing soft kisses against her lips, then her eyelids and nose, working his way down her face, Allar nibbled along her jaw to the sensitive spot behind her ear before returning to Renny's mouth, harder and more demanding this time.

Opening to Allar like a flower to a buzz-buzz, she tasted of honey and spices and warm woman. He'd never be able to get enough of her. Pulling back with a grin, Allar rested his forehead against Renny's. Whispered, "Woman, how could you doubt that I want you?"

Giving herself up to the wonder of Allar's kisses, feeling as if she'd been drugged, Renny felt bereft when he stopped and pulled away, both breathing hard. Blushing when she realized she was no longer sitting beside Allar but astride his lap with her arms twined around his neck and her tingling body pressed tightly to his, Renny immediately tried to wriggle off.

"Don't move. Just...don't move." Allar's urgent plea froze Renny in place.

Having been around men all her life, Renny didn't have to be told why. Besides, she could feel his *why*, pressing explicitly into her soft woman's place.

Her blush intensifying until Allar could feel the heat radiating off her, Renny's apology had him gritting his teeth. "Don't apologize, just sit still for a moment until I cool off or I'm going to embarrass us both. I haven't gotten this heated, this fast, since I was a green youth."

Allar didn't think it was possible, but Renny's face got even redder.

Nuzzling Renny cheek to cheek, Allar murmured, "You best be glad we're surrounded by men and dragons or I'd have your clothes off and this time… I wouldn't have stopped there."

Renny's eyes snapped to his, but she said nothing.

Zantha coughed discreetly, and when she was sure she had Allar's and Renny's attention, she informed them, "The others can't see you. I'm blocking their view."

Uttering a heartfelt thank you, Renny scrambled off Allar's lap. Tried to put distance between them but Allar refused to let her.

Standing when she did and grabbing Renny's hand before she could bolt, Allar kept her close. Cupping her face with his other hand, Allar brushed his thumb over her swollen lips, once, twice.

Mesmerized, eyes wide and lips parted, Renny stood still and let him.

Two DAYS more and Renny and Zantha decided Conthar could try a short flight. Up and walking around since Allar's speech and kiss, they were all more than ready to quit this place. Voya, unless he returned today with news, had found no leads.

Renny watched with her heart in her throat as Conthar slowly tested his wings, Zantha right beside him.

Landing triumphantly in front of Renny, she rushed to Conthar to make sure none of his wounds had opened and that he was truly fine. Passing her inspection with flying—haha—colors, Conthar dipped his head and Renny threw her arms around his neck.

"We did it! We really did it!"

Bursting with joy, Renny spun and leapt into Allar's arms, plastering kisses all over his face.

Allar held Renny to him, her feet dangling off the ground. Capturing her lips, he deepened the kiss.

Voya's chuckle broke their tryst.

Renny tried to wiggle down but gave up when Allar tightened his arms around her, opting for burying her face in his neck instead. Taking the opportunity while she had it, Renny nipped at the strong cords in Allar's neck.

"Sheesh! Would you two get a room!" Voya's eyes were sparkling in jest, a wide grin splitting his weathered face.

Arms full of his woman, willing at that, Allar grinned back. "As soon as possible, my friend. As soon as possible."

Reluctantly loosening his hold just enough for Renny to slide down his body and get a good feel for how happy he was at her predicament, Allar kept her in the circle of his arms.

Renny turned to face Voya and Allar pulled her back against his chest, tucked her head under his chin.

Losing his grin, Voya shook his head. "I wish I had good news to report, but...nothing. It's as if they don't exist. We questioned every village or croft we could find and no one, unless they're lying, has seen anything."

Allar shrugged. "We'll find them, it's just a matter of time. Conthar was the most important thing. Thanks to Renny he is alive and well. I'm sure Mithar already told you, but Conthar has just returned from a short flight. Depending on how he feels, we'll leave here as soon as he's able."

Conthar grumbled, "That would be never if the females have their way."

Renny lit into her dragon. "Just because I allowed you to make one short hop—if you think I spent all that time and energy saving you so you can crash and destroy all my hard work in one fell swoop...

Zantha hit Conthar smugly from the other side. "Renny can always drug you and have the dragons carry you back in a sling."

Looking from one to the other, dragon and human, Voya might not be able to understand Zantha and Conthar but he got the gist of it.

Looking pleadingly at Allar and Voya, both shaking their heads in amusement, Conthar said, "Help me out here. Demented—they're both demented."

Allar had to bite back his laughter. "Un uh. Renny's the Dragonhealer. What she says goes. You'll get no sympathy from me." Sobering, Allar looked to Renny. "All teasing aside, how long before you think Conthar can fly? We've been away from Dragon's Haven far too long."

Left to Renny, she'd've had Conthar stay ground bound much longer, until he was fully healed but Allar was right. The longer they stayed here, the more at risk they were. They had no idea where the dragonhaters came from or even how many there were.

Renny smiled grimly to herself, remembering how she'd reduced their numbers by quite a few. Decimated them, actually.

Stroking Conthar, evaluating, Renny nodded. "I think we can leave on the morrow and see how far we get, as long as Conthar promises not to shut me out. And as long as he also promises to let me know the very instant he feels any pain or fatigue. I won't have him stressed, not even to get back to Dragon's Haven."

Conthar made a rude noise. "As if I could get away with anything around you and Zantha. The two of you are in my mind like stick-tights."

Renny laughed, a delighted sound, as Conthar's grumbling conjured up images of the little flat burs capable of working their way under a dragon's scales. Impossible for dragons to remove without human aid, they'd been known to drive a dragon crazy.

"Ah, but you love it, you big lug." Patting Conthar's satiny hide, Renny loved being able to tease her dragon. Her dragon!

She could still hardly believe it. She, who'd never had a family or a home, now had the makings of both as well as a dragon!

Scratching Conthar's eye ridges, giving him a final pat as he sighed in pleasure, Renny stepped back reluctantly. "If we're to leave tomorrow, you must rest now and let the other dragons bring you more food."

Worn out from his short test flight, Conthar murmured sleepily, "I do love it, Renny. And you. I was beginning to despair of ever finding you." Eyes slamming shut, Conthar was asleep while the last words were still ringing in Renny's ears.

Giving Zantha a pat as she bedded down beside her mate, Renny left to make sure the other dragons were ready for the long flight home.

Renny checked the rest of the dragons—ecstatic to once again have all Renny's attention—one by one thoroughly from tip to tail, every single scratch and possible stick-tight, anything that would bother the dragons.

Not that their riders didn't do a fine job, Renny just wanted hands on, and reveled in the contact. Bena and Sher as well as the riders had looked them all over but Renny had to see for herself, be absolutely sure. Some of the poisons were slow acting, with nasty residuals.

The dragons talked to Renny non-stop, over the top of each other, interrupting and finishing each other's sentences. Renny lapped it up. 'Twas sheer joy to speak to a dragon that wasn't in pain or dying.

Mithar tried to be patient, but finally hushed the others so he could speak. "Renny, Mina and I... Thank you for Conthar. To lose a child is heartbreaking, and Conthar is the only one of ours to survive."

Renny caught Mithar's thought, hastily censored, of failed hatchings, of dragonlings dying in infancy of easily curable diseases simply because there was no Dragonhealer available.

Renny began hesitantly, "Some of those things are easily preventable. You don't need a Dragonhealer for…"

Tant broke in bitterly. "The old Dragonhealers were secretive and selfish, keeping their knowledge to themselves to better their status."

Clenching her fists, vibrating with rage, Renny narrowed her eyes. "Not everyone can reach a dragon mind to mind, but the salves and unguents should be common knowledge, available to everyone."

The ring of dragons gasped in unison at Renny's sudden ferocity, her dedication to dragonkind.

Mithar laid his head on the ground and the others followed suit. "If there is ever anything we can do to aid you or repay you, you have our dragon bond."

Renny caught the agreement of all the dragons present.

Mithar continued, "Mina sends her love, and we would both like to welcome you to our family. Yours must be very proud of you."

Uncomfortable with the praise the dragons were heaping on her, Renny fidgeted nervously. Zantha must not have told the dragons everything. They'd probably take back their kind words and turn their backs on her when they found out the truth.

Best to tell them now before she got used to being liked.

Not seeking pity, merely stating a fact, Renny shrugged. "I have no family. I am an unwanted orphan of unknown parentage, most likely a bastard."

At Renny's confession, the dragons erupted in a furious roar. They heard the old pain and knew the stark realities behind such an admission.

Expecting condemnation, heartsick at the thought of losing the dragon's respect but unable to lie to them, Renny at first paid no heed to their words.

They were furious alright—raging on her behalf. That anyone would abandon a child, especially a Dragonhealer child, was beyond their ken. When the dragons quieted somewhat, Mithar spoke again.

"Renny, that you have survived and become what and who you are with no guidance, no family, no love, speaks volumes. We are your family now."

Allar strode up behind Renny and slipped his arms around her. "Renny, your past matters not to us save that it has made you who you are. You will have to forgive us if that makes us a little overprotective of you. We can't bear for you to be in pain or hurt any more."

Feeling as if a great weight had been lifted off her shoulders, Renny relaxed into Allar's hold. She wasn't ashamed of her past, she'd had no control over it, but others hadn't been so understanding. That Allar and the dragons didn't care, were actually furious on her behalf and not angry at her...

While Conthar rested, Renny spent the remainder of the afternoon with the dragons, the men drifting over and joining them. For the first time in her life, Renny felt like she belonged. The men and dragons regaled her with tales of past exploits, each more unbelievable than the last.

Finally, unable to laugh any more, holding her sides, Renny rose and excused herself.

Stopping by the fire, Renny took the plate Allar handed her, ate it all and handed the plate back, her mind on Conthar.

Awake and stirring, he contacted Renny. {{*I want to try another short flight.*}}

Making her way to his side, Renny checked Conthar's wounds again, getting in a little close contact while she was at it, wishing she could nuzzle Conthar the way Zantha did. Prolonging her inspection, using any excuse to keep touching the big cobalt.

Patting Conthar's side, Renny acquiesced. "I don't think another flight will do you any harm, but stay close and no showing off. Zantha, stay with him."

Barely breathing, Renny watched with her heart in her throat as Conthar made a long, slow, swooping circle around the outer rim of the valley. Not quite as anxious as she'd been with the first barely-above-the ground flight, Renny was more than glad to see Conthar land safely.

Rushing to him, running her hands over him once again, Renny pronounced Conthar fit. Loving the feel of his soft scales beneath her hands, like stroking silk. Enjoying the vibrancy of his cobalt color, gleaming in the sunlight like a fine jewel.

Even his wounds and scars couldn't detract from Conthar's beauty. Drowning in sensation, Renny was startled when Conthar broke into her silent revelry.

He sounded…ashamed. {{*Renny, as your dragon, 'tis my right and my privilege to carry you. Thanks to you, I am much better, well on my way to being completely healed, but I cannot ensure your safety right now. Until I can be sure, I humbly request that you continue to ride on Zantha with Allar during our journey back to Dragon's Haven. Having only just found you, I refuse to endanger you, or Zantha and Allar due to my own selfishness. Please believe me, I can hardly wait. It already seems I have waited my whole life for you. I can wait a few more days. I promise you, as soon as I can carry you safely, I will.*}}

Overcome, Renny wrapped her arms around Conthar's neck and buried her face against his warm hide. While she couldn't force words out of her tight throat, when she could finally form a coherent thought again, Renny assured him. {{*I, too, have waited— forever it seems, without knowing what I was waiting for. And while I do not fear for my safety with you, I would never jeopardize you or Zantha or Allar. Tell me when you feel ready. Until then, I am content.*}}

Remaining as she was with her face tight against Conthar, inhaling his unique scent, Renny only became aware of Allar when he pressed his length against her back, trapping her between himself and Conthar.

"Hey, when do I get a turn?" Nuzzling his face into Renny's hair, Allar's deep voice soothed her and made her laugh.

Turning in the circle of his arms, Renny pressed her face into Allar's chest as she'd been doing to Conthar.

Allar's chest rumbled and vibrated. "You don't stroke me like that and my skin is as soft as his scales."

Fisting her hands in Allar's shirt at waist level to keep from doing just that, Renny leaned back to look him in the face, laughing again as Allar batted his eyelashes.

"My eyes are as beautiful a blue as he is."

Enjoying their sparring, Renny quipped, "Yeah, but can you fly?"

Zantha joined in, making no attempt to hide her amusement at their antics. "Face it, my human. You've been upstaged by a pair of wings."

The foursome's shared laughter echoed in the valley like a cleansing breath.

UP AND READY TO leave the next morning while the sky was still without color and the sun was a lighter colored darkness on the horizon, they flew slow and easy, stopping the instant Conthar felt any discomfort.

The other dragons, hunting on the fly, brought food to Conthar as soon as he landed. Out like a light as soon as he fed, the next several days were much the same, each day flying a little closer to Dragon's Haven.

Regaining his strength by leaps and bounds, on the fifth day, Conthar insisted on hunting for himself.

Renny agreed grudgingly. Not because she didn't think Conthar was healed enough, simply not wanting to admit she couldn't bear having him out of her sight.

Putting her foot down when they reached the lake shore, Renny insisted they spend two nights before Conthar endeavored to fly across the lake. Made Conthar rest and let the other dragons bring him food.

Giving him a thorough once over, Renny sat beside Conthar and awaited the other dragons' return, her mind in a turmoil. It'd taken the other dragons what seemed forever to cross the lake, and they'd been in excellent health.

There were no islands or shoals for Conthar to land on if he became too weak to make it. Chewing her lip, twirling a spike of hair around a finger until it threatened to create a bald patch, Renny stewed and agitated.

What if Conthar wasn't ready? What if his strength gave out? What if…

Unable to shut out Renny's worrying, Conthar asked gently, "Renny, did you not swim this same lake?"

At her nod, Conthar casually posed another question. "Did you know that while dragons fly across this lake all the time, never has a human even attempted to swim it?"

Renny shook her head ruefully. "You're trying to tell me I should stop worrying?"

Conthar nodded and nudged Renny. "Had I any inkling you'd do such a thing, I don't know that I'd've placed such an overwhelming compulsion in your mind to find Dragon's Haven. It never occurred to me you wouldn't at least try to find a village, or a fisherman. Build a raft. Make a signal fire. Something other than what you did. That you might try to swim across never entered my mind. That you succeeded is a testament to your stubbornness and will. My heart still stutters at the risk you took. I forbid you to place yourself in such danger ever again."

Renny grinned impudently. "I didn't swim all the way. Part of the time I floated."

Blowing Conthar a kiss, she left him in search of Allar.

Left Conthar shaking his head, trying to tease some sympathy out of Zantha and not making any more headway with Zantha than he had with Renny.

Renny didn't have to look far to find Allar. Standing on the shore, staring grimly out across the water, he turned as Renny approached. Opened his mouth.

Renny cut him off before he could berate her. "You're too late. I've already had this same lecture from Conthar. No need to waste your breath, at least on lecturing."

Snapping his mouth shut, Allar dragged Renny close and kissed her breathless.

When they finally came up for air, Renny burst into laughter. "There! Wasn't that much nicer?"

Grasping Renny's upper arms and shaking her lightly, Allar grimaced. "You will not disregard your safety in such a manner gain. My heart cannot take it." Resting his forehead against hers, Allar breathed Renny in. "I want your word you will not do anything so foolish again."

Looking Allar in the eye, Renny fervently promised, "I will not swim the lake again."

Allar groaned. "Who's incorrigible?"

THEY FLEW and flew and flew and flew some more, and still they seemed no closer to reaching the other side. The far shore was merely a hint of a shadow on the horizon when Renny's sharp healer's eye noticed Conthar slowly losing altitude.

Knowing there was nothing she could do except offer hope and encouragement, Renny kept up a steady patter, much as she had the night she'd healed him.

{{*Come on, baby, you can do this. We're almost there. Don't give up now. You promised you would be my dragon and I would be your rider. You promised.*}}

Zantha was doing the same, and so were the rest of the dragons. Renny could hear them all, droning like a cloud of buzz-buzzes in her head.

By the time they could make out individual trees, Conthar

was skimming just above the water, wingtips sending up spray with each stroke, Renny crooning non-stop as if her words alone could keep him aloft. Giving one last flap, gliding as far as he could before splashing down clumsily a few feet shy of the actual shoreline, he managed to drag himself mostly out of the water before collapsing on the sand to lie unmoving except for his heaving sides.

Renny scrambled off Zantha. Conthar conked out before Renny reached his side.

CHAPTER 16

*C*onthar didn't move, didn't wake until the sun was well up the next morning. Groaning, moving slowly and stiffly, he gradually pulled himself the rest of the way out of the water.

The other dragons had collected a veritable mound of herd-beasts. Good thing the beasts bred like hoppities, for dragon appetites were voracious, and Conthar was starving.

As she'd done each time before, Renny laced a carcass with medicines. Wolfing the pile down in quick, gulping bites, staggering a few feet to a patch of warm sand and stretching out, Conthar immediately fell asleep again.

Renny took the opportunity to rub more ointment onto every part of Conthar she could, going so far as to enlist Zantha's aid. Normally reserved for sore spots, Renny figured Conthar was just one big sore spot anyway.

The day they landed back on this side of the lake, Renny had sent several dragons to Lakeside to fetch large quantities of tallow. While they were gone, she'd recruited Bena and Sher to help her strip leaves from the waxy, menthol smelling shrubs along the shore.

Renny bit her cheek to keep from laughing when Sher innocently asked if someone had fleas or dragon mites. Shaking her head, she enlightened them.

"I know you think this plant is merely a weed, mostly used to repel insects, but it has many other uses. The most important being what we'll use it for. It not only heals on the outside, it soaks into the skin and eases aches and pains. It'll have more effect once Conthar is up and about. Body heat increases its effectiveness."

Lifting a handful of the pungent leaves to her nose, Renny grinned and confided, "It works on people just as well, if you can get stubborn men to use it. They'd rather suffer in silence than smell like this and have everyone know they're hurting."

Bena and Sher watched intently as Renny boiled the leaves to mush. Once the thick brew was partially cooled, she strained out any pieces that hadn't softened, mixed in the tallow and rubbed her concoction all over Conthar, even standing on Zantha's back so she could reach the middle of Conthar's back.

What was left Renny divided up and put in the thick clay pots with glazed interiors and tight stoppers that Bena and Sher used to store their medicines.

Finishing up, making sure none of the other dragons needed any ointment, Renny debated with herself. That patch of sun-warmed sand next to Conthar was calling her, but she hadn't had a bath since Allar soaked her to get rid of the poisons, and that didn't count.

Glancing around to see if anyone was paying any attention to her, Renny opted for the bath.

Like most dragonriders, the men were engrossed in taking care of their dragons or weapons. Allar was conferring with Voya and Awalt, heads together. Bena and Sher were sorting through their newly improved collection of herbs and making copious notes.

Conthar was out for the count and the other dragons were drowsing or splashing in the shallows.

No one would notice if she slipped off by herself for a bit.

Sighing in anticipation, Renny snaffled a clean shirt out of Allar's pack and headed off down the shoreline, intending to bathe in private.

Conthar would let her know when he woke, and she wasn't planning on staying gone long.

Deep in conversation with Voya and Awalt, Allar followed Renny with his eyes. Not that he'd taken his eyes off her for more than a blink anyway. {{*Zantha, what is Renny doing?*}}

Next to Conthar, Zantha was busily worming her belly into the sand, scratching spots she could never reach otherwise. Sounding more concerned with her belly rub than Renny's whereabouts, Zantha gave the equivalent of a dragon shrug. {{*Renny said she was going to slip away to bathe. You know how strange you humans are about bathing in front of other humans. Ridiculous, if you ask me, but… Ahhh.*}}

Having hit the right spot, Zantha's eyes were closing fast, content to nap beside her mate. Zantha sighed. Yawned. {{*Do you want me to go with Renny?*}}

Without answering Zantha, making no excuses to Voya or Awalt and leaving them mid-sentence, Allar left to pursue Renny. Slowing enough to snag a clay pot of Renny's ointment, Allar cradled it one-handedly and kept walking, a determined look on his face.

Exchanging amused glances, Voya and Awalt shook their heads. Man or dragon, males were the same in their single-minded pursuit of their mates.

No intentions of going very far, just out of sight of the camp, Renny had a lifetime of experience in hiding her female-ness, and old habits died hard.

Zantha'd promised to alert Renny if any of the men followed her, so Renny was being more lax than usual.

Not far from the camp, Renny found exactly what she was looking for—a small creek flowing into the lake.

Cocking her head to one side, hoping her ears hadn't deceived her, Renny turned and followed the creek a short way uphill into the thick woods. And there—a perfect waterfall spilling gracefully into a small pool! Bliss!

Locating a bit of soapweed growing on the creek bank had Renny humming to herself in satisfaction.

Taking a careful look around and seeing nothing but green trees and blue water and mossy rocks, Renny shed her clothes and stepped into the water. Placing her dagger on a rock within easy reach, Renny ducked under the waterfall and soaked herself thoroughly.

Coming out from under the waterfall long enough to retrieve her soapweed, Renny crushed and rolled the fragrant leaves between her hands until it bubbled into a froth. Raising her arms, elbows pointed skyward, Renny washed her hair.

The wound on the back of her head mostly healed, there was still a knot, tender to the touch. Rinsing her hair, rubbing more soapweed between her palms, Renny made enough bubbles to soap her body, going easy on the previously wounded areas. Although, once they'd found Conthar, and Renny had started working her magic on him, it seemed it rebounded, speeding her healing as well. She'd never recovered this fast. This newfound ability would've come in handy when she was younger and Orst was beating the stuffing our of her on a regular basis.

Standing under the pouring water, Renny let the water sluice the bubbles off and just enjoyed.

Allar followed Renny discreetly, but she never once looked back.

Watched as she turned into the woods and hopscotched along the bank of a small creek.

Watched as she stopped at a waterfall and draped her clean shirt over a large rock in a puddle of sunshine.

Watched as she stripped, picked some soapweed, and proceeded to drive him out of his mind.

Ogling Renny—mouth open and tongue hanging out as she washed her hair and then her body—Allar waited for her to come out, desire quickly supplanted by fury at Renny's carelessness.

Figuring she'd been gone long enough, knowing she'd better head back before they sent out a search party, Renny reluctantly left the soothing stream of water cascading over her head and shoulders.

Shaking her head, she sent a spray of water droplets in every direction. Tipping her head back, raising her hands to slick her hair back out of her face, Renny stopped mid-motion, elbows high in the air.

At the sight of Allar planted on the bank, booted feet spread wide and arms crossed, a dark scowl on his face, Renny fisted her hands on her hips and glared, too furious to speak.

Gaze locked with hers, Allar gritted out, "Come here."

When Renny made no answer and showed no signs of obeying, Allar reached down and pulled off a boot. Hopping on one foot, he tugged off the other.

Renny stood stubbornly mute.

Grasping the hem of his shirt and whipping it over his head, Allar had both hands on the laces of his pants and was undoing them when Renny finally reacted.

"What do you think you're doing?"

"What does it look like I'm doing?" Pants off, Allar stepped into the water and stalked Renny. "You take off without a word to anyone, with no thought or care for your own safety and I find you naked in the woods. Anyone, *anyone*, could've come across you out here like this and you're mad at me?"

Wanting to back up in the face of Allar's wrath, Renny

refused to let him see how much his words hurt her. "I am not accustomed to asking permission for my actions and I generally bathe naked and alone." Head raised high in defiance, Renny had to crane her neck to look at him, he'd gotten so close.

Allar crowded Renny until she could feel every hard line and plane of his body straining against hers. He bit out, "Had you asked, I'd've come with you and guarded you, with my back turned, and been a gentleman about it. Since you didn't—and are displaying your wares for all to see—all bets are off."

Grasping Renny's head between his hands, Allar slanted her face to his liking and kissed her. A hard kiss meant to punish Renny for scaring the life out of him. Renny's lips were cool and tasted of clean water—they were also totally unresponsive.

Renny didn't struggle, didn't move. She could feel Allar's pain and fear for her, radiating out of him and into her. She just didn't know what to do about it. Dragon pain she was most familiar with. This… This concern for her person, fear for her, was so far out of her league she froze.

When Renny didn't struggle, didn't move in his hold, Allar pulled back enough to see her face. What he saw splintered his heart. Anger he could deal with, tears he could've handled, but what he saw cut him to the marrow.

Renny's eyes were glued to his face, wide and blank, emotion buried so deep he couldn't see any. Immediately loosening his hold, Allar took a step back, turned away and whirled back to face Renny.

"Do you have any idea how precious you are to me?" Shaking his head, Allar answered himself. "No. Of course you don't."

Taking deep breaths, clenching and unclenching his fists, Allar tried to calm down. He could remain a rock in the fiercest battles, keep his temper no matter what happened at Dragon's Haven, but this one slip of a woman…

Gentling his tone, hoping to get through to Renny, Allar

tried to rein in his temper. "I watched you undress and bathe and at first all I could do, as Zantha likes to tease, was ogle you. Then I thought about you being out here by yourself and someone else watching you—someone who wanted to do you harm. I know you're used to taking care of yourself and I respect that, will even try to allow for it. You're going to have give a little and help me take care of you. I can't stand the thought of you being hurt. Besides the fact, which seems to escape you, that you mean everything to me, you are the *only* Dragonhealer left alive on this world. Do you have any idea how valuable that makes you, or how many people would kill you for that alone? If you won't think of yourself, think of me, and if not me, the dragons. Without you, we'd've lost Conthar for certain and losing him, we'd've lost Zantha as well. You cannot take such needless risks with your precious, precious life."

Another deep breath and Allar stepped closer to Renny. Grasped her shoulders, and as soon as his hands touched her skin, felt their bond sparking and arcing. "I am a warrior—it is my job, my duty, to protect you. Even were you not mine I would do so. You have to meet me halfway on this. Losing you would destroy me. Destroy me utterly. I've searched my whole life for you, and now that I've found you, everything else pales in comparison."

Turning her head to the side, Renny closed her eyes so she couldn't see the pain in his. Didn't help much. She could still feel his pain, battering at her, swamping her the way a dragon's pain did only worse. Much worse.

Told Allar tiredly, "I just wanted to bathe, and I did tell Zantha what I was going to do." Sighed heavily. "I've tried and tried to tell you, I don't know how to be mate to anyone. I've never had anyone who cared enough about me to worry where I was or what I was doing. Or even whether I lived."

Renny didn't move so much as a muscle but Allar could feel

her withdrawing. "Renny, we can work this out, I promise. Give us a chance."

Words weren't going to reach her. Renny'd been belittled and lied to all her life. Actions might reach her better.

Cupping her face with one hand, Allar turned Renny's face to his. Motionless and cold as a marble statue, she still wouldn't open her eyes.

Tangling his other hand in her hair, tugging gently, Allar tilted Renny's head back and began to brush butterfly kisses all over her face. Whisper soft, he started with her closed eyes, worked his way down her high cheekbones, her perfect little nose, brushed over her lips.

Sucking on them, coaxing her lips open, Allar took his time learning the tastes and textures of Renny's mouth. Nibbling his way down her neck, he traced her collarbone with little nips, soothing the nips with quick little flicks of his tongue.

Groaning, stopping while he was able, Allar buried his face in Renny's neck. "See what you do to me? I can't get enough, can't keep my hands off you. Tell me you don't feel anything, tell me you don't want this and I'll stop."

She said nothing, so he continued talking, voice dropping to a heated rumble. "I can't wait to get you away from the others and spend days doing exactly what we're doing right now."

Raising his eyes, Allar studied Renny's face.

Her eyes were still closed, her lips swollen from his kisses, a faint blush shading her cheeks. Brushing a thumb over her lips, leaving his thumb just at the corner of her mouth and cradling her cheek in his palm, Allar tucked Renny under his chin and just held her.

Hard to do with his naked body raging at him at their close proximity. Hard to stand, much less think when every fiber of his being was raging at him to possess his mate.

Allar's solid length pressed tight against Renny from the top of her head right on down. His chin over her head, his arms banded around her like dragonhide supports around a wooden mast. His hard arousal pressed into her softer belly.

Renny absorbed all that and more.

So much bigger and stronger, Allar could've forced himself on her at any time. And yet, he was merely holding her. Letting Renny decide for herself.

The roiling emotions inside Renny settled, like a vast whirlpool she'd swum through on her swim across the lake. Going round and round in dizzying circles until Renny couldn't tell which way was up and then...all of a sudden, spitting her out into still water. Burying that tidbit deep, so Zantha wouldn't rat her out, Renny settled.

Realized what she was feeling. Strange things for her, scary because of their very unfamiliarity. She felt... The same way she'd felt when she woke in Zantha's cave at Dragon's Haven.

In Allar's arms.

Loved. Protected. Cherished. Safe.

Without shifting position, Renny murmured against Allar's throat, "I am truly sorry for causing you such distress. 'Twas never my intention."

Softer then, so soft he almost didn't catch it, Renny whispered, "Teach me more about being your mate."

Leaning back, Allar tipped Renny's head up so he could see her face. Renny opened her eyes this time and the void that had been there was replaced with so much emotion Allar all but drowned in it.

Laughing, Allar held Renny tight against himself and spun around, water droplets arcing everywhere. Setting Renny on her feet Allar gave her a quick kiss.

"Don't move."

Renny watched as Allar made a mad dash for the shoreline, snatched up a fistful of soapweed and splashed back to her, throwing sprays of water high in the air with each step.

Laughingly protesting, Renny shook her head. "I already washed."

Eyeing Renny mischievously, Allar rubbed soapweed between his hands. Satisfied with the amount of lather, he began running his soap-slicked hands all over her.

Starting with her shoulders, he worked his way down her arms, picking up each hand and doing her fingers individually, turning her hands up and using his thumbs to rub circles in her palms.

Motioning for Renny to turn around, Allar soaped her back in long, lazy strokes, then scraped his fingernails gently back and forth and up and down.

Renny shivered in pleasure. Muscles she hadn't known she possessed, didn't know were aching, relaxed and surrendered—a lifetime's neglect and lack of touch made up for in this one shining instant.

Soft, so soft, everywhere Allar touched Renny was like warm silk beneath his hands. Running his slick hands down over her butt, trailing his fingers up and down her crease and under the curve of her buttocks.

Cupping and squeezing her sweetly rounded cheeks, Allar flattened his hands and slid them around Renny's hips in a slow glide. Guiding her back around, he gave her front the same thorough attention.

Spending a lot of time on her perfectly palm sized breasts, rubbing soapy circles, flattening his hands, then caging them in his hard fingers and drawing them to stiff peaks, Allar dropped lower to define her ribs with trails of bubbles.

Spanning her waist, he laved attention on Renny's taut belly, palms first before cruising the backs of his knuckles all over, dipping a knuckle in her belly button and swirling bubbles.

Guiding Renny back under the waterfall long enough to rinse her off, Allar joined her for a moment, picked her up and set her down on a waist high—to him—boulder.

Lathering more soapweed, Allar started over, on Renny's lower half this time. Gliding his hands up and down her sleek thighs, around her knees, the extremely sensitive backs of her knees, her firm calves.

Picked up each foot and gave it the same meticulous care he'd lavished on her hands. Working the soap between each toe, massaging the high arches of her small feet, trailing his fingers around her surprisingly delicate ankles.

Moving behind her, tilting her head back, Allar worked soapweed into her hair and massaged it into her scalp until Renny was so relaxed she could barely hold her position.

Practically purring, skin tingling, nerves alight, eyes languorous.

Scooping her up like she weighed no more than a child, making a slow, spinning pass under the waterfall and rinsing her off one more time, Allar sat on a lower rock with Renny on his lap.

Grinning wickedly, he picked up a small piece of soapweed.

Renny tried to squirm away as Allar began rubbing it in the silky curls at the juncture of her legs.

Allar was smugly pleased to note Renny was already slick there, the soap adding to the slippery sensation of his hand gliding over her most intimate parts.

Rubbing and stroking and teasing until Renny was squirming and panting and clutching his shoulders and right on the brink of tumbling over, Allar halted, so hard he thought he'd explode. The first time his mate came for him, he wanted to be buried balls deep inside her.

Wanted to capture those first breathless cries with his kisses.

Wanted to see every expression on her face and in her eyes.

Letting Renny slide into the water, keeping one strong arm around her, Allar bent and ruffled his hand through her curls and folds until he was sure all the soapweed was rinsed off and the remaining slickness was all Renny.

Pulling her back into his lap, kissing her, Allar put all the love he was feeling into their joined lips.

Breaking apart, gasping, Renny and Allar stared wordlessly at each other, the air around them sizzling and crackling.

When she could breathe again, Renny scooted out of Allar's lap and leveled a finger at him. "Stay right there."

Swiveling his head to watch Renny wade to shore but otherwise obeying her dictate, Allar grinned as she picked not merely several generous handfuls of soapweed but an entire clump and splashed back to him. Plopping the soapweed on Allar's rock within easy reach, Renny began working a handful into an overflowing wad of bubbles, never taking her eyes off his.

"Let's see how good a teacher you are." Standing between Allar's legs, Renny started in the same place he had. Spreading bubbles on his broad shoulders, she worked her way down his muscular arms to his hands, calloused and strong but oh, so gentle when they touched her.

Renny had to climb up on Allar's perch in order to reach his back. Long, slow strokes up and down, swirling around his ribs, dipping into his narrow waist. She didn't have much in the way of fingernails but she did what she could with what she had. Changing up a little, Renny washed Allar's hair while she could reach it.

On her knees, she tilted his head back, resting it against her breasts and massaging his scalp as he'd done hers. Running her hands through his inky hair, Renny took her time, loving the silky feel of it and the length, way longer than her own.

Renny's snicker startled Allar out of his stupor. "I can't pick you up. You're going to have to rinse yourself off."

Sliding bonelessly into the water, Allar went supine along the bottom, staring up at the wavering form of his mate, peeking over the edge of the rock and peering down at him. He stayed under so long, just staring, Renny reached down and hauled him up by a handful of the hair she loved to touch.

Allar sat up, spluttering and Renny jumped back in. Tipped his head back and finished rinsing the bubbles out. Stepping in front of him, she eyed Allar up and down, contemplating her next move.

"Do you want to stand first, or sit?"

Swallowing audibly, Allar croaked, "Sit," and used the rock to pull himself to a standing position.

Smirking, planting a hand in the middle of his chest, Renny gave him a shove in the direction of his chosen seat. Allar stumbled backwards and sat down hard.

Renny immediately placed herself between his legs and began soaping his defined chest. Loving the ridges and hollows of him beneath her hands, the crisp hair so different from her own fine down, as different as Conthar's silky scales to her human skin.

Where Renny's stomach was flat, Allar's was rippled as a windblown sand dune.

Hard. All his muscles were unbelievably hard. And warm, as if one of the sun-warmed boulders had been covered in the finest moss.

Renny stroked and petted until she knew his contours, every dip and hollow.

Teasing without touching, purposely ignoring what was right in front of her, Renny slid her hands up and down his thighs, knees, and calves as far as she could reach without going under water.

Eyes on her prize, delaying for a bit longer, Renny ordered, "Rinse off again and turn around."

Lathering up once more, Renny contemplated Allar's ass, and a very fine ass it was. He jumped when she made contact, shivered when she started making soapy circles in the indentions on both cheeks, exploring with just her fingertips.

Spreading her hands wide, Renny made larger circles before sliding her hands to his hips, across his lower back, then returning to her starting point. Mimicking Allar's earlier movements, Renny trailed her fingers down his crack and under the curve of his ass.

Scooping up water in her hands, she let it cascade down and take the bubbles with it. Tugging on one hip, Renny got Allar to turn facing her. Reaching past him for more soapweed, a devilish grin on her face and emerald eyes locked on target, Allar grabbed her wrist.

Jaw clenched, he said hoarsely, "Renny, I... You don't have to do this."

Her grin flickered but her eyes never strayed. "You're stopping me now?"

About to come out of his skin—Allar'd been with his share of women but never had the mere touch of one's hands set him on fire like this small bundle of female's could—he croaked, "I only want you to if it's what you want. I don't want you to feel like you have to."

"Well, then." Before Allar could dredge any deeper and attempt to remain a gentleman, Renny made a froth in her hands and proceeded to torment him as he'd tormented her earlier. Making sure her hands were plenty soapy and slick, Renny cupped his taut sac with one hand and stroked his rigid staff with the other.

Changed her attack and raked her short nails over both.

Gritting his teeth, Allar tried to think of something else, anything besides what Renny was doing to him with her magic hands, unlike anything he'd ever felt. Not the soft hands of the court ladies, but working hands, calloused hands, the calluses only adding to the multitude of sensations she was unleashing on him.

Innocent hands.

Inexperienced Renny might be, but her enthusiasm more than made up for it. Her exploring was going to be the death of him.

Swelling impossibly harder at her ministrations, Allar grabbed Renny's hands before he embarrassed himself. Bending his knees, he sank underwater. The cool water did nothing to lessen the heat coursing through him.

Straightening his legs, he caught Renny to him, picking her up so she wrapped her arms around his neck and her legs around his waist. Cupping his hands under her sweet little ass, Allar roved them up and down her back and kissed her breathless.

Stumbling to the shore with her most intimate parts rubbing against his most intimate parts was blissful torment.

Reaching out one-handed, Allar spread his shirt on the soft moss at the water's edge. Going to his knees with Renny beneath him, he covered her body with his own.

Nudged her thighs apart with his knee and moved one hand to stroke the wetness between Renny's legs.

Shifted his weight and heard Renny's soft grunt of pain.

That faint sound saved him, or her.

Renny was too inexperienced, too wounded still for the kind of rough lovemaking Allar had in mind. All he was capable of right now, when she so needed tender loving.

Rolling onto his back, lacing his fingers with hers, Allar covered his eyes with a bent arm and emitted his own groan of pain. When he could form a coherent thought again, he gritted out, "Renny. My Lady. Forgive me. I let this go entirely too far and that was never my intention."

Opened his eyes to see Renny propped on one elbow, staring at him. "I do not mind. That was…most enlightening. Especially since that's the first time I ever touched a man with no intent to do him damage." Indicating his man parts with a flick of her eyes, she shrugged. "That would never have fit anyway."

Allar laughed loud and long. "Oh, yes. Trust me, I will fit and fit well. If you weren't such a good student, I wouldn't have gotten so large."

Renny eyed him as if he'd lost his mind.

Dragging his pants on, Allar stopped Renny when she reached for her own clothes. Looking around, he spotted the jar of ointment he'd brought for just this purpose. Holding it up so she could see it, he cocked his head.

"I heard you tell the healers this could be used on humans as well as dragons. Will it harm your skin?"

Renny shook her head, eyeing Allar dubiously.

Waving his hand to indicate she should stretch out on his shirt, Allar proceeded to rub her body, front and back, with the ointment. Slowly smoothing and stroking, he paid special attention to the remaining bruises and mostly healed cuts, and the spots he knew were still tender.

Renny groaned in relief with each gentle swipe, as much at the touch of his hands as the ointment.

Knowing the answer, he asked anyway. "If this is such good stuff, why didn't you make some earlier, for yourself?"

Renny shrugged, a slight twitch of one shoulder. "There wasn't time, and besides, I had no tallow and no way to store it."

Making a derogatory sound, Allar stated reprovingly, "What you mean is; while you'll expend the effort to make this for the dragons, you don't think enough of yourself to take the time."

Cracking one eye, Renny evaded a direct answer. "And just who was I supposed to get to rub this on?"

Growling playfully, Allar gave Renny a quick peck and snagged a few leaves of soapweed, Renny's voice trailing him. "Wash well. You don't want to get that on your... On that."

Adding an entire branch of soapweed to his leaves, washing his hands long and well, Allar definitely didn't want to get this ointment on his *that*, as Renny so eloquently put it. Striding back and dropping down beside Renny, he curled himself around her, intending to let her sleep for a bit.

Her sleepy protest was barely audible. "Can't sleep long. Conthar will wake up soon. Have to...get back."

A jaw-cracking yawn and Renny was mostly asleep by the

time Allar crooned, "Rest now, baby. Conthar will call you when he wakes. We have time."

After the hot and heavy bout they'd just shared, it was no wonder Renny was exhausted. What was he going to do with her? Renny refused to take care of herself, took needless risks, placed everyone's welfare above her own. His mate was the most stubborn, infuriating, wonderful woman he'd ever known.

Allar would do the only thing he could. The only thing he was capable of doing.

Love her.

And that definitely included protecting her and taking care of her.

Someone needed to.

Holding Renny, thinking back on what they'd just experienced together, Allar smiled. No woman had ever turned him inside out like she just had, and they hadn't really done anything.

None had ever made him lose control like some green youth, just by smiling in his direction, and when Renny touched him…

Never had he met a woman with such sensitive skin or one who responded so willingly and eagerly to the slightest touch. But then again, Allar supposed if he'd never been exposed to any tenderness, any love, he might soak it up the same way she did.

Holding Renny close, Allar breathed in her warm woman scent and let her rest while she could.

They didn't have long to themselves. Sprawled in the warm sun, fast asleep, tucked close against Allar and dreaming the most magnificent dreams, Renny felt Conthar stir.

{{*Renny, something is wrong! My skin is all tingly and hot.*}}

Dragging herself up from the depths of a—unusual for her—good dream, Renny advised, {{*You're fine—'tis the medicine I rubbed on you. I did it yesterday but it'd worn off before you woke up. If you feel up to it, go for a short flight with Zantha. Movement will make the ointment work better to loosen stiff muscles and joints. I'll be there shortly.*}}

Content, Renny snuggled into Allar, on the verge between wakefulness and sleep. Let her thoughts drift and accepted what'd just happened for the wonder it was. She certainly hadn't meant to anger Allar but the results had been…spectacular and she'd learned a great deal.

Snorted to herself. She still didn't see how Allar could possibly fit, but she'd take his word for it and see what happened. If worst came to worst, she could take him down. Probably. Possibly.

Smiled. She had to agree with Conthar, her skin was all hot and tingly as well. Had been, even before Allar rubbed ointment all over her. So relaxed right now, Renny didn't think she could lift a finger to protect herself or otherwise.

Allar's growl startled her. "You're supposed to be asleep, so how come I can hear the gears turning in your head?"

Grinning, eyes closed, Renny smirked, "Conthar's awake. He informed me his skin is all hot and tingly. I explained why, didn't tell him I'm in much the same state. I doubt he wants to know."

Allar's voice dropped a notch, from watchdog to lover in an instant. "So tell me how come you're all hot and bothered."

Voice full of mischievous laughter, Renny asked, "Um… Because you rubbed ointment all over me?"

Opening her eyes to find Allar looming over her, Renny put her hands up to fend him off.

Catching her hands in one of his, Allar stretched them over her head and bent down until he could reach her lips. Started nibbling, tracing the shape of her lips with teeth and tongue. "Can you remember now?"

Renny shook her head breathlessly. "Because… I was sleeping in the sunshine?"

"Wrong answer." Allar covered her, careful to keep most of his weight off her, rubbing their hips together so Renny could feel his arousal. "How about now?"

Renny shook her head again.

Rocking, pressing himself against her much smaller form, hip to hip, Allar tried again. "Anything coming back to you?"

Laughing, gasping, Renny gave in, emerald eyes wide and innocent. "I remember, I remember! But you have your pants on and I didn't rub any ointment on you so how come you're all... hot and tingly?"

Growling, Allar buried his face in Renny's neck and cradled her as he rolled them both over so she lay sprawled on top of him.

Renny sat up, straddling him. At Allar's groan, she wiggled experimentally.

Grabbing Renny's hips to hold her still, Allar closed his eyes and gritted his teeth. Neither helped any. The vision imprinted on his eyeballs of her naked body perched astride his...

Not just imprinted, seared.

"Be still, woman."

Afraid the slightest movement on her part would push him over the edge, Allar tightened his hold on Renny's hips while he listed all the reasons he couldn't just take what he wanted right now.

First and foremost, Renny was far too wounded.

This was neither the time nor the place to take his mate for the first time. Renny deserved soft sheets and a soft bed.

They were far too vulnerable out here in the woods. Anyone could come up on them at any time. Hadn't he just chastised Renny for bathing alone? And here he was about to jump her.

Not happening. He'd endangered Renny enough. She was far too distracting, but he wasn't that far gone yet. Close, but he still possessed a modicum of sense.

Renny laughed at his obvious dilemma, the sound shivering through her and into him where they were joined.

No! Not joined! Where they were touching!

Allar opened his eyes in time to see Renny throw back her

head, laughter spilling out like water over the rim of the waterfall.

Running his palms up the curve of Renny's hips, the in-curve of her waist, gently over her ribs, Allar cupped her breasts and thumbed the peaks. He grinned as she arched her back, pressing herself harder into his palms, a moan escaping her lips.

Renny looked down at him, one slim brow arched. "Time for another lesson?"

Thumping his head back against the ground, Allar mock-grumbled, "I've created a monster. A sex starved fiend."

Tightening her thighs, Renny teased, "Well, since we haven't actually had sex yet… Besides, doesn't it take one to know one?"

Before Allar had a chance to defend himself against her latest threat, Renny cocked her head as if listening to something only she could hear and scrambled madly off him.

Alarmed, Allar went to his knees and looked around, expecting the worst. A horde of dragonhaters or brigands or… Reaching for his weapons while trying to put Renny behind him, Allar demanded, "What is it?" All traces of the lover disappeared, the warrior taking over instantly.

Sounding panicked, Renny gasped, "Conthar. He and Zantha are almost here. I told him to take a short flight so the ointment would work better. How was I supposed to know he'd decide to fly here?"

Frantically searching the ground for her scattered clothes, she scowled as Allar fell back on the ground and roared with laughter.

"Go ahead and laugh, you big oaf. You would think this is funny." Fuming, Renny dragged on her leggings. Had to yank them off and start over when she realized she'd put them on backwards. Hopping on one foot and then the other, stretching down for her shirt and trying to fasten her leggings at the same time, Renny almost toppled as she snagged her clean shirt.

Amused to no end, leaning on one elbow, Allar watched

Renny scurry around. "Why don't you tell Conthar we'll meet them on the shore? There's no good place for them to land here, anyway."

Stopping dead in her tracks, one arm in her shirtsleeve, breeches up but unfastened, Renny gaped.

Rising gracefully, Allar pulled the shirt back off.

"What are you doing?" Renny tugged on her shirt hopelessly. Giving up, she searched the ground for her dirty shirt. She'd left it right here. Somewhere.

"Renny. Calm down." Turning Renny's shirt right side out, he slipped it over her head and pulled her arms through the sleeves. "Whether we have clothes on or not, they'll know what we've been doing."

At Renny's horrified stare, he continued. "When we're as closely linked as mates and dragons are, you learn to be very discreet. You have to. Otherwise we'd all die of embarrassment."

Face bright red, Renny sat down hard. "I might anyway."

"Might what?"

"Die of embarrassment." Covering her face with her hands, Renny tore at his heartstrings.

She'd spent her whole life being singled out and ridiculed. Why would she think today would be any different?

Allar soothed, "Renny, love, if it bothers you that much, close your mind. Zantha says you have the strongest barriers she's ever encountered, and Conthar will respect them."

Crouching in front of Renny, Allar pulled her hands away from her face and cupped her chin, forcing her to look at him. "There was nothing wrong with what we did. We're mates, and mates enjoy each other's bodies. 'Tis meant to be so."

Renny swallowed, wanting so hard to believe him. "Truly? I have never done anything like that in my life."

Pressing a kiss to Renny's forehead, Allar breathed a sigh of relief and tried to lighten her distress. "That I am most thankful for. I would be very displeased if you bathed naked with every man you came across."

Snorting a laugh, Renny rolled her shoulders. "I guess I'm over-reacting, huh?"

Stroking her cheek with the back of his hand, Allar pretended to consider Renny's question. "Maybe just a tad."

Blowing out a deep breath, Renny got up and walked to the edge of the bank. Kneeling, she cupped her hands and splashed water on her face.

Standing up and shaking her head so water droplets flew in every direction, Renny turned to Allar, face still dripping. "The ointment is certainly working now."

Laughing, Allar used his shirt to dry Renny's face. Unable to resist, he kissed her long and deep.

Working her hands between them, Renny shoved. "I'm hot enough already. Keep it up and I'll rub some of my ointment on your…"

Grinning hugely, Allar clasped her hand in his and headed for the lakeshore. Breaking out of the trees, the humans were delighted to see their dragons doing a little nuzzling and necking of their own.

Pleased to see their humans obviously sharing more than a bath and some ointment, if dragons could grin, these two were. To her chagrin, Renny felt her face redden.

When no one said anything, human or dragon, she relaxed.

Renny walked up to Conthar. Her dragon leaned into her, butting his great head gently against her chest and she circled it with both arms, scratching the underside.

Taking a step back, Renny laughed when Conthar took one as well, keeping Renny just where he wanted her. Giving his nose a pat and a firm shove, Renny craned her head to see the rest of him. "Stop, silly dragon. I have to check your wounds."

Conthar nuzzled Renny again. "I'm fine—wonderful, in fact.

I'm well rested, my belly's full, and I have two beautiful females attending my every move. What more could a dragon ask for?"

Ignoring his protests because she had to see for herself all was well, running her hands all over Conthar's gorgeous blue hide and inspecting each scabbed-over cut, Renny finally agreed.

Conthar bobbed his head and blew puffs of air at Renny. "The short flight helped, as you said it would. Your ointment is truly a wonderful thing."

Leaned closer and sniffed, wrinkled his nose. "Allar rubbed some on you? Good! How are you feeling? Allar checked your wounds?"

Throwing a desperate look in Allar's direction, Renny squeaked, "I'm fine."

Sliding an arm around Renny's shoulders and pulling her close to his heart, Allar set her dragon at ease. "I've inspected her wounds. Several times, as a matter of fact."

As Renny's face once again attained the shade of a ripe apoma, Zantha took up for her mate's human. "Stop teasing, you two. Can't you see you're embarrassing our Renny?" Swinging her head to nudge Renny gently, silently conveying her gratitude and thanks, Zantha huffed, "Ignore them, Renny, they're doing it on purpose." Winking at Renny, getting in a dig for the girls, Zantha snarked, "Allar, Voya and Awalt said any time you can pay attention they are waiting to finish the discussion you were having."

Renny turned amused eyes to Allar. "You left your second and your arms master in the middle of an important discussion?"

"More like in the middle of a sentence," Zantha added smugly.

Opening his mouth to defend himself, realizing the futility of arguing with two females, Allar pointed an accusing finger at Renny. "You were heading off down the shore. By yourself."

Attempting to head off the imminent explosion, Zantha informed Renny, "I told Allar I would go with you."

Conthar hissed, Allar smirked. Conthar's single word conveyed a wealth of disapproval. "Alone?"

Exchanging glances over Renny's head, Allar told Conthar in a deceptively mild tone, "I already raked Renny over the coals. Your turn."

"Don't you start on me, too. I'm perfectly capable of taking care of myself." Renny faced Conthar, hands on her hips, a sassy three year old, not backing down but instead confronting the monster under the bed.

Taking a breath, preparing to tell Renny exactly what he thought about her going off by herself, before the first word passed Conthar's lips, Renny spun on her heel and stomped off rapidly down the shore.

In the opposite direction from camp.

Exchanging another look with Allar, who simply shrugged, Conthar took off after Renny. One hop and a short, circling glide later, he landed facing his rider. Keeping his wings flared wide so she couldn't pass him on the narrow strand of beach, Conthar begged, "Renny. Listen to me. I know you're used to taking care of yourself and I—we—have complete faith in your abilities. You'd never have survived the things you have otherwise. You are going to have to accept that we care about you. Sometimes it's harder to receive love than to give it. You have so much love inside you that you pour out on us—allow us to do the same for you."

Conthar waited, holding his breath. Their entire future hinged on Renny's response.

Renny stared back, hope and uncertainty vying to outdo each other. "The love I can accept. 'Tis a cage I cannot bear."

Creeping a few steps closer, Conthar crouched and made himself smaller, bringing his body closer to Renny's. "To you, it seems as if they are one and the same, but they are not. You have been so alone all your life. What you see as bars, we see as a means to keep you safe. What you see as restrictions, we see as precautions.

Conthar didn't take his eyes off Renny's face, even when Allar and Zantha joined them.

Hearing Conthar echo what Allar'd already said, Renny tried to see things from their point of view. Two headstrong, overly protective males confronted with an equally headstrong, determinedly independent female. She could see how that was a problem.

A recipe for disaster, more like.

Renny hesitated, not sure how to phrase what she wanted to say. "You two—three," with a nod to Zantha, "want to coddle me, prevent every splinter and skinned knee. If I can't appreciate the cosseting, I do at least acknowledge your concern. It isn't that I'm ungrateful..."

Renny trailed off, frustrated by her inability to put her feelings into words.

Thought about all the times she'd been utterly alone, all the times she'd wished for a family.

For someone to care about her, to care for.

Always she'd been the outsider looking in.

Conthar, Allar, Zantha—they were all trying to draw her in, make her part of their family. Had already accepted Renny as part of their family.

Maybe... Maybe Renny'd been outside so long she didn't know how to come in, even with the door wide open.

Sadness filled her at that thought, constricted her heart until she couldn't breathe. The opportunity she'd waited for all her life —maybe waited too long for.

So long that when she finally was granted her dearest wish, so used to being alone, she couldn't accept what the others were offering.

Didn't know how.

Conthar and Zantha crowded close while Allar wrapped

Renny in his arms and held her as tight as he dared. "Renny, you have to stop being so sad. You're causing all of us, especially yourself, unnecessary pain. We'll get through this together. That's what families do."

Taking a deep breath, Renny tried again to find the words. "I think part of this, a very large part, is I've only known you— known of you—for days. Those days have been…intense, to say the least. All of you have seen my memories so you know me far better than I know you. And the three of you have known each other for a long time. I'm still trying to find out where—if—I fit in your world. You three…just…accept this as if it's the most natural thing in the world."

She halted, her words drying up as she choked.

Rocking her softly, Allar finished for Renny. "This happened so fast, you're afraid to trust it, or us. Trust will come. For right now, just believe we love you."

Smoothing a hand down her back, nuzzling his head against her hair, Allar reiterated, "The rest will come."

Burying her face in his chest, her voice so low and muffled they could barely hear her, Renny's voice hitched. "What if I'm dreaming? I'm so afraid this is all a dream. And what if, when I wake, what if all of you are nothing more than a figment of my starved-for-love imagination? What if that blow to my head knocked something loose and this is merely another happily ever after fantasy of mine?"

A sob escaped her and Renny clutched Allar tighter. "Waking up, probably curled up beside a dead or dying dragon and finding out none of you are real… That I'm back to being alone, chasing down dragons I don't have a prayer of saving…"

Allar wrapped his body around Renny's shuddering form and Conthar and Zantha crowded as close as they could without crushing their humans. "Renny, Renny. We're real, and we're not going away. Most people don't share in an entire lifetime the up and down emotions we've shared in the handful of days since we

met. Just because you keep endangering yourself needlessly…
We're not going to stop loving you, no matter how upset we get.
You're tired and stressed and getting over being grievously
wounded, not to mention finding your dragon and your mate.
That's a tremendous amount of emotional upheaval in a very
short time."

Allar finished smugly, "Besides, if you dreamed me, you'd
dream some wimpy, easily led boy who'd fall at your feet and
hang on your every word. You'd never dream a great warrior
such as myself."

Renny laughed, as he knew she would. "You forgot obstinate,
possessive, over protective, arrogant…"

Allar laughed in turn and kissed Renny soundly before
framing her face in his hands. "Do you know that I have laughed
more in the short time I've known you than I have in…possibly
my entire life?"

Renny stared at him, astonished. "Me too."

Conthar nudged Renny and stated, "My turn."

Renny eyed her dragon from the circle of Allar's arms.
"What? You want to kiss me too?"

Zantha snickered and gently bumped Renny from the other
side. "Renny's warped sense of humor is more than a match for
the two of you."

"No. It is simply my turn to be with you." Conthar sounded
so serious Renny left Allar and moved to Conthar's side.

Puzzled, still not understanding what he meant and more
than a little worried about his state of mind, Renny comforted,
"You are with me. I'm right here."

Puffing up his chest, Conthar dipped his head to Renny. "I
am much recovered, and I promised you."

"Promised me?" Feeling like she'd missed something crucial,
as if she awakened in the middle of an important conversation,
Renny looked at Conthar in confusion. Glanced at Allar and
Zantha for help only to see both of them grinning. Evidently they

hadn't fallen asleep and they were privy to whatever secret Conthar was trying to divulge.

"You have waited long enough. I have waited more than long enough. It's time you learned to be a dragonrider."

Renny said nothing, only stared at Conthar in amazement, his words so far from what she'd feared for him they weren't making sense.

Drawing himself up, Conthar demanded, "Did I not promise you that as soon as I could carry you safely, I would do so? We will try a short flight now and see how it goes. If we are both comfortable with the results, I would be honored to be the one to carry my rider back to Dragon's Haven on the morrow."

Before Renny could fashion a reply or think to protest, Allar grasped her around the waist and lifted her onto Conthar's back. He vaulted onto Zantha and both dragons flexed their wings, taking off simultaneously and flying slowly out over the lake.

Over their private link, Conthar informed Renny, {{*I don't think you will, but just in case you fall, I would rather it be over water. Don't worry, I will not get far from shore, just enough to cushion you should you slip off.*}}

Too delighted, too awed to reply, Renny savored the feeling of riding her dragon—her dragon!!!—for the first time. Riding Zantha had been exhilarating, but Renny had no words for what she was feeling at this moment.

There just...weren't...any words to describe her joy at the smooth play of muscles working beneath her, the quiet shush of wings keeping them aloft, the incredible view.

The swelling in her heart until Renny thought it must surely burst.

Conthar banked slowly left, then right, trying to use as many muscles as possible. Zantha stayed on his wing-tip, mirroring his moves exactly. They flew in lazy circles and figure eights until Conthar was satisfied he'd worked all the kinks out.

Renny's ointment was like magic! As magic as the woman

herself! Delighted and awed at his rapid recovery, knowing exactly who was responsible for his health and his life, Conthar was certain sure he'd be the one to return Renny to Dragon's Haven.

Reluctantly heading back toward the camp, Conthar picked up speed for a moment. Feeling no strain, he flew a little faster and a little faster yet, until he knew the limits of his recovering muscles.

Slowing before he did any damage, Conthar arched his neck. {{*Well, Renny?*}}

Laughter erupted from her, bright and iridescent as bubbles.

Speech might be impossible for her, but Renny's joy radiated around the foursome like light from a sun-struck prism.

Circling the camp once, Conthar trumpeted loudly and eased down for a perfect landing to the resounding cheers of riders and dragons.

Landing amid the wild cheers, Renny's face was luminous, her eyes shining. Unable to form coherent thoughts, speech still evading her capabilities, Renny grinned.

Unwilling to lose contact with Conthar after she dismounted, Renny kept running her hands over him, finally settling between his front legs. Leaving her with Conthar to enjoy their newfound closeness, Allar drifted off for awhile.

Bringing food, dropping beside Renny, Allar matched her grin. "I looked and felt the same after my first ride with Zantha. Of course, you had the same awed look on your face at the waterfall after I…"

Laughing, looping an arm over Renny's shoulders, Allar pulled her close.

Making no protest, leaning her head on his shoulder, Renny sighed in contentment and fell asleep in the space between breathing in and breathing out.

CHAPTER 17

*I*f Renny thought the warriors and their dragons made a racket, it was nothing compared to her reception at Dragon's Haven.

Almost home, flying in tight formation, Allar at last allowed word of their triumphant return to be spread among the inhabitants and dragons. People and dragons poured out of the keep, lining the battlements and walkways, filling the courtyards and the skies, the roar deafening.

Conthar had returned—alive!—and with a rider!

A rider who also happened to be a Dragonhealer!

Allar had found his mate!

The best part being—all three were one and the same!

Days later, finished with his duties for the day, Allar found Renny right where he knew she'd be—right where he'd left her hours and hours ago, in the large courtyard in front of the dragons' caves. Conthar and Zantha flanked her.

Allar had spent a great deal of his mornings ordering a new wardrobe for Renny. Remembering with perfect clarity the look of rapture on Renny's face at the soft shirt he'd given her in

Zantha's cave, he specified her clothes be made of the softest, finest materials.

Underthings, comfortable tunics and pants, shirts and warm cloaks, a ceremony dress—with a split skirt—in vivid green to match Renny's exquisite eyes.

The four of them hadn't spent much time apart since their return, other than what time Allar'd allocated to his duties. All of them had, in fact, been spending nights together in Zantha's roomy den.

Time for that to stop. Allar was eager to spend some time alone with Renny, to finish what they'd started at the waterfall. Renny should be healed enough by now.

Allar would make sure she was. He wasn't about to risk Renny now, just because he'd been in a state of semi-arousal since he'd laid eyes on her.

He smiled as he saw first Bena, and then Sher, along with a couple more of the younger healers scurrying to do Renny's bidding. Bena and Sher had practically begged Renny to continue helping her with the dragons.

Securing Seon's permission, they and several others ate, slept, and dreamed Renny.

In a purely healing dragons, techniques and meds sort of way.

Techniques and remedies Renny gladly shared, as willing to teach as they were to learn.

Once word had gotten out of a Dragonhealer at Dragon's Haven, people and dragons had been showing up in droves, hoping for a moment of Renny's time and skills.

Renny diagnosed problems, and under her tutelage the healers went to work rubbing in ointments, dispensing herbs, making medicines. They'd never have Renny's innate ability with the dragons, but from the look of things, she was going to need all the help she could get.

The courtyard full of dragons, the ramparts fairly groaned under the weight of more. The sky stayed dark with circling dragons, like flocks of birds weaving and darting in complicated patterns, looking for a spot in the crowded meadows outside the keep wall.

Stopping beside Voya, Allar shook his head in amazement. "I had no idea there were this many dragons left in all the world."

Voya raised his brows in awed wonder. "Worlds, you mean. I doubt all these are locals, and legend has it the dragons came here from…elsewhere."

"Nothing yet?" Allar was beginning to hate that question and dread the answer.

Voya snorted, both knowing full well if there'd been any word on the traitors, Allar would've been among the first to know. "Unless you count the fights between the nearly wild dragons and anyone who gets close to them, nothing. Word of Renny has drawn even them in. They just arrived."

Tipping his chin, Voya indicated a tight cluster of dragons off to one side, a rough and motley looking crew.

The keep dragons, shiny and well fed, kept a wide berth around the scruffy, tattered, scarred and lean to the point of gauntness wild ones. The wild ones reminded Allar of the feral cats who haunted the streets of Lakeside, unused to any kindness, battle scarred from fighting for every morsel of food they could scrounge.

Voya sighed in frustration. "'Twould take more than one army to keep Lady Renny safe. I much prefer a known enemy to what we're facing here. All these strange dragons in and out, coming and going, getting so close to her—it's a security nightmare."

Agreeing completely, Allar clapped Voya on the shoulder. "If we forbid them entrance, Renny will no doubt go to them. That would be a true nightmare. As long as Renny is within the walls of Dragon's Haven, we have enough men and dragons to surround her. Outside… Thank you, my friend. You've done an excellent job of watching over her when I have to be elsewhere."

Voya snorted in amusement. "Lady Renny has already asked me at least a dozen times why, since I am your second, I seem to have nothing better to do than gawk at her when I should be helping you. She's not going to be very pleased when she realizes I am helping you. You might better tell her before she takes enough time away from her dragons and figures it out. She's liable to take a strip out of both our hides."

Grinning and whistling, Voya strolled off to take care of his other duties.

Conthar and Zantha, planted on either side of Renny like statues at the gateway to a sacred temple, were screening the humans as well as the dragons. Each powerful in their own right, the three of them together were a force to be reckoned with. Something about combining their talents…

So far, everyone was who they claimed to be with no motives other than to meet the Dragonhealer face to face.

There were just so many of them…

Allar could feel Conthar's and Zantha's weariness beating at him from another long day of reviewing supplicants.

If they were tired, Renny had to be exhausted. She'd barely slowed since first light, only stopping when someone else insisted she eat. Doing the same for days, standing in the same place, doing the same things over and over, and still… Renny greeted each dragon and human with a smile, a hug when the humans needed it, caresses and pats for the dragons, medicines and and advice where needed.

All the while Renny kept the healers in training scrambling to follow her orders until they fairly drooped. A tough taskmaster, but the healers loved every minute of it.

Watching Renny deal with the latest pair, human and dragon, before anyone else could approach, Allar stepped in and held up his hands, palms out. "That's all for today. Dragonhealer Renny will be back tomorrow. Thank you."

Renny didn't protest Allar's highhanded tactics this time. She simply sighed, washed her hands in the basin set there for that purpose, twined her fingers with his and let him lead her away. Leaning into him, she stifled a yawn. "Thank you. I could tell Conthar and Zantha and the healers were getting tired but I didn't want to say anything and embarrass them."

Prepared for a fight, Allar turned to Renny in surprise. Seeing the glint of mischief in her eyes, he let go her hand, wrapped an arm around her shoulders and pulled her close. Dropping a kiss on the top of Renny's head, he informed her, "We're staying in my quarters tonight, sleeping in my bed."

Renny started to pull away when Allar drawled, "Wouldn't want to embarrass Zantha and Conthar now, would we? They need some time alone, too."

At Allar's too innocent smile, Renny burst out laughing. "I was right. You're totally incorrigible."

"You're about to see how truly incorrigible I can be." Scooping her up, Allar kissed and nuzzled Renny all the way to his chambers. Her weariness beat at him and he could hear her stomach growling non-stop.

Good thing he'd already ordered a bath and food.

Opening his door one-handed, he kicked it shut behind them.

Renny looked around curiously. Very familiar now with the Healing Hall and the dragons' caves and their courtyard, not nearly as familiar with the kitchens as she'd like, this was the first time she'd made it this far into the personal areas of the keep.

This room was definitely Allar's. Heavy dark wood, and big. Every stick of furniture was built to accommodate Allar's size. The bed looked as large as a dragon, and the desk and the table and chair and… All had been built to match.

Renny burst out laughing. "I feel like I just stepped into a giant's room."

Wrapped her arms tighter around Allar's neck as he spun her in circles and growled. "You know what giants do to women they catch in their castles, don't you?"

A knock at the door interrupted their silliness.

Ignoring the knock for a moment, Allar resumed. "They eat them!" Making slurping sounds, he pretended to devour Renny.

Plopping Renny in a massive chair in front of the fireplace, Allar gave her a quick kiss and a hearty admonition. "Do not go to sleep!"

Opened the door to delicious smelling food. Tons of it.

Renny's eyes widened in amazement as the servants moved a table next to the chair and began placing dish after dish on it. Made a mental note to make time tomorrow to find the kitchen and personally thank the cook.

Looking at Allar, Renny managed to hold her laughter until the servants departed. The door closed and her delighted laughter pealed out until it filled every corner of the huge chamber.

Holding her sides, Renny gasped, "If I eat all that, I'll be as big as your bed!"

Allar's pitiful sounding rejoinder, "I was hoping you'd save a little for me," had Renny dissolving into merriment again.

Picking Renny up and settling back into the chair with her in his lap, Allar began picking through the delicious array. Batting her hand away when she reached for the food, refusing to let Renny touch any of it, he slipped morsels and tidbits into her mouth, kissing her between each bite.

Noticing Renny was thirsty, instead of handing her the cup, Allar took a sip and kissed her, letting the cool, sweet liquid trickle from his mouth into hers.

The next knock got nothing more from Allar than a gruff call to enter. Face flaming, Renny watched from her perch in Allar's lap as servant after servant came in. First with a huge tub, then bucket upon bucket of hot water.

Placing the tub in front of the fireplace, they erected a large screen painted with scenes of dragons and riders. Something else she'd have to examine in detail. Later.

Waiting until they were alone once more, Renny snickered. "Wouldn't it've been much easier to fly back to the waterfall?"

Allar vowed, "We will do that, too, My Lady, and I know where many others are located. We can try any or all of them. While I will never look at a waterfall the same way ever again, for tonight, I want you here. In my chamber, in my arms."

Allar's voice dropped into the smoky sultriness Renny recalled from waking up in his arms the first time.

Suppressing a shiver, she'd thought then he sounded like warm fires and long nights on soft furs. She'd thought exactly right.

Allar offered Renny another morsel from the still laden to the point of groaning table, which she reluctantly refused. "My compliments to your cook, but if I eat any more, I'm going to pop."

Smacking his lips in satisfaction, Allar motioned to the steaming tub. "Bath time, then."

Holding Renny in place with one strong arm banded around her, Allar tugged off her boots. Not letting her do anything for herself, he stood her between his legs and began to slowly undress his mate.

Reaching up beneath her tunic, Allar shaped her waist and hips with his hands, then slowly unfastened her leggings and dragged them down. Clasping one of her hands, he urged Renny to step out of them.

Bending, he ran his hands from her ankles, up over her calves and thighs, back to her hips. Not stopping there, he continued running his hands up her body, under her loose fitting tunic.

Cupping a breast in each hand, he rubbed his thumbs over her nipples until they were hard peaks. Withdrawing his hands, he grasped one sleeve and pulled an arm free before repeating the gesture on the other side.

Lifting the tunic over her head, he dropped it on the floor.

Keeping hold of one hand in case she decided to bolt, Allar leaned back in his chair and admired the view.

Fidgeting, starting to fret, Renny stilled at the male look of pure adulation on Allar's face.

He looked her up and down, the firelight delineating every soft curve and angle, gilding Renny, limning her so she appeared less substantial than a half remembered dream.

Motioning with his free hand, Allar waved her to turn in a circle.

She did so by slow increments, not sure what he was looking for, or at.

Upon completing her circle, Allar leaned forward with a groan. Wrapping his arms around her, he buried his face in the softness of her belly.

Renny hesitantly put her arms around his head and cradled him to her.

Breathing deep, having ascertained Renny bore no bruises or open wounds that would impede his plans, Allar turned his head to one side and just breathed in her warm woman scent. "Do you have any idea what it means to me to have you here like this?"

Not knowing what answer he was seeking, Renny held her peace. Shifting a little, she held Allar with one arm and stroked the fingers of her other hand through his hair in long, comforting sweeps. Raking her nails across his scalp, she could feel some of the tension he wore like a second skin easing out of him.

Going down on her knees, Renny cradled Allar's face between her hands. "I know what it means to me to be here."

Allar's gaze was hot, his voice husky. "You know there've been other women. I don't deny that. You are the only one who has ever been in my chambers, the only one that ever will be. The only one I've ever wanted to bring here."

Leaning into Allar, Renny kissed him as he'd taught her. Twining her arms around his neck, she put everything she was feeling into that kiss. Somewhere, amid all the kissing, Renny ended up in Allar's arms again.

The next thing she knew, she was being held against Allar with her feet dangling over the tub.

Letting Renny slide slowly down his body into the water, making sure it wasn't too hot, Allar urged her to sit. Taking a few steps, he went down on one knee to open a trunk.

Rummaging for a moment, finding what he sought, Allar turned to Renny with a wicked grin on his face. Kneeling beside the tub, he leaned in and kissed Renny thoroughly before letting her see what he held.

A bar, an actual bar of soap this time instead of soapweed. A bar that smelled like Allar, some concoction of woods and water and sunshine.

Renny grinned back. "Time for another lesson?"

"Aye." Already rubbing the soap into a lather, Allar proceeded to wash every nook and cranny, even washed Renny's hair as he'd done at the waterfall.

By the time he finished, Renny felt like a piece of used soapweed—limp and totally useless.

So relaxed she could barely keep her head above the rim of the tub, Renny didn't lift a finger as Allar scooped her up and stood her on her feet. Letting Renny lean all her weight against him, Allar dried what he could reach with a soft bath sheet, warmed by the heat of the fire.

Rousing a bit when Allar scooped her up again and laid her on the bed, on soft furs that caressed her sensitized skin, coming up on an elbow, Renny looked at him quizzically. "What are you doing, Allar? It's your turn. Or mine, whichever way you want to look at it."

Allar shook his head, dark eyes intent on her form. "Tonight's all for you."

Smothering Renny's half-hearted protest with kisses, Allar rolled her to her stomach. "Just relax and enjoy."

Choking on a laugh, Renny complied. "If I relax any more, I'll be a puddle."

Renny truly hadn't thought it possible to get any more mellow than she already was but Allar proved her wrong. Stroking, rubbing kneading, he massaged all her tired muscles until Renny felt so boneless she couldn't have moved if the bed caught on fire.

From the soles of her feet to the top of her head, Allar touched every muscle and nerve. That was just the backside.

Then he rolled her over and proceeded to give her frontside the same thorough treatment.

Tingling so much all over, it took Renny a bit to realize Allar wasn't touching her anymore.

Opening her eyes required too much effort. Slitting them a crack, Renny just could see the outline of Allar taking off his clothes.

Scooping her up once more, pulling back the furs with one hand, Allar put her in bed, climbed in after her and snugged Renny tight against his heat.

Tucking Renny close to his side, her head on his shoulder, Allar pulled the furs up and relaxed his whole body.

"Sleep, little love. Just go to sleep. We'll finish this another time when you aren't so tired."

Renny's drowsy murmur was barely audible. "But what about you?"

Allar gave a short bark of laughter. "You, my love, are exhausted. This is the longest I've seen you still since we arrived at the site of Conthar's supposed demise. I can wait. I want you, but I want you awake and participating."

An unintelligible murmur, and Renny went limp.

HIS MATE WAS GOING to be the death of him. Allar lay beside

Renny all night, his body hard and throbbing and demanding completion. He'd never wanted a woman as much as he wanted the small bundle in his arms. Gritting his teeth and shifting restlessly, he tried to think of something else. Anything else.

No matter what he thought of, everything circled back to Renny.

Dragons—he thought of Renny.

Finding out who was responsible—Renny.

Food! No dice. All he could see was Renny's thin form, and her enjoyment at the smallest hint of food.

The grand feast to be held in honor of... Renny. The one honoring her as a Dragonhealer and his mate and Conthar's rider.

Their official bonding ceremony, to be held at the feast.

The gown he'd commissioned for Renny.

He'd told her about the feast and the gown. She'd shrugged and nodded, too absorbed in caring for her dragons.

Allar chuckled to himself. Most women would be planning their ceremony down to the last detail. He doubted Renny had spared so much as a single thought to any of it.

If it didn't involve dragons, Renny couldn't care less.

So where did that leave him?

All of that put him right where he wanted to be—in his chambers, in his bed, with his woman in his arms.

That finally calmed Allar. Taking advantage of Renny's unusual stillness, he spent the time rubbing his hands up and down, gliding over every curve, every dip and hollow and swell.

Just before first light, Allar managed to relax enough to drift off. Having the most erotic dream—about Renny!—feeling her stir, Allar tightened his arms. Eyes shut, he rumbled, "Where do you think you're going?"

Taking him by complete surprise, Renny leaned up on an elbow and kissed Allar fiercely, running her free hand all over his chest—and lower.

Catching her roving hand before she found what she was seeking, wide awake now, Allar rasped, "What…"

The rest of whatever he'd been about to say was cut off as Renny came to life. Squirming in his arms, she straddled him, wiggling to find a comfortable position.

Allar's hands immediately latched onto Renny's hips, gripping her and holding her still when all he wanted to do was encourage her to move. His own hips were straining desperately to arch into her while he strained just as hard not to.

Renny laughed, a deep, throaty sound and leaned forward to kiss him, running both hands all over the topography of his chest.

Sweating, breathing like he'd been in a battle, he couldn't hold her hips and her hands at the same time…

"You said, when I was awake. I definitely remember that, and I'm definitely awake now. Why are you fighting me?" Voice a teasing purr, Renny stretched against him. "Besides. I might've been asleep, but I felt you all night, rubbing and stroking me. I had the most interesting dreams. So? What are you waiting for? Make my dreams come true."

Why was he fighting Renny's advances?

Allar couldn't remember anything past the sexual haze Renny was creating. He wanted to… Had to make sure… Didn't want to hurt her.

Slow.

Slow down.

Impossible with his body raging at him, with her small hands setting his skin on fire everywhere she touched him, her soft breasts dangling in front of him, then pressing into his chest.

Growling, in one swift move he reversed their positions. Catching both Renny's hands in one of his and stretching her arms over her head, knowing if she touched him he would lose his tenuous control, he pinned her hips with his own.

Just short of thrusting into Renny, he froze.

Holding himself taut, eyes closed, Allar swallowed repeatedly.

Tried to remember how to breathe.

Opening his eyes, Allar looked into Renny's trusting gaze. Forced the words out. "I don't want to hurt you. You're so damned small."

Accusing, as if Renny'd deliberately chosen to be small just to thwart him.

Renny met his burning gaze solemnly. "I trust you."

With those simple words, whether she knew it or not, Renny handed Allar her heart.

Her belief leashed his lust, enabled him to regain control.

He'd felt her moist heat sear his shaft when she straddled him, but he was going to make damn sure Renny was ready.

Rocking into her hips gently, rhythmically, Allar nuzzled the soft spot behind her ear, worked his way along her jaw line until he found her lips. Trailed down the other side of her neck and slid down so his face was between her sweet breasts.

Molding one with his hand, he lavished attention on the other with teeth and tongue. Switching sides, he repeated the gestures. Nipping lightly and suckling harder, he teased first one and then the other to stiff peaks.

Renny was writhing beneath him, panting and making soft moaning sounds that pleased him to no end. Slipping his hand between them, sliding his fingers through her moist curls into wet heat pushed his control to the limit. Settling the head of his shaft against her welcoming entrance, Allar pushed just a little and stopped.

Commanded, "Renny. Open your eyes and look at me."

He wanted to see as well as feel the first time, that first joining.

Wanted to see the need and the fulfillment.

Wanted to watch Renny's eyes glaze over with passion, watch the emerald splinter and fracture as she found her pleasure and they became true mates.

Drifting in an erotic haze, enjoying what Allar was doing,

Renny vaguely heard his whispered instructions, his praises and compliments. Her body wasn't hers anymore, responding instead to Allar's every whim.

Straining toward him, on fire with new sensations, reaching for...

Renny didn't know what she wanted or how to get it—but Allar did.

She became aware of the cessation of movement on his part, and then heard Allar's urgently repeated command.

"Renny. Open your eyes."

Incrementally, feeling as if a dragon was sitting on each eyelid, Renny forced her eyes open. Allar's gaze was as hot as the rest of him. She tugged at her hands, wanting to touch him, but he still refused to let go.

He wanted her like this, open to him, wanted this to last long enough to pleasure her as well as himself. It would never happen if those clever hands of Renny's stroked their magic over his skin.

Just the thought made Allar tighten his jaw and clench his teeth. Renny's hands on him—that he would savor another time.

Holding Renny's gaze, his heart in his eyes, Allar said, "This is going to hurt some. I, for obvious reasons, do not know how much. You are small and I... I will be as easy as I can. Seon's medicines and time have done a great deal to heal you but you must let me know if any of this is too much for your old wounds."

Totally bemused, straining uselessly against his hold on her hands, wanting to caress his face and remove the fierce frown of concentration from his handsome features, Renny gave in. "The only thing that hurts right now is the ache I feel because you aren't moving."

Renny wiggled herself closer to Allar's hard heat.

Allar looked so solemn, Renny couldn't help but tease. "If I said you were hurting me, you would truly stop?"

Tearing his gaze off Renny's face long enough to look down

between the length of their almost joined bodies, Allar pulled away a smidge. Shifting his eyes back to her face, catching the grin in her eyes, he knew she was playing him.

Two could play this game.

Remaining where he was, Allar used his free hand to stroke all of Renny's body he could reach.

Starting with her captive hands, he traced each finger and the palms of her hands, smoothed his fingers down first one arm and then the other. Lingered on the sensitive spots at wrist and elbow, the backs of her arms, the ticklish spots of her underarms, the outside curve of her breasts.

Allar traced Renny's collarbone, her jaw line, brushed his thumb over her cheekbones and brows, ran a finger lightly down the middle of her breastbone to her belly button.

All the while, the tip of him was throbbing just inside her, doing nothing to ease her ache but setting off a chain reaction of ripples and tremors that raged throughout her body.

Making Renny feel as if her heart was centered between her legs.

Renny wasn't sorry she'd started this, but she wished Allar would finish. Turning her head to the side, unable to take anymore, Renny panted, "I give. I give! If I feel any pain, I'll let you know. Please…"

"Open your eyes, my love."

Barely able to comply, Renny tried to focus.

Blue. All she could see was the intense blue of Allar's eyes.

A glint of emerald, then as Renny's eyes opened wider, a smug smile lit Allar's features.

Her beautiful eyes, normally as bright as the gems they resembled, were cloudy with desire. Slowly, slowly they focused until Allar was sure Renny could see him.

Locking eyes, pushing bit by bit, he stretched her, entering a little deeper with each rocking thrust.

Renny's eyes widened, blinked, widened more.

Allar paused, making certain it was caused by wonder and not pain. Murmuring soft words of encouragement, he eased in farther, never taking his eyes off hers until he was completely sheathed.

Resting his forehead against hers, he rocked his hips gently when his body was demanding he thrust hard and deep. Taking a breath, Allar looked into Renny's eyes once more.

Renny felt no pain, only extreme fullness and…wanting. "Allar, this feels really good, but I know there is more. Stop holding back. I am not some fragile doll that will break if you touch it. Show me how to please you."

Allar complied with a groan. Drawing almost completely out, he drove back in, over and over. Renny was so hot and tight and wet.

Pushing into her was like nothing he'd ever experienced.

Renny struggled to meet each thrust, trying to free her hands and hips so she could touch him, reciprocate.

Allar kept control, holding onto his by a thread, trying to prolong this until Renny found release.

Renny might not be able to move, darn him, but all the running she'd done had given her excellent muscle tone. Waiting until Allar thrust again, when he began to withdraw, she contracted her internal muscles.

Hard.

Sucking in a breath, Allar threw his head back, gritted his teeth. Tried to think of icy mountain streams, of fire-thorn, of battle wounds. Of Seon's foul potions.

None of it helped.

With a great shout and a shuddering groan, Allar spent himself.

Collapsing to one side of Renny, face down, bodies still fused, he draped an arm over her to keep her close.

Renny snuggled. Hands free at last, she caressed every part of

Allar she could reach. "That was…nice. You said it would hurt, but it didn't. When can we do it again?"

Voice muffled, Allar bit out. "If *someone* hadn't been so impatient, I'd've lasted longer and I assure you, it would've been much better for you than *nice*."

Renny laughed at his growling, her laughter contracting her muscles and inadvertently squeezing Allar's *that* again. "You seem to have enjoyed it immensely. That's enough."

Turning his head and opening his eyes so he could see her, Allar growled. Told her slowly and distinctly, "No, it is not enough."

Rolling them over, still joined, so Renny straddled him, Allar laced his hands behind his head and smirked. "Your turn."

He was going to lie still and let Renny set the pace, find her rhythm this time if it killed him. And it just might.

Allar began swelling inside her so she moved experimentally.

Bodies and body parts already slick were enhanced by the shared fluids they'd exchanged.

Renny sat up, bracing her hands against Allar's wide shoulders.

Wiggled her hips, shifted side to side, slid up and down.

Discovered quickly that sliding up and down his shaft while tightening her internal muscles at the appropriate time garnered the best results. Being on top was a whole different dragon race.

More movement, more control, and it put Allar inside her at a completely different angle. Absorbed in her learning, Renny moved fast, slow, whatever pleased her as she learned this new dance her body was teaching her.

Head tilted down so she could watch their joined bodies moving against each other, when she finally looked back up at Allar, his face was a taut mask of control.

Leaning forward, Renny pressed herself against his chest and peppered his face with kisses. Purred, "I like this much better."

Another growl. "I'm sure you do."

Laughing, sitting all the way up, Renny trailed her hands down Allar's rippled stomach.

Woohoo! This was way better! Renny flexed and rose slightly on her knees, tightening around him as she did so. Her body felt strange, not her own.

Hot, as if she balanced on the brink of some great discovery.

"Allar?" She looked to him questioningly.

Unsure if he'd survive her sweet torment, he encouraged, "You're doing fine, little love. Just fine. Just don't stop."

Renny squirmed, trying to reach... She didn't know what. Looking at Allar with beseeching eyes, Renny begged, "Do something. Put your hands on me. I can't stand this. I want... I need... I don't know..."

Allar grinned hugely. "I thought you'd never ask."

Gripping Renny's hips, Allar surged up into her, hard, over and over. Sliding his hands around and grasping her sweet cheeks, massaging them, running his hands up and down her back, Allar encouraged Renny with words and touches.

She was panting in earnest now, on the brink, eyes dark with her desire. Holding her down as he pushed up, Allar felt the first ripples of her desire as she looked at him in bewilderment.

"Relax, my Renny. Let it happen."

Renny exploded around him. All those years of living in the mountains, trekking up and downhill had given Renny wonderful muscles and all those deliciously tight muscles wrapped around Allar, squeezing and milking until he exploded too.

Renny collapsed on his chest, their breaths coming harsh and ragged. Each breath setting off aftershocks that echoed back and forth between them until Renny suddenly, unexpectedly, came again. She buried her face in Allarr's neck and rode it out, shuddering, caught between laughing and sobbing.

He stroked his hands up and down her back, slowly, soothingly, wrapped his arms tight around her, crooned softly to her. Words of love, of praise.

They lay unmoving, completely sated, utterly wrung out.

Incapable of movement, Renny hadn't been this tired when she crawled out of the Great Lake after her long swim.

Still trembling with aftershocks, their breathing somewhat less harsh, Allar heard Renny snicker.

{{*That was definitely much better than nice.*}}

Allar's smug {{*Told you so*}} resonated from his mind to hers before he could think about it.

Allar froze.

Renny hadn't so much as twitched and he definitely hadn't spoken.

She hadn't said a word! He'd heard her thoughts and responded.

As if…they were dragons and not humans.

Renny sprawled across his chest, unmoving, limp as a rag doll, his hands on her satiny skin.

He had to be mistaken. Mates couldn't hear each other, not like dragons could.

Could they?

He'd thought he'd heard her before, while she was healing Conthar, but that'd been because of Zantha and the other dragons.

Hadn't it?

Mentally shaking his head, Allar reminded himself.

With Renny, anything was possible.

{{*Renny?*}}

{{*Hmmm?*}}

{{*We're speaking mind to mind, not out loud.*}}

{{*So?*}}

Allar caught Renny's unquestioning acceptance, then undertones of unease, echoes of past hurts and oft repeated insults.

Freak.

Devil-child.

Witch.

Those and worse.

Appalled, Allar strove to calm Renny, wished he could wring the necks of everyone who'd been cruel to her.

{{*I must admit, 'tis a shock, but a most welcome one. Look into my mind, Renny, and see what a treasure I think—know—you are.*}}

Quiet for a moment, Renny snorted a laugh. {{*You must be thinking of some other woman, I'm not like that. Wait. Is that truly how you see me?*}}

{{*I assure you, the only woman in my mind is you. As for the rest, you are, and it is.*}}

Renny's sense of humor burst into blossom. {{*This could be handy if you ever think of cheating.*}}

{{*That could work both ways.*}}

At that, Renny laughed out loud and found the strength to roll off Allar. Struggling to her feet, she staggered to the tub.

Curious, Allar rolled to his side and watched. "What are you doing? The water is long since cold."

Renny threw a fulminating look over her shoulder. "What does it look like I'm doing? I'm going to wash. There's no way I'm going to treat dragons smelling of what we just did. Besides, I promised the wild dragons they'd be first in line today, and they're edgy enough as it is. Not like everyone won't know anyway." Still muttering, Renny picked up the cloth and soap.

Rolling off the bed and tottering to Renny's side, Allar snatched both away from her. Told her quietly, "'Tis my privilege to wash you on this first morning after. If you give me a moment, I'll call for hot water."

Renny taunted, "Afraid of a little cold water, are we?" Laughter pealing out at the pained expression on Allar's face, goading him, she taunted, "I'm kind of in a hurry here. Get on with it."

More laughter rang and echoed as Allar chased her around

the tub, then the chamber, amid many touches and hugs and kisses.

Allar would never get enough of skin to skin contact with Renny, and she had a lifetime of neglect to be compensated for.

They ended up calling for hot water as well as food.

Renny—meticulously washed, well fed, decently clothed, and thoroughly loved—cocked her head to look at Allar. Suddenly serious, she said, "I have a request."

Allar dipped his head to Renny, elated she finally trusted him enough to ask for something. "Anything that is within my power to grant, you may have."

His past experience with morning after requests ran to jewels and baubles, sometimes favors. Having no idea what Renny would ask for—a Healing Hall for the dragons, permanent residence for all the dragons camping out in and around the keep?—Allar was floored by her simple request.

"I would like to meet your cook. I know she's busy now with the morning repast, probably already started on the nooning meal, but later, this afternoon perhaps, when the kitchen isn't so hectic. I should like to thank her."

Allar could only stare, poleaxed. Any other woman would've asked for the world, Renny just wanted to thank his cook.

He'd've given her the moon on a chain for a pendant with bracelets of stars, and she wanted to meet the keep's cook.

Allar couldn't help himself. He burst into laughter.

Catching Renny up in his arms, he spun them in circles and kissed her until they were both breathlessly dizzy.

TRUE TO HER WORD, Renny treated the nearly wild dragons first.

Leftovers from the wars, refugees from destroyed keeps and human populations, most of them were like her.

Young dragons, orphans, surveying as best they could.

Eggs and baby dragons hidden in the wilds in hopes they might survive on their own, forgotten when their parents were killed.

And perhaps, just perhaps, as Voya had suggested, other worlds—now that it was common knowledge Dragon's Haven once more had a Dragonhealer. How they'd gotten word of her was a mystery for the ages.

While any keeps would've taken in the orphan dragons, and gladly, the wild ones had ended up so far from civilization and were so distrustful of humans, they were wary of any contact, preferring to stick to what they knew.

Without riders or even minimal human contact, the wild ones were infested with parasites, covered with raw wounds that were easily treatable—by humans.

Forbidding anyone else to come near—rightly afraid the wild ones would bolt—Renny spoke first to one, then another as she treated them. Scolded them gently, {{*Silly dragons, how do you expect to get help or find riders if you don't trust any humans or even other dragons?*}}

All of them tried to talk at once and their unexpected replies had Renny bellowing silently for Allar, as well as Conthar and Zantha. {{*Stay where you are, but listen.*}}

Opening her mind and propping the door open so she wouldn't absentmindedly forget and let it close, Renny continued questioning the wild ones while she treated them.

Living on the fringes, normally they didn't have much contact with each other, much less anyone else. A few of them had formed uneasy truces and small bands, hoping to stay alive.

They all told Renny tales, horrible tales, of traps and tortures and dead dragons.

Of dragons betrayed by humans and dragons alike.

The wild ones, with no one to protect or defend them, had been targeted far more than their tamer counterparts.

No wonder they were so skittish. They hadn't known whom

they could trust, any more than Renny had, so they avoided everyone.

Unable to pinpoint any specific locations because they came from such vastly differing areas, Renny kept questioning, hoping to find a common thread.

Opened her mind to them, letting them see what she'd seen.

Obviously terrified, it took a great deal of persuading and sweet talking on Renny's part to get the wild ones to admit to anything.

They, too, had seen the no-color. Didn't know where the dragon or rider came from.

Renny worked on the wild ones most of the day, only stopping when they'd all been treated and questioned and reassured. Urging them to be on their best behavior, asking Conthar and Zantha to befriend the wild ones, she quit for the day.

Allar shook his head in bemusement as Renny promised them all places at Dragon's Haven, at least until the torturers were caught. She had no idea of the logistics of housing and feeding so many additional dragons, but he had no doubt she'd go live in the wilds with them before turning a single one away.

Neither was an option.

Allar would add on to the keep and the quantity of herd beasts as much as he needed to in order to ensure Renny's happiness and safety. He understood, even if Renny didn't, why she loved all dragons but empathized so deeply with these particular outcasts.

Spotting Allar, Renny walked to him, pride in her accomplishments vying with weariness. She leaned against him, leaned into him, wrapped her arms around his waist and just absorbed.

His scent. His strength.

Allar wrapped her in his hold and let her, knowing she needed his strength whether she'd admit it or not. Started to press a kiss to the top of Renny's head and thought better of it as he examined—not too closely—what looked to be dragon snot.

Squeezed his love and switched gears. "I promised you a trip to the kitchen to meet the cook. Do you feel up to it or would you rather…"

Tilting her head so she looked Allar in the face, Renny grinned. "I need to wash up first. I may not have met her yet, but if she's like others of her kind, she'll kill me if I drag all this filth into her kitchen. What's her name? I can't very well call her cook."

Allar grinned back. "Yes you can."

Taking a step back, Renny ruffled up like a wet setting cluckity. "I most certainly will not. It's rude and disrespectful not to call the help by name. They are a most important part of any keep, especially the cook."

Grinning wider as Renny all but stamped a foot, Allar preempted the rest of her tirade. Dragons in flight, but he loved to rile her! It was worth it, just to see her eyes flash with temper and her body go all ready to fight.

Cupping Renny's nape, holding her in place, Allar's voice dropped into that sexy tone he only ever used with her. "Do you know that when you are defending someone, you light up? I keep expecting green sparks to come out of your eyes."

Renny eyed him warily, sensing a joke. Trusting Allar, and yet, she'd been the butt of enough jokes to last her several lifetimes.

Massaging, soothing, Allar nodded. "I agree with you on all counts. Have you heard any of the help here complain?"

Renny shook her head, still far too tense.

Allar sighed. "It's perfectly alright to call her Cook because that's truly her name. Mistress Cook, if you intend to be formal, but I have to warn you, she takes offense at it. Cook is her badge of honor and you will insult her if you call her anything else."

Blinking, clearly embarrassed, Renny relaxed under Allar's

expert ministrations. "My apologies." Hastily changed the subject. "I still need to bathe."

Allar cupped Renny's cheek. "No need to feel embarrassed, and it's never necessary to apologize for defending those under your protection."

Slinging an arm around Renny and tucking her close, Allar steered Renny toward Zantha's, and Conthar's, cave.

Retrieving a set of clothes from the storage niche while Renny submersed herself in the waiting tub and he tried not to watch, Allar tried not to think about Renny naked.

Renny and soapy water.

Renny defending Cook, sight unseen.

All of which made his heart—and other things—swell.

Mind on the upcoming meeting, Renny bathed quickly, totally oblivious to Allar's libidinous thoughts. Just as quickly donned clean clothes, leaving the blood and dirt stained ones at the door of the cave to be taken to the laundress.

Suppressing a grin, along with thoughts of Renny naked and in his arms, Allar shook his head. He'd had a fight on his hands the first time he instructed Renny to leave her dirty clothes in a pile.

She hadn't backed down until Allar informed her a laundress with no laundry to wash was useless, and therefore unneeded.

Giving in grudgingly, Renny had started to berate him about having so many clothes made for her.

Allar'd merely raised a brow and waited.

Renny got the message and clamped her mouth shut.

Sparks were truly going to fly when she saw just how many clothes had really been made for her. So far, she'd seen nothing but a few pairs of leggings, a handful of shirts.

She'd accepted them gratefully without asking for anything else, had yet to open the wardrobe where most of her clothes were stored.

Allar snorted in aggravation. Renny thought the pitiful few items she'd seen was far too much.

Smoothed his face as she came out from behind the screen and caught her hand in his.

Renny had a general idea where the kitchens were, but this would be her first visit. Unusual for her, she always made the kitchen one of her top priorities, right behind escape routes and bolt holes.

In her defense, she'd gotten kinda sidetracked this go round.

Approaching the kitchen, inhaling the delicious odors wafting their way, Allar doubted if Renny had any idea how tightly she was gripping his hand.

Hoping to calm her, Allar soothed, "'Tis no grand lady we're meeting, merely Cook. She will adore you in person more than she already adores what she's heard about you."

Rolling her eyes, Renny tried to snatch her hand out of Allar's. He acted as if he didn't notice. Either gesture.

Curled her lip. "Rank means little to me. Useful skills have far more merit than titles."

Allar silently filled in what Renny left unsaid. Cooking was at the top of Renny's list of useful skills.

Made perfect sense, when you knew her background.

They entered the spacious main kitchen, hand in hand. Normally a beehive of activity, things had slowed for the day. Morning and nooning were over, and most people only ate a light meal before settling into their evening activities.

Eyeing the large, rotund woman with her back to them, Renny stopped just inside the door and let out a relieved breath. She knew better than to trust a skinny cook.

A small girl-child, perhaps four summers, tugged on Cook's skirts to get her attention and pointed at Renny. "I know you. You're JusRenny."

Renny nodded but didn't move any closer, as if she'd be thrown out if she entered without permission.

Hand in the middle of her back, Allar gave Renny a gentle shove.

Cook spun around, surprisingly quick for all her bulk, a wide smile lighting her round face, crinkling her bright eyes and apple cheeks. Admonishing the child softly, under her breath—"it's My Lady Renny to you"— she dropped into a deep curtsy and tugged the girl down with her all in one movement.

"My Lady." Rising, keeping hold of the girl-child's hand, Cook continued, "We are honored. Please forgive my daughter. She's young yet, and…" A smile and a quick tug on the girl's hand had the little girl bobbing her head. "…forgets her manners."

Renny's laughter silvered the air, instantly dispelling any tension. "No harm. 'Tis my own fault. I fear I will never feel like anything but just Renny. Truly, I am the one who feel honored. I asked Allar to bring me here so I could thank you in person for the wonderful meals you provide."

Flushing at the praise, already rosy cheeks flaming, Cook beamed and proudly began showing off her kitchen to Renny.

Allar stood back and watched. Renny had a great talent for putting people and dragons at ease. Perhaps a part of her healing ability, perhaps an integral part of who she was.

In no time, Lissa, Cook's daughter, had untangled herself from her mother's voluminous skirts and was as close to Renny as she could get without crawling inside Renny's clothes.

He'd noticed that, too. The children of the keep were as attracted to Renny as the dragons and shadowed Renny every chance they got, gathering in knots and giggling groups, already playing Dragonhealer in their spare time.

Renny returned their adoration.

Allar had never seen Renny lose her temper nor tire of answering their endless questions.

She would be an excellent mother.

The thought of Renny, belly swollen with their child, or

cradling their babe in her arms sent a rush of love Allar hadn't known he was capable of burning through him.

Feeling his intense stare, without taking her attention away from what Cook and Lissa were showing her, Renny asked, {{*What is it?*}}

{{*How many do you want?*}}

Renny didn't pretend to not know what Allar was talking about. {{*As many as you will give me.*}}

{{*You will be an excellent mother. I can't wait to see you with our children.*}}

Cook felt the heat radiating between her Lord and Lady even with the width of the room between them. Hotter than the huge open hearth in her kitchen, their gazes locked on each other and they completely forgot the rest of the world.

As it should be for two people in love.

Renny hadn't actually considered it, but what they'd done did make babies. The thought of a babe of her own, their babe, to cherish and protect the way all children should be, was more than Renny could take and not be touching Allar.

Gently disentangling herself from Lissa, Renny met Allar halfway.

Allar caught her to himself fiercely and scorched her with his kiss.

Smiling hugely, fanning herself with one hand, Cook tucked Lissa's hand in hers and left them to it.

When he finally let her come up for air, Renny looked around guiltily. They probably shouldn't be doing this in the kitchen, much less in front of a small child.

To Renny's bemused surprise, Cook and Lissa were nowhere to be seen.

CHAPTER 18

That day set the tone for the following ones.

Mornings, Renny took care of dragons and Allar attended to keep business. Sometime after nooning they ended up in the kitchen where Cook always managed to have a special treat waiting for JusRenny.

Evenings, Renny and Allar spent time with Conthar and Zantha.

Nights—the long, wonderful nights—they claimed for their own and did their very best to make a baby.

Finished with the dragons for the day, her heart light, Renny was hurrying on her way to the kitchens to meet Allar. Wondering what treat Cook had come up with for today, thinking dreamily about the things Allar had done to her the night before and the way she herself had reciprocated, Renny almost ran slam over the unknown lady in the Great Hall.

Voya, shadowing his Lady as always, sent a quick mental bellow to Mithar for immediate assistance, knowing he'd relay the message to Conthar and Zantha, and thus to Allar.

They needed to locate Allar *right now*.

Fur was going to fly, or Voya wasn't Allar's second.

Automatically putting her hands up to catch the elegant lady, upon seeing the look of utter distaste cross the woman's face—despite Renny's freshly bathed person—Renny jerked her hands back down and fisted them at her sides.

She'd been the recipient of enough such looks to know neither protest nor apologies would change the woman's opinion.

Renny didn't even care to try. Backing up a step, inclining her head just a tad, Renny tried to go around the woman. She hadn't been introduced to this particular viaitor, but then, Dragon's Haven was full of people arriving, not merely to see the Dragonhealer, but for the upcoming celebration as well.

Renny's insides tightened at the thought of dressing up and having to be front and center, but it was her dragon's bonding ceremony, as well as hers and Allar's.

Blocking Renny's exit, the woman shuddered delicately. She obviously knew who Renny was. Looking down her patrician nose, the woman sneered, "I didn't give you permission to leave."

Arching a brow because she knew how much it would annoy the other woman, Renny grinned and answered cheekily, "I didn't ask."

Zeroing in and preparing to come between the combatants, Voya grimaced at the catfight about to explode in front of him. Give him a good, honest, guts and gore battle any day.

Planting her hands on her silk clad hips, the woman hissed, "You impudent, mannerless twit. Don't you know who I am? Allar will have your hide in strips for this outrage! Just because you're spreading your legs for him…"

Looking Renny up and down and finding Renny sorely lacking, the woman sneered, "Though for the life of me, I can't understand what he sees in you. You're filthy and unkempt and skinny as a rail."

The woman raised her hand to her mouth and tittered. "You look more like…a camp follower has-been than a lady fit to rule this keep." Stuck her nose in the air haughtily. "He'll tire of you soon enough."

Coming a stride closer, knowing it was too late, Voya mentally bellowed another heartfelt plea.

Renny stopped in her tracks, intuition blaring. This was one of the women Allar'd bedded in his past.

In. His. Past.

One who thought she belonged in Allar's bed still.

Crossing her arms, eyes cold and flat, Renny returned the scathing up and down.

A little on the plump side, exposing more cleavage than Renny possessed, rings on every finger. Jewels glittering everywhere, hair in some outrageous frou-frou considered the height of fashion, the tart looked more the lady of the keep than Renny's scruffy self ever would.

Filled out in all the right places, Renny could see why a man would want to bed her—at least until she opened her mouth.

Renny eyed the woman's load of jewelry thoughtfully.

The hussy preened beneath Renny's gaze, thinking Renny coveted her glitter.

Skin tingling, hair on end, Voya moved a step closer and froze, obeying the unspoken command in Renny's barely upraised pinkie finger. It didn't stop him sending out one more desperate cry for help.

Allar sped around the corner just in time to hear Renny say in a mildly deceptive tone, "I neither know nor care who you are. I do, however, know who you *were*. Allar told me that once he beds a woman, the morning after he always bestows a trinket as a parting gift. Seems all the other men do so as well."

Without waiting for a response, Renny turned her back to the woman and started to walk off.

It took a moment, but the enraged shriek behind her let Renny know her barb had found its mark. Smiling a satisfied cat smile, Renny met Allar's eyes.

The annoying screeching behind her continued to climb in volume. "At least he gave me something! You're not worth a gift."

Renny laughed joyously, her eyes never leaving Allar's face. "I don't need gifts. I have Allar."

Without taking his eyes off Renny's beloved face, Allar instructed Voya, "See that Cylla is returned to her home without delay. She has worn out her welcome here."

Voya leaped to do his Lord's bidding. Making no effort to hide his relieved grin, he clamped his hand around Cylla's arm and hauled her toward the exit.

The farther away Voya dragged her, the more Cylla's tirade increased in volume until the entire keep could probably hear her. "You're nothing! He'll come back to me. You're not fit to be lady of Dragon's Haven! Or any other keep."

Two steps and a jump, and Renny wrapped her legs around Allar's waist. Allar caught her and spun them into a niche in the hall leading to the kitchen. Pressing Renny against the stones, his erection to her warm woman's place, Allar kissed her thoroughly.

Pulling back a smidge, foreheads touching, Allar thrust against her and murmured, "Sure you don't want any gifts?"

Tightening her leg hold on him, Renny nodded without moving her head away from his. "You're the only gift I need."

Many long, satisfying kisses later, Allar let Renny slide to the floor.

Holding hands, laughing like children, slowing to exchange frequent kisses, they eventually made it to the kitchen doorway.

Coming up from yet another mind-blowing kiss, Renny smelled something delicious. Renny couldn't put a name to half the things Cook made for her but she enjoyed each and every one.

Looking around, Renny didn't see Lissa anywhere. The child was as much a delight to her as the food.

Shooing them both to the table, carrying a big bowl of

something gooey and sticky sweet, Cook placed it in front of them, along with a spoon.

It hadn't taken any of the keep's inhabitants long to figure out Renny had a sweet tooth bigger than any child.

Allar derived as much enjoyment feeding Renny as she did eating whatever Cook made. Sitting close together on the long bench, Renny opened her mouth like a baby bird. Sighed in delight at the first spoonful.

Smiling broadly, Cook turned back to her work.

Allar'd fed Renny perhaps half the concoction, stealing occasional bites for himself, interspersed with more than a few kisses, when Lissa came running in.

Scrambling up on the bench, in her haste to hug Renny, Lissa knocked the bowl and sent it spinning.

Renny watched in slow horror as the bowl tipped, the remainder of the syrupy contents covering the front of Allar's clothes.

Nice clothes.

Clothes fit for the Lord of Dragon's Haven.

Allar hastily jumped up and back, but the damage was done. Even as he raised a hand to swipe at the mess, Renny was on her feet instantly, pulling Lissa behind her.

Allar stared at Renny in disbelief.

She stood facing him, lips skinned back, teeth showing in a feral snarl, dagger pointed at his heart.

His disbelief turned just as quickly to anger.

Fury, even.

That Renny had grown up in a world where a child was beaten for something as accidental as spilling a bowl of food.

That she thought him capable of committing such a despicable act.

They stood, a frozen tableau, until Cook's mothering clucks broke the spell.

"Oh, dear me. Let me get a wet cloth. Lissa, apologize this instant!"

Eyes locked on Allar, Renny could detect no anger in Cook's gentle scolding.

Both behind Renny, Cook and Lissa hadn't seen anything out of the ordinary, just people jumping out of the way of a mess. Honoring Allar's and Renny's private time, no one else was in the kitchen.

Renny blinked. Came back to herself in a heated rush.

Felt all the blood drain out of her face and head to the south'ard.

Looked down at the dagger she held pointed at Allar, looked up at his harsh expression. With exaggerated care, she placed her dagger on the table and took a step back.

Then another.

Allar made no move to stop Renny as she backed away.

Blindly following twists and turns, Renny ended up in the huge courtyard. Her heart hadn't hurt this much since she thought Conthar'd died in the avalanche.

She'd really blown it this time.

Skirting around the edges in invisible mode as she was so adept at doing, Renny kept going.

She had to get out of the keep for awhile.

A familiar screeching caught Renny's attention. She watched dispassionately as the shrew who'd accosted her in the Great Hall ordered servants around and created general chaos.

Spotting Renny, the woman's shrill harping directed itself at Renny. "You! This is all your fault! Pretending to be lady. Pah! You're nothing but a common whore. Go back to the streets where you belong. Getting me thrown out of Dragon's Haven before the celebration. Ordering all the dragons to refuse to carry me and now… Now I have to ride in this…this…"

Words failing, the shrew stabbed a jewel encrusted finger at the rude farmer's cart overflowing with her belongings.

Personally, Renny considered the woman lucky to have bribed the farmer. He must really need the coin.

Spotting the hunched, arthritic man standing by the cart beast's head, wishing she had even some small largesse to bestow on him, Renny tipped her head in grateful acknowledgement.

He winked in return, gnarled hands softly stroking his beast's tattered ears. A sway-backed, spavined beast who looked to be at least as old as his master.

Renny frowned. The dragons sometimes carried passengers from one keep to another, at their discretion. As for Renny giving the dragons orders—the woman must be delusional. Renny hadn't spoken to any of the dragons since she'd left the dragon's courtyard for her afternoon snack.

Wouldn't have been that petty even if she'd thought of it.

Turning her back on the woman once again, Renny headed for the main gate.

The woman refused to give up. Stalking closer to Renny, she shrilled, ""Don't you turn your back on me, you shameless harlot."

Everyone in the courtyard stilled as Renny kept walking, over and done with the shrew's theatrics.

Screaming now, spittle flying, the woman kept plowing ahead. "Did you hear me? Don't you have the guts to stand up for yourself? Can't fight unless there's a big strong man to back you up, or a couple of your worthless dragons?"

Grabbing Renny's shoulder, spinning her, the obnoxious woman raised a hand.

Instinct took over.

Drawing back her fist in a lightning move, Renny landed a

solid punch. The shrew crumpled to the ground, broken nose spurting blood everywhere.

Thinking it was just anger roaring in her ears, it took Renny a moment to realize the sound was outside herself. Real.

Every dragon in the place was roaring, every person in the assembled crowd cheering.

Looking to the old farmer once again, Renny nudged the limp woman with the toe of her boot. "If she gives you any grief, I expect to hear about it."

Bobbing his head and grinning toothlessly, he motioned several of the younger men to pick up the unconscious woman.

One grabbed her ankles and one grabbed her wrists. With an expert one-two-three toss they draped her unceremoniously, precariously, over her bags.

Renny turned and continued out the gate, silently berating herself. One more strike against her.

Drawing a dagger on Allar—Allar!—as if he'd've laid a hand on Lissa, brawling in the main courtyard like a street urchin.

Smiling grimly to herself, Renny conceded that noxious woman was right about one thing at least—Renny didn't belong here.

REJOINING ALLAR in the Great Hall, Voya shook his head.

They'd searched the entire keep and the surrounding area.

Renny was nowhere to be found.

No one had seen her since she'd walked out the gate.

Voya hadn't been worried about keeping an eye on her because he thought she was with Allar.

By the time Allar had gotten away from Cook's ministrations, Renny was long gone.

The dragons were stubbornly mute on Renny's whereabouts.

Frantic now, Allar contacted Zantha yet again. {{*Are you sure you haven't seen Renny?*}}

{{*I give you my word—I have not seen Renny since she was tending the dragons this morn.*}}

Pausing to think a moment when everything in him was screaming for him to *find Renny*, Allar narrowed his eyes. Dragons had a most peculiar sense of truth. From Zantha's careful wording he deduced he wasn't asking the right questions. {{*Do you know where she is?*}}

Zantha's silence was answer enough.

{{*Zantha, I'm going crazy here. Help me out just a little.*}}

{{*Renny wants to be alone. Needs to be, until she can sort this out in her mind. She's heartsick about what happened in the kitchen, and that harridan's taunts struck deep. Renny thinks she doesn't belong here. In her pain, she has even shut out Conthar. Refuses to converse with him although he's still able to read the thoughts on the surface of her mind. She's not physically hurt, and she's close by. Conthar says...*}} Zantha paused as if listening to Conthar, {{*Renny's mind is different from most humans. Her walls are too strong to breach without hurting her.*}}

Allar fumed. {{*You're not telling me anything I don't already know. Renny shut me out in the kitchen and I'm not strong enough to open the pathway by myself. I can't read her thoughts like you can and I can only converse when she opens the door.*}}

{{*Allar, my beloved human, whatever Renny decides, she will let you know. Give her time and space.*}}

EVERYONE else long since gone to bed, Allar slouched alone in his massive, throne-like chair in the Great Hall, staring into the embers of the dying fire. He sensed Renny before he saw her.

She stepped out of the darkness, into the dim edge of the flickering light.

Allar blinked—was she there or not? He refused to look

directly at Renny, preferring to keep his sullen stare on the fire. He'd had plenty of time for his temper to build while hers had been cooling.

Renny plunged in headfirst. If her actions had been so unforgivable Allar no longer wanted her, she needed to know. She told him quietly, firmly, "You have my sincerest apologies. I didn't think... I don't... I *know* you would never strike a child, else I wouldn't be with you."

Allar glared moodily, torn between raging at Renny or wrapping her in dragonhide and throwing away the key to their chambers. "No. You didn't think. You reacted. That I can understand."

Growled louder. "What I can't understand is why you shut me out. Why you disappeared without a word." Voice going deceptively quiet, in a tone superbly effective on the most recalcitrant soldier, he asked, "Did you think I would stop loving you? Hate you? Kick you out of my bed and my life?"

Dropping onto a low stool, Renny stared into the dying fire. "I wasn't thinking about you at the time, except that I'd just drawn a dagger on the one person I care most about. That I came close, far too close, to using it on you. I might be able to live with you hating me. Knowing you were harmed by my hand... That would kill me."

Allar continued to brood, not helping Renny in the least, letting her get her thoughts and reasons out while his temper drained away.

Renny spoke again, vehemently. "I won't, however, apologize for that little fiasco in the lower courtyard. If she's any example, your past taste in women is atrociously lousy." Paused, marshaling her thoughts.

"At first, I agreed with her when she said I didn't belong here. Especially knowing what I'd just done to you. I had to get out for awhile and think. Out, because everyone here—and I already think highly of them—would've hounded me to death with well wishes and are-you-alrights. My going out hurt you, and I am most sorry I caused that hurt."

When Allar maintained his stony silence, Renny demanded quietly, "Would you like to know what I decided?"

Allar continued to stare at Renny, his heart about to burst out of his chest. She'd talked herself into staying—else she'd be long gone. He needed to sit still and listen to her reasons so he'd know better next time how to deal with her fears.

Renny crossed her arms over her chest, and had it been any other woman, Allar would've labeled it pouting.

Not his Renny. She didn't pout. Much.

More like a temper tantrum held in tight check.

"I can't be your lady..."

Allar paid her words no mind, the sudden lightness in his heart telling him otherwise.

"Not if it means being like her. I can't do the jewels, and the hair."

Allar suppressed a snicker at the feathered monstrosity he'd barely noticed perched atop Cylla's sour features. Bit his cheek to keep from laughing out loud as he recalled how Renny'd nailed the excessive jewelry Cylla was flouting.

Renny was really winding up now, springing to her feet and pacing, arms jerking, hands attacking the air with sharp cutting movements. "I can't sit around and do nothing all day and demand the servants wait on me hand and foot while I bitch and moan about what a rough life I have. I don't know how to be a useless bauble nor an ornament on a man's arm."

Breathlessly awaiting her answer, temper gone and absolute love filling the empty hole, Allar asked, "What kind of lady can you be?"

Renny blew out a breath. "If you still want me, the only kind I know how to be. I can't promise I won't lose my temper. There are many wonderful people here, but some of them, especially the ones from other keeps are..." Shooting Allar a don't-shoot-the-messenger look, Renny swallowed and tightened her fists. "…twits."

Wincing, Allar put a hand over his heart at her direct shot.

Flexed her hands until they were open and relaxed. Relaxing, not quite fully there yet.

"It's not likely I'll forget to eat, but I know I'll forget to change clothes and show up at some stupidly stuffy important dinner looking like I just came from the dragons. I'll probably always need a good haircut, and I'll never remember to walk instead of run."

Allar rose and stretched languidly. "I'll make sure you're wearing proper attire at all stuffy meetings and that your hair is…"

Renny shot him a fulminating glare and Allar hastily changed *the latest fashion* to "decently cut and combed."

Running her hands through the messy mop in question, Renny tangled her fingers at her temples and tugged hard at the silky strands.

Looked Allar in the eye. "I can promise you this—I will work hard to help rebuild the populations of dragons and dragonriders. I will be utterly faithful to you, and I will cherish all the children we make."

Stalking Renny, Allar growled. "You forgot the most important thing."

Trying to remember what she'd said and what she hadn't, pegging the intense look in Allar's eyes and realizing in a blinding flash what he was angling for, Renny asked innocently, "What? What did I forget?"

Taking another step, Allar shot her a heated look.

Definitely teasing now, Renny hemmed and hawed. "Umm, I promise not to bathe at any waterfall without you?"

Shaking his head, Allar advanced another step. Backing Renny up, he pinned her against the stones of the immense hearth, his arms on either side of her, bodies a breath apart. "I'm waiting."

Straight-faced, Renny countered, "I promise the keep will always have an excellent cook."

Pressing his forehead to hers, Allar rumbled, "Woman, you are killing me."

Voice full of laughter, Renny fended, "But those are very important things."

Jaw tight, Allar growled through clenched teeth, "Renny."

Giving in, Renny cupped his face in her hands and conceded joyfully, "Allar, I promise to love you."

Allar's answering bellow most likely woke the entire keep. "She loves me! She's finally admitted she loves me."

Hushing her love the only way she could, Renny twined her arms around Allar's neck and dragged his head down, plastering her mouth to his. Over and above Allar, Renny heard the ecstatic rumble of approval from the dragons.

CHAPTER 19

Cylla woke in a strange bedchamber, face throbbing.

Disoriented, she tried to remember what'd happened.

Part of it came back in a rush.

That bitch! That pitiful excuse of a female had...*punched* her! That's why her face felt as if someone was stomping on it. Cautiously ghosting her hands over her swollen nose, Cylla couldn't tell if it was broken or not.

Wait... How had she ended up...here?

Where was here?

Starting to panic—she wouldn't put it past that evil witch to have her kidnapped and held for ransom or something—a guttural voice came out of the shadows.

"Tell me what you know of the happenings at Dragon's Haven and I will see you are fully avenged."

No longer caring where here was, or even who the strange voice belonged to, Cylla preened and began to oblige, veritable founts of information gushing from her spoiled mouth.

CHAPTER 20

*T*ucking Renny closer to himself, Allar grinned as thoughts of the night before played front and center.

He'd carried Renny to their chambers, undressed her slowly and made sweet love to her for the remainder of the night. Extraordinary before, Renny's admission had added a whole new dimension to their lovemaking.

Grinned wider as he felt his love stirring. They'd slept late by Renny's standards—she was usually up and going at it hard before first light. Giving her a squeeze, Allar knew she'd needed the extra sleep after the day she'd had.

And the night.

Twisting so he could awaken Renny with a kiss, Allar jubilantly counted days. A few more and she would be his officially.

The ceremony was important so the rest of the world would know they were bonded. Allar didn't see how it was possible for him to feel any closer to Renny than he already did.

Awakening to Allar's kisses and caresses and a thorough bout of loving, added to the countless ones from the night before, Renny staggered to the wash basin.

Splashing warm—warm!—water on her face, Renny contemplated dressing versus going back to bed and Allar's arms.

There, on top of the chest where her clothes were stored and her clean ones were always magically laid out for her, Renny spotted her dagger.

The dagger Rand had crafted for her.

The one she'd pulled on Allar. Reaching out to touch it, Renny snatched her hand back before she touched the cold metal.

One of her most treasured possessions, if she couldn't use it responsibly she didn't need to carry it.

Rand's voice rang in her head, as if her mentor stood right there. *"Don't pull out a weapon you don't intend to use, and if you pull it out, be prepared to kill."*

Could she really have used it on Allar? Agitating, full of self-doubt, Renny dithered. She felt more naked without her dagger than without clothes.

Walking up behind her, Allar guided Renny's hand to the hilt.

He still trusted her! "Allar, I…"

Squeezing Renny, dropping his head to inhale her sweet scent, Allar pressed a kiss to the top of her head. "I know, little love. I wouldn't've returned it if I thought you truly meant to use it yesterday."

Since they'd missed their evening visit with their dragons, Renny insisted on going to see Conthar and Zantha first thing, practically dragging Allar in her haste.

Watching Renny run her hands lovingly all over both dragons, Allar was hit with a sudden inspiration for a perfect ceremony gift for Renny.

Their dragons, a waterfall, and just the two of them.

He was still grinning when Renny turned to him, flashing a

mischievous grin of her own. "All the desperately wounded dragons have been tended. You're the only one I've gotten to ride since we got back, and Conthar's been sorely neglected."

Grasping Renny's hips, Allar pulled her tight against his raging erection. "I'm in desperate need of some tending, Healer. I have this swelling that won't go away."

Rubbing herself against him like a pursim, Renny was practically purring. "Sounds like a personal problem to me. I don't think there's a permanent cure for what ails you, but I can do something about temporary relief. Any waterfalls close by?"

Over Renny's head, Allar saw Zantha and Conthar stop twining their necks and rubbing their heads together long enough to give him a pleading look. He stood no chance against any request of Renny's, but when all three of them ganged up on him…

Throwing his head back and laughing loud and long, Allar nodded. "Zantha, ask Mithar to send Voya here. He can handle things for a bit. We need some time to ourselves, just the four of us. Oh, and have Voya send our morning repast here as well."

A few moments later, a sharp rap, and Voya entered Zantha's den. Couldn't keep the delighted grin off his face if he tried. His Lord and Lady and their dragons had truly bonded.

Upon hearing Allar's request and travel agenda, Voya's grin widened until he feared his face would split and his heart would burst.

∾

FLYING FREE, Renny reveled. {{*My apologies to you, my Conthar. I've been so busy, I forgot how wonderful this is!*}}

Conthar's wings took great bites of air as he propelled them upwards, folded flat against himself as he reversed direction and dove. {{*You've been busy healing dragons, Dragonhealer. How can I take offense at that? We have all our long lives ahead of us. Besides, I've been getting to spend time with my Zantha.*}}

Zantha bugled joyfully and the four of them spun and twisted in a wondrous mid-air dance.

Renny shared a gleeful look with Allar and on his signal, they began spiraling down to a perfect lake. Small, but with a significant waterfall at one end.

They spent the morning there, splashing and swimming. Renny and Allar gave the dragons a good scouring, using handfuls of the white sand to clean and polish the dragon's hides.

Renny had just finished scrubbing Conthar, the two of them nose to nose as she scratched his eye ridges when Allar directed a huge font of water in Renny's direction with the flat of his hand.

Allar taunted Renny as she spluttered and wiped her face. "What was that you said last night? I believe I heard you say lousy—no, *atrociously lousy*. Don't like my taste in women, huh?"

Laughing, backing away and plotting on the go, Renny gasped, "Past women. I know I said past women. Your taste is much improved."

"Maybe I need another taste to be sure." Pinning Renny against Conthar's bulk, Allar pretended to bite her neck, nibbling and making Renny laugh until she braced her hands against his shoulders and pushed, trying to make enough space between them to breathe.

"How's that for taste? Or would that be tasting?"

{{*Allar.*}}

Turning to see what Zantha wanted, Allar took his eyes off Renny for the barest second.

Using the distraction to her advantage, Renny went limp, slid out of his hold like an eel out of a net, and disappeared under water. {{*Now, Conthar.*}} Coming up some distance away, Renny laughed until her newly healed ribs ached.

Both dragons, using their wings, were plastering Allar with great gouts of water.

Eventually tiring of their water play, they all crawled out to collapse on the sun-warmed shore, the dragons on the sand, Allar and Renny on a blanket.

When Renny's stomach rumbled, she realized Allar hadn't brought anything but clean clothes for both of them, and the blanket. So unlike his normal self—he always, *always*, made sure there was plenty of food on hand for Renny.

She'd gotten so used to him providing victuals, she hadn't paid any attention to the lack of full to the brim saddlebags.

Looking out at the lake, its surface glistening like it'd been dusted with diamonds, Renny shrugged. Maybe he was going to fish. Fish was good.

On the other hand, it wouldn't hurt her to miss a meal. She'd certainly missed enough in her lifetime. One more wouldn't make the slightest difference.

Cocking his head at the audible growling of Renny's tummy, Allar rolled over and swatted her on the butt. "Get dressed, woman, or we'll be late."

Sleepily eyeing the deserted shoreline and calm water, Renny rolled over. "Late? Late for what? Another bath? And, don't know if you noticed or not, but you're still naked, too." Snickered. "Didn't you get *bathed* enough?"

Laughing as he pinned her, Renny arched invitingly against Allar.

"Oh no, Renny my love. None of that right now. We'll save that for later. Rolling off Renny and to his feet in one smooth move that totally showed off his thigh, calf, and superb ass muscles, Allar snagged his pack.

Watching him draw clean clothes out for both of them, Renny eyed what he held out to her suspiciously.

Allar'd provided her with plenty of clothes, mostly utilitarian as was her wont, and all made of unbelievably soft materials. If she changed ten times a day, she'd never be able to wear half of them. For someone used to wearing the same

291

clothes until they were far beyond threadbare, the bounty was overwhelming.

The ones Allar held out to her now were fine, soft and beautiful. Still tunic and leggings, but designed for a Lady. The cuffs and collar of the tunic were embroidered finely, expertly, with alternating symbols for Healer and different colored dragons, interwoven into an intricate display of her status.

The side seams of the leggings bore the same.

Definitely not practical, so what was Allar up to?

Looking at Allar questioningly, Renny rolled to her feet and stepped back, hands fisted at her sides, shaking her head all the while. "Un uh. Not till you tell me what's going on."

Gazing at her perfect form, naked and defiant, Allar tried to convince Renny without giving himself away. "Renny, we are going to a nearby keep for nooning. 'Tis only fitting that my Lady wear clothes befitting her station."

When Renny still made no move to take the clothes, and didn't soften her stance, Allar arched a brow.

"Would you have people think I treat you badly? That I'm so miserly I won't spend coin to buy proper clothes for you? That the only reason I keep you around is to heal the dragons?"

Renny burst out laughing. "I should be clapping. You're up to something, but I'll go along with it. For now."

Waiting until they were both dressed, Allar pulled something else from his pack. Holding it tight in his fist, he looked at Renny with his heart in his eyes. The dragons stretched their necks and pushed their great heads near their humans, careful not to knock them over.

Stepping behind Renny, Allar ordered softly, "Close your eyes."

Taking a deep breath, Renny did, and thought how very far she'd come in such a short while—to trust this man enough to do as he bid without knowing why.

Renny felt Allar place something around her neck, felt it settle lightly at the top of the valley between her breasts.

Allar's love-filled voice whispered in Renny's ear, "You may open your eyes now."

Renny did so, and looked down. Took another deep breath and blinked rapidly.

An exquisitely crafted pair of silver dragons—twined one around the other, one with emerald chips for eyes, the other with sapphire—hung at the end of a four strand twisted silver chain.

Renny's eyes shimmered as she beheld Allar's latest gift.

"Allar, I…"

Spinning her to face him, Allar clamped his hands on her shoulders. Not enough to hurt, just enough to let her know he was serious. And to hold her in place should she decide to bolt. His words came out gruff, his tone hoarse.

"Do not refuse this gift."

Her voice full of sadness, Renny met his gaze. "'Tis beautiful, but I have nothing to give you."

Sliding his hands down to her upper arms, Allar gentled his hold. "Nothing to give me? You gave us Conthar's life back, thereby ensuring my dragon's life. You have given me back laughter when all seemed dark and dreary. You have given me Zantha's mate as well as my own. You have given Dragon's Haven, along with the rest of the dragon world, a Dragonhealer. How can you say all of that is nothing? 'Tis we who owe you an immeasurable debt."

Taking in Renny's not quite convinced look, Allar frowned, unsure how to get through to her, but at least she was listening to him. "Do you think giving you one bauble will pauper me? I have fought many battles, battles in which the victor claimed the spoils. Much tribute has been given to the warriors of Dragon's Haven for services rendered. I have spent little of mine for my own needs. Allow me to spend it on you. Whether you like it or no, you are mate to a powerful and wealthy Lord. Were you any other woman, you'd scarce be able to walk for the weight of jewel-gifts. I have given in to most of your wishes to remain plain and unadorned. Enough is enough. What's mine is yours, and this gift is not just from me, it is from Zantha and Conthar too. Do not shame me—us—by refusing to accept this gift from our hearts to yours."

Swallowing her pride along with her objections, Renny whispered, "Tell me about my pendant. I love it."

Allar and Conthar and Zantha talked over and around each other in their haste to speak.

"I located the gems in a hidden valley."

"I located the silver in a vein deep below the surface."

"I designed the pendant and chain."

Renny looked at the three co-conspirators wonderingly. "When did any of you have time to do this? What you've created is… Astonishing. Mesmerizing. Amazing."

The other three exchanged glances and burst out laughing.

Conthar tamped down his mirth enough to answer for all three. "Renny, when you are tending dragons you are oblivious to the rest of the world. You shut everything out, including us."

Renny's protest sounded feeble, even to her own ears. "No I don't. Do I?"

That set them off again. Renny stood there, face turning crimson as she realized they spoke the truth and nothing but. Opening her mouth to apologize, Conthar beat her to it.

"Do not even think to apologize. Healing is tiring, exacting work, and you would not be the Healer you are if you couldn't focus so completely. We are in no way chastising you, merely teasing."

Throwing her arms around her dragon's neck, then Zantha's, saving Allar for last, Renny thanked them each with a tight throat.

Holding Renny in his arms, Allar murmured, "There. That

wasn't so hard after all, was it? We give you gifts, you say thank you. Although if you want to pay me back in the bedroom…"

Muffling Renny's laughter with a long kiss, Allar pulled back and squinted up at the sun. "Enough of your delaying tactics. We are expected."

Renny rolled her eyes as Allar clasped her around the waist and boosted her onto Conthar while completely ignoring Renny's, "You still haven't told me where we're going."

Shrugging at Allar's close-mouthed tactics, Renny enjoyed the ride as they flew farther east than she'd ever ventured. This land was different, softer, rolling green hills interspersed with large pastures of different kinds of herdbeasts instead of the familiar— to her—peaks and valleys.

In the distance, she could see a large keep. Just as the land was less harsh, this keep was more castle than fortress. Still easily defendable, yet not bristling with in your face weapons and soldiers like Dragon's Haven.

With a bit of surprise, Renny realized Dragon's Haven must be an outpost, the first line of defense on the fringes of civilization. Huh. She'd just assumed all keeps were like Dragon's Haven. To her, after some of the places she'd grown up, it seemed like Paradise.

Wondered with a frown why the dragonhaters seemed centered on the mountains. These flatlands would be much easier to attack. Nowhere near as easy to hide dragon carcasses, though.

Nowhere for the vicious Orimjays to hide, either.

Watching Renny take in the sights the same way he was watching her—utterly absorbed and not missing a single thing— Allar hoped she wouldn't choose now to read his mind.

He'd deliberately not told her about his family, wanting Renny to see how other people lived, knowing she'd balk at leaving Dragon's Haven. Would have wanted his family to journey to Dragon's Haven, and they would have, gladly.

Allar wanted Renny to see for herself.

She wouldn't have believed him if he'd told her everyone didn't spend every waking moment prepared for battle. There was more to life than always fighting, always being on guard.

Relieved beyond measure Renny hadn't kicked up more of a fuss about the clothes and jewels, he didn't care what she looked like when she was healing dragons any more than the dragons did. He refused to introduce his mate to his parents looking like an orphaned waif. Allar would have his way in this, temper tantrum or no.

Casting Renny a sidelong glance—she was always beautiful to him—he wanted everyone else to see the same beauty he did. He'd had one of the keep's women trim Renny's ragged mop into some semblance of order so her gorgeous eyes were no longer hidden, but framed instead.

Knowing why she kept them so well hidden and wore the clothes she did broke his heart.

Sensing Allar's gaze, Renny turned those living emerald eyes on him. They weren't flying fast, more gliding, so they could hear each other. "What?"

Allar swallowed, swallowed again. "You are…amazing. Beautiful beyond belief."

Blushing a becoming shade of pink and turning her head, Renny frowned. The daft man had obviously lost his mind. Her? Beautiful? But still, it was a nice sentiment coming from her mate. Mates were obligated to say that sort of thing, they?

Allar reminded her gently, "Renny, I just gave you a compliment. A compliment is a gift."

Turning back to face him, eyes glowing with hope, threaded with insecurity, she smiled. "Thank you."

Landing in a large open space outside the castle walls, when Renny would've jumped down, Allar held out a hand.

"Wait, please, My Lady. Allow me the honor."

Shrugging, giving in, still bemused by Allar's attentions, Renny focused on a crowd of approaching people.

Crossing the space between his dragon and hers, holding his arms up to Renny, Allar spared the ever-growing crowd a glance and a grin. "'Tis fine. These people mean us no harm."

Sliding into his waiting arms, Renny pressed herself against him as she slid the rest of the way down. Allar went instantly hard, making Renny smirk at his groan.

"Woman, I will never get enough of you, but now is not the time." Giving Renny a quick but thorough kiss, Allar took a step back and began undoing the fasteners on her overtunic, the plain one save for the Dragon's Haven crest. Drawing it off, he folded it and draped it over his shoulder, hoped his own loose tunic would cover the evidence of his desire.

He could feel her mounting panic as the strange people drew closer and closer and he did nothing. Drew no weapons, assumed no position of defensiveness.

Renny focused on the crowd, looking them over one by one with a practiced eye. Allar insisted they bore her no ill will, but habit had Renny scanning—seeing who carried what weapons, who needed to be taken out first.

Her eyes locked on the two largest men, automatically deciding they were the most lethal, perusing them in earnest for weapons, attempting to shift her body in front of Allar's.

He might see no danger, but Renny's over-trained senses were screaming. These were warriors, whether he'd admit it or no.

Allar tightened his grip and held Renny to his side, knowing exactly what she was doing. Trying to do.

Renny wiggled her fingers, trying to loosen Allar's grip—he held her sword hand after all. He only held tighter. No matter, she was proficient with both hands.

Funny thing, the closer they got and the better Renny could see them, these people didn't seem to be carrying much in the way of weaponry. Smiling far too much, they looked far too joyous, to be harboring ugly thoughts.

She took another look, scanning faces closely this time instead of hands and sides.

Allar knew the instant Renny realized exactly who these strangers were.

How could she not see the resemblance?

Allar looked just like his brother, and both were carbon copies of their father.

He felt Renny relax slightly, and then tense back up, tighter than a drawn bow string, for another reason.

She was trembling—actually trembling.

Allar couldn't hold back his face-splitting grin.

That was his Renny.

Ready to face down a mob of people, willing to do battle and single-handedly protect Allar and her dragons without blinking.

Terrified to the point of fleeing at the thought of meeting his family.

Watching closely as most of the crowd stopped while two men and two women kept walking, Renny calculated the distance to Conthar. Decided if she could free her hand from Allar's unrelenting grip she could be mounted and gone before Allar could stop her.

Reading her mind, Allar leaned close and whispered, "Conthar knows my family. He won't help you, and they won't bite. You have my word on both."

Retaining his hold on Renny, Allar greeted his family with a lift of his other hand. Keeping Renny close by his side Allar didn't have to read her mind to know what she was thinking.

A whole family, and he hadn't said a word!

Like wind blown smoke over hot coals, he felt Renny's fear dissolve as those coals came closer to bursting into flame—to be replaced by fuming anger.

{{*Zantha, please tell Renny…*}}

Renny spat, {{*Do not even think to involve the dragons in this! You couldn't tell me you had a family? You don't trust me enough for that? Afraid*}}

I'll embarrass you?}} Renny's mental hiss of hurt condemnation blasted at Allar.

Holding a hand up to his family, pausing them in mid-step, Allar swung to face Renny and looked deep into her eyes. {{*Not because I didn't trust you, little love, and nothing you do will embarrass me. Because I knew how you'd react—exactly as you are—terrified and ready to bolt at the slightest opening. Answer me this—would you have come here today if I'd told you why we were coming, who we were coming to visit?*}}

Soothing Renny and himself, Allar ran his hands up and down her arms in long sweeps. {{*If I'd told you I had family I wanted you to meet, you'd've worried yourself to death about meeting them, made excuse upon excuse not to come. I'm proud of you, proud to introduce you to my—now yours as well—family. You're panicking, afraid they won't like you.*}}

Taking a deep breath, calling for Zantha's additional backing to read the truth in his mind and relay it to Renny, Allar vowed, {{*Their approval doesn't mean nearly as much to me as your love. If you don't like them, then we don't have to come, ever again. Will you at least give them a chance before you make up your mind?*}}

Renny's anger drained away as swiftly as it'd formed as she carefully considered Allar's heartfelt words.

He was absolutely right. She was panicking.

Feeling her anger dissipating to be replaced with guarded hopefulness, Allar stood still and let Renny find her own way.

{{*You really think they will like me?*}}

An unwanted orphan's heartfelt plea colored by a lifetime of rejections, Renny's pain-backed query squeezed and mangled Allar's heart. His assurance was swift and just what Renny needed to hear. {{*You are so exactly right for me, how could they not love you?*}}

Renny buried her face against Allar's chest. The mere idea that he would give up his family for her if she didn't like them… A family he obviously loved very much, and if the radiant faces were any indication, loved him just as fiercely.

Burrowing her nose into Allar's breastbone like she was trying to get inside him, Renny stammered, {{*I've never been part of a family before—what if I'm not any good at it?*}}

Arms tightening convulsively, Allar assured her. {{*Zantha, Conthar, and I are your family, and you do an outstanding job with us. We'll all help you with anything you're not sure about. I apologize most sincerely for withholding information from you. 'Twas selfish and cowardly on my part, a foolish attempt to spare you worry.*}}

How could Renny possibly hold on to her anger in the face of Allar's little speech? Not just pretty words, but deeply held sentiments.

Zantha's smug {{*I told you so*}} sealed the deal.

Conthar harrumphed, and Renny snickered.

Heaving a sigh of relief, Allar drawled, {{*Let's try this again, shall we?*}}

Turning to face his family once more, keeping his arm around Renny's waist—just in case, and because he could—Allar looked at his assembled family, waiting patiently.

Indicating Renny with a sweeping gesture, Allar announced proudly, "It is with utmost pleasure that I present to you my mate, Lady Renny."

Allar said other things—mother, father, sister, brother—but Renny was too busy panicking to pay him much mind.

Had Conthar not been planted firmly behind her, Renny would've backed up and run like a hoppity being chased by a red-fur. As it was, she flinched at the glad cries and squeals emanating from the two women.

Like what's her name at Dragon's Haven, these folks had a way better idea who she was than she did who they were. Renny only hoped she didn't have to break either of their noses. Allar probably wouldn't laugh that infraction away as he had the other.

Rushing Renny, the women enfolded her in perfumed hugs, chattering non-stop.

Renny watched helplessly, dagger hand twitching, as the two

men who looked like an older and a younger version of Allar did the same to him. Clapped him on the back with hearty blows that would've felled a lesser man.

Reclaiming Renny, Allar started toward the castle, stuck smack in the middle of what seemed to be a whole herd of strangers.

"We have much news to impart, news I wasn't comfortable sending by courier or even through the dragons. Besides, I promised Renny food."

Greeting the rest of the waiting crowd and others along the way, slowing but not stopping, Renny looked up when the shadows of Conthar and Zantha blipped over the humans.

{{*We go to hunt and then to the the dragon's courtyard. We'll meet you there, Little Warrior.*}} Dipping his wingtips in salute, Conthar led Zantha off to one of the teeming pastures.

Swept along, upon entering the Great Hall here, Renny stopped and stared. Dragon's Haven was solid and sturdy, but being a man's keep and having no lady, it was sorely lacking.

The garrison at Fort Helve had been even more spartan, the farm of the Old Mother that of comfortable albeit poor people.

Renny hadn't known anything could be as beautiful as what she was seeing.

Hadn't noticed the lack of beauty, because she'd never known any.

The beauty here pierced her heart like her first sight of Conthar. Renny desperately wanted Dragon's Haven to look like this.

Not just a keep, but a home.

Exquisite dragon tapestries on the walls, tapestries she was going to examine in minute detail as soon as she could.

Scented candles in niches, vases of flowers on the gleaming tables, intricate designs on the polished flagstone floor, inlaid with a plethora of multicolored stones, and telling stories as captivating as the ones on the tapestries.

Now Renny understood why Allar wanted her to dress up. He truly wasn't ashamed of her, knew just how out of place her regular garb would've been amongst this finery.

Renny hadn't spared a thought to the binding ceremony to take place in a few day's time, but suddenly she was filled with trepidation. What would Allar's family think when they saw Dragon's Haven?

They'd think Renny'd been utterly remiss, and they'd be exactly right.

Snatching her hand out of Allar's grip, Renny panicked as she sought his mother. *What was her name?*

Things had been so chaotic at the introductions, Renny couldn't remember. Couldn't very well address the richly dressed woman as Hey, you—Allar's mother.

At Allar's startled glance, Renny demanded, {{*What is your mother's name?*}}

{{*Renny, little love. Look at me. Calm down. Look into my eyes and take deep breaths. This is all new to you, and overwhelming. Think how well you did in the dragon's courtyard with all those strange dragons demanding your attention. This is the same, only with humans.*}}

{{*But I can't mind-speak with humans!*}}

{{*Renny. Deep breath. In. Out.*}}

Keeping eye contact until Renny's eyes stopped wheeling like a terrified Okumo, Allar praised her. {{*Good. Very good. Now tell me what's wrong.*}}

{{*Nothing! Everything! I need to speak to your mother and...*}}

{{*In. Out. In. Out. Show me how, love. In, out. There you go.*}}

Putting one of Renny's hands over his own heart, Allar covered it with one of his. Held it there until Renny's breathing evened out.

Dropping her head but not before Allar saw the embarrassed red creeping up, followed by white as the blood drained out of Renny's face, Renny admitted, {{*I don't know her name!*}}

Tilting Renny's chin up with a couple fingers, Allar waited.

When Renny finally looked up and into his eyes, he smiled and nodded. {{*Yes, you do. I introduced them to you earlier. Repeat after me—My father is Lord Gamron, mother is Lady Gemma, my annoying brat of a brother is Tellar, and my spoiled brat of a sister is Ninar.*}}

At the glint of humor in Allar's eyes, Renny almost changed her mind. Stiffening her spine like she was going into battle, Renny pulled away from Allar. Nodding, lips moving over and over in a silent repeat, Renny headed for Lady Gemma.

Wondering what in the world was going through Renny's mind, unable to mind-speak with her since she'd slammed the door—as she tended to whenever she was upset—Allar watched Renny approach his mother.

Waiting just out of Lady Gemma's line of sight until she finished with the servant she was speaking to, Renny stepped up and dropped a deep if somewhat clumsy curtsy. Rising, Renny looked Lady Gemma in the eye and locked her knees lest they betray her.

"Lady Gemma, I…need your help." Waving a hand to encompass the hall and all its accouterments, Renny started to explain.

Lady Gemma cut her off. "No."

Renny froze, all her insecurities rushing to the fore. This… this is what she'd feared, despite Allar's assurances to the contrary.

Lady Gemma laughed.

No, this was going to be far worse than Renny'd thought. She took a step back. She'd been right to think they wouldn't accept her. Stiffening, face going blank, Renny looked for the nearest exit, Allar be damned. She was taking her dragon and going home. And if he no longer wished to be associated with her, well, then…

She'd been rejected all her life, but this hurt, dammit. These were Allar's people, and important to him. Renny didn't want him to have to choose between them, because they'd all lose.

"Wait! That didn't come out at all right." Placing her hand on Renny's arm, Lady Gemma shook her head. "Forgive me. I am so excited—exultant!—that Allar has at last found his mate, that he has finally brought you here, I am beside myself."

Leaning closer, she whispered conspiratorially, "Downright addled, if you want the truth."

Renny stared, certain she'd lost her mind. As well as her hearing. She thought she'd heard Allar's mother—Lady Gemma —apologize to her. Renny.

Hooking her arm through Renny's, Lady Gemma began walking. And talking. "I am more than willing to give you any help you need. Am, in fact, delighted you asked. From what we've heard, you are most independent. Anything within my power, you have only to ask."

When Renny continued to stare, speechless, Lady Gemma laughed again. A high, delighted sound with no malice hidden anywhere.

"You're right to look at me as if I've lost my mind. What I meant to say a moment ago, was no, not Lady Gemma. Not to you. I was hoping you'd call me Gemma, hoping more you'd call me mother. But only if it doesn't make you uncomfortable. I'm rattling. I'll shut up now."

Renny's mouth dropped open. She couldn't help it, couldn't close it either. Couldn't say anything. Mother? She'd only just met this woman and already she was being invited to call her mother? Renny tried it out silently, loving the way it felt on her tongue and in her heart. *Mother.*

Getting no answer, trying hard to keep the hurt out of her tone and failing, Lady Gemma inquired, "Lady Renny? No matter. We'll come up with something else. Something we're both comfortable with."

That closed Renny's mouth and unfroze her. Wheezing with laughter, she replied, "Just Renny."

Not knowing what it was, sure there was a joke mixed in

there with Renny's acceptance, Lady Gemma sighed and smiled as she steered Renny toward the family table. "Now, what were you about to ask me for help with before I sidetracked you?"

Sobering, Renny let her eyes make another long pass around the hall and took her turn at rambling. "This... Everything is so... Our ceremony... In a couple day's time... Dragon's Haven..."

Swallowed and tried again. *Get it together, Renny! If you can fight dragonhaters and survive, surely you can string together a few coherent words.* "I have done nothing to the keep at Dragon's Haven. I don't even know where to begin."

Lady Gemma defended Renny, forever winning Renny's heart in the process. "You've been so busy with the dragons, Dearling, I don't know when you would've had time."

Pinning Renny with a look, Gemma arched a slim brow. "Allar didn't tell you about us, did he? He's certainly bragged to us enough about you. You've made him so very happy already. Thank you."

Gemma did a little foot shuffle-butt wiggle-hip shimmy-grinny/smiley thing. "Now I've got two daughters and two sons! You've made us all very happy."

Staring one more time—come on, Renny, use your words!—she made no answer.

Lady Gemma kept right on, as if Renny was actually contributing to this crazy conversation. "Is that hideous war chest still plunked in the main entrance?"

At Renny's look, torn between agreement and loyalty—she thought the thing was perfectly serviceable and accessible, and, yeah, it was herdbeast butt ugly—Gemma laughed.

"Don't worry, your answer won't hurt my feelings. I've been trying to get Allar to do away with that...thing for years. While he may not have mentioned us, as soon as he told us about you—I believe while you were still on the Healing Hall—we started packing things you'd need."

Renny made some sort of confused noise, nothing that could actually be considered in the category of a word unless you were talking to a days old babe.

Gemma smiled encouragingly. "The baggage wains should reach Dragon's Haven on the morrow." Sniffed in derision. "I've been to Dragon's Haven. It's not much of a place for a lady to reside. Allar was never interested in changing it until now. Said it kept the husband hunters to a minimum. I guess he figured if it looked that bad, no lady in her right mind would want to stay there."

Laughter pealing out, covering her now crimson face with her hands, Gemma peeked through her fingers at Renny. Fanned her cheeks and shook her head. "That didn't come out right, either. What I meant was, you are the perfect lady for Dragon's Haven and I'm glad to know it's Allar you love and not his wealth."

Coming up behind them, delighted Renny was getting along so well with his mother, Allar pulled Renny into his arms. Jibed, "It's not my wealth she's after, it's the dragons."

Renny drove a swift elbow back into his ribs, doubting if he even felt her attempt. Took a deep breath as a shudder rippled through her. {{*She asked me to call her mother.*}}

Allar felt the wonder in Renny's words as clearly as he felt Renny in his arms. Knew just exactly how much it meant to her. Gave her a brief, hard squeeze as Zantha and Conthar added their kudos.

"I don't know how you tend the dragons. I love them, but they're so big and fierce. I'd be afraid they'd snap at me in pain and swallow me in one gulp." With a delicate shiver, Allar's sister jumped into the conversation.

"Don't go all girlie on us, girlie. Why, I remember..." Allar's brother, grinning mischievously, started to add his two dragon mites' worth.

Not giving Tellar a chance to finish his tattle-tailing, Ninar hip bumped him out of the way and sought Renny's aid. "You don't have any idea what it was like to grow up with these two. I'm so glad to finally have a sister."

Smiling sweetly at her brothers, Ninar batted her eyes innocently. "Now they can't gang up on me so frightfully. I've got backup."

Sister. The word rang and echoed in Renny's head the same way *mother* had.

Allar squeezed Renny again in support and the dragons rumbled their approval.

Walking up behind Lady Gemma, Allar's father copied Allar, wrapping Lady Gemma in his arms and pulling her close, nuzzling her neck.

Renny stiffened in Allar's arms at Lord Gamron's approach, relaxed by slow increments as Lady Gemma returned the affection. Turning her face up to his, Lady Gemma reached up and caressed Gamron's jaw with one hand, a look of complete adoration on her features.

Allar squeezed again, conveying his pride in Renny to her. She'd always be wary of men, especially large strangers. At the thought of how much his diminutive Renny trusted him, Allar's heart swelled and he bent his head, nuzzling Renny's neck.

Lord Gamron met Renny's direct gaze, and hers didn't back down to his in the least. His approval of her, already high, went up. There were a great many men who didn't hold the courage his son's new mate was so fearlessly displaying.

A nod to Renny, and, "Gemma says she's asked you to call her mother. I'd be honored if you'd call me father."

Renny didn't give him a definitive yea or nay, but bobbed her head the tiniest bit as the bell sounded for nooning.

Seating the ladies first, the men took up positions alongside them.

Renny ate and listened to the teasing banter flying back and forth.

Family!

They had no idea what a blessing they possessed!

So this is what it felt like to belong, to be part of a family, and they'd accepted her unconditionally.

Heart full to bursting, Renny knew she'd do anything to keep them safe.

Anything.

After a most satisfying nooning, anxious to see the rest of the castle, Allar and his family—family!—walked Renny around.

Going first to the dragon's quarters so Renny could check on Conthar and Zantha, Renny had to stop and talk with the rest of the dragons.

Unlike Dragon's Haven, there were only a few. Excited to see Renny, vying for her attention, all were in excellent condition, obviously happy and well loved.

Renny tended a few minor complaints, more because the dragons craved the attention of the Dragonhealer than because they needed it.

Hanging back to give Renny some breathing room, Allar and his family kept their eyes on her and talked quietly.

Watching Renny peer into one of the dragon's mouths with no more care than if she'd been looking at a baby's toothless gums, Tellar ribbed Allar. "Brother... It looked as if your mate there was trying to protect you when she saw all of us stampeding your way."

Allar's, "She was," had all their heads swiveling to look at him.

Looking from Allar to Renny and back, Tellar laughed. "Her? She's too little to do any damage. What was she thinking?"

Allar's face harsh and grim, his voice full of pride, it would almost be worth seeing Tellar handed his ass, but... No. Allar wouldn't put that grief on Renny. She'd take it to heart and be too upset. "Do not underestimate my mate. Renny might be tiny but she has the heart of a warrior."

Let that sink in a moment before adding a casual, "Renny trained at Fort Helve, under Rand."

At the audible indrawn breaths of his father and brother, Allar took his eyes off Renny long enough to inform them, "Renny has better weapons and skills than most soldiers. Weapons crafted for her by Rand, skills he taught her."

Tellar managed to sputter, sure his brother was pulling his leg, "Rand doesn't teach females to fight."

"He taught this one. Renny could take you before you had a chance to blink."

At Tellar's snort of disbelief, Allar smiled grimly. "You don't have to take my word for it. But… If you value your life and your manhood, don't make any sudden moves around her, and whatever you do, don't raise a threatening hand to anyone, human or dragon, that she values. I won't come to your rescue."

Lord Gamron merely pursed his lips. "Rand, you say?"

Lady Gemma and Ninar merely exchanged a knowing look. No wonder Renny had no idea how to be a lady. On the far side of the lake, Fort Helve was far more primitive than Dragon's Haven.

Hushing as Renny gave the dragons a last farewell pat and a promise to return on the morrow, Allar said softly, "Mother, Renny really likes kitchens."

Renny rejoined them, glowing as she always did after a session with the dragons, eager to continue her tour. Listening to their conversation, occasionally contributing a quiet comment, they rounded a corner.

Renny stopped, completely motionless, as the others continued walking. Backing up to stand beside Renny, Allar looked at her and then where she was staring. Grinned. Swore he could hear the wheels turning in her head.

Staring, utterly transfixed, Renny stared. What a dummy! She'd always had to hunt and gather the things she needed. The thought had crossed her mind, but... She had no knowledge, had never stayed in one place long enough for it to be a possibility.

Getting his mother's attention, halting her wedding chatter with Ninar, Allar gave a chin lift at what held Renny's rapt fascination.

Dragon's Haven had plenty of room, and there was that one sheltered spot close to the dragon's caves... It would be perfect... Turning excitedly to Lady Gemma—mother!—Renny spoke fervently. "You offered help. I know how to use these. Will you teach me to grow them?"

"Certainly, Dearling. They're not hard to grow. I can give you starts off most of these, just tell me which ones you want."

"All of them!" Giving a whoop of delight, eyes shining, Renny set off to explore the weed patch, aka herb garden.

At his mother's baffled look over Renny's exuberant response, Allar had to laugh. "Do you know the only favor Renny's asked of me? The morning after she truly became my mate, she asked for..."

A totally besotted smile on his face, Allar's eyes stayed locked on Renny, blissfully darting hither and yon like a nectar drunk bright-wing. "I'd've granted her anything. Most women would've asked for jewels or clothes and yet it was a battle, practically a war, to get her to accept the clothes and the pendant she's wearing now."

Allar swallowed hard and sucked in a breath as his mate bent over some dusty colored weed, stretching her leggings over her sweetly curved derrière, making his mouth water and all his blood head south. "The only thing she's asked of me is to meet my cook so she could express her thanks."

They all stared at Allar in astonishment, then turned to watch Renny happily identifying weeds. Sniffing and cupping, carefully noting where each was growing so she could duplicate siting.

Gemma gave a little laugh. "The Healers buy most of their

herbs from peddlers and fairs. Few bother to grow their own, but Renny is the Dragonhealer, after all."

Finishing Renny's tour, which included a lengthy stay in the kitchen and Renny wrapping the castle's cook tightly around her finger, Gemma and Ninar begged off.

Stretching up on tiptoe, giving Gamron a peck on the cheek, Gemma sank back down and teased, "Do not lock yourself away in your study for too long, or I shall have to…"

Hooking an arm round Gemma's waist, Gamron pulled her back up for a real kiss. Letting her slide back down till her heels touched the floor and she was steady once more, even if her eyes were a bit unfocused, Gamron chuckled. "Care to finish that thought, my lovely lady?"

Patting his muscular chest, Gemma smiled seductively. "Later, my dear one. Later." Flouncing off, she flung back over her shoulder, "After the children have gone to bed."

Renny goggled at their affectionate display.

Ninar huffed and walked off in the opposite direction, rolling her eyes and muttering about parents acting like moonstruck herdbeasts.

Tellar elbowed Allar and, with a sappy look, mimed winding a string around his finger. Catching Tellar's head in a ruthless grip, Allar bent his brother over and proceeded to make Tellar's hair stand on end with the rough side of his knuckles.

Oblivious through all the byplay because she was intently focused on Gemma and Gamron's display, Renny stayed with the men when the groups split, not yet comfortable enough to go with the women and needing to contribute to Allar's grim news.

Renny told her tale succinctly, then left the men to their discussion.

While they talked, Renny wandered around the study—library!—heart singing at the multitude of books and scrolls. Occasionally offering a comment, hands tucked carefully behind her back, she perused the weapons displayed and—the books!

311

Allar hadn't asked, hadn't even thought to, but from Renny's intent scrutiny of the covers, he'd bet anything his Lady could read. She would never cease to amaze him.

Wait'll he showed her the library at Dragon's Haven. Not as well stocked as this one, perhaps, but a sizable one nevertheless. Not as diversified either, more war oriented—tactics and battles and...

{{*Allar, it's getting late.*}} Returning his stare, Renny's gentle reminder cut through his plans. {{*I've enjoyed this day tremendously, but don't we need to be going?*}}

Allar's answer stroked Renny like a caress. {{*Sometime we will ride our dragons at night, beneath the full moon and the stars. 'Tis magical— a whole different world. Tonight, though, we will stay here. Voya knows not to expect us until the morrow.*}}

Harumphing as Allar trailed off in the middle of a sentence —yet again!—Gamron grinned. "That's enough for today. We'll talk more tomorrow. Renny, feel free to read whatever books you like. If you want, we can have some of them sent to Dragon's Haven."

Yanking her eyes off Allar at Gamron's more than generous offer, not altogether sure she liked him paying such close attention to her, Renny bobbed her head, all the movement she seemed capable of with Allar's father.

Ninar burst into the room carrying a ribbon and ruffle bedecked gown across both arms. Holding it up, measuring Renny against the dress, she nodded. "I am sure this will fit you if you don't mind wearing one of my old gowns. Mother kept them all and..."

Perusing Renny head to toe, Ninar pursed her lips. "You're so little, none of my recent gowns will fit you and there's no time to have a new one made."

Staring at her new sister by marriage, wide eyed and slack jawed, Renny almost turned and looked over her shoulder to see if Ninar was addressing someone else. Too bad there was no one else in the room save the three men.

Gamron interceded on Renny's behalf. "Take Renny to your mother, Ninar. Now. And calm down. You're scaring her."

Looking from her father to Renny to the dress, Ninar frowned. "Scaring Renny? Nothing to be scared of. Mother is merely throwing a celebration for the two of you. A pre-ceremony bash, if you will. Hurry, or we won't have time to dress properly."

When Renny still didn't move, Ninar stepped closer and snagged Renny's hand, tugging her out the door in a flounce of ruffles and lace.

Renny threw a beseeching look at Allar. He just shrugged and held up his hands in surrender.

Safely gone, Allar blew out a breath and quipped with a crooked grin, "That's a battle I'd pay to see. I haven't been able to get Renny into anything but leggings and tunics. I had the keep's seamstress make her piles of clothes and she has yet to so much as open the doors to her wardrobe."

Clapping him on the back Tellar mocked, "Must be tough having a woman who doesn't demand expensive gifts with every breath."

Allar punched his brother in the arm as they left the study. Tellar laughed and said in a high falsetto, "Let's go find something for you to wear. I'm sure some of my old clothes will fit. You're sooooo…little."

Tellar dodged the second punch, dancing out of the way and backing down the hall, making come hither movements with his fingers.

Bounding after him, intent on murderizing the annoying so and so, Allar retorted, "You little jerk. Emphasis on little. Or would it be on jerk?"

Fondly watching his boys sparring good naturedly until they

were out of sight, shaking his head and grinning, Gamron followed them. Some things never changed.

Dressing quickly—in his own clothes, thank you very much—Allar went in search of Renny.

Figuring they'd holed up in Ninar's room, Allar knocked.

Ninar opened the door a crack and her agitated face appeared just long enough to hiss, "Go away! We'll be out in… We'll be downstairs in a while. Shoo!" The door slammed in Allar's face and he heard the bar drop into place.

Fine. Allar could wait a bit to see his wife. Taking up a station at the bottom of the stairs, he refused to budge.

CHAPTER 21

"*I* am not wearing that!" Renny was politely adamant, and Ninar was pulling her hair out.

Renny'd outed the servants and vetoed every single gown Ninar'd suggested. Desperate, Ninar sent for her mother.

Lady Gemma swept into the room, sized up everything in a glance and set to work.

It certainly wasn't the barely worn gowns Renny was objecting to—just the gowns in general.

Neither Gemma nor Ninar had ever met a female who didn't like fancy clothes—until now. The gown Ninar held—as were all the ones scattered around the room—was all wrong for Renny. The wrong colors, and definitely too many frou-frous.

Renny needed something simple that would show her off while staying within her comfort zone.

Cocking her head, Lady Gemma had an inspiration.

"Ninar, go fetch that silver gown you wore to the mid-winter festival several years ago. It's in the trunk in…"

Ninar left in a flurry of skirts.

Lady Gemma paced around Renny, considering. She doubted

if Renny had ever worn a dress, much less a gown. This was going to take some delicate negotiating.

Lady Gemma coaxed gently, "Renny, think of this as a battle. Would you go into battle unprepared, with no weapons? All the other women will be dressed up. If you are not, it puts you at a great disadvantage. Weaponless, if you will. Women wield their beauty and wiles much as men use their strength and swords."

Miserable, Renny looked at Allar's mother and tried in vain to stop her fidgeting. "I have no wish to embarrass Allar, or you. I tried to tell him I know nothing of being a lady. He won't listen. I know nothing of wiles, or beauty, or gowns or manners or polite company. I say what I think and most of the time, I react before I think. I will not start a fight, but neither do I refuse to defend myself. I do not want to cause a brawl because some twit Allar once bedded thinks she is better suited to being his lady."

You know nothing of being a female, Lady Gemma thought. Her heart hurt for the spirited young woman standing in front of her, baring her soul.

Giving Renny a quick hug, Gemma stepped back and smiled, her hands on Renny's shoulders.

"Renny, you are a gem and a treasure. Just as precious stones need polishing to reveal their inner beauty, so do people. You are exquisite inside, you just need to let some of that beauty shine through. Trust me—after the antics of my three…nothing you do will embarrass us. I know nothing of fighting, but I do know about being a lady. Let me help you."

Ninar came back, the gown she'd been sent for draped over her arm. "It's been in storage so it smells like red-wood. There's no time to air it." Frowning down at what she held, Ninar looked back to Gemma. "Mother, are you sure? This gown is so…plain."

Nodding, Lady Gemma pushed Ninar firmly back out the door. Closing the door and shutting out Ninar's protests, she smiled at Renny. "The two of you are close in years but not in age. Ninar has led a very sheltered life, and is, I'm afraid, just a little on the spoiled side."

Holding up the silver for Renny to look at, Gemma explained. "She never liked this gown because it's too plain for her tastes. My beloved daughter has yet to realize that just because a gown is covered with ribbons and crusted with gems, doesn't make it, or her, more beautiful. On the other hand, this gown will show off your beauty to perfection."

Handing Renny an under-shift so soft and fine it could've been made from wisps of clouds, Lady Gemma shook out the gown while Renny donned the under-shift.

Turning to Renny, sucking in a breath, Lady Gemma had to bite her lip to keep from crying out. Allar had told them Renny was a warrior but until this moment Gemma hadn't fully believed him. Very nearly transparent, the under-shift hid nothing. Renny's body bore a multitude of scars, more evidence of her harsh life.

Hearing Lady Gemma's indrawn breath, Renny stiffened. She would not be pitied!

Reaching out a hand, stopping just short of touching Renny, Lady Gemma drew her hand back. "Renny, child, I am furious— furious—that there was no one to protect you as you deserved to be."

Renny watched in surprise as a tear tracked down Lady Gemma's cheek. To Renny's knowledge, no one had ever shed a tear on her behalf.

"I guess I didn't do a very good job." Eyes meeting, both women laughed.

Holding the silver up to Renny, checking the fit and murmuring to herself, Gemma missed Renny's deep inhale and satisfied smile as the scent of red-wood filled her lungs.

Relaxing, Renny went along with Lady Gemma as the woman helped Renny don the gown. Rummaging through Ninar's baubles and trinkets until she found the perfect silver ribbon to pull Renny's hair back from her face, Gemma stuck her head out the door and sent a servant scurrying to her own chambers for a jeweled girdle and dancing slippers.

Through it all Lady Gemma chattered while Renny mostly listened, thoughts whirling through her head with the ease of each stroke of the brush Gemma used to tame Renny's hair.

She'd never spent so much time, one on one, with any adult female other than Cook. Not even the Old Mother. They'd spent time together, but it'd been instructions for Renny to go and fetch this herb or that, and how to use what she found.

Satisfied with the results, brimming with happiness that Renny, fey creature that she was, had permitted Gemma to transform her, Gemma stepped aback to admire her handiwork.

Allar was going to be picking his jaw up off the floor. Grinning wickedly, Gemma confided, "Renny child, Allar was never one to share well. You are so beautiful he will not want to let anyone close to you. Think he can make it through the evening without starting a brawl?"

Both laughing, hooking elbows, they started for the door.

Lady Gemma watched in fascinated silence as Renny stopped, picked up her small dagger and cunningly strapped it to her calf. Hidden, but within easy reach.

Lady Gemma reminded Renny gently, "No one will hurt you here."

Giving Lady Gemma a long, level look, Renny shrugged. "I know that in my heart and I do not doubt your hospitality, nor the safety of these walls." Shook her head. "I cannot be without a weapon. I cannot."

Sighed resignedly. "I fear I will never be comfortable without a weapon close at hand."

Contemplating her son's mate, Lady Gemma bestowed a brilliant smile on Renny. "Then by all means, wear your dagger. Let's go join the celebration!" Holding out her hand, Gemma waited.

Hesitating but for an instant, Renny wove her strong, scarred fingers through the long, elegant ones of Allar's mother and they set off down the hall.

Renny, only half jesting, said, "You've managed to get me into a gown, how about a crash course in manners?"

Gemma responded instantly. "Don't maim or kill anyone, try to keep Allar from the same, and whatever you do, don't copy anything you see Ninar do!"

Renny laughed, as Gemma intended. Squeezing Renny's cold fingers, Gemma finished, "If you need help, I'll be close by. You are so beautiful and graceful, just be yourself. Everyone who doesn't already will love you."

Renny made a wry face. "JusRenny, huh?"

"Absolutely! You are perfect just being you."

Renny hunched, then straightened, head up, eyes to the fore, preparing for battle.

Lady Gemma cocked her head, fully aware of Renny's uneasiness and her determination. "I've told you several times you're beautiful. You shine, love. Positively glow from inside. If you don't believe me, you have only to look at Allar's face."

Stopping at the head of the stairs, with a tilt of her chin, Lady Gemma directed Renny's gaze to the bottom, where Allar impatiently stood guard.

Standing statue still, Allar fumed, eyes going to the top of the stairs with every other blink. What could be taking so long? Ninar'd come down ages ago and informed Allar that Mother was helping Renny.

He'd known Renny would balk, but this was ridiculous. Having just made up his mind to go and get both of them, a sudden hush fell over the assembled crowd.

Focusing on the top step, Allar's eyes swept the women just beginning their descent. His mother and another beautiful woman.

Allar's cobalt eyes locked on…

Was that…his Renny?

The woman slowly floating down the stairs looked…ethereal. Watching in awe, Allar had known his Renny was beautiful, but his mother had wrought a miracle.

Renny wore a simple floor length silver gown, a bejeweled girdle encircling her tiny waist and winking ruby and emerald and sapphire with every breath. Somehow, his mother had talked Renny into wearing a ribbon that held her hair back out of her face, leaving wisps of her bangs to showcase her astonishing emerald eyes and show off the lines of Renny's elfin face.

The only true jewelry Renny wore was the dragon pendant Allar and their dragons had gifted her with at the lake.

Unable to take his eyes off his breathtaking mate, Allar wouldn't've been surprised in the least if she suddenly sprouted gossamer wings and disappeared, leaving nothing but a poof of silvery fairy dust behind.

A sharp elbow to his ribs got no response. Snickering, Tellar reached over, put a hand under Allar's jaw and closed his mouth. "You're drooling, brother."

Allar gave no sign he even noticed Tellar's presence or teasing. Stepping to the mid point at the bottom of the stairs, Allar blocked the way.

Cobalt staring up ensnared emerald staring down. Without taking their eyes off one another, Renny descended, halting two steps above Allar so they were eye to eye.

Time froze. For a long moment neither of them moved or spoke.

Allar broke first, reaching both hands out to touch Renny. At the last instant, he reverently sketched her outline without touching her.

"Renny." Just her name, all the speech he was capable of.

Bracketing Renny's face with his hands, Allar kissed her. Slowly, thoroughly. Putting his whole heart into that one meeting of lips.

Renny returned his passion tenfold.

They surfaced to thunderous cheering.

Allar gazed down into Renny's eyes and she read his lips, no way she could hear anything over the roaring crowd.

"My heart, you are beautiful beyond belief."

Renny's smile lit her face. Burying herself against his chest, she held onto Allar like a lifeline as his arms surrounded her tightly.

Looking up into his mother's teary eyes, Allar dipped his head in silent tribute. Mouthed, "Thank you."

The rest of the celebration passed in a blur. Unsurprisingly adept at dancing, Renny managed to keep Allar from killing every man who had eyes, even managed to keep Tellar alive by expertly deflecting his incessant teasing.

Secure in Allar's love, Renny didn't even attempt to throttle the multitudes of women making eyes at him. 'Twas a surety Allar didn't notice them.

Much later, celebration in full swing, Allar whisked Renny away and up to his chambers.

Kissing and laughing, they stumbled inside. Lips still locked, Allar backed Renny against the door while he barred it. Moving Renny aside and breaking the kiss, Allar slid a heavy chest against it as well.

"Expecting an invasion?" Brows arched, Renny couldn't help but laugh at Allar's grimace.

"Tellar." Heaved another smaller chest on top of the first one. "Likes to play practical jokes." Contemplated the barrier like he was planning on adding to. "Lots of practical jokes." Heaved a sigh. "This probably won't stop him but it might slow him down long enough to give us some warning.

Eyes sweeping the room, grunting with effort, Allar added another chest in front of the two already there.

Returning his attention to Renny, Allar clasped both her hands in his and held her arms away from her sides. Stood there, simply taking her in. "From the first days I beheld you, battered and bruised, you were beautiful to me. But this... You take my breath away."

Renny shook her head. "I had nothing to do with any of this. 'Tis all your mother's doing."

"I must remember to give her something, something extravagant as a thank you. I didn't think I'd ever see you in a gown."

Renny chuckled. "I don't have any. Would you have me borrow one of Cook's?"

The mental vision of Renny swallowed inside one of Cook's voluminous dresses made Allar grin. "You haven't looked inside the the big wardrobe in our chambers at Dragon's Haven."

Confusion and a dawning horror on her face, Renny asked, "Why would I? Aren't...your clothes in there? You said I could keep mine in the chest at the foot of the bed."

Allar's grin widened at the suspicious panic lacing Renny's tone. "I keep some of my clothes in there."

Renny hadn't been ignoring his gifts, truly hadn't known they were there. Allar had to keep reminding himself Renny wasn't like other women—she'd never dream of snooping nor of looking through other people's things without asking, and she would never ask. All her new clothes would've turned to dust long before she examined the contents of that wardrobe unbidden.

"Never mind. I want to show you something." Catching Renny's hand, Allar pulled her over in front of the huge cheval nestled in a corner. "I had mother put this in here for you. For us."

Mellow light came from a softly burning fire and a scattering of candles throughout the room. Positioning Renny in front of him so they were both reflected in the mirror's depths, Allar put his hands on her shoulders and commanded softly, "Tell me what you see."

Renny fidgeted, not knowing what he wanted. "You, me?"

Standing tall and proud behind her, Allar dipped his head and nuzzled Renny's hair. "Yes, but more than just the two of us. Look at yourself. See how I see you—how beautiful you are."

Renny gazed a moment more, mostly at the tall, handsome man behind her. Her love and her life.

Dragged her eyes off Allar and looked lower.

It seemed impossible that the fairy tale woman in the mirror could be herself. Renny studied the reflection critically, trying to see herself as Allar—and others—saw her.

Looked past the visible scars and the too-old eyes, past the strong limbs and alert stance.

Saw a rather small woman in a borrowed silver dress with borrowed gems sparkling at her waist. Large, somewhat sad and definitely wary green eyes, eyes that'd seen too much sorrow and pain looked back at her.

Those same eyes lit on her dragon pendant and softened. A tangible reminder that she was loved, twinkling at the hollow of her breasts. Looking deeper, Renny saw Allar, surrounding her with his love.

That's what he wanted her to see—love.

"Love. I see love."

Allar brushed a kiss across the top of her head, his eyes never leaving hers. "Promise me something."

Answering breathlessly without a trace of hesitation, Renny knew she'd do anything for this amazing man. "Anything."

"Wear this dress for our bonding ceremony. I had a green one made to match your eyes, but I don't see how you could be any more beautiful to me than you are right now."

Renny's breath caught. "If your mother and sister are agreeable. These things belong to them."

"They'll agree. They, like myself, would give you the world if you asked for it, and more if you'd let us."

Renny swallowed. "You truly had a gown made for me? I

don't know what…" Straightening at his sharply raised brow, Renny finished. "Thank you."

Allar kept his smile to himself as he thought of all the clothes waiting for her. *A gown?* Renny was going to pitch a fit when she opened that wardrobe. He couldn't wait to see it, or her, in the clothes he'd commissioned.

Couldn't wait any longer to see her *without* clothes.

Unfastening the jeweled girdle, he slowly slipped it off. Spanning Renny's waist with his hands, he slid his hands around to caress her flat belly. Still looking into the mirror, both of them watching his hands, Allar whispered, "Think we've made baby yet?"

At Renny's indrawn breath, Allar nuzzled the sweet spot on her neck. "Even if we have, we won't know for awhile. I think it's best if we keep trying. Just to make sure."

Bemused, Renny could only nod.

Lifting the shimmery gown bit by bit, Allar pulled it over Renny's head. When he would've dropped it on the floor, Renny caught it and draped it over one corner of the mirror frame.

Her movements highlighted by the firelight, Allar stood staring in shock. Where had his sister—his baby sister—gotten this under-shift? What was his mother thinking to allow a little girl to wear something like this?

Mentally changing gears, on the other hand, Allar was very pleased Ninar had lent this to Renny. Ninar might not get it back.

Undergarments like this were only meant to be seen by a mate, and what a sight his was.

Renny stood before him, glowing from his adoration as well as the soft light. The fabric was so sheer it hid nothing while accentuating every curve, every hollow, every rise.

Allar could see the delicate outline of Rennie's bones, the dip of her belly button, the sweet swell of her breasts and hips.

The dagger strapped to her calf.

Bursting into laughter, he shook his head. "Only you. I

should've known better than to think you'd be caught weaponless. Planning on using that on me?"

"Having ideas about another female?"

Allar's laughter boomed out. "Renny love, if a man can look at you standing there like a dream come true and think of another woman, then he's not much of a man. I'll wait till at least tomorrow morning."

At his teasing, Renny smiled evilly and parried, "Keep talking like that and I'll side with Tellar against you." Allar's horrified look was all the leverage Renny needed.

Wincing, holding up his hands in surrender, Allar shook his head. "You don't know what you're saying. Don't give him any encouragement. He's…horrible."

Renny winged a brow, her voice dripping with sweetness. "Incorrigible?"

Laughing, Allar whisked the gauzy nothing of a shift off, scooped Renny up, took a couple strides and tossed her on the bed.

Scrambling to her knees, Renny held up one hand, palm toward Allar. "I want to undress you."

Walking forward until his thighs pressed against the bed, Allar spread his arms out to the side and gave Renny a come and get me grin.

Sitting back on her heels, Renny gave Allar a thorough once over.

Wearing a sapphire doublet shot with silver threads, combined with his brilliant blue eyes and inky hair, it made Renny break out in a full body shiver. Knowing what was underneath caused another shiver.

Reaching up, she slowly undid the elaborate silver frogs, starting at the top and working her way down. The last frog was positioned close to the bottom of his doublet, covering the top of his leggings.

Pretending to have trouble undoing the last one, Renny

fumbled and spent an inordinate amount of time with her hands in close proximity to Allar's groin.

Peered up at him from under her lashes. "Did I tell you how extraordinarily handsome you looked tonight? Good thing what's her name was nowhere near or I might've broken her nose again."

Allar unclenched his jaw enough to say, "I'd've like to have seen that."

Renny snorted, "What? Your mate brawling in the courtyard like an ill-mannered urchin? I tried to avoid it, and her, but she left me no choice." Her hands stilled and she told him earnestly, "I can't promise you I wouldn't do the same thing again."

Going down on one knee, Allar put a hand under Renny's chin and lifted her face. "I don't want you to. Never, ever, apologize for defending yourself. Nobody thinks you're ill-mannered, least of all me. In fact, many of my people wanted me to give you a medal. Cylla has been a thorn in my side ever since... Thank you. I don't think she'll be coming back any time soon, if ever."

"You truly don't mind? Her screeching I could ignore, but she raised her hand to me and I... I saw red. Literally. There was blood everywhere." Laughter filled Renny's voice as she related that tidbit. That had been a most satisfying punch.

Sounded bewildered as she asked, "Why would she think I told the dragons not to carry her? I have nothing to do with whom they take as passengers. That's their business."

Allar mentally shook his head. Renny would never understand how important she was to him—to the dragons. Everything, *everything*, that affected her affected them all. "Renny love, the first time she lit into you, she doomed herself—if she's lucky—to farm carts for the rest of her life. She's fortunate the dragons didn't take her for a ride and drop her in the middle of nowhere. As in, do a quick loop-de-loop and accidentally on purpose unseat her cloud high."

Stroking a hand down Renny's cheek, Allar smiled at her. "All the dragons, especially Zantha and Conthar, keep tabs on you all the time. Our two can usually read your thoughts unless you shut them out, the rest can if you're close enough and they all have a general sense of your whereabouts at any given time."

"They do that? Why?" Renny sounded as surprised as she looked.

"Renny." Allar felt so much love for this small woman welling up, he could do nothing but kiss her. Which he did, most thoroughly.

A short time later, divested of their clothes, Allar murmured against Renny's lips, "Let's practice making a baby. Practice makes perfect, you know."

Easing his mate back until she sprawled on the bed, Allar let his eyes wander and feast. Trailed his hands everywhere. Licked and kissed, cupped and kneaded and massaged until Renny's body was limp, on fire with need.

Lifting heavy lidded eyes to his face, Renny protested, "You're having all the fun."

Without missing a beat in his explorations, Allar agreed. "Oh, yeah."

"I want a turn."

Blue eyes met green and Allar grinned wickedly. Stretched out beside Renny and watched as she sat up. Dragons, but the woman was a fast learner. Of course, she had a certain natural talent that, once unleashed, ran rampant.

Renny turned Allar into a pile of mush.

When he could stand it no longer, Allar surged up in one swift move and pinned Renny under him, nudging her legs apart as he did so. Positioning himself above her, Allar waited until Renny met his eyes before driving inside her slick heat.

He pulled back, almost out, going for a repeat stroke, when the most awful caterwauling erupted outside their door. The door handle rattled as thump after thump vibrated the thick wood.

Allar froze and started to pull out, Renny locked her strong legs around his waist and clamped down.

Shifting from passion to anger in a blink, Allar snarled, "I'm going to throttle that little weasel. Let me up."

Renny tightened her hold, ran a hand up and down Allar's chest. Back down and stroked his shaft. "I happen to like you right where you are." Timed her strokes to her casual words. "Tellar is not yet mated, is he?"

Grinning down at her, pushing deeper again, Allar nuzzled his face in her breasts. Lifted his head. "Woman, I love your devious mind nearly as much as your luscious body."

Then he groaned and gritted his teeth as Renny's laughter spilled out and tightened her internal muscles around him mercilessly, caterwauling forgotten.

CHAPTER 22

"She raised a hand to you?" Allar's bellow woke Renny. Cracking her eyes open the teeniest bit, surprised they'd obey at all since they hadn't stayed closed much the night before, Renny rasped groggily, "What?"

Right in Renny's face, Allar hissed, "Last night. You said Cylla raised a hand to you. Why did you not tell me immediately? She would have been sent away in disgrace. I was not informed of this or I would have banished her from Dragon's Haven forever." {{*Zantha! See to it! Let everyone know!*}}

Managing to pry her eyes all the way open, Renny yawned and stretched before answering. "Why would I have said anything? 'Twas my problem and I took care of it. She was plenty humiliated, and her nose will never be straight again. Every time she looks in the mirror, and I'm certain she does so on a regular basis, she'll be reminded of her humiliation. You don't have to worry about her coming back."

Allar gaped. "I expect you to let me know any time you're at risk. You are not alone anymore. I am responsible for your well-being."

Renny snorted. "I am responsible for myself. Not you, not anyone else. I told you I'm perfectly capable of defending myself. I've been doing it all my life."

Allar growled. "That was when you had no one. You have us now and we will protect you, whether you want us to or not. Anyone, male or female who raises a hand to you—raises their *voice*—who even thinks of doing so, will be banished or executed."

Renny's turn to gape, she was tempted to say *you can't be serious.* The grim look on Allar's face enough to convince her otherwise, she was saved from answering by a knock on the door.

"Wake up, sleepyheads. We're all ready and waiting on you." Tellar's cheerful voice singsonged through the barricaded door.

Renny switched her gaze to the door as if it might bite. "Waiting for us for what, Allar?"

Temper dissipating like windblown smoke at the mildly panicked look on Renny's face, tempted to tease her, Allar drew in a deep breath. "A morning meal with the family for us, nothing more. You don't even have to dress up, and after that we're leaving for Dragon's Haven."

"Going home? So...soon?" Trying to sound upset, Renny couldn't pull it off. At Allar's knowing grin, Renny said defensively, "I like it here. I've enjoyed meeting your family."

Giving her a quick kiss, heart soaring at the casual way Renny'd said *home*, Allar finished for her, "But you're ready to go home?"

Renny nodded.

"There's something else."

Renny eyed him warily.

"They're all going with us for the ceremony."

"Your family will all be there?" Delighted at this unlooked for bonus, Renny wrapped her arms around her middle and beamed at Allar, framing and lifting her sweet breasts unintentionally.

Eyes on the prize, hardly able to talk for the view, Allar said, "They're your family now as well."

A slow grin wrapped Renny's face. "I like that idea very much." The grin disappeared, chased away by a resigned shrug. "I never thought to live long enough to find a mate or have a bonding ceremony, much less a family to attend and witness. I always figured if the dragonhaters didn't kill me first, I'd eventually go crazy from not being able to help the wounded dragons."

Renny's blasé acceptance of an early death or a lifetime of lonely insanity had Allar swearing and Zantha and Conthar bellowing in protest. Renny faintly heard the castle's other dragons protesting too.

Directing her thoughts to Conthar and making a point of opening her mind to Allar, Renny asked, {{*How is it that now I can hear dragons that aren't in pain? I never could before.*}}

{{*Before what?*}}

Renny considered Conthar's question carefully. {{*Before I met you. I knew there were other dragons, healthy dragons, but I could never speak to them.*}}

{{*Mind to mind, or using actual speech?*}}

{{*Mind to mind. I never got close enough to an unwounded dragon to speak out loud to them.*}}

Conthar began, feeling his way like a human crossing a stream on moss covered boulders. A step, a hesitation, another step. {{*I have given this a great deal of thought. When I came to from the dragonhater's...spell, for lack of a better word, I sensed you immediately. I could tell you were aware of me but you didn't show any signs of recognizing me as your dragon. I was terrified for you, afraid to bond in case I couldn't get away, unwilling to doom you with our bonding. You'd've felt crippling pain anyway, but had we been bonded, my death would've pushed you completely over the edge. I do not know how you held on as long as you did by yourself.*}}

Conthar's open admiration wrapped around Renny like a

warm cloak. {{*When exactly was the first time you heard another—not wounded—dragon mind to mind?*}}

Renny didn't have to think about it, so fresh was the memory. {{*The very first time was the no-color in the valley where they trapped you. After that, Zantha warned me about Din. She wasn't wounded but she was in danger, so I didn't pay it much attention. I heard her loud and clear, so loud I thought my head was going to burst.*}}

{{*Apologies, Renny. I thought only to warn you.*}}

Giving Zantha a mental pat, Renny kept on. {{*When I awoke after, in Zantha's cave, I could hear all the dragons at Dragon's Haven a little, like the murmur of a distant conversation. Now—I can hear them all as clearly as I hear you. After we healed Conthar and left the valley, I could hear dragons from all over. I thought it was because I was so linked with the other dragons and we'd tried so hard to save you.*}}

{{*How can you hear that many?*}} Allar questioned Renny eagerly. {{*I have never heard of such a thing! 'Tis extraordinary! Most people can only hear their own dragons, and if they're very lucky, their mate's dragon. I had read in some of the ancient scrolls that Dragonhealers could converse with any dragon, but only if they were face to face, or known to each other.*}}

They all felt Renny's mental shrug. {{*I can't explain it. Once I hear a dragon's voice, it creates a...doorway. That opens to a trail, a path, and all I have to do is follow the path to the dragon. The dragons seem to be able to open the doorway to reach me with no trouble, often dragons I have no connection to.*}}

Renny paused a moment, obviously puzzled about something. {{*If people couldn't talk to the dragons mind to mind, why didn't they just ask them with real speech?*}}

A concerted indrawn breath was her answer. The truth hit her like one of Rand's training blows to the stomach, catching Renny off guard and stealing her breath. {{*No one else can understand the dragons when they speak, can they?*}}

"Renny, you can understand the dragons either way?" Allar

was so excited about the discovery he forgot they'd been using mindspeak.

Renny looked warily defiant, as if she thought she'd be in trouble for this latest admission.

Allar shook his head. "I can hear Zantha, of course, and since you and I bonded I can also hear Conthar, but I can't understand any other dragons."

Zantha chimed in, sounding awed. {{*No wonder you shut us out sometimes, with all the voices in your head.*}}

Renny agreed and apologized guiltily in the same breath. {{*Sometimes I just need quiet.*}}

{{*Renny, when you were healing me, when you came after me into the dark place where I was trapped and we bonded… It somehow changed your mind. Even before we bonded, I felt you. I could see your light, surrounding me and keeping me safe. I was in too much pain to fight you. Somehow you took my pain and sheltered me close to your heart. I was almost at the end of my endurance, but after we bonded, I was even more determined I would not let you down, wouldn't drag you down with me. I had to live, for you as well as Zantha and Allar.*}}

Conthar's heartfelt speech resonated in Renny's soul, binding them even closer.

{{*So what you're saying is…*}}

{{*I think our bond opened your mind, freed it. Strengthened it to possibilities that were closed off before. I think… You needed to hear the wounded ones so you could hear the unwounded ones later.*}}

Pondering those truths, Renny was lost in thought when Allar jibed, "You planning to go down stairs like that?"

Throwing a pillow at him, Renny followed it with her body. Allar caught her mid-leap. She wrapped her arms around his neck and her legs around his torso.

Allar was instantly hard again.

How could Renny get to him so fast? It wasn't as if they'd been apart for months, they'd spent the entire night making love.

He shouldn't've been able to get out of bed, much less be considering diving back in.

They didn't make it back to the bed. Allar took Renny against the wall, hard and fast, making the pictures rattle and leaving them both breathless and trembling.

Letting Renny slide off him and down his body, they stood with foreheads touching, trying to catch their breath.

Knowing Renny would want to wash, Allar staggered to the door, shoved the chests aside. Unlocked the door long enough to bellow for hot water, then hurriedly closed and re-barred it.

Grinning at Renny, leaning against the door, Allar crossed his arms. "So… Tell me what evil plans you have in mind for Tellar when he finds his mate."

RENNY AND ALLAR entered the Great Hall hand in hand to find everyone else already there.

From across the room, Tellar spotted them first and quizzed —at the top of his lungs—"What took you so long?"

That set the whole room laughing.

Renny threaded her way to him purposefully, Allar right behind her and grinning ear to ear, not knowing what retaliation she planned but more than willing to aid and abet. Stopping so close to Tellar she had to crane her neck to look up at him, Renny smiled. "I would like to thank you for the serenade last night and the wake-up call this morn.

Tellar smirked at Allar.

Reaching up and grabbing double fistfuls of Tellar's hair, Renny tugged his head down to hers. Giving him a smacking kiss on the cheek, she stepped back until her back pressed against Allar's front. Told Tellar sweetly, her tone and her mischievous eyes at total odds with one another, "We can't wait for you to find your mate so we can return the favor. Oh, and… The dragons want to help."

Tellar blanched and Allar hooted with laughter.

Gamron and Gemma looked at each other and rolled their eyes. Renny was going to—already did—mesh with their family perfectly.

Tellar looked over Renny's head at Allar. "I'm in love."

Wrapping his arm around Renny and pulling her back against himself, Allar growled, "Find your own mate. This one's mine."

Leaning down, kissing Renny over her shoulder, Allar looked at his brother and smiled evilly. "Take all the time you want finding a mate. Renny has a memory like a dragon."

Breakfast over, accompanied by any who wished to go, they flew in a grand, leisurely procession back to Dragon's Haven. Tellar and Ninar weren't dragonbonded, but stray dragons had appeared, seemingly from nowhere, enough to carry those without their own dragons, so the dragons had been keeping their own count of the humans.

Arriving at Dragon's Haven, the convoy was greeted joyfully, noisily by the keep's inhabitants and even more new dragons.

Renny excused herself and disappeared shortly after landing to care for the new arrivals. It pained her, but she skipped nooning, opting instead to grab a quick bite and finish with the dragons so she'd have the evening free.

Remembered, barely, to change her clothes before heading to the Great Hall. Stepped in and stopped.

True to her word, Gemma had wrought a miracle. What had been an austere and functional room two short days ago had been transformed into a warm and welcoming home.

Renny surveyed the changes with delighted awe.

Like a dream come true, Dragon's Haven was well on its way to resembling Lady Gemma's home. Tapestries hung on what had been bare stone walls, sweet rushes covered the floor, everywhere flowers and candles.

Renny sighed. She was going to miss this stuff when Lady Gemma returned home and took her beautiful things with her.

Lady Gemma spotted Renny as she entered the Great Hall and the look on Renny's face made every bit of the effort worthwhile. Everyone in the keep had been pressed into service in some capacity to make this happen.

Making her way to Renny, Lady Gemma made an extravagant gesture that encompassed the entire hall. "What think you?"

Eyeing Lady Gemma uncertainly, what Renny wanted was to throw her arms around the older woman in gratitude. Not taking Gemma's familial offer lightly, Renny asked shyly, "May I hug you?"

Opening her arms and embracing her newest daughter, Gemma was careful not to let Renny know how livid Renny's question made her. Gemma could scarce imagine a child, a woman, so starved for love—so unsure of her reception—that she would ask permission for a hug.

Remembering Allar's oft repeated instructions upon receiving gifts, Renny whispered quietly, so quietly Gemma wasn't sure she heard aright. "Thank you, Mother Gemma."

Squeezing Renny tighter, Gemma squinched her eyes shut hard in order not to cry.

Inhaling deeply, Renny tried not to tremble, wanted to stay right here for a long while. Other than the keep's children and Allar, not many hugged her, and she so enjoyed it.

Not wanting to wear out her welcome, still unsure about her place in this family, Renny pulled back far sooner than she wanted to.

Watching from across the room as his mother took Renny under her wing, Allar balanced on the balls of his feet, fully prepared to jump to Renny's defense the second she got too overwhelmed. His mother's back to him, Renny faced Allar during the hug the women shared. Renny's face, so full of longing and hope it made him want to go out and pummel something to a pulp.

Looking back and forth between Renny and Allar, Tellar started shaking his head. "I've seen that look on your face before, brother. Go find someone else to spar with."

Without taking his eyes off Renny, jaw clenched, eyes blazing, Allar asked Tellar, "How could anyone treat a child the way Renny was treated? Not only starve her by begrudging food, but by withholding love and affection. It breaks my heart."

"It appears our Renny has much to make up for." Tellar trailed his fingers across his cheek. "I shall treasure this morning's kiss even more."

Allar landed a firm slap on the back of Tellar's head. "Yeah, well, don't get used to it. Renny saves her kisses for me."

The brothers spatted good-naturedly, and kept an eye on Renny and their mother.

Keeping her hands on Renny's shoulders, not allowing too much distance, Lady Gemma indicated the hall with a glance. "I am so glad you like it. This is our joining ceremony gift to you and Allar. If there's anything you don't like, you have only to say so and we will change it."

Renny smiled, already internally lamenting the loss of the beauty Lady… Mother Gemma had wrought. "Thank you for the loan of your beautiful things and all your work. It's hard to believe what a difference they make."

Lady Gemma's laughter had heads turning. "Child, we're not *loaning* these things to you. *They're yours.* To keep. *That* is our gift. I've been planning this day for years! I've just been waiting for Allar to find his mate so there would be someone here to care for these things. The only stipulation is, if you don't like something, you have to let me know so we can exchange it for something you do. Something more to your tastes."

Renny shook her head, certain she'd heard wrong. Allar's parents were…*giving* all these beautiful things…to *her*? The thought of ruining any of this…splendor out of sheer ignorance because she sure didn't know how to take care of any of it petrified Renny. She protested weakly, "Lady Gemma, I don't know how to…

"Oh, Renny child." Lady Gemma gave Renny a quick, hard hug and hooked her arm through Renny's. "You are such a treasure. There's nothing you can do to hurt any of it. I just wanted someone who would love and appreciate their beauty, as you do. Men seldom pay any attention to their surroundings, as long as their bellies and their beds are well filled. If you have any questions, you have only to ask."

Steering Renny toward the stairs, Gemma confided, "I have some things for your personal areas as well. I've seen Allar's chambers. There's nothing in there fit for a female unless she's a troll or a giantess. Let's go look, shall we, and you can decide what you want where."

Renny promised fervently, "Lady Gemma, I give you my word I will take excellent care of everything, and I do appreciate it. More than you know."

Exerting pressure on Renny's arm, Gemma pulled her close so they touched heads. "I never doubted you would." Gemma told Renny in a conspiratorial whisper, "I like Mother Gemma much better."

ALLAR ENTERED his chamber and stopped in shock, much the same way Renny had when she'd gotten her first eyeful of the Great Hall. His mother had been busy. Very busy.

Renny turned to him, wide-eyed. "Allar, your mother *gifted* us all these beautiful things!"

Throwing her arms wide, Renny twirled in a slow circle, showing him the bounty as if he couldn't see for himself.

Soft rugs on the floor beside the bed and the fireplace, brightly colored pillows on the bed, a tapestry on one wall depicting Belingrad, the first dragonrider.

Renny spun to a halt, a worried frown on her face at his lack of response.

Allar dispelled any doubt with his sincere words. "None are half so beautiful as you."

Renny stammered her thank you and then, "Look!"

Looking where she pointed, Allar saw the silver gown.

Scarcely able to contain her excitement, Renny bubbled, "I asked, and they said yes!"

Unable to touch Renny without bedding her this instant, it was Allar's turn to point, to the huge wardrobe taking up most of one wall. Voice thick, he told Renny, "Your gown belongs in there, not on a hook on the back of the door." Taking the filmy fabric down, Allar held the gown out to Renny.

Looking at Allar questioningly, Renny took it. She hadn't given the huge wardrobe another thought since she'd asked Allar if she could keep her clothes in the chest at the foot of the bed.

Recalling that conversation and the one last night, Renny remembered the strange look on Allar's face both times.

Cautiously opening the wardrobe—like she was springing a trap—Renny stood as if turned to stone, making no move to hang up her gown.

Really, there wasn't room.

Gown upon gown, clothes upon clothes in bright jewel tones filled the wardrobe from side to side, top to bottom. Renny reached out, not quite letting herself touch them. The silver slipped to the floor to puddle unnoticed at her feet.

Renny stretched out one finger to lightly stroke the emerald green gown, front and center.

{{ *This is the one you had made for me for our ceremony?*}}

{{*Aye.*}}

{{*I should like to wear it this evening.*}}

{{*So you shall.*}}

Taking a deep breath, Renny smiled at Allar, her eyes brimming with love. {{*I adore the smell of red-wood. It always reminds me of Rand. And now you.*}}

CHAPTER 23

*T*he celebration was in full swing by the time Allar and Renny made it back down stairs, Renny looking like a woods elf this evening, all greens and browns.

Loath to let go of his mate, but since Renny was in high demand as a dance partner, Allar stood to the side, watching. At the moment, Renny was teaching Tellar a new step, and how was that possible? Tellar should've been teaching her!

Gemma and Gamron joined Allar, and they stood in companionable silence watching Renny's antics in the midst of an admiring circle.

Putting a hand on Allar's forearm, Gemma beamed. "Renny called me Mother Gemma today."

Allar looked at his mother, his delighted grin matching his mother's smug smile.

Gamron harrumphed. "The most I can get out of her is *Sir.* With that, he moved off to see if he could steal a dance with his new daughter.

Critiquing Tellar's footwork, explaining why he was having so much trouble and laughing all the while, Renny looked up in surprise as Lord Gamron appeared in front of her.

Bowing slightly and holding out his hand, Gamron swept Renny into the stream of dancers. They danced without speaking, Renny trying desperately to think of something, anything to break the ice.

"I've been watching you dance, and you're a natural. Relax, child. I won't attack you."

Renny threw back her head and laughed as Gamron whirled her. "That I would know how to deal with."

"Allar tells me you trained at Fort Helve under Rand. I fought beside him some in our younger years. He is a good man and an excellent teacher. Does he still…"

Allar had been without Renny far too long. Renny was his, and 'twas his turn to partner her. Breaking in smoothly, Allar held Renny too close and rubbed against her repeatedly, suggestively, all the while fending off other men trying to break in.

Refusing to relinquish his hold.

Seeing Renny's longing glance toward the food as they whirled and spun, Allar steered them in that direction.

Loading a plate with fruits and cheeses and sweets, the pair found a secluded corner. Backing Renny into the corner, Allar blocked her in with his big body.

Laughing and carrying on like children, they sampled the treats. Holding a tidbit to Renny's lips, Allar teased, knowing Renny's loyalty ran bone deep. "Cook is beside herself. Foods are pouring in from all over, ceremony gifts for us. She's afraid you'll like someone else's cooking better than hers."

Nibbling at the treat, getting a good taste of Allar's fingers, Renny licked her lips. "Not a chance."

Laughing, starting to say more, Allar popped a small piece of cheese in her mouth. Renny chewed and swallowed, her face undergoing several startling transformations before settling on a sickly green.

Allar heard the dragons' protests as Renny's ripples of unease spread.

"Renny, what is it? Talk to me!" Allar handed her their drink, ready to bellow for Seon. Conthar and Zantha added their pleas. Catching the eye of some of his most trusted soldiers, Allar nodded and they immediately took up extra-protective stances, eyes roving and hands on their sword hilts.

Almost strangling on the words, Renny raised tormented eyes to Allar's. "This…cheese."

Allar's immediate thought was *poison*. All this food coming in was a perfect way to slip poison into the keep. Even though he'd ordered all the food routed through the dragons' courtyard, where the dragons checked it for poisons.

In all the excitement over their ceremony, how could he have forgotten Renny had enemies? That someone wanted her dead?

Drawing a breath, Allar bent to scoop her up, intending to find Seon.

Holding out her hand, Renny shook her head. "This is it."

The dragons' uneasy roars subsided and Allar stilled as understanding dawned. {{*Zantha! Tell Mithar to find Voya immediately and send him to me.*}}

Appearing almost before Allar finished his order, taking a look at Renny's face and then the plate Allar had set down on a small table, Voya's face tightened. "Which one?"

Renny shrugged apologetically. "I wasn't paying attention."

Cupping her face, Allar glared. "Don't you dare apologize."

The three of them made their way slowly down the food table, Allar and Voya flanking her, Renny sampling cheeses. Keeping their backs to the crowd, it appeared as if they were merely enjoying the many delicacies.

Upon identifying the right one, no words were necessary. Renny closed her eyes, head back, face awash in pain.

Allar and Voya exchanged a long, telling look over Renny's head, knowing if they so much as turned their heads, she'd be gone, attempting to locate and destroy the dragonhaters by herself.

Hefting the whole platter, Voya headed to the kitchen. Cook would know exactly who had sent what, if only so the senders could be properly thanked.

The soldiers Allar had singled out earlier moved closer, warily ready. Renny would just have to get used to the extra guards.

Waiting a bit, pretending to sample more, Allar held Renny back from following hot on Voya's heels. They'd gone only a short distance down the hall to the kitchen when Allar clamped Renny's arm in an unbreakable grip and stopped her, held tight when she tried to follow the now out of sight Voya.

Eyes flashing, the budding woman of the last few days vanished and the battle hardened and battle ready waif reappeared in the blink of an eye. Taking in the men following and preceding them, Renny's eyes shot daggers at Allar as she hissed, "Let me go. I have to know where that came from. Who's responsible."

"Renny. Listen to me. It's what the dragonhaters want, to draw you away from us so they can torture and kill you. Think how you felt when you came across the dead and dying dragons. That's exactly how all of us would feel if they got their hands on you, except a million times worse. The mate bond can be our greatest blessing, or our worst curse. None of us will survive without you."

Conthar and Zantha echoed Allar's words until Renny's head rang so badly she shut them all out.

Renny glared at Allar so hard his skin should've been smoking. "I swore vengeance on the perpetrators to all the dragons, the ones I couldn't save as well as Conthar. I will not break my word to any of them."

How to get through to her? "Renny love, none of us are denying you your vengeance or asking you to break your word. You told me Rand always said for you to use your brain. Use it now.

Whoever sent that cheese doesn't know you're able to identify it. If you go rushing after them, they could get away. I know you don't want that to happen. All I'm asking is that you give us enough time to reconnoiter. To plan."

Calming somewhat, Renny tried to consider Allar's word rationally, with some part of her brain other than the one screaming for justice. Eyes huge in her pale face, voice cold, she rolled her shoulders as if shifting an unbearable weight. "We have to know for certain if the people who sent the cheese are the ones who committed the crimes. They could be merely buying and selling the cheese."

{{*That's my girl! Use that fine brain of yours!*}} "Then we'll find out who they sold it to and who they bought it from. Renny, we will find them. I will make certain there is no question as to the identity of the guilty party or parties before exacting retribution. We will figure out a way to destroy the dragonhaters. We want them as badly as you do."

Renny barked, "You cannot possibly want these people dead as much as I do. This is my battle—I've been fighting alone for years and I will accept your assistance, but I refuse to let you protect me and keep me from fulfilling my oaths."

Added eagerly, albeit futilely, "Use me as bait. You said yourself 'tis me they want. Use me to draw them out. I trust you to keep me safe."

At the thought of Renny in the hands of the dragonhaters, Allar's rage blossomed. Allar, Zantha, and Conthar were united in their vocal disapproval—using Renny as bait was not an option.

Allar snapped at her, his voice frigid. "That will never happen! You will not think to place yourself in danger. Otherwise I *will* order you restrained. Your safety is paramount."

Renny's temper, barely held in check, sparked like dry tinder. "Allar, I swear to you, if you attempt to restrain me or shut me out of this in any way, I will never trust you again. Never forgive you."

Allar matched her ire with his own. "If keeping you alive means you hate me for the rest of our lives, then so be it. I make no promise to you save this—you are my mate and I will protect you as I see fit. If that means locking you up to keep you safe, I will not hesitate to do so. If you try to escape the guards assigned you, they will be punished. Severely."

Glaring at each other, one very large man and one diminutive, determined woman, toe to toe, sparks filled the air around them. The spark burst into flame and a wise man would've looked for water, not more fuel.

Holding Renny's shoulders, Allar growled, "I want your word that you will accept adequate guards and that you will take no risks."

Radiating fury the way a burning coal threw off heat, Renny spat, "I need no babysitters. Your men have far more important tasks than me. Did you think I wouldn't notice Voya following me around like a puppy? He didn't become your second so he could watch me pamper dragons all day. 'Tis past time you let him resume his duties. You need him beside you, now more than ever. I can take care of myself."

Allar's eyes were hard and cold, all warrior now. "You are his duty. If I cannot be at your side, he is to be. There is nothing —*nothing!*—more important than your safety. Do not go behind my back on this—do not even *think* to enlist the help of my people or any of the dragons. Anyone, human or dragon, who helps you will be banished from Dragon's Haven immediately and forever. Anyone."

Spinning on his heel, Allar stalked back out into the Great Hall.

Renny could see several soldiers close ranks at the entrance. Looking the other way, same-same. And Voya was in the kitchen. Even supposing she could slip past the soldiers...

Renny paced, livid. How could Allar do this to her? Didn't he know how much this meant to her? A chance to find out who was responsible, to finally end this once and for all, and he wanted to coddle her.

Conthar nudged the barrier in her mind, asking for admittance.

Grudgingly letting him in, Renny continued to pace, kicking the stones of the wall in frustration every couple of steps.

{{*Renny. Think. That's all we're asking.*}}

{{*Leave me alone until I calm down. I thank you for your concern, but I am not fit company for anyone right now.*}}

{{*Renny. Allar is right. We cannot risk losing you. You are far too important. He is not trying to shut you out. He simply wants to protect you. Losing you would destroy him, destroy us, completely.*}}

The truth in their words was a bitter pill for Renny to swallow. {{*Do not try to comfort me right now. I swore an oath to the dead dragons and to myself, swore to you, that I would make the dragonhaters pay for every foul, atrocious deed they have committed. That oath is not something I take lightly. Would you have me break my word? That would make me no better than them.*}}

Conthar sighed. {{*I would have you alive.*}}

{{*Conthar, I do not want to lose you either. Try to understand—all my life I have had precious little save my honor. If Allar takes that away from me, it is as if my entire life was wasted, as if every thing I fought so hard for was without meaning.*}}

Conthar's derisive snort came through loud and clear. {{*Little Warrior, no one could be prouder of your accomplishments than we are. The only way your life could be wasted is if you let the dragonhaters get their hands on you. Your honor is not in question here—your safety is. You have to trust us to take care of you. That is what you are having so much trouble accepting. The oaths you swore were when you were alone, when you expected to die trying to fulfill them. You have much to live for now, so change your plans to include us.*}}

Renny slowed her pacing and kicking. {{*But…*}}

347

Relieved Renny was at last listening, Conthar repeated some of his earlier points, added a few new ones, hoping to sway her further toward their way of thinking. {{*They will pay, make no mistake on that score. I know you feel the need to do it all, but think on this —you have single-handedly done more to thwart the dragonhaters than any army. Before, you had nothing to lose but your own life, which you deem so unimportant. You. Are. No. Longer. Alone. Everything you do has consequences, repercussions. If they hated you before when they were uncertain of your identity, think how much more they must hate you now that they know who and what you truly are. If they get their hands on you now, they will make certain your death is slow and excruciatingly painful. Zantha and I, and Allar, will feel every torture inflicted on you. All the dragons on the planet will suffer right alongside you. I know you do not want that.*}}

Renny shuddered at the thought of Allar and the dragons having to go through even once what she'd endured each and every time a dragon died. Wouldn't wish that on the dragonhaters.

Head pounding, suddenly weary, tired of hurting, of being hunted, Renny was more than ready for this to be over.

Almost ready to concede she needed help, still amazed by the promise.

She needed to be with Allar and Conthar and Zantha.

Conthar ventured, {{*Renny, that man, the one who tried to kill Zantha at Lakeside.*}} Stopped as a long, rumbling growl emerged. Tried again. {{*He was going to kill you as well.*}} Another growl, longer and louder. {{*He didn't care if he died doing it. Zantha has shared her memories, and yours. She picked up enough from him to know he was terrified of letting you live, of having to report that he failed to kill you, which means he wasn't working alone. He was following orders to kill dragons—and you. The one we want is the one giving orders. Whoever it is will stop at nothing to finish the job.*}}

Renny nodded, all the while kicking herself for one more bad decision in a long line of. She should have… {{*In the tavern, when Din met the other man. It looked like Din was giving a report and taking orders. The man giving the orders seemed like a lord, or at least some high ranking official. It was dark and he was sitting in shadow, but I'm sure he's the one we want. We need to find him.*}}

After a quiet pause while they both pondered this newest bit of the puzzle, Renny came to life. {{*Thank you, Conthar. You did comfort me and I appreciate it. May Allar and I sleep in your cave with you and Zantha this night? I need to be close to all of you.*}}

A quiet presence until now, Zantha chimed in. {{*Both of you are always welcome, Renny. No need to ask.*}}

Renny sighed a heartfelt thank you and went in search of Allar. She had some major sucking up to do. Letting her pass, the guards fell into step right behind her.

Taking a few steps, Renny turned to face them, hands on her hips.

They glanced at her warily and the largest one said, "Lady Renny, Lord Allar gave us strict orders. If you so much as think about ditching us and disappearing, we're to lock you in your chambers."

Renny held up a hand in a peaceful gesture. "I give you my word I will not get you in trouble. Can you walk beside me instead of behind me? I feel like a prisoner."

Smiled winningly and the two big strong warriors almost turned to mush. "Inform whomever has night guard, we'll be spending the night with our dragons and not in our chambers."

Both nodding, one managed to stammer, "'Twill be no problem, My Lady."

Allar and Tellar watched from across the room. Allar was still fuming and Renny's little display with two of his fiercest guards fanned the flames.

Tellar asked mildly, "What do you think she just promised them?"

Allar growled his response. "I have no idea, but I already warned both parties what would happen if Renny attempts to bribe them or if they let her out of their sight."

Grim faced, Allar remained seated while he watched Renny's progress toward him.

Tellar stood beside his brother, grinning like a fool. "Trouble in Paradise already, Brother?"

Coming to a stop in front of Allar, eyes glued to his face, Renny ignored Tellar and the guards completely. Plopping in Allar's lap, Renny wound her arms around his neck.

Allar sat as if frozen in place.

Renny apologized in one long rush of words. "You were right, I was wrong. I'm as sorry as I know how to be. You have my word I won't try anything. Can we please spend the night with our dragons? I need all of you close."

Tellar's grin widened as Allar's besotted expression mirrored that of the guards. Tilting his head close for a kiss, Allar didn't move otherwise.

Renny kissed him, hard, then buried her face in his neck.

Allar's arms closed solidly around his love, his life, as he clutched her to himself and stood up.

As Allar carried her off, Renny snickered at Tellar's plaintive, "Are you sure you don't have a sister?"

They completed the long trek to the dragon's caves in silence, Renny content to snuggle in Allar's arms. The cadence of his steps and the feel of his strong arms banded around her, his warmth surrounding her, lulled Renny until she was nearly asleep.

Holding Renny with one arm, Allar pulled back the covers with the other. Placing Renny on the raised platform that served as their bed here, Allar took his time stripping Renny down to her under-shift.

Smiled wickedly to himself. Renny had taken his mother and Ninar's teachings to heart. The under-shift she wore was, if not the same one she'd borrowed, definitely its close cousin.

Rolling to her side, making no attempt to hide her jaw cracking yawn, Renny mumbled, "Sorry, Allar. Too...tired."

Brushing a kiss across her forehead, Allar soothed, "Hush, little love. I'm just making sure you're comfortable."

Stretching out beside her on the thick feather mattress, Allar pulled Renny close. Zantha and Conthar nestled close on either side of their humans, their heads and necks entwining at the foot.

CHAPTER 24

Something was wrong.

{{*Renny! Awake!*}}

Renny remembered going to sleep in Allar's arms, their dragons close by.

{{*Renny! Now!*}}

Why was Conthar trying to wake her? Not just Conthar—all the dragons were clamoring at her.

Maybe she was caught in a nightmare. Dragons knew, she'd had more than her share of those and dragon screams always figured prominently.

{{*RENNY!*}}

She kept trying to wake up, but the very air was…thick, too thick to breathe. Struggling in earnest to obey Conthar's summons, feeling caught in one of her endless running and getting nowhere nightmares, Renny forced her eyes open enough to see orange light flickering on the walls.

{{*Conthar? Zantha?*}} Where was Allar?

As if her thoughts conjured him, Allar appeared beside her.

Panting, he gasped out, "Renny—fire!"

Helping Renny up, they staggered to the cave entrance. The world had turned to flames.

Renny stared in horror.

The keep was stone, the dragons could fly, the material things could be replaced.

The people! They had to get the people out of the keep, their own and all the guests.

Even as they took in the living nightmare, the dragons had roused all the riders, who in turn roused others. Bucket brigades were forming in the hardest hit areas. Some of the outbuildings were already engulfed.

Renny started forward, only to have Allar grasp her arm and jerk her back.

"Get dressed. Zantha and Conthar will take you to safety."

Determined not to be shuttled aside like some useless damsel, Renny shook her head. "Allar, I can help."

Giving her a quick kiss, Allar cupped her cheek. "I know you can, but you can help more from outside the keep. I need you as Lady of Dragon's Haven and a Healer, not another body in the bucket brigade. Conthar's going to take you to the edge of the big landing field, close to the biggest dragon-fruit tree. We'll bring the wounded to you. Keep your mind open to me. Don't leave without... There's Voya. Clothes. Hurry. I love you."

Allar was gone, plunging into the conflagration before Renny's answering *I love you* feathered the air.

Whirling, she grabbed the first clothes she came to on the shelf. Got her hands on the big satchel that was stuffed with as many medicines as she could cram into it, dropped her dagger into her boot sheath, ran outside and vaulted onto Conthar.

Airborne while she was still settling onto his back, Voya and Mithar flanked her on one side, Zantha on the other.

The damage far more evident from the air, it seemed as if everything at Dragon's Haven was on fire.

Conthar was still back pedaling his wings, legs outstretched, when Renny bailed. {{*Go, Conthar!*}}

Mithar and Zantha left with Conthar in a heated rush of wings.

Renny gathered anything that would burn, the irony smacking her in the face like a wet blanket. Voya used his sword to hack whole branches from the dragon-fruit tree to serve as torches. Once lit, the waxy, dragon shaped seedpods would burn for a long while.

Voya stobbed the branches into the ground and Renny lit the first one with a flint and striker she kept stashed in her medicine bag for just such emergencies. Voya lit the others from that one in turn, outlining a landing pad for the dragons and marking off safe areas for the wounded, the very thing destroying Dragon's Haven exactly what they needed to save its inhabitants.

The dragons kept up their usual running commentary in Renny's head, keeping her informed.

Many of the guards were missing, the gates and doors had been blocked off and fires lit in front of them to keep the people trapped inside. Renny caught a stray thought...*one of the biggest piles had been in front of the door to Allar's chamber.*

The only way the people could get out was to reach the ramparts and wait for the dragons to airlift them away from the hungry flames.

Consoling the dragons, Renny's heart ached for Allar. He'd worried from the first an insider was helping the dragonhaters. Looked like he'd been right.

As more and more people arrived, Renny was kept busy tending them. Mostly frightened and disoriented, a few with minor burns and smoke inhalation, Renny did more comforting than healing.

Seon, along with Bena and Sher and more apprentice Healers, scattered out among the crowd and began tending the wounded. Renny was more than glad to turn the human wounded over to him, as her healing talent didn't encompass non-dragons.

A large group of dragons landed, one by one in the field marked off by the torches, bringing a huge influx of people, some badly wounded. Voya was helping them dismount when Mina landed, carrying Voya's mate.

Both were burned and coughing up thick black smoke.

The pain radiating from them already swamping Renny, Mithar screamed from inside the keep, a cry of agony. His pain, added to theirs, drove Renny to her knees.

Amid the screams and cries and general confusion, someone tugged at Renny's sleeve. Gasping like an Okumo had kicked her in the ribs, raising her head, Renny beheld a raggedy little urchin. No one she recognized, and not one of the children from Dragon's Haven or the surrounding area, it was like looking into a mirror and seeing her younger self.

"The little girl—she needs you. She's in a bad way."

Renny didn't move, didn't blink as she called to Conthar and Allar. {{*The dragonhaters are here.*}}

{{*DO NOT MOVE! We are on the way.*}}

{{*They're using a little girl as bait.*}}

Conthar's bellow drowned out Mithar's.

Renny did a little bellowing of her own. "Seon! I need a Healer over here! We have a wounded little girl!"

Gently cupping the thin shoulder, narrowed eyes taking in the instinctive flinch, Renny assured, "I'll get you help. The Healers will take care of you."

Bait that she was, the little's girl's eyes flared in panic.

Renny had no doubt a severe punishment had been threatened if the little girl failed in her mission.

"What's your name?"

The little girl stared mutely, obviously terrified.

A tall form came out of the darkness to kneel beside Renny, and Bena added his calm tone to Renny's. "Where are you hurt?"

"Not…not me. Some other little girl." Stammering and trying unsuccessfully to worm away from Renny, the little girl tried again. "You have to come. Nobody else. Just her. The Dragonhealer."

As if they'd needed confirmation.

Gathering a generous fistful of the over-large shirt the girl was wearing, cranking down with a twist of her wrist so the girl couldn't slip out of it, making sure she had a good grip on the raggedy cloth, Renny stood and jerked her thumb towards Bena. "He heals people. I heal dragons."

Handing over custody, striding off toward Mina, Renny checked in with Allar and Conthar, both a constant presence in her head and vying for space with Mina and Mithar and all the other dragons. {{*I'm fine, my loves. Crisis averted and I didn't use myself as bait.*}}

{{*Where's Voya?*}}

{{*Calm down, Allar. Mina just landed. She and Latia are wounded. Voya is with them, as he should be.*}}

The closer Renny got to Mina the worse the pain got. Locking down her mental barriers and yet allowing Conthar and Allar to remain, Renny assessed the damage.

Hands skimming the air around the burns on Mina, even as she plucked the memories out of Mina's mind, Renny demanded, "What caused this?"

{{*Dragonhealer…something…exploded and when this touched me…it stuck and the burn keeps going deeper. Help my rider. She caught the blast as well. Help Latia. Help…*}}

"Shh, shh. Easy Mina. Bena and Seon are taking care of Latia. Thank you for the vote of confidence but you know I'm much better with dragons than humans. Mithar got into this same stuff?" Renny spoke aloud, soothing and calming Mina, already knowing full well exactly what had happened to Mithar.

Knowing as well that none of her carefully hoarded

medicines would help with this newest torture from the dragonhaters.

Finding a patch of undamaged skin, Renny placed her hands on Mina. {{*Conthar! Zantha! I need you! Link with me! Link now!*}}

Diving into Mina's essence like she was diving into a bottomless burning pool, Renny made her way to the worst damage. Mina was exactly right—the…whatever it was was eating Mina's flesh.

How did you put out fire? Water?

Renny pushed a wave of metaphorical water toward the burning…sap.

Mina screamed in agony as the viscous matter splattered and *chomped.*

Hastily pulling back, *sorry, sorry, sorry,* Renny wracked her brain.

Water hadn't worked, had merely spread and intensified the burn.

Sap was like grease, wasn't it?

How did you put out a grease fire?

Smother it.

Sand? Dirt?

Not in a fresh wound.

Think, Renny!

Fight fire with fire!

Summoning a blast of heat, Renny pushed a wave of heat at the burning sap.

It took a moment, but the sap stopped advancing, just sat there bubbling and frothing.

Now, how to get rid of it.

Push it out and incinerate it.

Not sure if the words came from her own mind or the minds of all the dragons she was currently linked with, Renny pushed with all her might.

Surrounding the evil substance with a wall of heat, Renny pushed.

And pushed, and pushed, and pushed.

Pushed until she thought her eyeballs and eardrums would burst.

With an audible *pop!* the remnants left Mina's body and plopped onto the ground, hissing and spitting.

Hands on her knees, Renny gasped for breath, wondering how in the world she was supposed to expel the vile sap from Latia?

Renny couldn't heal humans, couldn't get into their minds like she could dragons. Had to heal Latia or she was going to lose Mina despite her best efforts.

Staggering to Latia, still trying to catch her breath, Renny nudged Bena.

"Just Renny! You saved Mina!"

Shivering, drenched in sweat that was rapidly cooling, Renny gasped, "Latia?"

Patting his motionless patient, Bena nodded, cluelessly. "Much better now that Mina isn't in so much pain. What did you do, and how did you do it?"

{{*Mina?*}}

{{*Help her, Dragonhealer. The poison acts slower in humans but it's still eating through her flesh.*}}

The poison had to come out before it reached a vital organ.

Think, Renny! You helped Mina, do the same before it's too late for Latia.

Mind flipping through possibilities like a dedicated reader flipping through a book for a specific passage, Renny threw out mentally and verbally:

{{**"Does Dragon's Haven have a glass blower?"**}}

Allar's hand dropped on her shoulder just as dragons and humans alike hit Renny with affirmatives. Twisting her head, Renny pressed a kiss on his hand. "I need him. Now. If he can blow, he can suck. I need this poison sucked out. Bena and Seon and Cher can treat the wounds but we have to get the sap stuff out!"

"Kelos, and she is on her way."

"We need a fire, like the forge fire, to incinerate…"

"Renny. Take a breath."

Leaning back against his hard form, Renny melted into Allar for a moment. {{*How long?*}}

{{*Not as long as you think. You will be able to heal the next one faster now that you've figured out how.*}}

{{*Gather all the dragons who are wounded…*}}

"Renny my love." Allar cupped Renny's shoulders, ran his hands comfortingly up and down her upper arms. Pressed a kiss to the top of her head and rested his lips there. {{*You are no longer alone. Breathe. Zantha has Kelos and they are almost here. All the dragons who've been touched by this foul concoction are being directed here, where you have the most light and the most help. Breathe, love.*}}

Renny sucked in a breath, blew it out.

{{*But you already know all of that. Your connection with all the dragons is beyond amazing. That you saved Mina… And figured out how to so quickly… The dragons are just as connected to you. They're carrying out your wishes before you complete the thought. Do what you need to and we'll take care of the rest.*}}

Turning into the circle of Allar's arms, Renny dropped her forehead to his chest and just breathed him in. {{*This is bad, Allar. Bad. What if I can't…*}}

{{*You already did, love. Stop second-guessing yourself and do what you do best—heal dragons.*}}

Another deep breath and Renny waded back into the fray.

Mithar was next, the dragons having already ferried him in a sling the way they'd done Conthar in the valley. The way they were becoming altogether too adept at doing.

Renny somehow compartmentalized the dragon's pain and managed to push the poison out. Mithar was far worse than

Mina, having been closer to another evil device when it detonated. The absolute only saving grace was… In their warped drive to prolong the torture, the dragonhaters had devised a slow-acting poison.

When Renny surfaced at last, Kelos was working hard, cheeks hollowed. Sucking the poison halfway up the clear glass straw, she was carefully moving the poison-filled tube to the side and then blowing it back into a glass container.

Face red, streaming with sweat, Kelos nodded at Renny.

Renny nodded back and headed for the next patient. "Take care."

Striding past the humans Kelos had already helped, Renny eyeballed them approvingly. She was gonna have to step up her game to keep up with the gray-haired glassblower.

Here, there, everywhere, tending new dragons and rechecking the ones she'd already seen, Renny stomped and hustled and cussed a blue streak when she ran out of the one ointment that seemed to do the most good.

In the middle of one of her whirling movements, she ran smack into Allar. "Allar! I need more fire-thorn! It grows wild, find me a patch."

When Allar only stared, Renny smacked him on the arm. "Now!"

When he continued to stare stupidly, Renny shook her head. "Never mind." {{*Conthar! Take several dragons and riders and get me as much fire-thorn as you can carry! Don't go far and hurry back!*}}

Allar stared, his face screwed up in distaste. "That's stuff's a vile, noxious weed. We made sure there isn't any close to Dragon's Haven. It keeps trying to take over, we keep burning and digging and eradicating. The harder we try, the faster it grows, or so it seems, like it's trying to get to the dragons." Allar shuddered in distaste and spat, as if he'd gotten a face full of the thick kazas smoke.

Renny stared, slack jawed. "Have you lost your mind? The

fire-thorn *is* trying to get to the dragons. They need it. It's a symbiotic panacea. It's the basis for most of my salves and…"

"You didn't say anything about that when we were talking about fire-thorn."

"Why would I? You said the dragons wouldn't help you destroy it. That should've been your first clue." {{*Conthar, I need fresh leaves, and the berries, if you can find any. They'll do the most good, the fastest.*}}

{{*On it, Renny.*}}

"How do the dragons pick the fire-thorn? You can't get within two dragon's length of that stuff without the thorns leaping out and stabbing you."

Renny blinked, biting her tongue against the caustic reply hovering on the tip. "The juvenile form is the only one that has thorns. The older it gets, the less thorns. The thorns are to protect the young plants." {{*Zantha, please explain fire-thorn harvesting to Allar.*}}

Leaving Zantha to her excited explanations of the dragon's mouths reaching out and raking great swaths of the leaves and berries off the plants, Renny snickered at Allar's plaintive, {{*Why didn't you tell me? All those pricks and sticks and smoke…*}}

Renny laughed out loud at Allar's whining and Zantha's {{*You never asked why we wouldn't help you destroy kazas. We just thought pulling and burning it was a stupid human thing.*}}

Going back to pushing out more poison until Conthar returned, Renny set to. Indicating a large piece of dragonhide spread on the ground, Renny had the dragons spit out the fire-thorn. They'd done a good job of masticating the leaves and berries, helping Renny immensely.

"Bena, Sher! Take this!" Swiping a thick piece of the loose, curling bark from the dragon fruit tree and using it for a makeshift scoop, thrusting the cud-like mixture at the Healers, Renny fired orders.

"Don't worry about making an ointment out of this. We don't have time. Just plaster it on the wounds and pack it in."

Eyeing the slimy, reeking mess, Bena swallowed uneasily. "JusRenny. We need gloves for this. Fire-thorn's…"

Grinding her jaw, Renny shook her head. "Don't get squeamish on me now! Once the dragons chew it, fire-thorn won't burn humans. Haven't you ever noticed…" Muttered to herself, "Of course you haven't."

Pointing to Conthar, Renny waited.

Licking his lips like a contented feline, Conthar settled on his haunches, eyes glassy. Claws kneading the ground and a low, rumbling purr emanating from deep in his thorax.

"He's… Conthar's sick! Blasted fire-thorn! I told you…"

Renny shook her head, an amused smile lighting her features. "Look again."

All of them focused on Conthar, and Zantha too, as both tipsy dragon's heads began weaving and bobbing and… Was that drool?

A chuckle started low in Bena's throat and quickly worked its way to a full belly laugh. "He's… It's like a pursim with pursim-nip. He's drunk!"

Renny beamed at her prize student. "Exactly!"

Slipping an arm around Renny from behind, Allar mused, "I've never seen…"

Renny snickered. "Probably not. Most dragons don't overindulge when their humans are around because they don't want to look like nincompoops. The only reason they're so bad off now is because they brought me a huge amount and had to keep it in their mouths for so long. Couldn't help but swallow a large quantity of the juices."

{{*Zantha, why didn't you tell me how important fire-thorn was to you?*}}

Zantha's dreamy answer floated to them on a satisfied purr.

{{*You never asked, my amazingly wonderful and humanly dense human. You only asked why we wouldn't aid you.*}}

Frowning, Allar tried again. {{*Why? All you had to do was tell us not to destroy it because it was important to you.*}}

Giving a very dragonish shrug and almost tipping herself over in the process, Zantha stropped herself sinuously against her mate, her mind obviously far from this inane conversation and locked on something much more important. {{*We figured it was like your stupid human habit of cooking your meat and making it inedible. And it's not like there isn't tons of the stuff growing everywhere.*}}

She hiccuped and draped her head over Conthar's shoulders before twining her neck with his.

Enthusiastically returning the affectionate gesture, Conthar made a distinctively male sound of possession.

Laughing softly at their besotted antics, Renny spun and froze.

A circle of dragons faced her, all with their mouths dripping fire-thorn slobber.

Eyes tearing up at their gesture of solidarity and support, with a wave of her hand, Renny showed them where to drop their gleanings. {{*Thank you. Thank you all.*}}

Arms crossed, booted feet wide, Allar demanded petulantly, "How come the smoke doesn't affect them?"

Renny shrugged. "Different form, different results."

"They could've said something. Do you have any idea how hard we've worked to get rid of that stuff?"

Tipping her head to one side, Renny made a face. "Why?"

Allar blinked, opened his mouth, shut it. "I have no idea, save the weed is invasive and nasty."

Renny made a noncommittal sound. "If you'd left it alone, the dragons would've kept it under control. The harder you try to destroy it, the faster it grows."

Eyes narrowing, Allar stepped closer, attempting to intimidate Renny as a thought suddenly occurred to him. "Which one told you? There's no way you'd be this rubbing-it-in-my-face-smug if you'd known all along."

Renny burst into laughter, drawing all eyes, her own dancing mischievously. "Gotcha!" Sobering, she covertly stroked a hand down Allar's chest all the way to the top of his leggings, mimicking Zantha's attentions to Conthar.

"I long ago figured out it was a balm for the dragons. The wild ones just told me last week that fire-thorn had…other uses." Renny continued dryly, "Evidently the wilds discovered it all on their own. Quite by accident."

Face tightening, Renny growled, "Conthar tells me the old Dragonhealers knew this, and deliberately withheld the knowledge from the general public."

Grasping her arms, Allar demanded, "Why? Why would they…"

Renny shrugged and pretended Allar's grip didn't hurt. "I cannot say for certain, having never known another Dragonhealer. Conthar says…" Cocked her head as if listening. "The dragonhealers wanted to be revered."

Loosening his grip at Zantha's delayed prompting, rubbing Renny's arms in apology, Allar shook his head. "What do you mean, *wanted to be revered?* The old tales tell of immense wealth and favors bestowed upon the Dragonhealers. They had everything they could possibly want handed to them on golden platters."

Working her shoulders, Renny tipped her head the other way. "Not merely revered, they wanted to be…gods. The dragons revolted."

Allar finished incredulously, "They wanted more? Wait. The *dragons* revolted?"

Half turning her head, listening to more and more dragons as bits and pieces of the truth filtered in from some of the more ancient dragons, Renny's face hardened and her eyes filled with tears. "The Dragonhealers began to withhold treatment if the dragons wouldn't comply. No, a faction of the Dragonhealers. They split, the ones who loved the dragons and the ones who felt they deserved to be worshipped."

"And so they became Dragonhealers and dragonhaters."

Renny nodded and dropped her head against Allar's chest. "Until there were no more Dragonhealers. The dragons…tried their best to protect the true Dragonhealers, but somehow, the dragonhaters can conceal their true hearts. The same way they lured Conthar and others in so they could torture them."

"What you're saying sounds impossible."

Renny jerked. "You doubt me?"

"Do not even…" Allar jerked right back, yanking Renny tight against himself and wrapping his arms around her in an unbreakable grip, dropping his head over hers. "All of this seems so farfetched and yet… It seems the dragon wars have gone on forever when in truth, it has only been a few generations. Our world has very nearly been destroyed and much knowledge has been lost, or skewed beyond recognition."

Both looked at the pile of fire-thorn mush.

Renny rubbed her cheek against Allar's shirt, wishing it was bare skin. "Deliberately, I'd say."

Allar spat, "So we're back to traitors in our midst. How are we going to rout them? The dragons can't sense them. We don't know who they are. They've survived this long with their agenda intact. Who knows how much longer they'll be able to keep on fooling us?"

Renny smiled, a dangerous smile her dead enemies would recognize without hesitation. "You didn't have me. Now you do. My offer stands."

Cranking down on Renny's slight form until she squeaked, or maybe it was her bones protesting his fierce hold, Allar barked, "No! I told you I will not allow it!"

Uneasy bellows and grunts from the dragons confirmed his statement.

Burrowing closer to him, wrapping her arms around his waist and squeezing back, Renny nuzzled her face into the hard muscles of Allar's chest. "I'm not some helpless damsel. I'm a trained warrior, and besides, they won't hurt me." *Much.* "They'll want to convert me to their side. Think how much damage I could do to the fragile balance between riders and dragons and the general populace. To the dragon population. Think what a terrible figurehead I'd be. Beloved by all the dragons. No one would suspect me until it was far too late."

Allar's thundering heart tried and failed to drown out Renny's words. "No. NO. **NO!**"

Blowing out a warm breath, fitting herself closer to Allar's form and burrowing her face in the warm spot she'd created, Renny sighed. "You might as well give in, my beloved. It's only a matter of time until they kidnap me. It'd be much better if we orchestrated it from our end instead of trying to figure out…"

Allar went so rigid in Renny's arms, it was like hugging a statue.

Sliding a hand under the hem of his shirt and touching warm skin, Renny grounded herself. "I'm not used to waiting, my love. I'm used to being preemptive. I've only held back as long as I have because you and the dragons asked me to. This…"

Waving her other hand at the field hospital even though Allar couldn't see her motion behind his back, Renny shook her head. "This…abomination. I won't stand for it. I've given you my word. Don't make me break it. Work with me."

Grasping at straws, trying not to let Renny's unaccustomed use of endearments and her outright threats sway his decision, Allar gritted out, "The girl knows nothing. Has no idea who is using her, only that she's more terrified of him than anything we can do to her."

Renny's voice remained determinedly patient, each word like a drip of water wearing down rock. "Yet another reason for me to hurry and get this over with, Allar. It's only going to get worse.

They'll keep trying and keep trying and keep trying until Dragon's Haven is rubble, the people wounded and cowed and all the dragons dead. I can't bear to watch another dragon die, or another child, or another warrior. Not when all this is my fault."

Heart in his throat, knowing what was coming, Allar did his best to sidetrack Renny, to delay the inevitable. "Think highly of yourself, don'cha? This war was started long before either of us was born and will…"

Renny straightened, all warrior, her eyes cold and dead serious on his. "…end now. No more, Allar. I may not have started it, but I can end it. He knew the child would fail. That was merely a trial run. He's going to keep upping the stakes. What do you think I would sacrifice for your life? Or Conthar's? Or…Lissa's? Or any of the dragons, wild or tame? This has become…a game to him. He'll just keep picking off things I love, one by one, until I am so damaged as to be useless."

Pressing his forehead to hers, Allar breathed Renny in. Her warm woman scent calmed him and drove him wild at the same time. "Just the thought of losing you… We can't lose you."

Renny blew out a heavy breath. "If you don't let me at least try it my way, you're going to lose me for certain. That decision has been made for us. The only thing left for us to decide is whether it's to be as quick and merciful as possible or as long and drawn out as he can make it. We all know which he'd prefer."

Breath coming in harsh gasps like he'd just come from a battle, Allar used their private link. {{*You could hear the dragons when we were in the valley, even when their riders could not. You can hear all the dragons, not just our own.*}}

{{*There is that.*}}

{{*And you can hear me and speak to me.*}}

{{*I can. And no one save our dragons knows about that. 'Tis our ace in the hole.*}}

{{*You have to fight. Know that we will come for you, no matter how far they take you.*}}

Petting Allar, stroking him like she did the dragons to calm them, Renny soothed, {{*It won't be too far away, my love, and probably far closer than you'd like.*}}

At Allar's reluctant capitulation, Renny began firing orders over their dragons' uneasy rumblings.

{{*Conthar, see that all the dragons partake of the fire-thorn, a well deserved reward for all their hard work. I need them drowsy and off their game. For this to succeed, all must know I've been taken and be unable to track me.*}}

Conthar's furious reply blasted Renny like wind driven sand in one of the ferocious summer storms that plagued the planet.

Zantha added her distressed call.

Renny stood firm. {{*Slow, piece by piece, or over and done? I'm not easy to kill. The dragonhaters haven't managed to kill me when I was on my own, what makes you think they can now that I have all of you?*}}

CHAPTER 25

*R*enny came back to consciousness bit by bit.

She could smell smoke—fire—but there was fire at Dragon's Haven.

Contorted into an uncomfortable position, weighted down, she couldn't move, couldn't see, could barely breathe and whatever was beneath her was heaving like a foundering ship.

Was she trapped?

Had there been another explosion?

Her head was throbbing.

Maybe she'd gotten hit on the head again.

Renny remained still—not as if she had any choice in the matter—her mind struggling to put the facts together.

Suddenly her position made sense.

She lay facedown over the shoulders of a dragon in flight, hands tied behind her. Gagged and blindfolded, enveloped. Wrapped in some heavy material, a cloak or a rug or thick furs.

Had no memory of how she'd gotten here.

Did it matter?

Mission accomplished.

She'd been kidnapped by the dragonhaters.

Reached out instinctively for Conthar.

Even knowing she'd most likely draw a blank, the nothingness nearly stopped her heart.

Taking as deep a breath as she could, Renny reached for Allar.

Like her time in the lake, it seemed she swam forever. Mentally this time.

Whatever the dragonhaters had used on her was potent indeed.

But not nearly as strong as Renny's heart. Her mind.

Her love.

{{*Allar! There you are!*}}

{{*Renny! Renny my love!*}}

{{*Allar! Calm. Find your center and remain calm!*}}

{{*Hard to do when the dragons are circling aimlessly, spreading out in all directions and hunting blindly for you. When my heart is alternately beating out of my chest and not beating with fear for you.*}}

{{*I am unharmed. Restrained and blindfolded, but unharmed.*}}

Allar's rage came blasting down their link, making Renny jerk in her bonds.

{{*We knew this would happen, Allar.*}}

{{*Knowing and experiencing are vastly different, Renny.*}}

{{*Know this my love: Nothing will keep me from you or our dragons. This is just a detour. A skirmish, if you will.*}}

{{*You sound...far away.*}}

{{*They drugged me. I can taste it in my system. There is something else impeding our link... Can't tell exactly what. The connection is...sporadic. Promise me not to panic if I can't hold our link. I swear I will not intentionally shut you out. Be patient...*}}

The link snapped audibly and Renny couldn't reconnect no matter how hard she tried. A product of her head wound or some trick of the dragonhaters? Bereft, had Renny been any other female, she'd've wailed out loud.

Being Just Renny, she internalized the silent sound, used it as intangible fodder to fuel her anger at the ones responsible.

The rider of the no-color, the no-color himself if he was doing this of his own free will.

Him.

The one Din had reported to.

The orchestrator of all this insanity.

Who could possibly have such a vendetta against dragons?

Renny didn't know, couldn't imagine, but she would find out.

Mentally going over options, she figured the guards would rough her up when they got her to…wherever.

Then they'd take her to whomever was in charge and he'd play dumb. Scream at his idiot minions for daring to touch her and then offer succor.

Like Renny'd be stupid enough to fall for any of that.

CHAPTER 26

$\mathcal{A}$ smoky dawn highlighted a war zone: fires out, the wounded tended, the dead awaiting burial, a pall of disbelief and grief hanging over all.

Overwhelming all the deaths, the loss of property and goods, the sheer trauma of such a secure stronghold being attacked from within…

Renny's kidnapping.

Word had spread like wildfire.

The Dragonhealer.

Conthar's rider.

Lord Allar's mate.

Gone, stolen away—from under their very noses—by the Dragonhaters.

Ignoring the pitying looks and half-glances aimed his way, the hands reaching out and snatching back before they made contact —because, really, words and touches were all they had to offer, inadequate as they were—Allar struggled to keep his steps even as he headed for the huddle of humans and dragons he'd targeted. Voya and Mithar and…The pain swirling in the air—

magnified by the bonds between the two mated pairs, between the foursome—a grim harbinger of what lay in store for Allar's own foursome if they failed in their mission to find Renny.

If any one of Allar's four died, the other three might live but it would be as damaged, hollow shells of their former selves, much like Voya and Mithar right now.

"Voya." Pained and smoke-strangled, Allar's voice cracked and he tried again, loud enough to be audible this time. "Voya."

On his knees, looking up slowly, like he was hundreds of years old and nearly calcified by arthritis, Voya attempted to find his feet. Even if his body hadn't refused the order, Allar's heavy hand clamped on Voya's shoulder held him in place.

Head bowed, Voya apologized. "I failed you, my Lord. You and Lady Renny. I'm relieving myself of duty and accept whatever punishment you choose to mete out. I have no right to ask, but… I have to stay with Mina and… At least until…" Choked, unable to continue.

Dropping to his knees, wrapping Voya in a tight hug, Allar shook his head and wallowed in his own part of this deception. Losing Voya's trust would be like losing Renny, but if Voya hated Allar after… Allar would bear that hate. "There will be no punishment. This was a hideous and well laid plan. I do not hold you responsible. Stay with your mates while you can."

Silence for a long moment as Voya digested Allar's words, his battered brain trying to make sense of what his lord was saying and what he wasn't…

A spark, a glimmer of disbelief quickly shuttered, and Voya lifted his head a bit to meet Allar's eyes, unspoken communications flying back and forth.

Allar nodded and squeezed Voya's shoulder once more, a command to keep silent. "I will have need of you soon and then I must ask that you leave them and follow me. Others will guard… them until we return."

Voya's eyes burned, with knowledge and rage. Still knee to

knee with his lord, Voya nodded. So close none other could hear their words, seeming to be two males comforting each other for their losses, Voya fiercely pledged his continued allegiance.

"Lady Renny did her utmost to save my mate and my dragon's mate. There is nothing I would not do for her, and for you. We will be avenged and then I will return here and take care of my…" Reaching out a shaking hand, Voya gently tugged the blanket up around his wife's shoulders and tucked it close.

Patting the air over her barely moving chest as if afraid an actual touch would stop even that shallow, erratic movement, Voya nodded to himself.

If his Lord and friend was asking Voya to leave his dying mates, then that's what Voya would do. He'd long ago pledged to be Allar's right hand through thick and thin.

He would honor that pledge until his dying breath.

Gaining Voya's compliance and hating himself for even asking, Allar wondered grimly, who to trust? Voya, obviously. But who else? Which others? There was no doubt this had been an inside job. If Allar trusted the wrong person, all Renny's plotting and planning and sacrifice would be for naught.

Voya's pain would be for naught, a forever stain on Allar's soul.

Allar walked among his people, giving Voya as much time as possible.

Renny was alive.

Allar held onto that thought as he surveyed the damage in the light of day, his resolve solidifying with each wound, each body. A word here, a touch there. Said all the right things, made all the appropriate gestures. Held himself together through sheer will.

Came to a stop facing a ring of soldiers, some his, some from other keeps. Strong men, battle hardened warriors.

Allar stared at them, they stared at him.

Each and every one knew what it cost Allar to hold it together, to not rant and rave like a lunatic. Most had been in battle situations with Allar before, though none with such horrific consequences for failure.

Unable to say anything, there was nothing they could say that would help.

Cook bustled over, Lissa close on her heels. Curls a tangled mess, stumbling and rubbing her eyes, the child was obviously just waking up.

Cook encouraged, "My Lord, please. Sit, eat. You've been fighting fires all night. You'll need your strength for...later." A quick glance down at Lissa kept Cook from finishing her words.

Letting go her tight hold on her mother's skirts, Lissa marched over to Allar and stood with hands on her hips glaring up at him through eyes red rimmed from the smoke, or perhaps from crying. Stomping her foot, she demanded, "Why aren't you getting JusRenny back from the bad man? He took her and put her on a bad dragon. She wasn't moving, 'cause he did something to her and then tied her up. He flew away. I tried and tried to find you."

Frozen in place, the men were holding their collective breaths. Cook clapped both hands over her mouth, her eyes huge.

Torn between grabbing Lissa and shaking her/hugging her tight/interrogating her/ smothering her with kisses, Allar knelt on one knee and asked gently, "You saw the man who took JusRenny?"

Nodding, Lissa offered nothing else, obviously miffed that none of the adults had listened to her.

Afraid of spooking the small girl into incoherent tears, trying not to bellow in frustration, Allar cocked his head. "Can you show me where you saw the bad man?"

Taking him by the hand, peering around to ascertain her bearings, Lissa wended her way into the woods. Stopping at the verge of a small clearing, she pointed. "I was scared and Momma was losted. I saw JusRenny and I was going to stay with her 'cause I knowed she'd keep me safe. I heard the bad man say *I* needed help. JusRenny taked off running this way and I couldn't keep up."

Sobbing now, barely able to talk through the fat tears streaming down her face, Lissa hiccuped, "When... When I caught up he was putting Renny on the dragon. She wasn't fighting or yelling or nuthin. That's how I know he hurted her. They flew off that way."

Lissa jabbed her finger at empty air and wailed, "Now I really do need help! You have to get her back! You have to!"

Picking Lissa up, comforting her, Allar faced the men gathered around him. Head buried against his neck, arms wrapped tight and sobbing in earnest, Lissa pulled back enough to tell him, "I tried...to find you...but I got losted in the woods for awhile...and then I couldn't find you. I kept asking and asking...but everybody kept telling me you were in a different place. Then...then I was so tired I falled asleep...and I just waked up and...and it's all my fault."

That was the last coherent thing they got out of the distraught child.

Cook sobbed as Allar handed the child to her. "My Lord, she kept asking for you and jabbering about Lady Renny but I thought... I wasn't paying attention. I truly thought she'd just had a nightmare after last night's...excitement."

Giving Cook a hard hug, Allar kissed Lissa on top the head. "You both did fine. Lissa, what you did was very brave. JusRenny will be very proud of you when I tell her."

"What do we do now? We know which direction they went and that a dragonrider took her. What do we do?"

Looking at the soldier from another keep who'd voiced the question—Levat, if Allar remembered aright—sweeping his glance over the other hardened, desperate faces awaiting an answer, Allar took his time. "We wait. We rest. We prepare, and we wait. Renny will contact..."

Allar wound down to a halt, unwilling to lie and refusing to spill the truth. "Renny will make contact as soon as she's able."

Swords were sharpened, quivers filled, bows and shields inspected, armor checked and rechecked, mounts readied, supplies gathered and packed. Mindless tasks most of the warriors could've performed in their sleep were a necessary buffer, a mental shield to keep them from losing their minds while they waited.

All eyes stayed on Allar, awaiting his signal, ready to leave on a moment's notice.

Everything now was hurry up and wait.

Settling close to Zantha and Conthar, all three of them feeling like they'd been sandpapered and salted, Allar kept his voice low, unwilling to chance one of the no-colors or one of the traitors overhearing any mental convos.

"None but the four of us know Renny can mindspeak with me, that she's already contacted me. I can feel her life essence but…"

Taking a deep breath, making sure they were still well away from any prying eyes and cocked ears, Allar continued, "I'm hoping… I'm betting our gamble doesn't cost Renny her life. If I'm wrong…"

Nudging him, one from either side, Zantha and Conthar breathed warm breath on him, subtly reprimanding their human.

Renny was alive.

Dropping his head back against Zantha and closing his eyes, Allar's internal voice prodded and poked.

Alive—but in what condition and for how long?

CHAPTER 27

Stomach bottoming out and pushing up in her throat, Renny let out an oof as the dragon landed and she was roughly shoved off to land in a crumpled heap.

Smoothly rounded stones—cobblestones?—beneath her.

A courtyard?

Voices, echoey and warped confirmed her guess. From the sound, an empty courtyard. Like an abandoned house, devoid of all furnishings, nothing to break up the sound patterns and yet distorting them beyond recognition.

Trying to wiggle her hands and feet, possibly loosen the knots, a hard kick and a curse from her captor disabused Renny of that notion.

Picked up and slung over her captor's shoulder, Renny's nausea increased to terrifying proportions as his shoulder dug into her stomach with each step.

Fighting it back, Renny was thrown down, landing on smoother and more regularly shaped stones than the previous irregular ones. Rolled out of whatever was covering her by the force of the throw, Renny heard the door thud shut as her captor left—without loosening her bonds.

Squirming and twisting, Renny attempted to free herself. The ropes were too tight, the knots expertly tied. Concentrating, she could see Allar's light shining dimly, like candle glow around a door not properly shut.

Left it that way, knowing with that little bit of contact he would sense her presence but not feel her pain, unwilling to add her pain to the misery he was already experiencing. Pain she was absolutely certain sure was about to get way worse.

Evening out her breathing, Renny calmed herself, reminded herself—*Conthar buried himself under half a mountain for you and stayed that way, filled with poisons for a long while so you could have time to make it to Dragon's Haven and get Allar. They'll be here to end this—as soon as you let them know where here is. Stay alive and find out everything you can. Give them something to work with, the way Conthar's compulsion led you back to him.*

Ceasing her fruitless fighting against the unforgiving bonds, Renny concentrated on her surroundings.

Flat, square flagstones. She must be at ground level or below. The upper floors would have wooden flooring. Judging by the jarring each step had caused her, they'd gone down.

Casting her senses further, Renny recoiled.

This place felt…wrong.

Had been wrong for a very long time. Long enough for the wrongness to seep into the very stones and permeate everything.

Listening, Renny heard nothing but her own harsh breathing and the slow drip of water, reminding her how thirsty their poison had made her. Squirming until she found a wall, Renny pushed herself into a sitting position.

Drip, drip.

Breath in.

Drip.

Breath out.

Drip, drip, breath, until the sounds became her world.

A world infected with a deadly poison, the poison seeping out of the stones around her, soaking into Renny.

A while later—could've been moments, might've been days—the door opening sounded loud as a battle.

In her rolling and twisting, Renny'd ended up opposite the door.

Footsteps, coming closer, thudding like the footfalls of angry giants.

Her blindfold was yanked off, hard enough to bang Renny's head back against the wall. If the utter blackness of her blindfold and the darkness of her prison conspired against her sight, the torch in the doorway finished her off.

Renny could see nothing.

She could, however, feel.

Monstrous evil.

Just like the rider of the no-color who'd interrogated her for Din. Felt him pressing against the edges of her mind the same way. Might even be the same evil rider.

Had to be.

Knowing she couldn't actually hear her dragon, Conthar's words still rang in Renny's head.

Your shields are the strongest I've ever encountered—USE THEM!

Giving a little smirk, Renny closed her eyes and thought of… nothing. A void so complete it embodied nothingness.

An enraged snarl, and two sets of hard hands grabbed her arms, pulling Renny upright.

She blinked, trying to focus, but…the light.

Held her thought of the nothing.

A sharp blow caught her across the face, then another and another, all over her body, until she lost count.

Without the disembodied hands of the second guard holding her, Renny would've crumpled to the floor. The bright light was now overlaid with stars and spots, shot through with jagged bolts of lightning.

The blows slowed, slowed, and finally stopped.

Vision tinged with red, Renny couldn't focus at all.

The hands let go and she slid down the wall.

Ears ringing, even over her own labored breaths, she still heard the furious hiss.

"You think you're so clever, telling me your name was Birdie. Well, Lady Renny, 'twas a clever play on words. Renny, Wren, Birdie. How's this for a play on words? Dragon, girl-child, death. Your dragon, Conthar, is dead. He tried to save some stupid little girl-child from the living fire and got himself as well as the child cooked in the process. Of course, if the *Dragonhealer* had been doing her job, she might've been able to save him."

Refusing to use Allar's name in case the evil rider picked up on it, she sent a desperate thought winging. {{*Conthar?*}}

Jerking upright, Allar gasped.

Everyone else, focused on him, came to attention and the dragons began bugling.

Blasted by her pain, he picked up immediately on what Renny needed. {{*Not a scratch.*}}

{{*My thanks.*}}

Renny hurriedly re-closed her mental door with Allar until aught but a crack remained.

COMING TO HIS FEET, a hand on both dragons, Allar looked at his family clustered around him and eagerly awaiting, swept his gaze farther and took in the soldiers.

Kept his tone purposely low so it wouldn't carry beyond his family. "They've started torturing her."

Lady Gemma stepped forward and wrapped her arms around his waist. "You'll find her. Renny's brave and she's tough.

You men go on as soon as you can. Ninar and I will stay here and do what we can on this end."

Allarr looked at his father and brother, his face grim. Their faces were equally grim, full of dark promise. "She's in a dungeon, and she doesn't know where."

Clapping Allar on the shoulder, his father consoled, "Renny was trained by Rand, and she's one of the best fighters I've ever come across. Added to that, she's far more intelligent than her captors. Hold on, son. Hold on. She'll get the information to us."

RENNY HAD no way of telling how long, but some time later her tormentors came back for round two. This time they threw the blanket back over her head. Grabbing her arms, they dragged her out of the cell and up endless stairs.

Listening hard, Renny could hear nothing but her own harsh breathing and her captors' footsteps.

Hanging between them like wet clothes on a line, Renny heard a knock and then a door creaking open. Dragging her inside, balancing her on her still bound feet, they whipped the blanket off and gave Renny a shove.

She landed painfully, taking the brunt of the fall on her knees and one shoulder, rapping the side of her head hard on the wooden floorboards.

One of the captors turned her head until her neck creaked in protest and removed the gag.

Renny tried to swallow, to work some moisture into her parched mouth. What little vision she had was blurry and the room was dark except where she lay, close to a fireplace.

She could make out nothing helpful from here.

A voice came out of the darkness, a voice she recognized.

The same person who'd been at the tavern with Din!

Cursing herself soundly for not staying long enough to see his face, she missed his first words.

A hard kick to her ribs made her eyes water and concentrated her attention.

Harsh hands dragged Renny to her knees, a hand tangled in her hair jerked her head back. "Answer when you're spoken to!"

"Have you tried contacting your dragon yet?" A chortle, and then, "Of course you have. What did you find out?"

Renny wanted to kill the owner of the voice at his smug question. She wanted to kill him anyway. She settled for glaring in his direction.

Wanting to surge to her feet, effectively immobilized, Renny settled for another glare.

Evil laughter lauded her effort.

"Untie her. It's not as if she can do anything. Can you, *girl?*"

Renny froze at that one word. She'd heard that word, in that tone, before.

Before what?

Before she had time to puzzle the whens and wheres, her arms fell forward. Too fast to have been untied, they must've slashed her bonds with a dagger. If she could just…

Yeah, right.

She couldn't feel her arms or legs.

Knew for a fact when the feeling came back, it would be nothing but pain.

Nothing more was said for awhile, long enough for the tingling to start.

Keep stalling, Renny-girl. Surreptitiously working her fingers and toes, encouraging blood flow, Renny waited.

She could hear the sounds of eating, reminding her she hadn't eaten for…how long?

Get a grip, Renny-girl. You've been hungry and in pain before. This is nothing. Find out something useful.

Interrupting her scrambled thoughts, a piece of meat, nearly

383

raw, landed on the floor in front of her. Tracking it with her eyes, Renny didn't move otherwise.

Slurping sounds, the clink of silverware on fine china, the rasp of fine linen being dragged over beard stubble. "Not hungry yet? You will be. Would you like to know what kind of meat you'll soon be begging for?"

Dread swirled low and settled in Renny's stomach at the gleeful tone.

Lips smacked in enjoyment, and then, "Any dragon meat is good, but wild dragon has a special piquancy. A little salt and…"

Renny's limited vision grayed, her stomach lurched and had there been anything in it, she'd have vomited. Any further words were lost to the roaring in her ears.

Swallowing bile, Renny tuned back in in time to hear, "No need to look so horrified. I promise you, dragon is quite tasty. Eventually, you will eat it—it's the only thing you'll be offered. And if you refuse to eat on your own, why, rest assured, my men are experts at forcing compliance."

Knife against plate sounds, more smacking sounds, swallowing sounds like he'd taken a sip of wine to wash down his…

"I've waited too long to get my hands on you to let you starve yourself to death. When I found out there was a Dragonhealer, I couldn't wait to get started on you. A healer to torture—what exciting entertainment!"

Talking around a mouthful of food, he continued. "But, a funny thing… Din was chasing someone he *swore* was the warrior who'd been causing me so much trouble. Turns out, I only had to capture one small woman to get both of my fondest desires. I owe you for all the trouble you've caused me, for the men I've lost, for all the fun you've ruined. For Din. Quite the righthand man. Pity."

Silence except for the sounds of someone enjoying a delicious meal.

Or not.

Renny wished he'd start talking again, if only so he'd stop…

"Would you like to know what's in store for you?

Haven't you learned, Renny-girl, to be careful what you wish for?

Snapping his fingers, something crawled on all fours out of the darkest corner of the room. Thinking at first it was a large hunt beast, Renny's eyes quantified it before her brain did, but some extra sense had her screaming silently in denial.

The creature that bellied into the light was barely recognizable as human. Female, judging by the long, straggly hair. It came to a cringing halt at the foot of his chair, head bowed. His hand came into the light, patted the creature on top of the head.

Tangling his fist in the lank locks, he jerked the victim's head up.

Renny recoiled in horror, at least as far as she could with the guard standing right behind her, holding her in place.

It was the woman from Dragon's Haven, the one who'd accosted Renny! Cylla!

Renny was sure only because the creature's nose was still swollen, her eyes black and blue rings.

The woman was otherwise unrecognizable.

The perfectly coiffed, slightly plump, extremely vain woman had been replaced by a cowering, hollow-eyed scarecrow. She looked decades older, her hair gray, her skin as wrinkled as the Old Mother's.

"Take a good look." Tightening his grip, moving like a baby with a rattle-pan he shook the woman's head for emphasis. "She, stupid selfish wretch that she is, lasted no time before she gave in. You, on the other hand…"

He chortled again. "With all your experience… It will be most interesting to see just how long before you start begging for mercy. That's the only reason we're not already force feeding you."

Casting the wretch away from him and snapping his fingers, Renny watched in horror as the shell of a human scrabbled across the floor and greedily snatched up the piece of meat. Sinking her teeth in and latching onto it, she growled like a starving dog with each tearing gulp.

Snapping his fingers again, the wreck of Cylla immediately dropped the meat and wrapped her arms protectively around her head, rocking and keening.

Dark laughter filled the room.

The chair creaked, and Renny knew if she could see him, he'd be leaning back, belly full, looking like the pursim who'd gotten the cream.

"I have waited long and long to repay Allar for his misdeeds. While you're nothing more than an urchin who can hear dragons, you are the perfect vessel for my retribution. "

Urchin who can hear dragons...

An echo sounded in Renny's head, and her hatred quadrupled...just before her heart exploded in joy. She'd beaten this man at his own game before.

"With you unable to contact your dragon, no one will ever find you. When we have tortured you beyond reason, when there is nothing left of you but a broken shell, I will "find" you. Return you to Dragon's Haven so Allar can experience the results of his meddling firsthand, and he will be forever grateful to me."

Like a bloated toad, drunk on his own sick humor, he kept gloating. "Your loving mate will be so sunk in his own grief, so glad to finally have you back, to know your fate, he will not question me too closely on just how I happened to find you. The best part is, he will never suspect me because all along I will go to him, tell him how very sorry I am to hear of his loss, what a tragedy, blah blah, blah."

A demented snicker rang out. "I will console him as a grieving father and, because of the stone in my ring—he will never know I am one of the ones responsible for your torture and his demise. Even the dragons cannot hear my thoughts while I wear this."

Tossing another scrap of meat Renny's way, he laughed until he snorted. "What? Pursim got your tongue?"

While each round of his laughter served to increase the darkness in the room, when Renny's rang out it seemed the shadows lightened and fled. The low fire chose that moment to flare up, whether by chance or by design, furthering the illusion.

Not even repeated blows to her back and ribs had any effect.

Her words... Her words were like the sun. "I know you. I've been besting you since I was a small child. This time will be no different, save that it will be the last time. This time... I will destroy you utterly."

His chair screeched back and fell over with a clatter. "Take her to the... To him. Let him soften her up for awhile. Then we'll see how defiant she remains."

His pitiful attempt at a commanding roar sounded more like his chair and only made Renny laugh harder. The blows stopped for an instant and then redoubled before the blanket was thrown back over her head. Grabbing her still mostly numb arms, the two minions hauled her off.

A different way this time, longer, and far more stairs, still being dragged. At first because Renny's legs weren't getting any signals from her brain, and then because she figured she'd make them do the work and let them think her still incapacitated.

Arriving wherever they'd dragged her to, they stopped and hesitated, arguing amongst themselves.

"I say we take her before we put her in there. He'll never know. She's a prime piece of tail, unlike that other useless bitch." Pressing Renny up against the cold stone wall, he ran his nasty hands up and down Renny's body.

She twisted, trying to get away, but there was no direction she could move. Two guards crowding her from behind, an unyielding stone wall in front of her.

The more evil of the two, the second man ran his hands over Renny as well. Squeezing, pinching, considering. "Nah. Not worth taking a chance. If he finds out, he'll put us in there." Lust got drowned out by fear, if the evil rider's tone was any indication. "There'll be plenty of time. After. And by then, she won't be able to rat us out. Doubt if she'll be able to form a coherent thought, much less string intelligible words together."

Both of them laughing, they opened a door and shoved Renny inside.

What could the two of them possibly fear so much? More than they feared the man above stairs?

Another shove and the blanket was yanked off as Renny and the covering went in opposite directions. The door slammed quickly behind her and not one, but several heavy bars were dropped into place, a sound Renny was all too familiar with. She'd spent enough time in locked rooms when she was little.

Staggering, managing to keep her feet, Renny took stock. This was a much larger chamber. She didn't need the light of the sputtering torch to tell her that.

The dim light didn't extend far, but even so, Renny picked up the glittery shine from the slimy walls. Those damnable rocks again!

The stench hit her. Fetid. Rank. A lair long overdue for cleaning.

Standing motionless, Renny heard rustling. Turning more toward the sound, wishing she had any kind of weapon, she just could make out a large shape.

Eyes. Huge eyes. One blink. Two.

Renny's brain kicked in, identifying the misshapen lump.

A dragon!

Why would the guards fear a dragon?

Why would they imprison a dragon?

What could they possibly have done to…

Renny's mind sheared away from the answer to that question.

Did she really want to know what atrocities they were capable of inflicting on a trapped and confined dragon?

As the dragon focused on her, a wave of malevolence hit her.

Renny had her shields up, high and strong, so it took a moment.

The trapped dragon was radiating extreme emotions, emotions that swamped Renny with their intensity despite her shields.

Fear. Hatred. Rage. Pain.

The very walls were saturated with evil.

This dragon hated humans.

As he roared and screamed in agony, Renny's last coherent thought shrieked out a warning. Renny collapsed, unconscious from the intensity of the emotions blasting at her.

GRABBING HIS HEAD, Allar fell to his knees. Every blow, the pain in Renny's bound limbs, the absolute horror of the man's words, the guards' hands on his mate.

Allar felt each and every indignity inflicted on his mate.

The dragon's hatred was the last straw.

Mercifully, he slipped into unconsciousness along with Renny.

CHAPTER 28

*C*oming to, afraid to move and hoping her last impression had been wrong, Renny rose to one knee and waited for the room to stop spinning.

How could it be that this dragon hated humans?

On the other hand, in this keep, any horror was a possibility.

Renny stifled a desperate laugh. The dark lord thought the dragon's desolate emotions would overwhelm her, drive Renny stark raving.

It would've worked on any other human.

He didn't know Renny's will had been forged in the fires of Hell. It would take more than one dragon in pain to break her.

Calling on all her years of dealing with dead and dying dragons, blocking her own pain, Renny focused on dispersing his. Poor dragon.

Renny tried to get closer to him, but with each try the dragon growled and snarled and gnashed his teeth.

An unknown time later, no closer to reaching her objective, Renny was soaked with sweat and shaking, desperately in need of something to drink.

Tried mindspeak again and again but the paths were completely jumbled, all crossed wires and dead ends. He'd snapped his massive jaws at her with each intrusion.

She'd tried singing to him until her voice was scratchy and barely audible. Sometimes that worked. No go this time, although he seemed a little calmer.

Sitting with her back to the wall of their prison, Renny murmured assurances for what seemed days, telling stories, talking nonsense through her parched throat.

Rising, Renny began pacing back and forth, whispering now. "Dragon, do you have a rider?"

That got his attention.

Lunging, the dragon pinned Renny to the wall with his head.

Over his roaring, Renny heard the rattle of chains.

Chains?

Struggling for breath, unafraid in the least, Renny reached out both hands, thankful she'd regained feeling and movement.

Cupping the dragon's face, sending gentle beams of healing through her touch, Renny demanded gently, "Who did this to you?" The angry compassion in her tone hit a nerve and set the dragon in motion.

Evidently she was getting through to him a little or maybe her touch was working miracles, because instead of incoherent ramblings and guttural noises, he actually used words this time.

Easing back a little, the dragon answered. "Why should you care? If I don't do as they command, they'll torment me more. Wait—how is it that you can speak with me?"

"I am the Dragonhealer." Renny's newfound breathing space disappeared as the dragon put more pressure on her already abused ribs. Renny swore she heard them creaking with the weight of the dragon's head, but she gave no sign he was causing her discomfort.

The dragon snarled in outrage. "Liar!" Bellowed until the walls shook and Renny's ears rang. "What is this? Some new deviltry to make me come to heel? There are no Dragonhealers left. Even if such an impossible thing were true, none would ever aid me."

Blackness was closing in fast when the dragon let up on Renny's ribs this time. Sucking in several deep breaths, Renny waited until she was no longer seeing spots before conversing with the dragon again. "I am the Last Dragonhealer, whether you believe it or no."

As his words sank in, Renny's heart wrenched. What had they done to this poor dragon? No matter, it would be avenged. "Why would you think a healer wouldn't attend you?"

The confession torn from him shredded Renny. "I…killed my rider. They said… They said…in one of my fits I killed him and…killed him and ate him."

Hiding her shock and horror behind a veil of fury, Renny's coaxing tone held no condemnation, only empathy. "Tell me more, dragon. I don't believe that for a moment."

"I have no memory of it. They told me I killed my rider. I remain locked in here because… 'Tis part of my punishment."

Knowing full well who *they* was, Renny asked anyway, anything to keep the dragon speaking to her. "Who told you that?"

A shudder wracked the dragon's emaciated frame. "The man. He comes sometimes and…watches. I never see him but… I should know his name…" The dragon trailed off, his thoughts scattering like leaves in a fall storm.

Stroking without ceasing, Renny soothed, and dug. "You said part of your punishment. What is the other part?"

Gathering his thoughts, the dragon replied in a mortified tone. "The man uses me to torture prisoners. He puts them in here and doesn't feed me." Jerking back as if he couldn't bear Renny's loving touch, the dragon indicated a dark corner.

Glancing at the pile of bones, glimmering faintly in the torch light, Renny placed her hands firmly on the dragon.

Flinching as if expecting a blow, the dragon cowered.

Petting him with hands and words, Renny calmed him until he no longer shivered. "Dragon, open your mind to me. I can ease your pain." Renny smiled to herself as she repeated Conthar's words.

Butting her softly, pulling away reluctantly, the dragon urged, "Step back into that corner as far as you can. My chains won't stretch that far. When I try to remember, I go berserk."

Renny's heart melted more, the dragon sounding as ashamed as Renny had when she'd admitted to Conthar her part in helping the dragonhaters.

The dragon crouched down, pinning his ears back and switching the tip of his tail like an angry pursim.

Renny'd thought she was prepared but the onslaught of pain was like nothing she'd imagined.

Years worth of pain, stored up and released in a geyser of emotion.

Even Conthar's pain hadn't been this intense.

The dragon roared and bellowed, spittle flew along with incoherent words.

Absorbing his unfathomable pain along with his memories—hearing the guards outside the door gloating, enjoying the commotion and cheering the dragon on—Renny dropped like a stone.

EAVESDROPPING shamelessly on Renny's conversation with the dragon, Allar listened closely, hoping for a clue. The man's manic voice earlier had had a familiar ring but Allar hadn't quite been able to place it.

Another wave of pain hit him, spread to Zantha and Conthar like spilled honey, the cloying darkness clinging to human and dragon alike. The three of them caught Renny's pain, shared it, stretched it thin until it was manageable.

The pain gradually receded as Renny did something…miraculous.

Through their link, Allar tried to lend her his strength, hoped she could feel his love, hoped it would be enough to last until he got there.

As soon as the dragon began sharing his memories, Allar knew who held Renny. His triumphant shout rent the air. Warriors were mounted and dragons were airborne while Allar's cry still echoed.

CHAPTER 29

The man stood impatiently in the hall outside the dragon's cell. She'd been in there a good part of the night and most of the day, more than long enough. As soon as the dragon's horrendous noises had stopped blaring from the other side of the heavily reinforced door, the guards had brought word to Him and left for their own quarters, as they'd been ordered to do.

He'd taken his time getting down here, wanting Allar's mate to suffer as much torment as possible. Eventually she'd see Him as her savior from all this insanity and pain. Then her madness would be complete.

And his plans could progress apace.

The man's maniacal laughter rang and echoed off the walls. A master of manipulation, he could accomplish much with little, mere suggestions placed in the right ear.

For instance, the imprisoned dragon had never actually eaten a human. He'd been told so often enough, and thanks to his blackouts caused by pain and isolation, and a pile of bones strategically placed…

The same way the victims placed in the cell with the dragon believed the dragon would eat them. Something about a dragon snapping and snarling, threatening to devour, tended to cow the hardiest soul. The dragon roared and carried on, the victim screamed and begged for mercy—for awhile.

All that was in addition to the full roster of violent emotions swirling darkly in the confines of the cell.

More chortles as he patted himself on the back for finding out about the sparkly stones. Not only did they block the dragons calling for help, they intensified emotions. And no one else knew. Not for…years. Decades. He could continue with his master plan until all the dragons were insane or dead with no one the wiser.

Lady Renny—ha! She was no lady or he'd give up eating dragon meat!—might be a Dragonhealer, but even she couldn't heal this dragon. Years of torment and darkness had taken their toll.

Funny, the guards hadn't said anything about Renny screaming. Maybe the dragon actually had eaten her. Huh.

They'd reported the turmoil that'd taken place earlier and he fully expected to see her cowering, mind fractured, curled on the floor in the fetal position when he opened the door. As strong as she was, as strong as her mental shields were, it would probably take multiple sessions to completely break her.

Rubbing his hands together in glee, he slid the first bar out of the way. He didn't want her mind too shattered, not quite yet. Not with all the excruciating plans he had in mind with her name on them.

This upstart supposed Dragonhealer had been a thorn in his side for far too many years. First as the warrior who plagued him, thwarting his plans and killing his men. Then as…Dragonhealer? When he'd done his very best to eliminate each and every one?

When his patient waiting was finally coming to fruition?

Not only would he destroy the very last Dragonhealer on the

planet, thus ensuring the dragons' ultimate demise, but he'd get to watch Allar wither, so devastated he would never recover.

The dratted man had too much honor to die outright, too much responsibility toward the dragons.

He relished the thought of Allar living in torment for the rest of his life, as had he. And if Allar wallowed in misery because Renny's insanity left her alive and yet made her unreachable, Zantha and Conthar would be in agony as well.

Four for the price of one.

His glee nearly uncontainable, he moved the last bar out of the way and opened the door.

SORTING through the dragon's memories, Renny found the ones that were real and discarded the rest, the ones induced by drugs and pain.

She knew exactly who the dragon was, and his rider.

Allar would be here soon. All she had to do was hang on a little longer.

Unable to see the dragon's wounds with any clarity, Renny had run her hands all over the dragon's entire body, seeing the damage by touch as the sputtering torch had long since gone out.

Some of the wounds she could only fix when she got her hands on her medicines. He had a broken wing that would have to be re-broken and set to make it right, and Renny was *not* looking forward to that. Even with that extreme measure, Renny wasn't sure the dragon would ever be able to fly again.

Renny's temper boiled over at what this dragon and all the others had suffered at the hands of madmen. Especially the one above stairs.

No one had gotten close enough to the dragon before to try freeing him. The crude fasteners on the chains were a simple matter for someone with opposable thumbs and a dagger to undo, even in pitch blackness.

Renny couldn't believe her captors hadn't caught her liberating one of their daggers, but she wasn't complaining. They'd been too busy pawing her to notice her clumsy attempts, nothing like her usual smooth extractions.

Speaking of extractions… How in the name of all that was good was she going to get the dragon out of here?

Making short work of the chains, crooning soothingly and sharing her good memories, Renny distracted him a little from the pain of what she was doing. The chains had cut deep grooves in his legs, grooves currently oozing with infection.

The infection she could heal, given enough time and salves.

The scars…

Those he would always bear.

He'd been starved, for food and companionship and sunlight.

Glancing in the direction where she thought the door was— the very human sized door—Renny frowned. "Dragon, how did they get you in here?"

Lifting each freed leg in turn, the dragon bumped her gently with his head in gratitude. "Directly behind me is a tunnel that leads to the outside. It has not been used since they imprisoned me. I have no idea whether it's still usable or not."

Renny scratched him under the chin, drawing a low, ragged purr. "Only one way to find out."

ALREADY GLOATING, opening the cell door and holding a torch high, gleefully anticipating seeing a broken Renny, he stared in shock.

Not only was Renny nowhere to be seen, the dragon was gone as well. The only thing left in the cell were the chains that had bound the dragon for so long.

Impossible!

Bellowing for the rider of the no-color, he kicked impotently at the pile of herdbeast bones, scattering them every which way with hollow clatters as he waited impatiently for the guards. They would track her down and this time they would maim her so she couldn't move.

Deep in the tunnel, Renny and the dragon heard the enraged roar as their absence was discovered.

Pacing by the grievously wounded dragon's side in the stygian dark, one hand on his flank, the other outstretched and trailing along the wall, Renny cocked her head. "Can you move any faster, dragon?"

Pacing slowly, dragging his injured wing, they weren't making very good time.

Continuing a single step after the dragon stopped, Renny warned, "Don't even think what you're thinking."

"Leave me, Dragonhealer. You can move much faster without me. Go find help and bring them back here. I will hold them off."

Renny snorted, "I'm not leaving you. You couldn't hold off a stiff breeze. Pick again."

Shaking his head, the dragon stayed planted like a tree.

"Don't make me get behind you and push, dragon, 'cause I will."

About to argue more, the dragon's head came up.

Renny readied herself. Not that one dagger stood much of a chance against two armed soldiers but, hey, she'd faced worse odds.

Looking ahead and not behind, voice filled with wonder, the dragon stated, "My rider. I can sense my rider! He's close by. How can that be?! Dragonhealer, have I completely lost my mind?"

Patting his side, Renny silently urged him to keep moving. "Dragon, I hoped your rider still lived. I suspect he's been told the same lie—that he killed you. He's probably not in much better shape than you."

Suspicious again, both of his sanity and Renny's validity, the dragon swung his head to her. "If he's been close all the time, why couldn't I sense him? Or he, me?"

"Those sparkly rocks in your prison? They keep riders and dragons from speaking to each other. In all the valleys where I found dead or dying dragons, those rocks were in evidence. The traitor wears a ring made of the stone."

"Is that why you can't talk to your dragon?"

Renny shrugged, puzzled but not too worried. Her line to Allar was still open, so… "I suppose so, although if you can sense your rider I should be able to contact my dragon."

Not like Renny hadn't been calling out to Conthar off and on the entire time.

Jerking back to her surroundings as she heard a scraping sound in front of her, holding her dagger at the ready, Renny positioned herself in front of the dragon.

Expecting the worst, Renny was baffled for a moment when the dragon nudged her out of the way. Picking up on his joy, understanding the source, together they watched as faint torchlight wavered closer, growing stronger.

Bobbing and weaving, a misshapen figure slowly appeared, wavering in the flickering light. The light stopped moving and a quavering voice spoke.

Stepping to one side, Renny watched as dragon and rider were reunited, their glad cries tinged with shock and disbelief.

"Grenith?"

"Tobold?"

And then both at the same time, speaking over each other and using the same words, "They told me you were dead," and "They told me…I feasted on your remains," and "They told me the same."

Renny's hatred and desire for vengeance upped several notches with each heartbroken admission.

Grenith. Renny hadn't pushed for the dragon's name, knowing why he was reluctant to give it. Would never use it without his permission.

Letting them have a moment, Renny watched Grenith's and Tobold's reunion with her heart in her throat and tears in her eyes. How could anyone, much less a father, be so hateful as to keep a dragon and rider apart, be so deviant they'd tell a dragon and rider they'd cannibalized their partners?

Grenith and Tobold couldn't stop touching each other, each afraid the other was merely a figment of their imagination.

Delighted they'd found each other, Renny sent out call after call for her own beloved dragon. Befuzzled, Allar was still the only one she could reach, and she was beyond glad for that contact. He was already on his way with a huge contingent of dragonriders.

Warrior that she was, Renny was becoming more and more antsy. Allar would be here soon, but if her little trio didn't get moving... She needed to get them somewhere defensible, not trapped in this tunnel.

"Guys, I hate to break up your party, but we need to go."

Dragon and rider turned their attention to her.

The dragon—Grenith—cocked his head and recoiled, his suspicion and fear returning full force. "Dragonhealer. You wear a pendant of the sparkly rock."

Clasping what should have been her treasured dragon pendant, what Renny held instead was indeed a chunk of that damnable rock. Yanking it over her head, Renny flung it back down the tunnel as hard as she could.

Following its progress in the flickering torch light, farther back down the tunnel they could see more of the sparkly rock imbedded in the tunnel walls. It seemed to stop about two dragon lengths back, about where Grenith had sensed his rider.

The instant Renny discarded the rock pendant, Conthar sprang to the forefront of her mind, Zantha right behind him, and multitudes of other dragons hovered around the edges.

All demanding she answer their pleas.

Renny opened her heart to them.

{{*Hold on, Little Warrior. We are on our way. Stay away from those rocks! My heart cannot stand such as this again.*}}

Conthar's imperious order warmed Renny as nothing else could have.

Holding back from Allar, trying to spare him her pain, Renny now opened fully to him as well. {{*Allar? Allar my love, I am...*}}

Now it was he who was holding back, wedging the door between them shut. Renny could feel him, feel his livid fury like a flaming wall of fire, but he wouldn't answer.

Hurt, Renny turned to the dragons.

Zantha filled her in. {{*Renny, Allar is not so much angry at you as he is at what was done to you. He has not slept and has barely eaten since you were taken, and he is aware of everything they did to you. He does not want you to witness his battle rage.*}}

Renny's heartfelt laughter lightened the tunnel more than the torch. {{*He has yet to see my battle rage.*}}

CHAPTER 30

$\mathcal{A}$llar hadn't spoken a word, not to his dragon and not to the men he led, since he'd informed them who was responsible and where they were headed.

Raging, coldly furious, his emotions so raw and roiling so close to the surface, the other riders kept a goodly distance between themselves and the smoldering cloud surrounding Allar.

Mind and heart filled with thoughts of revenge and bloodlust, how dare the man kidnap and attempt to kill Allar's mate? How could he betray Allar and all other dragonriders?

After all that had been done for this lord—after all Allar had done for him—this betrayal was bitter indeed.

Had Renny not been able to keep the lines of communication open with Allar, had she not been able to communicate with the wounded dragon, they'd never have found her. Never.

Her captor held her, not at his main keep, but a smaller, secondary keep long thought abandoned. One that would never have fallen under suspicion.

As soon as Renny had said tunnel, Allar and his soldiers had switched direction and were flying hell bent for leather.

Only one keep had a tunnel from the dungeons to the dragon's quarters. A maze of natural caves, enhanced generations ago by the smuggler occupants of the keep and enlarged to permit the dragons clear passage.

Close now, Allar and his men would obliterate the main keep along with this lesser one as soon as Renny was safely back at Dragon's Haven. All traces of this lord and his minions would be thoroughly wiped from the face of the earth. The land would be salted and the name of this lord forever forgotten.

As the betrayer's keep came into sight, Allar's rage escalated, peaked, focused—became an icy, lethal calm. {{*Zantha—tell Renny to hold on, lay low for a few moments more. Tell her—we've arrived and we'll need a bit to secure our position and draw attention away from her.*}}

Renny answered, without giving Zantha a chance. {{*We're coming out of the tunnel. Don't worry about us. Take care of yourself. I'm going to be furious if you get hurt. You owe me a bonding ceremony night. And I will help take this place down. You owe me that as well.*}}

Allar didn't answer, too busy trying to discern if the empty appearing keep was a trap, or truly as deserted as it seemed. He hadn't been here in years beyond count.

What had once been a busy, vibrant keep was now a pitiful relic of its former self. Tall weeds grew in the cracks of the main courtyard paving stones, the battlements were unmanned and in disrepair, the surrounding fields untended and gone to weeds. Strangely—no, not so strange now that Renny had explained—no fire-thorn.

The once well tended and well filled dragon's quarters empty, the whole place looked desolate. Forsaken. Abandoned.

Battle ready, men and dragons landed warily, ready to fight.

There just wasn't an enemy to be seen, no one *to* fight.

~

ENCOURAGING Grenith and Tobold to hurry, neither was in any shape to accomplish much more than a shamble. Much the way Renny had entered Lake Town.

Renny could hear the guards, the sounds of their progress echoing in the tunnel, could feel the evil rider close on their heels and getting closer. Trying not to panic her two charges, Renny inquired, "How much farther to the end?"

Tobold answered. "Not much farther now. It comes out close to the dragon's quarters."

A shudder in his voice alerted Renny to bad news. She knew these two couldn't stand up to the evil dragonrider coming up behind them, not in their fragile state. How could whatever they faced at the other end be worse?

"So, what aren't you telling me?" About the time she asked, she thought, dragonrider equals dragon. Had to be one of the no-colors.

Tobold replied hesitantly, confirming Renny's thought. "The dragon's quarters are mostly empty."

Seriously considering jabbing both of them in the rear end with her dagger, Renny kept her tone calm. "Is there another way out? How'd you get in here?"

"There is another way out at this end, but only for humans. I'll die before I leave my dragon again."

Grenith's soft chuff seconded Tobold's statement.

Tobold blew out a breath and moved a little closer to Grenith. "They're getting close, aren't they."

Renny figured no answer was answer enough, wished she had her weapons. Her bow, her sword, heck, a big stick would feel mighty good in her hands right about now.

Surprising her with his question, Tobold asked, "Are you any good at fighting?"

Renny replied grimly, "I can hold them off for a bit, long enough for you two to get out." Ignored Conthar's and Zantha's rumbles of disapproval. "I have a small dagger. It's not much, but I'll do what I can. You two need to get out and... Help has arrived. Stay alive for a bit and this will all be over."

Conthar's and Zantha's rumbles were becoming roars.

Huffing and puffing, Tobold offered, "If we can make it, there's a small armory close to the tunnel exit. I think it used to be a guard house. There were weapons there the last time I looked."

Staring at him in astonishment, realizing she could really see his features, Renny grinned. "Lead on!"

Her grin fading, Renny waited expectantly for the bad news.

"There's also a dragon in the dragon's quarters. It sides with them."

Tobold claimed no sex or color for the dragon, so yeah, one of the no-colors for sure. There would be no help from that direction, not that she'd expected any.

The clattering evil was drawing closer, too close for comfort, the healthy guards making way better time than her band of stragglers.

Renny'd have to deal with the no-color later. She needed weapons *now!*

Prodding her charges into a shambling run, they rounded one last corner and saw a circle of dim, blessed day light ahead. "Hurry, guys! Move!"

Staying with them as long as she dared, waiting until they were as close to the light as she could, Renny sprinted ahead.

ALLAR LANDED outside the wide open gates along with a chosen few. The rest had orders to hover close. The battlements would've made perfect lookout points, had Allar been willing to trust any dragon's life to their crumbling state.

With the unknown state of affairs, no way was he asking any dragons to land in the dragon's courtyard.

Dismounting, sword at the ready, his swordsmen did the same. The most expert of his archers had bows drawn, arrows nocked, other archers hovering close overhead. Spreading out carefully across the deserted main courtyard, some to the stables and other outbuildings, the largest contingent entered the double doors leading to the Great Hall.

The inside looked as deserted as the outside, furnishings gone, the entire place sacked and gutted.

Mentally smacking himself for a fool, Allar tagged Zantha. {{*Ask Renny how many people are here.*}}

Zantha's amused snort grated on Allar's already shot nerves. {{*Renny said ask her yourself and she'll answer.*}}

{{*RENNY!*}} Allar's mental bellow had her replying, the fake sweetness making Allar grimace.

{{*Yes, my love?*}}

Gritting his teeth, grinding his jaw, Allar thought hard about padded rooms. Locked rooms, and he held the only key. With Renny inside.

Renny's laughter rolled across him in waves. {{*Aren't you the one always fussing at me for shutting people out?*}}

{{*You can berate me later for being furious because my mate willingly put herself in such a dangerous position. Answer me!*}}

Renny's smug tone grated even more, and he could actually see her shrugging, totally unconcerned with the danger to herself. {{*It worked.*}} Getting serious, Renny imparted, {{*Two guards, one's the evil rider of the no-color I told you about, and Him. But you'd know all that if you hadn't shut me out. Oh, and…Cylla.*}}

Renny sounded as puzzled as Allar felt as she imparted that last bit.

Allar didn't have time to worry about why Cylla was here. He had to get to Renny. Now.

Allar swore and tried to remember the fastest way to the dragon's quarters. Abandoning the need for caution, they ran through the empty maze of rooms and hallways, heading up and up until they burst out into the dragons' courtyard.

CHAPTER 31

*R*enny heaved a sigh of relief. There were weapons here still. Dusty, rusty, unused for a long while.

Although, Renny mused, if you were going to kill someone, it didn't matter if your weapons were on the dirty side.

Rust was another matter.

Hurriedly digging through the leftovers, looking for something small enough for her to wield and as shiny-sharp as possible, she found a sword. A little too big, but it would have to do. She swung it experimentally, slashed it back and forth, stabbed out with it.

A couple more daggers here and there and she was set.

Stepping out of the guardhouse to find the young man and dragon waiting for her, Renny got her first good look at Tobold.

Renny knew he couldn't be nearly as old as he looked. Was in fact, just a little older than Ninar.

Bent and twisted, he looked like an old man suffering the ravages of arthritis. Lank hair hung around a thin, sallow face that was creased and lined, deep grooves fanning out around his eyes and bracketing his mouth.

A once handsome face, lined from pain and anguish, not age.

Renny switched her gaze to Grenith. The dragon looked every bit as wounded in the daylight as he'd felt in the dark beneath her wandering hands.

A movement across the yard caught Renny's eye, and she couldn't help but call out. {{*Allar!*}}

Turning in Renny's direction at the sound of his name, Allar could see his beloved mate and the young man and his dragon.

He took one step in Renny's direction, and chaos reigned.

Zantha and Conthar landed in the dragon's courtyard just as a no-color came streaking out of a dark cavern in the dragon's quarters. Two men boiled out of the tunnel entrance, heading straight for Renny and her charges. Allar and his men broke into a run across the courtyard, the no-color went after Zantha.

Conthar placed himself squarely between Zantha and the no-color. The two huge dragons clashed, chest to chest, wings beating ferociously, massive jaws snapping, talons grabbing and rending.

Skirting around the edges, Allar and his men tried to get past the dueling dragons as Zantha took to the air to give Conthar more room to maneuver.

Taking in everything in a single glance, Renny knew what she had to do—protect Grenith and Tobold. They'd suffered too much already. Herding them into a corner, Renny stood tall and proud in front of them, facing down the guards.

Ignoring his dragon's plight, the evil dragonrider jeered, "I suppose you think your dragon or your mate will rescue you. Think again. You'll be long dead and so will the two cowards hiding behind you before anyone gets past my dragon."

Renny didn't take her eyes off the evil rider to look at Conthar. She had no doubt as to the outcome of that fight. Conthar was defending not only both his females, but a wounded dragon and an equally wounded rider.

She parried with the tip of her sword, a fey smile on her face.

"You, of all people, should know I don't need anyone, man or dragon, to protect or defend me. How many times did you return to the scene of a dragon's torture to find all your men dead, their fun and games ended along with their lives? You, with all your men and a dragon, couldn't catch one puny female on foot." Grinned wider as her taunts struck home.

Motioning the other guard to stay back, the evil rider launched himself at Renny. Sidestepping neatly, expertly, at the very last minute, she thrust her sword at his ribs.

The evil rider screamed as Renny's well calculated strike hit bone and, despite the dull and rust, ripped a long slash in his side. Not allowing him any closer to the two she was protecting, Renny spun and slashed again, with her—sharp and shiny— purloined dagger. Sliced his arm this time, cut to the bone again, left another long, bleeding gash.

Voice harsh, Renny taunted more. "Did you truly think I would allow you to live after what you've done? The only thing I regret about your death is that I can only kill you once. You deserve to die slowly and painfully, again and again, for all the pain you've inflicted on the dragons and their riders."

A quick, dancing step, a spin, another thrust and another slash.

The evil one faced her, incredulity stamped on his face. He was a great warrior. There was no way a mere female could defeat him! Besides, she was too little to do much damage.

Accurately interpreting his look, Renny laughed. "Keep thinking what you're thinking. It's what got your men killed. It's what got Din killed. The only thing better than watching you bleed out slowly and painfully would be some of your own poison on my blade, so I could know you died in as much agony as you caused the dragons."

Another rapid fire jab, another wound, while he gawped slack jawed.

"You can't do this. You can't take life. You're a healer, sworn to protect life." Eyes bugging out, blood flowing, gasping for breath, he stood still.

The idea that this deviant thought everyone else should adhere to normal rules was the funniest thing Renny had heard in a long while.

Renny corrected him. "*Dragonhealer.* I've kept my word, and my vows. My first allegiance is to the dragons, not humans. That means I will do whatever is necessary to serve, protect, and avenge."

The evil one gestured, and the other guard leapt into the fray. Both rushed Renny, prepared to hack her to pieces.

Stubbornly standing her ground, Renny distantly heard Allar's fierce bellow of denial.

A deafening sound, like thunder and lightning happening at the same time, made all of them look up.

Wild dragons! The sky grew dark with their numbers, all of them roaring. Dropping out of the sky like raptors after hoppities, talons extended, two of them plucked the evil rider and the guard from in front of Renny, leaving naught but their swords clattering on the stones and their fading screams to mark their passing.

Dragons and prisoners were gone in a blink, the sudden silence as deafening as the noise had been.

Renny shook her head and looked around.

Conthar pinned the no-color on its back and as she watched, ripped out its throat. Tearing her gaze away from that, she turned to Allar.

Close and getting closer and still beyond furious.

Radiating fury.

If the wild dragons hadn't shown up when they did...

Renny could feel the two behind her, their apprehension at the huge man's approach, their anguish and dread beating at her in crashing waves.

{{*Allar. Stop, my love. Please. Grenith and Tobold are terrified. They've been through enough. Let me sort this out and I will come to you. Please.*}}

His reply snarled and growled in Renny's head. {{They've *been through enough? I can't decide whether to strangle you or kiss you. You are not allowed out of my sight, ever again. I'm seriously considering chaining you in my chambers for the rest of your natural born life.*}}

If she hadn't already been head over heels for her man, his next actions sent her tumbling.

Grumbling, Allar reluctantly changed course, stomping to the far side of Zantha instead, peering around the emerald's bulk. Arms crossed and eyes locked on target. As promised, not letting Renny out of his sight.

Laughing at his empty threats, Renny blew Allar a kiss.

The grim faces on either side of him and behind him relaxed and grinned at Renny's gesture. Tellar grinned and winked, Lord Gamron raised the tip of his sword in salute, lips twitching.

Renny turned to Grenith and Tobold, a smile on her face.

The duo remained frozen in place, eyes huge, more scared of Allar's fury than they'd been of the evil dragonrider.

Crooning softly, quietly, Renny calmly coaxed the two to look at her. "There's nothing to fear now. Allar will keep you safe."

Shaking his head, Tobold answered for both of them, "He's the one who did this to us." Indicated his crippled limbs and his dragon's sorry state with a flick of his hand.

Anger surging, Allar's shock beating at her back like she'd been kicked by an okumo, Renny managed to keep her voice light. "Why would you think that? Allar is the one who found you! He rescued you!"

Cringing closer to Grenith, Tobold shook his head harder and Grenith made a pitiful attempt at a roar. A thrust of Tobold's chin and he said bitterly, "He's the one who caused this. This is all his fault."

Walking fearlessly up to Grenith, Renny put her hands on either side of his head. Ignoring the commotion happening behind her, she knew without looking that Tellar on one side and

Lord Gamron on the other both had a tight grip on Allar's arms, preventing him from advancing.

"Let me show you Allar and Zantha's memories."

Renny opened her mind.

Memories flowed like a raging flood seeking the sea.

Excruciating memories of Allar's and Zantha's search for a young boy and his dragon. Finding them. Boy and dragon shattered, in unimaginable pain. Unable to call for help, powerless to help each other. Going out of their minds, neither strong enough to block the other from feeling the pain, making the pain rebound in a vicious, endless loop.

Conthar and Zantha air lifting the wounded pair, listening to their screams until boy and dragon passed out from the pain.

Finishing, Renny took a step back.

Tobold slanted a look at his dragon, shifted his gaze to Renny. Pointedly did not even glance in Allar's direction. "This...can't be. He... Father said Allar knew where we were and he left us in that valley so long on purpose because he was angry at me for causing Grenith to be hurt. Allar's the one who ordered me sedated. The medicine made me... I was confused for a long time. When I regained my senses, they told me I'd killed Grenith and..."

At Renny's emphatic head shake, Tobold fumbled to a halt. Renny's voice was gentle, her eyes compassionate. "They lied to you about your dragon's death. Think, Tobold. Why would Allar leave a dragon and rider in pain? Allar is the greatest champion the dragons have. Allar ordered the two of you sedated because together you were only increasing each other's pain. It was only meant to be temporary, just until both of you recovered a little. Until you could handle it. Your father's healer was supposed to take care of you after that."

"I...don't know why Allar would do such a thing." Tobold considered, then barked, "If Allar didn't do this, why did he never once come to see us? Me? Everyone said he was a great warrior, that he loved dragons, but he never ever once came to see me, to ask about Grenith." Tobold sounded purely miserable, his voice full of a young man's pain at betrayal by someone he respected.

Without Tobold or Grenith noticing, Allar had eased closer. He spoke softly, from just behind Renny. "Tobold. I came to visit you at your father's main keep. Many times. Your father always told me you refused to see me, that you blamed me for everything. That my presence caused you too much pain. Your father cut off communication with all Dragonriders. He told us it was too much to expect him to keep hosting dragons and riders when his own son would never ride again. He sent word your dragon, and then you, had died. Refused to let us attend the funerals."

"Father refused to let you see me? Told you we were dead?"

Allar nodded, eyes locked on Tobold's.

Switching from disbelief to challenge, Tobold cocked his head. "So you say. How do I know you're not lying?"

Putting a hand over his heart and dipping his head to Tobold, Allar vowed, "I swear to you on my dragon's life—on my Renny's life—that I had no part in this after we brought the two of you back from the valley. Had I known, I'd've taken you back to Dragon's Haven. I would never have left you alone. Never."

The two males stared at each other, Tobold unwilling to drop his gaze, seeking truth. Allar because he had nothing to hide.

Taking advantage of the lull, Renny checked with Conthar. {{*My dragon?*}}

{{*Unharmed, My Human, but my heart hurts for the two of them and for any unwitting role I played in this tragedy.*}}

{{*Mine too. You have nothing to regret. You did your part. Don't forget, I have seen your memories, as you have seen mine. Stay vigilant. There is another no-color and his rider around somewhere.*}}

Renny reclaimed Tobold's attention by the simple expedient of waving her hand in the air. "Tobold. Your dragon told me he thought you were dead, thought he had eaten you. You said the same thing."

Tobold and Grenith shivered and moved closer, so close now that one had to breathe in when the other breathed out.

"I need to know who told you that. Justice will be meted out."

Grenith spoke. "The rider you just bested, and Tobold's father."

Tobold echoed, "My father."

"Tobold, Dragon, you have my word."

Grenith wrapped his tail around Tobold's slight form. Voice raw and strangled, he hiccuped and asked, "Healer, do you despise me so much for what I have done you cannot call me by name? Are you going to punish me?"

Leaping the small distance between them, Renny pressed her face to Grenith's head. Circled her arms and hugged him tight. "Punish you? *Punish you?* All you were doing was trying to survive and I told you—many of the things they said you did were nothing more than drugged memories. More torture for their sick pleasure. You both have held out against impossible odds. You are strong, and you love your rider. They couldn't break either of you, so they lied to both of you. Most important, I know what evil they wove, just by knowing a dragon's name. For that reason, and no other, I would never use your name without your permission."

Seeking to reassure him, Renny opened her mind to him again, this time to share some of the horrible things she'd done. The dragons she'd killed, her self loathing at doing it. Releasing her hold a little, so quietly no one else could hear, Renny murmured, "Do you hate me now? Do you think I should be punished? After all, I have killed many dragons, and far more men, and I was never drugged. I knew exactly what I was doing."

Making a pitiful moaning sound, Grenith leaned into Renny. Tobold joined them on one side, Allar on the other.

In the same soft tone, Renny urged, "Talk to Conthar. When

we met, I thought he would feel the same disgust for me, because of the things I'd done, that you fear I feel for you. I didn't think anyone could care for me."

Heart brimming over, she continued in an awe filled tone. "He doesn't hate me at all—Conthar loves me."

Allar's hand squeezed Renny's shoulder, Conthar's and Zantha's love washed over her.

Patting Grenith, Renny offered, "Give us a little time to sort all this out and apprehend the culprits. I will do whatever I can for your wounds. I cannot promise you will ever fly again, but I can ease the pain." Head drooping, Renny sounded so discouraged at her admission, Allar couldn't stand to not be touching Renny any longer.

Wrapping his arms around his love, he held her tight.

Tobold gave a shaky laugh. "Let us get used to living again, to each other. I'm not sure either of us will ever be up to flying again."

"Renny."

Just her name. That's all he had to say.

All he could say.

Spinning in his hold, Renny buried her face in Allar's chest.

When Allar could pry her far enough away from himself to see her, he framed her face with his large hands and examined every bruised inch.

Pulling her closer, Allar tucked Renny under his chin and banded his arms around her. Forgetting the rest of the world, he rocked her. "I'm serious about locking you in my chambers. My heart cannot take this."

At their distraught sounds of protest, Renny hastened to assure Tobold and Grenith. "Allar is jesting. He would never…"

Allar growled, "Don't be too sure of that."

Renny laughed in his face and snuggled deeper into Allar's hold. From her secure position, she watched as Conthar and

Zantha picked up the carcass of the no-color and disappeared over the walls with it.

Allar didn't relinquish his hold as he addressed Tobold and Grenith, not even when he passed Renny a canteen full of cold, clear water. "The wrongs done to you can never be undone. The wild dragons have taken care of several of our problems, and rightly so. They have suffered more than most at the hands of the dragonhaters. That still leaves one no-color and his rider as well as your father. As soon as we find your father, he will be executed for his part in this disaster—for what he has done to you and for the other crimes he committed."

Tobold tipped his head in acknowledgement. "If he's still here, he's probably holed up in his chambers. I saw him here earlier, but he could be anywhere, could be gone."

Craning his neck so he could see around the couple in front of him, taking note of all the soldiers, Tobold shrugged. "Or not. I have no idea where the no-color and his rider are."

Out somewhere torturing another dragon, no doubt.

Renny didn't say it out loud, didn't have to.

They were all thinking it.

Twisting in Allar's arms so she could see Tobold and Grenith, Renny gave them a nod. "Stay here. We'll wait until Conthar and Zantha return to guard you, but we have to find him. This has to stop, here and now. I'll tend you as soon as it's safe."

Fuming silently, Allar wanted to forbid Renny to help in the search, but he couldn't. Not without staying here himself. She wasn't getting out of his sight again, even if he had to chain her to his side.

Popping over the edge of the battlements, Conthar and Zantha landed nearby, moved slowly toward Grenith and Tobold.

Giving a glad cry, Renny slipped out of Allar's arms to assure herself Conthar was unharmed. Satisfied, she threw her arms around Conthar's neck and squeezed tight, pressing her face into his satiny hide and inhaling his unique scent, replacing the last of the dungeon reek with clean, healthy dragon.

Using mindspeak so Tobold could understand her through his link with Grenith, Zantha spoke to Grenith. {{*Younglings, it is good to know you still live. You must believe what Allar told you—we had nothing to do with your torture. Allar and I would have done anything to spare you the torment you have endured. If not for Renny, we would never have known either of you still lived. Renny will heal you, Grenith. You must trust her. She is the greatest Dragonhealer this world has ever known. She healed Conthar when none of the rest of us dared hope it possible.*}}

Blushing at the praise, Renny held herself tight against Conthar. Taking a deep breath, keeping one hand on Conthar, she turned to Allar. "Let's finish this. I need to leave this place. The echoes of evil—I'm being suffocated. It's embedded in the very stones of this keep. The sooner we find the guilty parties and leave, the happier I'll be."

A sudden thought struck Renny. "Allar, we have to find Cylla. You should see what he did to her. I barely recognized her."

Leaving a contingent of soldiers with Tobold and the dragons —with instructions for the dragons to airlift Grenith and Tobold to the large field outside the keep—Allar, Renny, and some of the most seasoned warriors set out to search. Renny was sandwiched between Allar and Voya in the front and Tellar and Lord Gamron in the back.

Moving as a unit, they scoured from top to bottom, discovering more than a few gruesome remains, but no living souls except Cylla, and at the very last, the old man who'd transported her in his cart.

Falling to her knees, Renny ran her hands up and down, all over him. The elder didn't seem to be harmed much, just starved and dehydrated. It looked as if they'd thrown him in the cell and just forgotten him.

Reaching out a bony hand, he tried to speak. Clasping it

gently, Renny leaned close, knowing he wouldn't rest until he told her what was on his mind.

"Ambush. Too many of them. Mercenaries from the south. Knew you'd come. Cartbeast—find my cartbeast." His head fell to one side and he was instantly unconscious.

One of the soldiers picked up the old man, cradled him like a newborn and headed outside to find Seon.

The old man had fared far better than Cylla.

They found her in one of the pantries off the kitchen, rooting through empty baskets and barrels. From the looks of it, this place had not seen food in more than a little while.

Worse off than when Renny had last seen her, Cylla seemed to have aged even more and the insanity had taken a much firmer grip. Hissing and spitting like a feral pursim, attacking the men with teeth and nails, she fought them off.

Unwilling to hurt her any more than she already was, one of the men finally scrounged a ragged blanket and threw it over her head, wrapping her tight to carry her out.

Emerging into the main courtyard, into the cleansing sunlight, Renny heaved a sigh of relief, heard it echoed all around her. Tipping her face to the sun, Renny located Conthar and Zantha hovering overhead. Slowing, watching a kicking and screeching Cylla being carried out the main gate, Renny stilled.

Allar knew that look—wheels were turning. Knowing where the majority of Renny's thoughts were, he pointed with a thrust of his chin. "Your satchel awaits you."

A curt nod of thanks, and Renny picked up her pace. "I have to tend Tobold's dragon. Tobold won't let Seon near him until I'm there to work on his dragon."

That's what she *said*. Allar eyed her closely, indicated with a twitch of fingers and head for Voya to gather several others and *watch her!*

Eyes locked on Renny, Allar waited for whatever was percolating in her brain to make itself known.

Allar and an exorbitant number of soldiers made a loose ring around them just in case, whilst Renny tended the wounded dragon, keeping up a steady patter of soothing nonsense the entire time. Kept a thoughtful eye on Tobold as much as she could.

When both she and Seon—here despite his aversion to flying dragon-back—had done all they could and Tobold and his dragon were settled comfortably, Renny crouched beside Tobold and looked him in the eye.

"Tobold, how did you find your dragon today? I'm more than glad you did, but surely you haven't been a prisoner all this time. You must've had plenty of opportunity to explore the keep."

Tobold whitened but didn't utter a word in his own defense. Pulled a crumpled note out of a pocket and held it out to Renny.

"You're right not to trust me. I wouldn't in your position. This was in my sleeping chamber when I woke. I seldom leave my chamber, except late at night, and then only to go to the kitchens. When I first came back to myself I was here, at this keep, and Father said it was because I looked so hideous no one at the main keep could stand the sight of me."

Drawing in a shuddering breath, Tobold looked away, looked back. "Every time I ventured out in the daylight… I wasn't a pretty sight. Everyone feared me, ran from me. I thought it was because they knew I killed… Then there weren't any servants left and Father told me because of my appearance and because I'd committed such a heinous crime, they'd all run away. He only comes here once in awhile to bring me supplies. I've been scrounging food from the storerooms for a long while, but even they are empty now."

Trailing off, looking inside himself, Tobold came back with a head shake. Told them wistfully, "I can't remember how long it's been since I had cooked food."

Heart going out to the pain-filled young man in front of her, Renny decided being an orphan was looking better and better.

Smoothing the crumpled parchment, she scanned the note she held.

Watching her closely, Allar nodded. He'd thought she could read, that night in his father's study.

Renny finished, read it again, and looked into Allar's eyes, her own so full of pain it almost broke his heart. Closing her eyes, tipping her head back, she thrust the note blindly in Allar's direction.

Reaching out to take it, Allar wondered what it would take to make his mate cry.

By the time he finished the few scrawled words, his blood was boiling. No wonder Renny looked so wounded. On her knees now, arms wrapped around Tobold, Renny was holding the boy and rocking both of them, Tobold's dragon keening softly in the background.

Passing the note to Voya, Allar didn't need to look at it again. The words were burned into his mind.

FOLLOW the tunnel that starts in the dragon's courtyard. There's a hot meal waiting at the end.

INNOCUOUS SOUNDING WORDS TO hide so much evil.

Someone had obviously wanted Tobold to find his dragon, hoping one of them would be so hungry the other wouldn't survive.

Another torment, a different torture.

A bond between boy and dragon that should have brought nothing but boundless joy had been been twisted into something so hideously malevolent as to be an unrecognizable abomination.

Conthar and Zantha, indeed all the dragons, rumbled their anger, fruitlessly seeking a target.

As soon as Allar could separate Renny from Grenith and

Tobold, he made sure Seon gave her a thorough going over. Checked for himself and backed that up with Zantha's and Conthar's opinions.

Settling down to a hot meal, unfortunately not one of Cook's hot from the kitchen offerings, merely simple camp fare.

Seon doled out portions to Tobold, fearing the youth would cause himself harm.

The dragons hunted herdbeasts for Tobold's dragon and coaxed him a little way from Tobold so they both could eat.

Having the men bring her bucket after bucket of hot water which she infused with herbs, and then fine sand from the nearby river, Renny washed Tobold's dragon gently and thoroughly. Rubbed salve in all his wounds while Seon offered a bath and healing to Tobold.

Allar doubled the usual amount of guards. With Renny and Tobold and his wounded dragon protected in the very middle, the rest of the men and dragons circled them and tried to sleep.

They would leave on the morrow as early as they could, Grenith in a dragonhide sling.

CHAPTER 32

$\mathcal{W}$aking to the soft gray light of early dawn, snuggled between Allar and her dragons, Renny rose and checked on her charges. Both were still sleeping soundly, Tobold curled between his dragon's front legs.

Allar rose with her, waking Tellar and Voya with a nudge of his booted foot.

Having awakened with their humans, Conthar and Zantha leapt into the sky, circling lazily over their humans.

{{*Renny, we're going to fetch some more laxamuls for...*}} Conthar's words cut off as Zantha's piercing cry struck fear into all their hearts. {{***Zantha!*** *Renny—she's been struck by an arrow!*}}

The humans watched in horror as Zantha spiraled clumsily to finally tumble end over end toward the ground. Renny took off running, intent on reaching Zantha.

Grabbing for Renny a split second too late, Allar missed her by a hair and sprinted after her.

Forsaking the safety of the camp without a second thought, eyes on Zantha, Renny ran smack into a man who rose up in front of her from a slight depression. Knew who it was without looking.

Struggling to get to her dragon's mate, Renny fought furiously.

Cuffing her hard enough to make Renny see stars, he spun her until she faced Allar. Yanking her back against his chest, he locked an arm around her throat and pressed a dagger under her chin.

Renny fought, kicking and scratching madly.

Lifting her off her feet by the arm around her neck, shaking Renny, he choked her into submission.

Glaring at Allar, he gloated, "Because of you, I've lost everything. Let's see how you like it. If either one of the females dies, you and your dragon will spend the rest of your lives in excruciating pain, just as I have. Which will it be? Your mate, or your dragon? That arrow was slathered in poison. If the healer can't get to your dragon shortly… Drop your weapons and back away, call off your dogs, and I'll let the healer go as soon as I'm far enough away to be safe."

Regarding him with a look that would've petrified a sane man, Allar pointed his sword at the blackguard's heart. "Anything you lost, you lost on your own. There is nowhere you will be safe from me. You betrayed your son as well as all other dragonriders. You *will* die by my hand. The only choice you have is the manner of your death."

The arm around Renny's neck tightened more. If she could somehow get him to loosen his hold, even a little…

Going limp, Renny became a dead weight. Grimaced to herself over her bad choice of phrasing.

Zantha's cries of pain and Conthar's echoes were driving Renny mad.

Think, Renny!

Hard to, with blackness closing in around the edges of her vision, breathing constricted.

There! He'd given her a minimal bit of breathing room.

Twitching her hands spasmodically as if struggling feebly, Renny sucked in as much air as she could.

Lifted the hem of her tunic with one of her spastic twitches. Grasped the dagger in her belt and plunged it backward with all her strength. Feeling her dagger strike bone, Renny twisted as hard as she could.

Surprised, disbelieving, he dropped Renny to clutch at the dagger imbedded in his hipbone.

Hitting the ground hard, Renny landed on all fours, trying desperately to find some air, to draw breath into her lungs.

Her throat felt swollen closed, her lungs like she'd been dropped from a goodly height and landed flat on her back.

Renny'd had the breath knocked out of her before. Hadn't liked it then, didn't like it now.

{{*Move, Renny!*}}

Crawling blindly, oblivious to the drama enacting just above her head, Renny had given Allar the opening he needed.

Allar didn't even bother to come closer, merely tossed his sword up, changed his grip as he caught it. Waiting until Tobold's father looked up, Allar launched his sword like a javelin.

It came to a quivering stop, buried to the hilt in the blackguard's throat.

Tobold's father was still falling when Allar reached Renny. Scooping her up, cradling her to his chest, Allar urged, "Breathe, little love. Breathe."

Tightening the band of his arms when she struggled, Allar ordered, "Be still. I'm carrying you to Zantha."

By the time she could breath easily again and the black spots had disappeared from her vision, Tellar was there with her satchel.

Pouring something over the blade of the dagger Allar extended to her, Renny raised it, paused. Looked at Conthar. "This is going to hurt. Hold Zantha as still as you can."

White and shaking, Renny steadied her hand and used the dagger to cut the poisoned arrow out of Zantha. Flushed the wound as well as she could with a salt solution, and packed it with the same poultices she'd used on Conthar.

Satisfied she'd done everything she could, shaking again, Renny glanced up. Looked around to find she was the bulls-eye in a watchful circle of men and dragons, weapons pointed outward.

Blinked, surprised to find the sun had barely risen. This day already seemed ages old.

Allar stood within touching distance. Without being asked, he poured fresh water on the stinging hands she stretched them toward him. Waited until she'd scrubbed thoroughly with the bit of dried soapweed he also provided, then rinsed Renny's hands twice, thrice, to make sure no taint of poison remained.

Reaching out a cleansed hand to Allar, Renny let him pull her to her feet.

Pressing her head hard against his chest with the hand tangled in her hair, Allar laid his head over hers and vowed, "Chains. In my chamber."

Renny snickered and replied throatily, just loud enough for Allar to hear, "I've never liked being tied up or imprisoned, but with you, I think I could learn to like it. And the thought of you, tied up, helpless and at my mercy while I… You know what a fast learner I am."

Allar choked and clamped his arms so tight Renny was plastered to him.

A discrete cough had Allar snarling.

Seon coughed once more, trying to cover a snicker. "Let me examine Renny and you can have her right back."

Loosening his hold enough so Renny could turn and Seon could check out her throat, as soon as Seon proclaimed Renny fit, Allar hauled her back against himself, under his arm, next to his heart.

Visibly shaking, Tobold shuffled closer, looked to Allar and then to Renny. "I am so sorry for what my father did to you, to the dragons. He was a great man, once. I don't know how such a great man could fall so far. Become so twisted and evil."

Looking every bit the Lord of Dragon's Haven, champion of dragons, Allar voiced his decree. "You are right. He was once great. I do not know either. Something changed him. What was his should be yours, but the keeps will be destroyed in payment and in warning."

"Even the one on the far shore of the Great Lake?"

Shooting a look at Voya, Allar snapped to. "Your father had a keep on the far shore?"

"I…thought you knew. He goes there often, stays there the most. He said it's easier, since there are less dragonriders…" Tobold's shoulders sagged as he realized the import of his words. "I'm guessing from your demeanor, he didn't mean that in a good way. I'm going to hazard another guess and say he commandeered one of the no-colors to carry him to and fro, even though he said he never wanted anything to do with dragons again. The ships take too long. "

"Not your fault, Tobold. And yes, that keep will definitely be destroyed." Grim-faced, Allar softened his tone. "You are more than welcome to come and live at Dragon's Haven."

Color washing his pale face, Tobold stammered, "You would invite me to your home, knowing what you know about me?"

Renny rasped, "If that's the only way I can get your dragon to come and stay until I do what I can to heal him."

At the startled look in Tobold's eyes, Renny laughed, more a strangled wheeze, and Allar explained, "The Dragonhealer's got a warped sense of humor."

Grenith shifted closer and cocked his head questioningly. Incredulous, he asked Renny, "You were serious about healing me?"

Renny tried to go to him but Allar wouldn't let go of her.

Instead, she reached out a hand to him, motioned him closer. "Grenith?"

At the dragon's nod of acceptance, Renny repeated his name. "Grenith, you have seen nothing but the violent side of me, and I apologize if that frightened you. I swear I will do whatever I can to heal you, and Seon will do the same for Tobold. 'Twill be easier done at Dragon's Haven but if you're not comfortable with that, we'll work something out."

Wrapping his stick-like arms around his thin frame, Tobold shuddered. "What if... What if I frighten everyone away at Dragon's Haven like I did here?"

Prying herself from Allar's hold, Renny locked her arms around Tobold. "Oh, sweeting. That was a lie, Tobold. Your father lied to you about that as well as everything else. You are not some hideous ogre or revolting troll. You are simply a wounded young man. An extremely valiant young man. You and Grenith will be welcomed, I promise you."

Shrugged. "There will be people who stare. The same way they stare at any wounded warrior. 'Tis their problem, not yours."

Tobold hugged Renny back, speechless.

Renny's head came up as if scenting the air, suddenly hyper-alert.

Picking up on her alarm, the soldiers immediately closed ranks, weapons at the ready, expecting the worst.

Before Renny had a chance to tell them everything was fine, Allar thrust Renny and Tobold behind him, between himself and Conthar, ringed by Tellar, Lord Gamron, Voya, and a couple other huge warriors.

Everything was fine.

Better than.

As the wild dragons filled the air, Renny didn't have to say anything.

Placing her hands on Allar's waist, Renny pressed herself tight against his back. "The wild ones have much to tell us."

Several of the wild ones landed, remaining warily on the outskirts.

Allar crossed his arms and his voice boomed out. "You must come to Renny."

When the dragons only shifted uneasily, Renny broadcast, {{*An attempt was made on Zantha's life, and mine. The perpetrator is dead.*}}

A dark amber Renny had treated at Dragon's Haven, obviously the spokesman for the wildlings, bellowed out his fury when Renny explained what had just happened, the rest of the wild ones following suit.

The amber paced the aisle the soldiers opened up for him, straight to Renny. Halting in front of Renny, the amber bowed his head.

Rising, he held eye contact with Renny.

Taking a deep breath, Renny gave life to the dragon's words. "He says to tell you all… The evil men and the no-color have been taken care of. The no-color was hunted down and dispatched, along with his rider, their saddlebags full of poisons and instruments of torture destroyed."

Unclenching the talons on one front foot, the amber released something into Renny's outstretched hand. Her dagger—the one Rand had crafted for her—and her dragon pendant!

Dropping the dagger into its accustomed sheath in her boot and slipping the chain around her neck, Renny sighed as she felt the familiar weights settle home.

Mindful not to spook him, Renny put her arms around the amber's neck and hugged him, whispering words of praise.

Tobold cleared his throat. When everyone looked at him, he paled but stood his ground. "If the dragons are willing to help, Grenith and I would like to tear this keep down today and scatter the stones. There is so much evil here, nothing except total obliteration can ever cleanse this place."

Shifting uneasily as men and dragons and one small woman stared at him for a long moment, Tobold swallowed audibly.

ZANTHA INSISTED ON HELPING, overriding Renny's protests.

The arrow hadn't hit anything vital and Renny had removed it before the poison had spread any at all.

The warriors started on the lower places they could reach. The paving stones in the courtyard, and the steps.

The wild ones and the rest of the dragons started at the top and worked their way down, dismantling the keep stone by stone.

Faster than any would have believed possible the stones were scattered to the four winds, no two touching. Others—clean stones from the river with no taint of evil—were carried back to fill in the remnants of the tunnel and dungeon.

Shortly after nooning they called it quits.

Where once a proud if dilapidated keep had stood, now nothing but a broken field remained.

Allar remained true to his vow, even with all the flying and maneuvering the men and dragons had done all morning.

Renny hadn't been able to take a deep breath without nudging either Allar or Voya or Tellar or Lord Gamron out of the way first.

Taking a break, eating a cold meal of biscuits and dried meat from their saddlebags, Tobold spoke to Renny and Allar.

Seeming to have gained stature in just a few short hours, Tobold stood straighter and actually made eye contact when he talked.

Petting Grenith, marshaling his thoughts, Tobold looked into Renny's green and Allar's blue. "I've been thinking some. I know I can't change what my father did, but I would like to make reparations. I'd—we'd—like to help the wild dragons, after Grenith and I get back on our feet. They told Grenith they need a home, that they're tired of living in the wilds, and they want to be close to the Dragonhealer, but they don't want to crowd Dragon's Haven."

Taking careful stock of the unbroken young man in front of them, Allar considered him diligently, not wanting to needlessly raise Tobold's hopes. "If you are willing to work hard," he held up a hand before Tobold could prematurely agree, "there are several empty keeps fairly close by. Is there anything you want from your main keep before we raze it?" Tobold shook his head and Allar continued. "The empty keeps need a lot of work before they can be made livable but you are welcome to take your pick and we will help you all we can."

Tobold frowned. "Empty?"

Allar nodded grimly. "Either the inhabitants were killed in the dragon wars or they were too few to defend their keep and so merged with a larger one for protection. There is no one left who can lay claim to these abandoned keeps. We would be honored to have you and the wild dragons fill one or more of them. A promise from you first—I would have you and Grenith fully healed before you undertake such an immense task."

"You have my—our—word, Lord Allar." Bowing low, Tobold straightened, eyes shining as he and Grenith exchanged a hope filled look. "For what you have done for us, there are no words to express our gratitude. If we can repay you in some small way by serving you and dragonkind, then it would be our great joy and utmost pleasure."

CHAPTER 33

*T*hey arrived back at Dragon's Haven well before dark.

While Allar's group had been deconstructing, everyone at Dragon's Haven had been equally busy reconstructing.

Lady Gemma had wrought miracles.

The piles of burned brush had been removed, the sooty places on the paving stones scrubbed clean, temporary doors installed. Other than the outbuildings, there had been very little actual damage inside the walls of the keep.

The ones who'd set the fires had been more concerned with ensuring people didn't get out than making sure the keep was destroyed.

Renny figured the smoky tang hanging in the air was a small price to pay.

Thanks to the vigilance and dedication of the men and dragons, very few lives had been lost. Most of the dead were guards, struck down at their posts before they could sound the alarm.

The recurring thought, *insider*, beat at Renny with each step she took, each person she greeted, each dragon she tended.

Renny greeted and was greeted warmly by Lady Gemma and Ninar, as well as Cook and Lissa. Thanked them profusely while trying to make light of her bruises so they'd quit fussing. Assured them that, no, the blood spatters on her clothes, which she'd barely noticed until now, were not hers.

Would've been hard pressed to admit it, but it was nice to have someone care enough to fuss. Surrounded still by Allar, Voya, Tellar, and Lord Gamron, starting to champ at the bit, Renny managed to move her entourage around enough to check on Mithar's and Voya's mates. Praising Bena and Sher for doing such a terrific job tending Mina and the other few wounded dragons while she'd been gone, Renny gave the dragons a thorough going over and many words of encouragement.

Checking on Zantha last, Allar made the rest of Renny's overlarge entourage wait outside Zantha's cave so he could have a moment alone with Renny.

Casually, as if he didn't care one way or another, Allar asked, "Do you feel up to it tonight?"

Hands stilling on Zantha's emerald hide, Renny slanted him a look. "What? Tying you to the bed and having my way with you? Oh, yeah. I think I can manage that."

Renny would've sworn Allar was blushing, but it was hard to tell in the muted light of the cave.

Giving her an interested grin, speaking calmly as if his ability to breathe without pain didn't depend on Renny's answer, as if he wasn't going to lose his mind if he had to wait any longer, Allar smirked, "That too. I was asking about our ceremony. The one we were supposed to have? I was wondering if, and for how long you wanted to postpone it. Mother needs to know."

Ceasing fussing with Zantha, Renny gave Allar her full attention. Panicked quietly. He sounded…off.

Was he backing out now? This last escapade of hers had been too much and he'd changed his mind?

Knees weak, stomach roiling, Renny was afraid to open her mind and confront his rejection. "You want to…postpone it?"

Allar shook his head, knowing something was wrong, frustrated Renny had thrown up her walls and shut him out. Didn't she want to go on with their ceremony? Was she too tired? Had she changed her mind?

Zantha chided softly, {{*Renny, how could you think he doesn't want you? Allar's desperate to have the ceremony this eve but he thinks you're too wounded and too tired.*}}

Taking a deep breath, feeling her stomach settle, Renny flashed Allar a brilliant smile. Took a few running steps and a flying leap, utterly confident he'd catch her.

Allar did, her arms going tight around his neck, legs clamping around his waist like a beginning dragonrider on his first flight. Foreheads touching, Renny teased, "If I gave you any more time, you'd probably change your mind and run screaming."

Holding Renny close and kissing her, mindful of her bruises and wounds, Allar used his lips to tenderly explore her whole face. Had her pressed against the cave wall, his hands under her tunic, one hand splayed across her back, one roaming her front and rocking the most intimate part of him into the most intimate part of her, when the sound of cheering and clapping intruded.

Pulling back, he looked into Renny's eyes, sparkling with laughter.

She burst out laughing. "I'm thinking that fair haired girl, the one with blue eyes."

Joining her, Allar laughed as he threw an evil grin over his shoulder. "The one who giggles all the time and asks incessantly about Tellar's whereabouts?"

The two of them laughed harder as Tellar shot them a horrified look and took off running, laughter trailing in his wake from inside and outside the cave.

Renny indulged in the merriment before tangling her fingers in Allar's hair and tugging his head down for another long, drugging kiss.

~

Voya stepped up beside Allar. "In addition to the cadre of guards Lord Gamron assigned to your mother and sister days ago, I've posted double guards and the dragons are scanning, as well as flying overhead, posted extra men at all the entrances and exits with more sweeping the crowd.

The two huge warriors stood in silence a minute, eyes scanning. "Lady Renny's going to use herself as bait, try to draw out the ones here who want to kill her.

Allar nodded. "Someone inside these walls betrayed us. Until we find them…"

Voya shuddered and agreed. "My heart stopped when Tobold's father got his hands on her. Lady Renny handled herself remarkably well but her little stunt took ten years off my life."

"Mine as well." Allar shook his head slowly, thinking out loud. "She's survived this long because everyone underestimates her and because she's so small and quick. You look at her and think *helpless female.* By the time you blink, she's pulled a dagger from somewhere and… Poof! You're gutted."

"So, how many is she carrying this eve?" Voya chuckled at the wry expression on Allar's face.

~

Deep in her own thoughts, her own agenda, Renny had asked Allar for a bit of time to herself, or as much to herself as she could be in this crowded hall.

Renny hadn't asked the wild ones what they'd done with the evil rider and his dragon but she hoped whatever it was had involved intense pain and a slow, lingering death. Tobold's father had been dispatched a great deal too quickly to suit her but there was nothing she could do about that. Not when Allar was involved and she'd been in the hands of a madman.

The old man was recovering nicely from being imprisoned and starved, but the dragonhaters had killed his cartbeast, and he was mourning the loss.

Tobold and Grenith were settling in better than she'd expected. Conthar and Zantha were watching out for them, had found them a sheltered nook out of the mainstream of dragons and people. The two of them weren't ready for total exposure just yet.

Cylla… Renny was almost sorry, for just an instant, that she'd punched the silly twit. Nah, Cylla had more than deserved it. Hadn't deserved what the dragonhaters had done to her, would probably never recover from her ordeal.

The whole group of dragonriders had made a small detour on the way back to Dragon's Haven and dropped Cylla off at her father's keep. She'd screamed the whole way, was still screaming when they left, despite having been given a heavy dose of sedative by Seon.

Renny's eyes scanned the crowd. Someone here was still guilty, and she fully intended to find out whom. Really tired of living her life looking over her shoulder and besides, now she had a whole keep full of people and dragons that were important to her.

No way could she keep an eye on all of them all the time.

What she had to do, and quick, was figure out who was going to be the next target and focus on protecting them. Still in her leggings and tunic, she might wear them to her ceremony.

There wasn't much of anywhere to conceal weapons in a dress that fit like a second skin, not anywhere that could be easily accessed.

Renny needed to talk to Conthar. Just the thought of her

dragon warmed Renny all over. Saving him had gathered all the scattered pieces of her soul and woven them back together. Saved her life and her sanity.

Conthar.

Renny's heart stuttered and skipped before taking up a mad drumbeat of terror. Would he be the next one targeted?

Conthar's beloved voice filled Renny's head, soothing and comforting. {{*Renny, calm down. I am fine, and I intend to live a long time with you and our mates and our offspring.*}}

{{*Conthar, you were so right. This was much easier when I only had myself to worry about. Now... I don't know who to keep an eye on or which way to turn. Everyone thinks the dragonhaters are after me, but...*}}

Whatever was going to happen would happen soon.

Renny wandered among the guests trailed by her three burly guards, eyes constantly sweeping, thoughts churning. Speaking when spoken to, mostly listening to the conversations flowing around her, making her way slowly to the spot where Allar's family was gathered.

A group of soldiers drinking and telling tales caught her attention. She smiled to herself as she eavesdropped. Renny'd grown up listening to tales such as these, each more outlandish than the last.

A weathered soldier was narrating this tale, reminiscing about a particularly violent and bloody battle.

Renny slipped closer so she could hear better. Allar hadn't spoken much of his battle exploits but he had as many scars as Renny did.

"And Lord Allar, he's standing there, sword in hand, icy fury radiating from him, looking like an avenging angel. The dragons were hovering high up because the dragonhaters had archers almost as good as ours and the fighting was too tight for the dragons to help anyway." Taking a slurp of his ale, waving the mug around for emphasis, he jumped back in, his voice reverent.

"We were close to being defeated, vastly outnumbered, but

Lord Allar wouldn't give. He stood there, rallied us to him, and we won the day." Another slurp, and the soldier blew out a yeasty breath.

"He was covered in blood. We all were. He just wouldn't give up. Wouldn't allow defeat. Wouldn't allow anything but victory. That's why we follow where he leads, without question."

A long moment of silence, and another soldier started his tale but Renny was no longer paying attention.

She knew who the dragonhaters were after.

Just as she suspected, not her at all.

She'd been an excellent decoy.

Would have been an immense feather in their caps, but she wasn't their primary target, hadn't even been a target until recently.

{{*Conthar! It's Allar! They're after him, not me. Help me!*}}

Kicking herself for not picking up on it earlier, Conthar's words when they first met rang in Renny's head.

Trust Allar—he's the greatest champion the dragons have ever known.

Zantha had said the same.

Renny had repeated it unquestioningly to Tobold and Grenith.

She should have seen it earlier.

Allar'd been in the spotlight much longer, had thwarted many of the dragonhaters' plans, destroyed their armies and their hiding places time after time. Had fought in untold battles long before Renny had become a known threat to the dragonhaters.

The attack on Conthar had been deliberate and well planned — even if they hadn't intentionally targeted him—knowing they could poison Conthar and keep him alive for weeks, if not months. Allar would never have stopped searching for Conthar and finding the dragon in such dire straits would've devastated Allar.

The dragonhaters intended to destroy Allar completely and Renny was just another way to get to him.

Especially since Allar and his men and Renny had thinned the dragonhater's ranks again in the last few days, completely demolished one of their hideouts, destroyed one of their best inside sources for information.

No way to know much information had been leaked by Tobold's father, how much damage he'd done, but where had he gotten his information?

Continuing to make her way to Allar's family, mentally forming plans, Renny would need all the help she could get. She'd never convince Allar he was the target, that he was the one who needed to be guarded.

Catching Allar's eye from across the Great Hall, Renny smiled at him and held to her course.

Allar smiled back, and clenched his hands until they creaked.

Voya, looking from his lord to his lady and back, asked, "Another guard? Or two?"

Allar grunted. "More. Three at least. Renny's definitely got something up her sleeve."

"Besides her daggers?" Snickering at his jest, Voya signaled more guards to surround their lady.

Dammit! Renny'd known it was a mistake to make eye contact with Allar! Couldn't imagine how many guards he'd've sent if she hadn't.

The extra guards reached Renny about the same time she made it to Lord Gamron's side. Any more, and she wouldn't be able to see for the wall around her.

Greeting her soon to be parents by law, Renny caught and held Lord Gamron's eye even as she accepted Lady Gemma's hug and absorbed the soft scolding that came with it.

"Child, whatever are you thinking? It's almost time for your ceremony to begin and you're not even changed yet! Would you... I would love to help you."

Taking a moment to bask in Lady Gemma's motherly concern,

Renny shook her head. "I'm heading that way now, and I thank you for offering, but no. I do need to speak with Lord Gamron, if you would be so kind as to let me borrow him for a bit."

Quickly hiding her dismay that Renny would choose a male over a female for help on her ceremony day, Lady Gemma shot her husband a confused look and gave in graciously. "Don't be too long, either of you. I'm not sure Allar's heart can take it if you're out of his sight for more than a few dragon breaths."

Exchanging a long wordless look with Tellar, Lord Gamron held out his arm to Renny.

Giving a barely perceptible nod, one hand going to the hilt of his sword, Tellar moved closer to his mother.

Taking the arm Lord Gamron offered, surrounded by her hulking retinue, Renny made for the stairs. Two of the guards went ahead of them, the rest trailed behind.

Leaning in close, Lord Gamron confided, "I hoped I would get a moment alone with you before the ceremony. I would be most honored to be the one to escort you to Allar's side."

Renny smiled hugely. "I am the one who would be honored. I accept, most gratefully." Tried to look around but all she could see was…large men. Very large men.

She laughed, a delighted sound that carried across the hall and tightened Allar's groin, made everyone else turn in Renny's direction. "These good folks are going to think I mean to run away and leave Allar standing by himself."

Lord Gamron's answering laughter boomed out. "He's not taking any chances with you. You've given Allar enough gray hair."

Renny sighed. "I'm afraid I'm going to give him more. I'm not the target, he is. I've been considering who the attacker might be, but I draw a blank every time. I simply don't know these people well enough. Voya's the obvious choice, but he's more loyal to Allar than anyone, even Zantha. It takes a great deal of faith to leave your wounded mate and your mate's dragon and follow someone into battle."

Lord Gamron listened intently as his soon to be daughter by law reasoned out her thoughts. "His other soldiers are almost as loyal. None of the dragons would harm Allar. The servants are the happiest, most content I've ever seen. If it was one of his past women, they'd go solely after me, like Cylla did. After what Tobold's father did to him and Grenith, they'd be logical suspects but Conthar and I have scanned them repeatedly and neither harbors any negative feelings about Allar."

Renny shook her head in disgust. "All the dragons have scanned ceaselessly All the soldiers know to be on the lookout for rings or pendants, anything made of the sparkly rocks. The answer is right here in front of me and I can't see it. If I don't figure it out, and soon, they're going to try to kill him."

Whilst they'd been talking and walking, they'd reached the door to Allar's and Renny's chambers. Two of the guards insisted she wait in the hall while they made sure the rooms were safe.

Renny cocked her head thoughtfully. "If..." Swallowed hard as her heart nearly stopped and the air had suddenly turned to burning cinders. "If Allar...dies. What happens? Who gets Dragon's Haven? I know Dragon's Haven isn't like the other keeps with leadership being passed down from father to son. I think...whoever's behind this sees himself as a hero and seeks to put himself in Allar's place."

Getting closer, Renny could feel the rightness of her conclusions, she couldn't just quite grasp the last piece. A piece that eluded her like the insubstantial memory of a dream, just beyond recall.

As soon as the guards emerged and gave Renny the nod, she slipped into her chambers to change.

Well used to his women taking forever to to ready themselves, Lord Gamron leaned against the wall and prepared himself for a long wait.

The door opened a scant few moments later, and thinking Renny needed assistance, something fastened or…

Lord Gamron's jaw dropped when Renny stepped out, completely ready. Dropped farther when he saw that instead of the customary bouquet, she carried her bow, quiver slung across one shoulder.

His booming laughter could be heard down below in the Great Hall, making Allar wonder uneasily what Renny had done to elicit such a response.

Giving Renny a quick hard hug, Lord Gamron chuckled. "You, my dear, are priceless. I hope you breed sons and daughters just like yourself. If you give Allar gray hair, several more of you will make him pull it out."

Still laughing, he draped an arm around Renny's shoulders, tucked her close, and headed back to the Great Hall.

Leaning into his bulk, Renny smiled. "Thank you. Allar says compliments are gifts and I should always remember to say thank you." Stopping, Renny looked up into Lord Gamron's handsome face, so like Allar's, merely older.

"I would thank you also for welcoming me into your family. If there's ever anything I can do to repay you…"

Lord Gamron eyed Renny speculatively. "There is one small thing."

"Name it and it's yours." Renny's solemn tone and fervent look assured him of her sincerity, not that he'd doubted it for an instant.

"Call me Father."

"Done." Renny held out her hand.

Instead of taking it, Lord Gamron pulled Renny close for another hug. Patted her back and pulled away to look Renny in the face. Placing both hands on her shoulders, he beamed. "I couldn't be prouder of you or love you more if you were my own."

Raising up on tiptoe as he leaned down, Renny shyly kissed his cheek. "Thank you. Father."

Hooking his arm through hers once more, his smile lit the hallway. "Renny girl, you've made me a very happy man. Family is so important. So many families were torn apart, lost or destroyed during the wars. Much like what happened to yours, I suppose."

Lord Gamron's voice faded as the full import of his words struck Renny like the flat of a sword on unprotected skin, stinging and resonating bone deep.

{{*Conthar! Did Tobold have any other family than his father?*}}

Without waiting for her dragon's answer, Renny hurried Lord Gamron toward the hall, asking him the same.

{{*Conthar! Tell Mithar to alert Voya…*}}

{{*Already done. Allar has more guards than you.*}}

Snorting her disbelief at that impossibility, Renny moved faster. The guards refused to let her outpace them and Renny was frantic she wouldn't get there in time.

"Renny." Lord Gamron had to call her name twice more before he could capture her attention. "Tobold had an uncle and an older brother. They went off to war and were never heard from again. They weren't dragonriders so we couldn't keep track of them that way. It was just assumed they died in some nameless battle."

Renny replied grimly, instincts cementing into hard facts. "They didn't. One or both are here now." {{*Conthar, the old man that agreed to transport Cylla mentioned mercenaries from the south. Tell me about them.*}}

{{*Mercenaries?*}} Pictures flashed in Renny's head, reaffirming her thoughts. {{*They have helped the dragonhaters before. They bear no love for dragons, for whatever reason. Dragons will have nothing to do with them, and so the south'ards use every opportunity to help the dragonhaters. 'Twas thought they'd been cowed, their leaders killed and their numbers*}} *depleted, but it seems we were wrong about that. They are easily roused to fight, easily led.*}}

{{*Like many that I killed for torturing dragons.*}} Renny knew none of the swarthy, smaller in stature mercenaries were within the keep's walls—they'd stand out like a herdbeast in a cluster of dragons.

{{*Conthar, do you or any of the other dragons have any memory of what Tobold's brother and his uncle looked like?*}}

A picture formed instantly in Renny's mind, nothing remarkable or outstanding about either man, and Conthar sounded apologetic. {{*I have not seen either for many years. If they still live, they probably look completely different.*}}

{{*Scan for them anyway. I'm positive one or both are here. They've got some of that damnable rock on their persons.*}} Renny's tone was grim, her thoughts grimmer.

Trying another tack, Renny hailed Grenith. {{*Grenith? Can you tell me anything of Tobold's brother or uncle?*}}

{{*They still lived when when my rider and I had our accident. I have no idea if they still live, or where they would be.*}}

{{*Can you remember anything about them? Anything at all?*}}

Renny felt Grenith take a deep breath, felt his pain like she'd struck him with a whip. {{*You think they are here?*}} Catching part of Renny's thoughts, Grenith gasped, {{*You think they are the ones trying to harm you?*}}

{{*Not me—Allar.*}}

Another gasp of agonizing pain from Grenith. {{*I can't remember much, my memories are but scraps and tatters. Everything is still—scrambled, but I remember this—neither were dragonbonded. Instead of being happy for Tobold when we bonded, they were very jealous. The two of them refused to even see us off for our first flight.*}}

Using Grenith's link with Renny, Tobold spoke up. {{*Renny, they seemed upset that I had bonded with a dragon, but I didn't pay any attention. I was too wrapped up in Grenith and our joyous feelings. My brother and my uncle*}} *were always close. My brother is quite a bit older than me. I was so happy to have found Grenith... Uncle grudging told me where to go on my first flight, as if he didn't want to share dragonrider secrets. I had no reason not to listen to him.*}}

The three of them contemplated that for a long moment. Renny, well used to betrayal from adults who were supposed to guard and nurture children, didn't find it as shocking as Tobold did that the uncle had deliberately sent a first time rider and dragon to a treacherous area, knowing what would happen.

Opening fully her path to Allar, before she could warn him his words chilled Renny to her very soul.

{{*Renny, stay where you are! DO NOT come to the Great Hall.*}}

That could mean only one thing. Tobold's uncle or brother, perhaps both, were here.

Allar hadn't warned her through Zantha because whoever was in the Great Hall had one of those damned stones—and Allar.

{{*Allar...*}}

{{*Whatever you're planning, I forbid it.*}} Allar's tone brooked no disobedience.

Closing the mental pathway between them, Renny smirked to herself. She'd never been good at following orders.

Having slowed her pace while she was conversing with the dragons and Allar, Renny came to complete halt so fast the guard behind her ran smack into her.

One look at her face and Lord Gamron knew it was bad.

He and the guards had slowed when Renny did, suspecting the worst but not knowing.

Renny confirmed their fears. "They're here, in the Great Hall. Allar can't talk to Zantha and he refuses to talk to me so I don't know exactly what's going on."

Frowning, she tried again to talk some sense into her mate. {{*Allar, listen to me. If you don't tell me what's going on, I'll march right down these stairs and find out for myself.*}} Crossing her arms, Renny waited.

{{*Stay where you are. Better yet, get to the dragon caves and stay with Zantha and Conthar. Have them take you into the sky, far up, out of reach of arrows.*}}

Hearing the strain in his voice, making hers as persuasive as possible, Renny tried again, hard headed men and their orders be damned. {{*Tell me what to expect.*}}

{{*DO NOT COME DOWN HERE! The dragonhaters have Tellar and Ninar, as well as Mother. You and Father are the only ones of my family not in their clutches. He's sending men after you as we speak. GET TO THE DRAGONS!*}}

The last was the strongest order Allar'd ever given her.

Renny grimaced to herself. If they were going to be mates, he'd better realize she didn't respond well to orders and less to threats.

Never had, wasn't about to start now.

Knowing they were nearly out of time, looking at Lord Gamron, Renny asked, "Do you trust me?"

At his instant nod, Renny outlined her plan as they retreated quickly down the passageway.

Handing her bow and quiver to Lord Gamron, Renny slipped back into Allar's chambers as her guards and Lord Gamron secreted themselves in several rooms on either side.

Snorted a grim laugh.

If the dragonhaters didn't already know which door led to Allar's chambers, it wouldn't take them long to figure it out.

The beribboned garlands stuck out like a sore dragon claw.

Sitting down in front of the mirror, looking like a normal female attempting to fiddle with a ribbon in her hair and in actuality running through battle scenarios, when the invaders crashed her door open, Renny grabbed a dagger and turned to defend herself.

A ripple of laughter ran through them as a thorough look around the room showed no guards, just Renny.

The invaders laughed again unpleasantly as they disarmed

Renny—she got in a couple good swipes—three of them were bleeding before they managed to subdue her.

The biggest, ugliest attacker got right in her face. "You're wanted downstairs, *Mi'lady*. First, a bauble for you so you can't be calling your nasty dragons."

He dropped a heavy cord with one of the sparkly stones around her neck. "We're carrying plenty ourselves, but we want to make sure."

Jerking Renny along, he demanded, "Where are your guards?"

Arms locked behind her, held in place by one of the invaders, Renny struggled futilely. "My guards were in the hallway. How did you get past them?"

Big and Ugly leaned in close and whispered evilly, "Looks like all of Allar's guards deserted you for the party below stairs. Makes my job much easier. Remind me to thank them."

Running his hands roughly all over Renny, lingering unnecessarily, he found the dagger she'd strapped to her calf. And the one in her boot. And the one in her sleeve.

Smacking Renny upside the head—pissing her off as the damned ribbon she'd worked so hard on was knocked loose and fluttered to the floor—Big and Ugly leered. "We've been told you like a fight. I'm thinking you'll get all the fighting you can stand later tonight. Might be a little one sided."

All the men grabbed their crotches and laughed lewdly.

Dragging Renny out into the passage, Big and Ugly twisted one of Renny's arms up past her shoulder blade. Surrounding her in a mockery of her guards, they steered her toward the Great Hall.

Their little cavalcade had passed two doors when they heard a sound behind them. Whirling, using Renny as a shield, they faced the disturbance.

One of the dragonhaters raised his sword to kill the terrified servant who'd opened the door. Before he could follow through, the servant scurried back into the chamber like a frightened mouse and slammed the door.

Big and Ugly ordered, "Get him!"

Most of his minions jumped to obey.

Paying them no more mind, intent on the havoc he was about to wreak, Big and Ugly spun Renny and aimed for the Great Hall once again, keeping Renny close in front of himself.

Pretending to trip, Renny twisted and cursed them loudly as she went down hard, in a movement so swift Big and Ugly almost tripped over her.

Yanking Renny back to her feet, he shook her hard. "None of your tricks, you hear me? Or your dragon gets it. Slow and painful."

LOOKING up in despair as someone appeared at the top of the stairs, heart sinking, Allar knew it had to be Renny. Why couldn't she just have listened for once?

He and his men would've figured out something.

Maybe.

The stairs were shadowy so he couldn't make out all the sordid details, could only hope his father had gotten away in time, although he couldn't imagine his father leaving Renny to the butchers without putting up a fight.

Knew his men would lay down their lives for Renny, probably had.

Allar's heart constricted as his eyes confirmed they did indeed have Renny. Looking past her small form, he could see no other captives, only guards.

Black rage consumed his vision.

CHAPTER 34

Surveying the Great Hall from her vantage point at the top of the stairs, Renny noted that the dragonhaters had insinuated themselves with the real guests and now they held Allar and his family captive.

Scattered throughout the crowd, they were holding women and children hostage, knives to their throats.

Lady Gemma, Ninar, Cook, Lissa. The list went on and on.

Allar's warriors stood stock still, hands figuratively tied.

A true standoff, Allar's men wouldn't drop their weapons, the invaders wouldn't release their hostages.

All eyes were on Renny as she was forced down the stairs. All of her captors except the one who held her stopped at the bottom of the stairs and fanned out along the walls.

Big and Ugly frog marched Renny to the middle of the hall and halted her in front of the man who had to be the ringleader.

Looking him up and down, Renny curled her lip in a sneer, face distorted as if she were looking at a particularly revolting piece of pond scum, or fresh dung stuck to the bottom of her new boots.

She knew him.

Micat, Assistant to Blan, Master of Supplies.

The toad might not have a dragon, but he had access to travel, contacts everywhere, much freedom and little accountability. With the aid of his damping stone he'd infiltrated and betrayed with impunity. Had used Allar's and Renny's ceremony as cover to bring in his trusted minions.

Renny's heartache eased a little, knowing it wasn't one of Allar's trusted inner circle who'd betrayed them.

Correctly interpreting the look on Renny's face, Micat stepped forward and backhanded her. If Big and Ugly hadn't held tight, the blow would've knocked her to the floor.

Bellowing in rage, Allar lunged forward against the tight circle of dragonriders surrounding and protecting him.

Pointing at one of his men, Micat grinned smugly as the man sliced the throat of his hostage and dropped her body to the floor. Quickly reaching out, the man snatched another woman from the crowd.

The Great Hall, which had rung a moment before with screams and cries, instantly went silent.

Allar froze.

Micat sneered at Allar's distress. "Struggle all you want. Every time you do something that displeases me…" Turned his attention back to Renny.

Wondering whether this was the brother or the uncle, deciding it didn't matter—Renny faced him fearlessly, her heart breaking with what he'd just done.

She had to buy time.

"Do you think to kill everyone here?"

"If I so desire." Taking a leisurely stroll around Renny, he returned to face her. "You are such an insignificant mite to have caused so much trouble. If you hadn't shown up, we would have destroyed Allar in our own good time. We'd made a good start already."

451

Reaching out and cupping Renny's swelling jaw, he dragged his fingers down her face in a parody of affection. Ran them back up and pushed hard on her bruised cheekbone.

"As hard as Allar has struggled to save dragons, we have fought twice as hard to eliminate the dratted nuisances. My brother banished dragons and riders from his keep. With no dragons or riders flying in or out, it was a perfect place for our base. My brother was free to come and go, free to plot his revenge. Everyone figured he was deranged from his losses, and he was. He was also the mastermind behind our army. I gathered information and he utilized it."

Uncle, then. Sorry, worthless waste of a human either way.

Renny eyed him coldly. "You are the one who's deranged. Did you presume you could kill dragons forever and not get caught?"

Micat gloated, "If not for you, yes. We could've continued until every last one was wiped off the planet. Would have. You... You will suffer greatly for the trouble you have caused me."

Renny made a disbelieving noise.

Narrowing his eyes at her, Micat bared his teeth. "Even as we speak, your dragon is being hunted, trapped in his cave and shot full of poisoned arrows. All the other dragons will suffer the same fate, drawn here to try and rescue the Dragonhealer. If my men don't kill you later with their sport, I'll remove the damping stone around your neck and have you tied out in the dragon's courtyard so you can feel their pain as they die slowly."

Even knowing he was lying through his teeth, Renny's heart cramped and spasmed with unbearable pain.

Tipping his head back, smiling at the ceiling, Micat turned that same demented smile on Renny. "That's the only part of the damping stones I regret. The dragonriders can't share their dragon's agony. But then, I'm sure you can imagine exactly what he's going through. You've watched enough dragons die to know how very painful a death it is. You failed. You couldn't save your dragon, nor can you save the others."

Sounding bewildered, Renny asked, "Why do you bear such hatred for the dragons? They've done nothing to harm you, indeed, our lives would be much poorer if not for the dragons."

Micat sneered. "Yours maybe. I intend to eradicate each and every one of those rats with wings. I loathe them. Their existence is an affront to humans."

"But why?" Renny kept her eyes on his, made sure his attention was centered on her.

Voice rising, heading directly for screech territory, Micat spat, "How about this? Why do the dragons permit only a chosen few to become dragonriders? Do you think it fair that not the oldest son but the one who becomes a dragonrider inherits? Why should dragonriders be accorded special privileges?"

Micat paced away a step, paced back. "If not for my brother becoming a dragonrider, I'd've been lord. My eldest nephew suffered the same fate. Raised and trained to be lord only to have it snatched away by some capricious dragon. My youngest nephew, betrayed by his own dragon and deserted by the dragonriders, a useless cripple for life."

Glaring at Renny, Micat snarled, "And you—you're the most nithling thing there's ever been and even you get a dragon."

Jealousy, then, was what fueled his insane hatred. Renny drew a deep breath. Just a few more moments…

Her laugh cut the dark air like the deciding flash of sword gleam on a battlefield. "Dragons aren't free to choose, any more than people are. Riders and dragons just are, like mates. The more dragons there are, the more riders there can be. But you—you will never be a rider, no matter how many dragons live."

This last earned Renny another backhand that rocked her back against her captor. Raising her eyes, she smiled her feral hunting smile, though she wasn't sure her battered facial muscles would respond.

They did.

Good. Keep him focused on her.

Soon, soon.

{{*Allar, hold!*}}

She couldn't look in Allar's direction right now, could only beg him not to draw attention away from her.

Micat was screeching now, spittle flying with every word. Renny just could hear him through the ringing in her ears. She shook her head, trying to clear her vision and hearing.

"Lousy, no good…"

Her hearing faded, came back. She taunted, "Good enough for a dragon."

Micat raised his hand.

Renny taunted, still smiling, "One you'll never get your filthy hands on. All the dragons are gone from Dragon's Haven."

On the heels of her pronouncement, one of the dragonhaters came barreling back into the Great Hall, his shouts confirming Renny's words. "My Lord, all the dragons are gone! All of them!"

Micat's face flamed, a hideous burgundy suffusing his features until he looked ready to explode. "You! You did this!"

Renny smirked. "They're all waiting for you to leave the safety of this hall. Whatever you do to the people here will be returned upon you tenfold. You may be able to hide your true thoughts thanks to your damnable stone, but through me, the dragons have seen the face of each dragonhater here. There is nowhere you can hide, for your evil deeds have doomed you."

Micat hissed and spit. "Impossible! You wear a damping stone! There's no way you can contact your dragon!"

Renny shrugged nonchalantly. "If you say so." Repeated snidely, "But there are no dragons left at Dragon's Haven."

In the dead silence that followed Renny's pronouncement, a voice rang out. "Uncle! Has your jealousy wrung everything human and decent out of you?"

Micat spun to face this newest threat. "Ah. So my brother's whelp grows a spine at last. Twisted and deformed, but you have your dragon to blame for that. I should've killed you long ago, but it was so much more fun to watch your father torturing you. I couldn't bear to deny him the only pleasure he had left. This was all your father's doing, you know."

Straightening as much as possible, Tobold faced Micat bravely. "Liar! It was you. Father held true, even after he was wounded in battle and lost his dragon, even after my mother and her dragon succumbed to their loss and he lost her as well. You are the one who corrupted him, twisted his thinking until he hated dragons, hated me."

Chest heaving with effort, Tobold shook his head. "Had you but asked, I would have abjured, even as Lord Allar did with his father's keep. Would have gladly given my brother everything. I never wanted any of it, nothing but Grenith."

Came a halting step closer, one shoulder hitching higher than the other, his face a mask of pain. "You have betrayed your family and your name. Even should you survive this, no one, Dragonrider or dragonhater, will have anything to do with you, for none can trust a liar and a thief."

With Micat's focus elsewhere, Renny sought Allar. If she thought Micat livid, it was nothing to the waves radiating off Allar.

{{*Allar, listen please. I had to buy time, and letting them get their hands on me was the only thing I could think of. Your father and my guards are fine, as are all the dragons. Even Grenith. Your father is over against the wall. He and my other guards overpowered the ones sent to fetch me, save the one behind me, and he never even noticed his men had been replaced. Your father and your men await your signal.*}}

He waited so long to answer, she didn't think he was going to.

{{*You are not fine.*}}

{{*Bruises only. They will heal.*}} Renny couldn't help but glance toward the dead woman on the floor. That death was on her, but for the life of her, she couldn't see any way she could've prevented it.

Following her gaze, Allar spat, {{*That is not your fault. All the hostages would've been killed anyway. How. Many.*}}

Renny blinked. {{*How many?*}}

{{*Daggers.*}}

Renny's lips twitched. {{*Just one. That's all I need.*}}

The root cause of her little clumsy spell upstairs had been dagger retrieval. When she pretended to trip, one of her own confiscated daggers had found its way into her sleeve.

Wonders never ceased, and being a pickpocket had its advantages.

One would be enough. The idiot holding her had her right arm twisted at an unmerciful angle, thinking he'd disabled her sword hand.

Hmph. Rand having seen to it Renny was proficient with both, she was merely biding her time.

Micat was advancing on Tobold. Brave, foolish boy, he wasn't backing down.

Refusing to let Tobold be hurt any more than he already had been, Renny's laughter rang out, startling everyone.

Micat swung toward the sound, eyes darting this way and that and bugging out, trying to see what was Renny found so funny.

"You thought," Renny was laughing so hard now she could barely speak. "You thought with Allar out of the way, with all the dragons dead, you would somehow become the Lord of Dragon's Haven. *Lord of Nothing* is all you'd've become. How did you think to hide the small fact of all the dragon and dragonrider deaths? How did you imagine all the other dragons and riders on this world would not destroy you in retribution?"

Renny laughed again, scornfully. "Lord of Dragon's Haven isn't a position that can be passed down in a family or won by treachery and murder—the dragons choose who will protect them. Only the bravest, strongest, most honest and most valiant warrior can be lord here. You are none of those things. You are not fit to tend herdbeasts. The dragons would never choose you, and no matter what foul deeds you committed, you would never be the true lord of this keep—not even if you were the last human on this planet."

Renny's laughter chimed pure and sweet until it filled the Great Hall. Gradually, as a trickle becomes a stream and a stream becomes a river, the inhabitants and honored guests joined in Renny's laughter.

{{*NOW, ALLAR!*}}

Renny sent her message winging as Micat closed his fingers around Renny's slender throat, intent on choking the laughter—and the life—out of her.

Renny had kept track with her peripheral vision of Lord Gamron and her guards working their way through the crowd, killing the attackers one by one and freeing hostages. Seeing what they were doing, Allar's men moved to aid them as soon as they could without endangering the rest of the hostages, taking up the infiltrator's positions with no one the wiser, the fallen bodies quickly hidden by the crowd.

Just before Renny's vision grayed out completely, she saw Lord Gamron—Father!—free Mother Gemma. With that sight imprinted on her eyeballs, Renny let her dagger slip from her sleeve and slashed it wickedly in Micat's direction. Swiftly reversed it and stabbed behind herself.

The unrelenting pressure on Renny's neck let up. The man behind her released her arm and Renny fell to her knees, gasping, trying futilely to draw air back into her starved lungs, trying to clear her vision.

Trying to get her right arm to function. Again.

Hadn't she done this enough already?

A firm hand landed on her arm, the one that held the dagger, but before she could strike Tellar exclaimed, "Hold, sister. I like my parts attached and my guts inside."

When she'd regained enough breath to lift her head, Renny looked him in the face, his teasing words belying the worry etched on his features.

Renny grinned and rasped, "Rescuing damsels in distress? You're ruining my image of you as just another pretty boy."

Grinning back, Tellar helped Renny to her feet. His sword hung from his other hand, dripping blood. Renny looked from it to the body on the floor.

"I owe you my thanks, Tellar. I couldn't figure out how I was going to take out Micat and the guard. Not the way he was holding me."

"You'd've thought of something." Praising her, Tellar pressed a kiss to the top of Renny's head.

Leaning on Tellar, borrowing his strength, Renny surveyed the Great Hall. Most of the traitors were dead, those that weren't soon would be.

Searching for Micat, Renny's breath hitched and her heart stuttered. Her aim had been off, or perhaps he'd sensed her attack and increased the distance between them just in time, but she'd done no great damage with her preemptive strike.

Micat carried a bloody stripe across the front of his tunic to mark their encounter, but it sure wasn't slowing him down any as he and Allar circled each other, swords busy.

If anything, like swatting at a buzz-sting, it'd only enraged him more.

Spewing venom as the circled, Micat hissed, "I'd've had you if not for that detestable healer. She's been nothing but a torment for a long while now. Had Din done as ordered and killed her, I wouldn't be fighting you because you'd already be dead."

A bleeding gash opened on Micat's arm.

As cold as Micat was hot, Allar made no verbal reply. Letting cold steel speak for him, Allar struck out swiftly with his sword.

Feint. Thrust. Parry. Contact.

For every insult hurled, Allar demanded payment in blood.

"I had my own brother believing you and the dragons were responsible for his son's accident. That the only way to absolve the blood debt was to destroy you along with all the dragons."

Slash.

"Your beloved Zantha would be in torment because Conthar would be dead."

Stab.

"I would already be Lord of Dragon's Haven, and my first order would be to kill all the dragons."

Slice.

"Your woman would be screaming beneath me."

"Never!" Allar quit toying and shoved his blade home. Shoved it to the hilt into the blackguards' heart and twisted. Withdrew and thrust again. Pulled his weapon free, spun all the way around.

Used his momentum and his great strength and swung his sword with all his might.

Watched as head was severed from body to roll across the floor.

Turned his back while the body was still standing.

Sword point down, sides heaving, Allar locked his gaze on Renny. What he saw didn't soothe his temper any.

Renny, looking back at him, flanked by his brother and his father, both of them looking like they were protecting her.

From him.

Unacceptable.

Allar took a step toward Renny.

His father and brother both took a step forward and shifted closer together, almost obscuring Renny.

Ignoring them for the moment, Allar focused his glare on Renny.

On her face.

On the fresh bruises overlaying the earlier ones.

On the dark smudges ringing her throat. Again.

The temper he'd tamped down while fighting burst to the surface.

Since his men had let him out of their protective circle, Allar'd had his sword in his hand and had been working his way to Renny, stopping only long enough to dispatch Micat.

To see her thus, hiding behind his family, as if she were afraid of him...

Was she going to run now? Decide she couldn't be with him, couldn't be mate to a man who had twice let her be taken prisoner, from his own keep? Couldn't be mate to a man who couldn't even protect her?

Staring back at Allar, Renny didn't need to read his mind to know exactly what he was thinking. Placing her left hand on Tellar's arm and leaning close to Lord... Father, she spoke softly to them.

They shifted, barely, and Renny slipped between them to advance steadily in Allar's direction.

She'd've laughed if not for the terrible look on Allar's face, the same one she knew was plastered on hers.

He was afraid she didn't want him, and she was afraid he'd be so mad at her for placing herself at risk again...

Walking fearlessly up to his temper, Renny laid her head on his chest, her left arm curling around his waist. "Thank you, again."

Standing like that for what seemed forever, Allar finally relaxed and wrapped his free arm around her, dropped his head over hers and heaved a breath that seemed to emanate from the depths of his soul.

When he could speak past the lump in his throat—most likely his heart—Allar tipped Renny's chin up. Scrutinized every bruise and mark, looked deep into her eyes. "You. Can't. Do. This. Again."

Renny shook her head and buried her face against his chest,

mumbling apologies. He caught *sorry, your father, the dragons, my fault.*

Winding the fingers of one hand through Renny's hair, he tugged her head back enough to see her face. "Renny, none of this was your fault. If you want to blame someone, blame me. I'm the one who let you, let everyone down. I was too cocky, too confident that the dragonhaters couldn't breach the security of Dragon's Haven. I'm the one who let them in, practically welcomed them with open arms. If it hadn't been for you… How did you know the dragons were gone?"

Renny blinked up at him, and remembering, ripped the hated dampening stone from around her neck and gave it a toss. Instantly, Conthar and Zantha filled her head with anxious queries. She automatically soothed them while pacifying Allar.

Swallowed and looked him straight in the eye. "You couldn't have known—no one blames you. This was as well planned as the fire. When you said not to come down, I almost listened to you, but… I couldn't do it. I couldn't leave all of you to them, to be butchered. They weren't after me, not really. They were after you, just using me to bait their trap."

Petting his chest like she would a distraught dragon, Renny kept going with her tale. "I made all the dragons leave before they put that stone around my neck. They did the sling thing and got Grenith out, went far enough away the dragonhaters couldn't get to them. They're all on their way back as we speak."

Giving a word of approval—knowing better than to come up behind Renny unannounced—Lord Gamron placed his hand on her shoulder in a gesture of solidarity. Told Allar with no small measure of pride, "Renny masterminded this whole rescue. She got us to hide in several of the empty rooms along the passageway. The traitors, morons all, must've come up the back stairs. They went straight to your chambers, guess they figured we'd all come back downstairs to join the party, 'cause that's what they'd've done.

Renny let the dragonhaters capture her and head back this way. We sent one of the servants who happened to be above stairs out as a decoy and replaced their guards with your men. When we reached the bottom of the stairs we spread out so we could get closer to the men holding the hostages. Everyone was so engrossed in Renny's drama they paid no attention to us. Very well done, my dear."

"Thank you. Father."

"I'm not finished with you, young lady. I forbid you to ever do anything so stupid again."

Renny's meek sounding, "Yes, sir," didn't fool anyone.

Allar's tension relieving laughter boomed out and drowned out the rest of his father's admonitions.

THE GREAT HALL WAS CLEANED—YET again.

Looking around at all the wetly gleaming surfaces, Renny was willing to bet this was the cleanest it'd ever been.

While the men had toted bodies out and water in, the women had scrubbed bloodstains.

Once removed from the hall, the carcasses had been piled onto dragonhide tarps. Several of the dragons had picked the tarps up and disappeared.

Standing tiredly beside Mother Gemma and Ninar, Renny swept the space once more with her eyes. Wondered if anyone would still want to have the ceremony this eve.

As if sensing her thoughts, Allar appeared beside Renny. Not that he'd gotten far from her, had barely taken his eyes off her while they were setting the room to rights.

Slanting Renny a grin, Allar gave her a slight bow. "Ready when you are, my love."

Glancing down at her bloody clothes, taking in the ruined silver dress, Renny grimaced. "Give me a moment to…"

Shaking his head vigorously, Allar denied her. "No way. You are not getting out of my sight again. Not even to change."

Lady Gemma protested vociferously. "Allar! You can't expect Renny to wear those filthy clothes to your bonding ceremony!"

Eyes locked on Renny, Allar refused to budge. "You have two choices; what you're wearing, or naked. I care not. I want this done now."

Smiling mischievously, Renny grabbed a fistful of Allar's shirt and pulled him nose to nose. So close no one else could hear the words she whispered against his lips. "And if I choose naked?"

Had the distinct pleasure of seeing Allar's eyes heat, and feeling the heat course through his body, and the answering heat in hers.

THE WOMEN WON OUT, but Allar got his way, too. He insisted on helping Renny bathe and dress, had half the soldiers in the keep stationed outside the door to their chambers and strung down the hall.

Renny reciprocated, helping Allar bathe and dress as well.

Engrossed in each other, they'd've been late to their own ceremony if Tellar hadn't…hurried them along with his… frequent reminders.

Leaving their chambers, heading back to the Great Hall, part two, Renny worried her dagger between her fingers. "I don't want to hurt your mother's feelings—I already did when I refused her help, not once but twice, getting dressed—and she did such a magnificent job decorating the Great Hall…"

"But?" Allar prompted, having a pretty good idea what was going through Renny's mind.

"It seems wrong somehow, to celebrate there tonight."

Stopping, turning Renny to face him, Allar cupped the less-bruised side of her face, stroked his thumb along her cheek.

Pressing her soft skin into his calloused palm, Renny pursed her lips at him.

"Renny love, I wasn't sure about doing this right now either. Almost called it off." Twisting his hand so his knuckles brushed her cheek, keeping the caress going until he cradled her head, Allar swallowed.

"Ranto, the husband of the woman who was killed, came up to me while we were cleaning. Said he wanted us to continue with our plans, that his wife would've wanted it so. She—Pentra—thought highly of you and he didn't want you to..."

Renny strained against Allar's light hold. Asked bitterly, "To what? Grieve? How can I not? She—Pentra—would be alive and they'd be together now if I hadn't..."

Continuing as if Renny hadn't interrupted, Allar touched foreheads with her. "Ranto didn't want you to feel responsible. He said to remind you, if not for your courage, many others would be suffering this night, human and dragon. Ranto also said you have come too far, accomplished too much, to let the dragonhaters win now. He asked that you not let Pentra's sacrifice be in vain. Make it instead a victory."

Pondering Ranto's words conveyed through Allar, Renny accepted the loss and sorrow along with the wisdom. "Very well, then. But not in the Great Hall."

Looked at Allar and said hesitantly, "What about the dragon's courtyard? It's large enough and that way... The dragons could watch as well."

Allar's smile lit his face. Kissing her bruised cheek gently, he agreed. "I think that's a fine idea. I'm sure the dragons will approve most heartily."

CHAPTER 35

*A*nd so they gathered, at twilight, in the dragon's courtyard.

The twilight of a long, hard day, with friends and family and dragons surrounding them, to speak their vows.

Allar let go Renny only long enough for Gamron to escort her back to his side—where Allar stood waiting impatiently at the front of the crowd.

Lord Gamron was chuckling as he placed Renny's hand in Allar's.

Raising his brows in question, Allar chuckled too as his father indicated Renny's bouquet.

Nestled among the flowers, Allar could just make out the gleam of Renny's favorite dagger.

Renny repeated the words and promises she'd given Allar in the Great Hall the day Cylla attacked her, made sure she included love in her vows.

Allar vowed Renny his promises, including love, just as darkness fell and the light from the torches flared bright.

The ceremony was brief, the congratulations lasted much longer.

Everyone wanted to talk to Renny, touch her, as if to assure themselves she truly was here and fine.

Allar couldn't blame them—he felt the same need himself.

That wasn't the only need he was feeling.

Voya brought them a plate of tidbits, and Renny shot him a grateful look at his thoughtful gesture, another when she saw that he hadn't included any cheeses. Didn't think she'd be able to stomach cheese for a long while.

The cheese Renny'd identified had indeed come from the keep of Tobold's father.

Nibbling, Renny's thoughts strayed to Tobold and Grenith. It would be a long road to recovery for the youth and his dragon, but they were young and regaining their strength, and now they had the backing and support they'd lacked all their lives.

Renny had seen Tobold a short while ago, deep in conversation with Ninar. Her frivolity and lightness would do Tobold a world of good, prove to the lad not everyone was hateful. Had even seen Ninar give Grenith a hesitant pat.

Grenith didn't seem any the worse for wear.

The dragons were getting good at hauling him around in a sling. They'd even lifted him up to the dragon's courtyard so he wouldn't be left out of the festivities.

Over there, barely visible in a dark corner, Renny sent Grenith an encouraging thought. {{*You're dong fine, big boy!*}}

Conthar and Zantha had patiently waited their turns, and Renny and Allar headed in their direction. No words were necessary.

Renny walked up to Conthar, stopped in front of him. Conthar blew a soft breath out his nostrils, a warm breath that caressed Renny's face and immediately eased her aching bruises, then dipped his great head and bumped Renny gently.

Circling his head with her arms, Renny scratched while Conthar hummed blissfully.

Allar did the same to Zantha, getting the same response.

Renny had enjoyed this gathering, as much as she could with her heart heavy from all the events of the day, but she was more than ready to get away for awhile.

Needed desperately to be with just her mate and her dragons.

{{*Allar?*}}

{{*Already taken care of, my love.*}}

Turning to say their goodbyes, they froze.

The entire assemblage faced them. Not a whisper, not a cough, hardly a breath stirred the wall to wall crowd.

Voya stepped forward. "We would like to congratulate you on your binding ceremony. Some of us were beginning to wonder if you'd ever complete it."

A ripple of amusement ran through the crowd.

Waiting until it quieted, in no hurry to end the sorely needed laughter, Voya raised a goblet high. "To our Lord Defender and our Lady Healer, may blessings shower upon you for all of your days. May your lives be long and prosperous, filled with love and laughter and many children. May the four of you remain together until you go into that great sleep that awaits us all, and may you all go as one."

As one, every single person took a knee and bowed their heads.

Even the dragons, hulking around the shadowy perimeter, dipped their great heads.

Renny threw a quick glance over her shoulder to see Conthar and Zantha, necks bowed gracefully.

Reaching out a hand to grasp Allar's, Renny looked on in utter amazement as all and sundry paid homage to their Lord and Lady.

Scooping Renny up, Allar seated her on Conthar and vaulted

onto Zantha. They took to the air amid wild shouts and cheers and trumpeting.

Conthar and Zantha flew sided by side, slowly, leisurely.

Flew for a long while, enjoying the peace of the night.

Not the dark, for the full moon lit the world.

Had it already been that long? That the moon was full again?

So many days had passed in a blur, with so much happening.

Allar had been right when he told Renny flying by moonlight was a whole different experience. The dragons seemed content to ferry their riders through the bright beams, perhaps all night, but Allar called a halt.

There would be other full moons, and Renny's weariness was beating at him, beating at the dragons as well.

DISMOUNTING, Allar held his arms up to Renny. Sitting on Conthar's broad back for a long moment, enjoying the beauty of the place they'd landed, Renny eased into Allar's arms.

He let her slide down the full length of his body, so she could feel every hard muscle and he could feel every soft place.

Renny gazed around in delight. Allar knew her so well.

A wide waterfall dropped in stages to a large pool, the whole gilded by moonbeams. The water gurgled and chuckled endlessly, repeating secrets to itself in some long forgotten tongue.

The spray from the waterfall reflected and refracted the moonlight giving the whole place a magical look, as if fairies and elves might burst forth any moment in wild celebration, or perhaps a mythical creature might step out of the forest to drink from a quiet edge of the pool.

A cozy tent was set up in the small clearing, no doubt chock full of goodies.

Feeling better already, some of her tiredness dropping away, Renny heaved a sigh of contentment. "Allar, I love your family and all our people at Dragon's Haven but I have been alone so long, sometimes it's hard to be around so many people all the time. I'm glad we're alone now."

Allar considered, for the space of a dragon blink, telling Renny they weren't alone, hadn't been since that first thoughtless foray he'd taken her on to the valley.

Considered and rejected the idea just as quickly—he *liked* his head attached to his body.

Renny did not need to know that wherever they'd gone, an entire squadron of dragons and dragonriders had been somewhere close by. Even now, they were camped just out of sight, surrounding his and Renny's camp.

The dragons had agreed early on not to contact Renny, and Zantha and Conthar hadn't wanted to give away their part in the deception. Although, technically, none of them had actually lied to Renny, merely invoked their dragon version of don't ask, don't tell.

Twining their fingers, Allar led Renny to a path off to one side of the waterfall.

Walking a short distance, Renny's eyes lit at what Allar showed her. Small pools, ringed by smooth boulders, highlighted by the moonlight and perfect for bathing.

It was late, though, and chilly.

Renny sighed and supposed they'd have to wait until the morrow.

Allar grinned, knowing what she was thinking. Tugging Renny down beside the closest pool, he touched her hand to the water.

Renny grinned back in utter delight.

The water was bath-warm.

Leisurely stripping each other's clothes off amid much kissing and touching, holding hands, they stepped down into the pool.

Reaching behind a boulder, Allar revealed a soft cloth.

Renny laughed in delight, wondered what Allar'd produce next. This place was magical, and nothing would surprise her.

Watched with great interest as he reached behind the boulder again, this time going back with soap.

Real, honest to goodness soap, not a handful of soapweed.

Renny smirked, "You truly have a cleanliness fetish, don't you? We just finished bathing a short while ago."

Allar crooked a finger and Renny laughingly moved closer.

Rubbing the soap into the cloth until he had a goodly amount of bubbles, what Allar really wanted was to touch Renny, reassure himself she bore no more wounds.

Seon had checked her out, and Allar'd examined her minutely when he'd bathed her earlier, but... That'd been hours ago.

Renny's mention of their ceremony had Allar's eyes going dark and sultry. He'd never thought mere words could make them any closer, but he'd been wrong.

Upon the completion of their vows, as close as he'd been to Renny and their dragons before, Allar had felt the very fabric of their lives intertwine, as if they were a tapestry in the making. Could feel the warp and weft, the shuttlecock filled with vibrant colors shooting back and forth, the tamping down and solidifying of the emerging pattern.

Seating Renny on an underwater boulder, Allar stretched out one of her arms and soaped from her shoulder to the hand he still held. "Not only is this water warm, even in the cold season, it also possesses healing properties."

Soaped her other arm in the same leisurely manner.

Working his way back to her shoulder, he ran the bubble covered cloth up her neck. "Tip your head back and close your eyes."

Swirling the soapy cloth over her face, then rinsing it, Allar hummed softly, lulling Renny.

Setting the soapy cloth on a convenient protrusion on one of the boulders, Allar reached for a clean cloth. Swishing it in the water, wringing it out, he gently placed the warm, wet cloth over Renny's face, over the worst of the bruises, leaving her mouth uncovered so she could breathe.

And so he could steal little nibbling kisses.

Picking up the soapy cloth, he nudged Renny's legs apart and stepped between them. Took his time, hands busy under the water, stopping every so often to rewarm the cloth over her face.

Beneath the double onslaught of warm water and Allar's hands, Renny melted, boneless as heated wax. Didn't think she could stay on her rock much longer.

Allar kept up his motions, watching Renny relax. That was exactly what he wanted; for her to forget for awhile, to feel nothing but his ministering hands soothing her.

Sitting on a rock lower than hers, Allar pulled Renny into his lap so she was up to her chin in the warm water. Wrapping his arms around her, tucking her head against his shoulder and running his hands all over her, he took great pleasure in murmuring love words in her ear.

Using explicit terms, Allar told Renny exactly what he was going to do to her, what he wanted her to do to him. Even over the heated water, he could feel her body flush in arousal as his words took root.

They would do all these things and more.

As soon as Renny was rested.

With her ass pressing back against the hard evidence of Allar's need, Renny sighed. Knowing that once again, no matter how much she wanted him, she was about to fall asleep and leave Allar wanting, she offered a sleepy protest he chose to ignore.

Rising with his sleeping woman in his arms, he wrapped a blanket from his stash around Renny before she had a chance to get cold and carried her back to their tent. Nudging the tent flap aside with one shoulder, Allar placed Renny under the furs on their makeshift bed. Dried himself off before slipping under the furs with her, pulled her close and tight, her back spooned against his front.

Fast asleep, she didn't acknowledge his presence except to wiggle her sweet ass closer to his aching groin.

Allar bit back a groan. Renny was making a habit out of wearing herself out and making him wait. There would be no sleep for him tonight, but he'd take it any day over the alternative.

Hard and aching with want, that wasn't what was keeping him awake. He reviewed the day's events, each scene playing over and over in his mind.

Renny, battered and bruised, again.

Placing herself in danger, again.

Trying to protect everyone else at her expense, again.

And after all that, playfully threatening to attend their ceremony naked.

Shaking his head and muttering, Renny's selflessness was going to be the death of him.

Zantha mumbled sleepily, {{*Will you please go to sleep? Your mental anguish is keeping us awake.*}}

{{*Sorry, Zantha. It's just… She's just…*}}

{{*We know, Allar. Rest.*}}

The thought that finally made him grin and settle down and at last allow all of them some rest was *how* he was going to wake his beloved mate.

Letting Renny sleep a few hours, until he felt she'd rested some and he just couldn't wait any more, Allar instigated his plan slowly.

Still spooned together, he began nuzzling her neck. Sweeping his hands down as far as he could reach and then back up, cupping her warm breasts in his calloused palms. Thumbing her nipples, running his knuckles back and forth across the soft undersides.

Pressed a palm flat against her taut belly, wondering as he did so if their babe was growing inside, safe and warm and already loved.

His wandering hands froze as a harsh though insinuated itself, one that'd tormented him earlier to no end—what if…

What if…Renny'd been carrying, what if they'd violated her, harmed the babe before he'd been able to rescue her from her kidnappers? Either time?

Would he ever have been able to forgive himself? Allar had no doubt Renny wouldn't even have thought to blame him.

He was in such turmoil, projecting such turbulent emotions, Zantha and Renny both woke and responded at the same time.

{{*Allar, 'tis over.*}}

{{*Allar, why would I blame you?*}} Turning in his arms, Renny cupped his cheek tenderly. "You did everything you could. Since I have known you…"

"Since you have known me, you have been endangered constantly, your life at risk over and over." Allar's voice rang harshly, full of self recrimination.

Renny shook her head. "My life has always been at risk. Since I have known you…" Unable to put her feelings into words, Renny turned to mindspeak, knowing Allar would be able to feel her emotions, the truth of what she felt for him.

{{*Protected. Safe. Well fed. Taken care of. Beloved. Cherished. All these and more. No one in my entire life has taken care of me the way you do. You make me feel special, as if I am worth more than how much work I can do, or how well I can fight. You have given me my fondest dreams on a silver platter—a dragon, a home, a family, a mate. Think on this—if not for you I would still have been captured—it was just a matter of time. If not for you, they would've done all you've imagined and worse, and I would have endured it for as long as possible, knowing there was no one who cared enough about me to help. Knowing my life would end in great pain—and never knowing any of the blessings you have bestowed upon me.*}}

Sensing Allar was softening, Renny shoved on his shoulder until he grudgingly rolled onto his back. Straddling him, Renny put her hands on his shoulders as if to pin him in place. "You are not to blame because Tobold's father and uncle were insane. They were clever enough to make everyone think they were still on your side, all the while committing their atrocities. Conthar told me the no-colors acted as they did because their hearts were dead. I don't know if the dragons or riders were corrupted first, or if, between the damping stones and Tobold's kin and the evil dragonrider the dragons were convinced everything was hopeless... I don't know. We'll probably never know all the details. How was the evil dragonrider able to exert control over the dragons? I''m telling you again—I was there when the evil dragon rider did—whatever to Conthar."

Renny swallowed hard, the memory of Conthar's cobalt body falling senseless to the ground nearly stopping her heart. "Conthar went down without a whimper, just folded up where he was, instantly unconscious. I couldn't reach him for the longest time. The evil dragonrider tried to get into my mind while they were torturing Conthar. I felt him prying, like he was trying to get a lid off a stubbornly sealed barrel. Had I given him my real name when he asked, I truly believe I wouldn't be her now. He tried again when they took me to the keep we dismantled. Even though he'd found out my name, my shields had become too strong by then for him to breech."

Voiced something she'd been considering, turning over and over in her mind. "Perhaps he was meant to be a healer, but instead of healing, something went wrong and he became a destroyer."

Renny shook her head again. "I just don't know. It doesn't matter. We won, they lost. That's all that matters." While she'd been talking, Renny's hands had been busy. Cupping Allar's face, tracing his features, stroking his hair back, running her fingers through the silky black strands.

Catching her roving hands, Allar brought them to his lips. Sat up in a swift motion so Renny was astraddle his lap, knees on either side of his hips. Letting go her hands, he ran his hands down her arms to her elbows, then up over her shoulders to cup her face gently, so gently for a long kiss.

Fisting her hands in his silky hair, Renny drew Allar close, until there was no space between them, only skin, and still they were too far apart.

Allar cupped Renny's naked buttocks, ran his big hands up her back, stroked them down her sides to cup her ass again. Palmed Renny's hips and traced her hipbones with his thumbs while he deepened the kiss. When Renny moaned and shivered in response, he traced her hipbones again, delighted to have found another sensitive spot.

His mate was absolutely the most responsive partner he'd ever had, as if her skin was one big bundle of nerves.

{{*I know you're not thinking about other women with your hands all over me.*}}

Renny's throaty laugh made Allar smirk.

{{*My love, I confess I was—but only comparing how much better you are than any other, how much more I enjoy you.*}} Allar's confession was followed by wicked laughter and sudden movement.

Renny's world spun and suddenly she was beneath Allar, soft furs under her, hard hot male covering her.

Continuing his exploring, mapping all Renny's most sensitive spots, marking them with hands and lips and tongue, Allar rose above Renny. Locking her fingers in his, palm to palm, he slowly slid home.

Renny's incoherent cries rang out, blended with the gurgling waterfall, filled the air with the sweet music of love.

Allar gave Renny that first stunning release, made her work for the next ones.

Changed position again and again. Took her to the razor edge of pleasure/pain over and over. Held Renny there as long as possible before leaping over with her, only to climb up onto the edge again, barely giving them breathing room in between.

Allar showed Renny what it meant to be truly bonded mates, to be loved.

Renny took all that he gave and returned it tenfold.

Only when they were both sated, pleasured beyond belief, did Allar ease up on either of them. Curling against him like a contented pursim, already drifting into sleep, Renny barely moved when Allar picked her up and held her close to his chest as he exited their tent.

They ended up back at the warm pool, Renny cradled in Allar's arms. He stepped down into the pool, Renny's silvery laughter matching the waning moonlight.

"Allar, three baths in one day?!"

As Renny's laughter rang out, Allar felt himself growing hard again.

Shouldn't have been possible, no way, no how, but the warm woman in his arms combined with the heady scent of their loving drifting up from the warm water bypassed Allar's brain and zinged straight to his groin. Renny's ripe essence surrounded him, more intoxicating than any wine.

Over Renny's laughing protests, he turned her so she straddled his lap once more, knees propped underwater on either side of his hips on the same boulder he was sitting on.

Looping her arms around Allar's neck, Renny pressed her forehead to his, touching noses. She could feel him, hot and hard, pressing against her slick entrance.

Shifting until he slipped inside, Renny lay against Allar's chest and just let him throb inside her, even that small movement teasing her over-sensitized flesh and nearly sending her over the edge again.

Rocking back, sliding up and down in minute increments, tightening her internal muscles, Renny teased Allar until he was practically begging.

The warm water lapping softly with their movements added to the stimulation.

Renny rubbed the tips of her breasts across Allar's chest, leaned back and cupped them in offering.

Allar obliged, most willingly. Suckling and licking and kissing, each contact twanged the nerve between Renny's legs until she was the one begging.

Weaving his fingers through her hair, Allar tipped Renny's head back. Slanting her head to his liking, he kissed her until they were both breathless.

Capturing Renny's soft cry as she let go, Allar joined her.

Nearly boneless, Renny slid off to one side and settled in the water beside Allar, one arm draped around his waist. He slung an arm around her shoulders and kept her close.

Lazily reaching out his other hand, Allar settled it between Renny's legs, cupping her mound.

Squirming at his light touch, head nestled on his shoulder and eyes closed, Renny's protest had him grinning. "Allar, even I know if you play with a new toy too much you'll wear it out."

"Hush, love. I'm only going to rinse you off, then we'll go back to the tent and sleep—for awhile."

"Hmmm." Her non-committal answer reached Allar's ears at the same time her hand dropped to his hardening shaft.

Allar couldn't say anything else, just gritted his teeth as she reached out a small hand and began to mimic his movements.

Finally managing to rinse each other off, they stumbled out of the pool together. Scooping her up, Allar pretended to stumble just to see if he could get a reaction out of Renny.

Tightening her arms around his neck, she hitched closer but refused to open her eyes. Muttered, "I'm asleep. Leave me alone."

Almost back to the tent, Conthar contacted Renny, sounding as smug as Allar. {{*Renny, I hate to interrupt you and we won't keep you long, but Zantha and I would like you and Allar to join us at the top of the waterfall. 'Tis almost sunrise.*}}

Instantly awake, Renny struggled to free herself from Allar's hold.

Setting Renny on her feet, Allar shrugged at her questioning look.

Haphazardly pulling on clothes, hand in hand, the humans hurried to do as their dragons requested.

Arriving at the top of the waterfall, breathless, Renny started to immediately go to their dragons.

Gazing up at the sky, without turning his head in their direction, Conthar commanded, "Stay."

He and Zantha took to the air as one.

The flat boulder Renny and Allar stood on was still cloaked in shades of gray, the fine mist from the waterfall adding one more layer of colorlessness.

Wrapping his arms around Renny and pulling her back against his chest, Renny and Allar watched as the dragons flew up and up, the high, early sunlight catching their jeweled tones, sparkling and reflecting myriad shades of cobalt and emerald.

Conthar and Zantha looped, flew down toward their humans and back into darkness. Made a low pass over Renny's and Allar's heads, dipping their wings in salute before swooping back up.

Suddenly, Conthar and Zantha were joined by other dragons, what seemed like hundreds—perhaps thousands—flying up in a twisting spiral led by Conthar and Zantha.

The jewel tones of of their individual dragon hides sparkled and glittered, each a different color. They made continuous loops and swirls, flying in and out amongst each other in intricate designs and creating a living kaleidoscope.

Heads tipped up, Renny and Allar watched in delighted awe as the dragons presented them with a ceremony gift, a gift of love and homage unsurpassed.

Safe in the circle of Allar's arms, Renny indicated the endless blue sky and the vast, never ending space beyond with a lift of her chin. "There are others out there. Other dragons who need our help. Other dragons I must heal if we are to save our own from extinction."

Not doubting his wife in the least, Allar squeezed her a little tighter, pulling her back closer against his front. Nuzzling her hair, inhaling her beloved scent, he looked to the twinkling colors far above, and further.

"Call them home, Dragonhealer. Call them home."

"The time is not yet come, but soon."

The dragons performed for a long time, and then, led once more by Conthar and Zantha, they made a long, tall column straight up.

Conthar and Zantha were the first to head down, the rest trailing them, winking in the sunlight like a waterfall of jewels. Pulling up just short of crashing, each dragon made a pass overhead before disappearing back to wherever they'd come from.

Landing in front of Renny and Allar, Conthar and Zantha once more bowed their heads to their riders.

Laughing and clapping, hearts full to bursting, Renny and Allar ran to their dragons. Renny had to touch Conthar, had to let him feel the joy she couldn't express in words.

Allar caressed Zantha the same way, and then put his arms around Renny from behind, the four of them standing in a close circle.

Conthar and Zantha returned the love, silent messages zinging between the close knit foursome.

Leaning into his rider, Conthar made a coughing sound. Lifted one taloned claw and held it out to Renny. Waiting until she held her hand out, palm up, Conthar delicately placed a silver ring in the middle of Renny's palm.

Cupping her hand, examining her gift, Renny turned wondering eyes on Conthar. Knowing, despite the beauty of the scrolled dragons etched into the metal, there was far more to Conthar's gift.

"'Twill call dragons from other worlds and bring them to you to be healed. You have only to invoke your will."

Taking it from her, Allar slipped the ring on her finger. "I, too, have a ceremony gift for you, my love. I had the chamber next to Zantha's outfitted for us, and Zantha created a passage between the chambers. No more sleeping far away from our dragons."

Heart full to bursting, sucking in a breath and looking at the dragons with shining eyes, Renny caught Zantha's brief nod and Conthar's wink, before Allar picked up on their message to her.

"Allar, remember how upset I was that I had no gift for you?"

Renny felt his nod, but he said nothing, waiting for Renny to explain herself.

Placing both his hands over her belly, Renny covered them with her own. "I have one for you now." Waited a heartbeat. "This past night, we made a babe."

Turning Renny in his arms so they were face to face, Allar took his time perusing her bruised and battered features, her cheeks wet with tears. His brave, fearless Renny, who wouldn't cry in pain or fear, cried now with joy.

Standing at the top of the waterfall, bathed in the bright light of a new day, showered in prisms created by the fine mist. Flanked by their dragons and wrapped in love, Allar kissed Renny.

His woman, his mate, his love. Soon to be the mother of his children—Lady Renny, Dragonhealer Extraordinaire.

ALSO BY H S SKINNER

Like Renny?

The Last Dragonhealer is Book One in the Dragonsisters Trilogy.

Also by H S Skinner…
Jennilee's Light
Amelia's Echoes
Willow's Green Man

And Young Adult published under Heidi Skinner…
Jilly's Mural

The sequel to Jilly's Mural, **O'rian's Key**, should be published in May of 2020!

Thanks to everyone who read and enjoyed my books! I love introducing my imaginary friends to my real friends!

Stay tuned to my FB page, H S Skinner for upcoming announcements!